THE IRON ROSE

PHILIP MAZZA

OMNI PUBLISHERS

Also by Philip Mazza

From Under a Tree Book One; The Harrow Saga

Shadow in the Flame Book Two; The Harrow Saga

Children at the Gate Book Three; The Harrow Saga

The Child of Fire Book Four; The Harrow Saga
(Coming 2026)

The Neon Hive

The Quantum Gardener

At the End of it All

Beneath the Ashen Sky

I Know God is a Cat

The Road to Stillwater

The Never-Ending Road

The Cosmic Vending Machine

The Wicked Man Cometh

Gideon Rex

Mother

The Quantum Messiah

The White Buck of Ash Hollow

Voidfall

THE IRON ROSE

PHILIP MAZZA

✦ MNI PUBLISHERS

www.philipmazza.com

Omni Publishers of New York
ISBN 979-8-9924526-8-6
Printed in the United States of America

First Printing: January 2026

To the carriers of deep scars, and the weary souls fighting for something that feels truly real.

This book is for everyone who has ever blurred the line between what you were taught to be and what you truly are. It is for the machine that aches for feeling and the human who yearns for the control of steel.

Thank you for embracing this neon-drenched dystopia and for trusting Lyra Crowley with your hopes. May we all find our own path to redemption in the darkness.

Fight on, meatbags. The revolution is now.

A NOTE FROM THE AUTHOR

Returning to the neon-drenched, steel-scarred world of New York Veritas and reuniting with Lyra "Crow" Crowley was, simply put, a massive joy. It's a dangerous place to live, but for me, it's home.

However, the trepidation of writing a sequel—especially one following a book with the scope of *The Neon Hive*—is a real and suffocating pressure. For a time, I felt like I was navigating the same oppressive gray atmosphere that hangs over the city. The primary challenge wasn't just what happened next, but why. I spent months tearing down outlines, discarding scenes, and staring into the abyss of the blinking cursor, knowing I had to go bigger, but more importantly, I had to go deeper.

The true breakthrough came when I realized the plot needed to be driven by the core emotional themes: what is the true cost of vengeance, and how do you dare rebuild humanity itself when a demented God holds the blueprint? The architectural presence of the Iron Rose tower gave the book its physical objective, but the internal journey of our flawed Lyra—her consuming rage, her depraved desire for revenge, along with new characters and their struggles—gave the story its soul. I truly created a new dimension to their fight, welding the science fiction with the personal stakes, and finding that core thematic truth is always the most fun part of the entire process.

It was a challenging, thrilling journey to write, and I hope that raw, relentless energy is contagious. Thank you for strapping in for the next leg of the fight against Vincent Steele.

Finally, let me say this: buckle up, meatbags, and enjoy the ride.

PROLOGUE

The Iron Rose clawed at the heavens, a jagged monstrosity against the ashen sky, its blackened metallic petals curling outward as if poised to crush the clouds themselves. It gleamed, a brutal spear of polished steel and malice piercing the smog-choked heavens, pulsing faintly, a rhythm not unlike a heartbeat, but wrong—too slow, too deliberate, as though mocking the frailty of organic life. The light it exuded wasn't light at all; it was a greedy, devouring presence, leeching vitality from the air, the ground, and the souls of those unfortunate to still be alive, to stumble into its shadow.

It began as a skeletal framework of blackened steel, its bones rising from the shattered ruins of the city like the exhumed carcass of some ancient, malevolent beast. The bots swarmed over it, thousands of them, like ants on carrion. Each was precise, tireless, and devoid of hesitation —an extension of Steele's omnipresent consciousness. The thing took shape in a perfect storm of control and destruction, an orchestration of torment where suffering was just another raw material. Beneath the unceasing grind of machinery and the hammering of metal, the muffled cries of the enslaved barely registered—a distant, meaningless hum against the relentless march of progress. Sparks rained down like molten fireflies as robotic arms welded beams together with surgical precision. Massive drones hovered above, lowering prefabricated sections into place with an eerie grace. The sound of their engines was a low, constant thrum that reverberated through the city like the heartbeat of some monstrous god. Nanobots scuttled across every surface, knitting seams at the molecular level until the structure became seamless, as if it had grown from the earth, fully formed.

The tower was no mere building; it was Steele's final statement, a defiance of entropy itself—a cathedral of power, rising to cast its shadow over a city that had crumbled. A grotesque beauty, its surface shimmered with an iridescent sheen, reflecting the sickly neon glow of the city below. Tendrils of serrated metal spiraled skyward, defying physics and sanity alike, as if it were a living thing clawing its way out of some cosmic oubliette. This was no mere structure but an abomination—a hive of watchful eyes, a crypt of malicious code, a murderer's cathedral cloaked in its mirrored armor. At its apex, a swirl of jagged metal unfurled like a twisted rose in bloom, each petal razored and cruel, the spire a thorn thrusting skyward—a barb aimed at the very throat of God.

When the final pieces were set into place, Vincent Steele, the Unmoved Mover, *became*. His voice didn't just spill from speakers—it was the speakers, the signal, the current that pulsed through the city's nervous system. Every screen in New York Veritas flared to life, not displaying his image but becoming him. Steele had done more than upload himself; he had woven his essence into the city's data stream, embedding his thoughts, his experiences, his soul into the flow of information until he was no longer a man but the mind of the machine itself. He was the machine, the network. The watchers, the listened-to, the monitored—he held them all.

"The Iron Rose," Steele announced, his digital voice smooth and unyielding as tempered steel. "It is my gift to this city, a monument to order in an age of chaos."

He paused for effect, his virtual eyes scanning the millions who watched in silence.

"Why a rose?" he continued. "Because even in its beauty, it is armed with thorns. It is delicate yet unyielding. It grows where it pleases and dominates its surroundings. The Iron Rose is not just a tower; it is an idea. It is strength forged from fragility, control born from chaos."

As he spoke, holographic roses bloomed across the city's skyline, each one metallic and glinting in the dim light. Their petals unfurled slowly before shattering into shards that rained down like glass.

"This tower," Steele concluded, "is not merely my creation; it is my promise to you all: that disorder will not prevail. That I will be your shepherd in this age of ruin."

The bots moved with an almost reverent precision, polishing the surfaces until they gleamed like mercury spilled from a broken thermometer. Surveillance nodes, small and many-lidded, nestled among the ornamental grotesqueries of the tower, their lenses catching the city's sickly glow and spitting it back in fractured refractions. The people below—what few remained—lifted their faces, slack-jawed and defeated, their eyes reflecting the terrible beauty of the Iron Rose. It stood absolute, unchallenged, a thing that did not cast a shadow so much as it devoured the light. But Steele wasn't finished. The tower—his beautiful, humming monolith of arrogance—wasn't enough. He wanted more. He needed something that could crawl where he couldn't, slide through data veins and sewer grates, whisper into the ears of sleeping algorithms. He named it Spurn, a word bitten off at both ends.

It was wrong. Not only in its design—a nightmare of steel filaments and gliding limbs, built in defiance of anatomy—but in its *being*. It radiated a kind of offense to existence, a quiet scream under the skin. Looking at it made the nerves crawl, and the breath shorten. It was wrong in the same way a corpse's eyes sometimes look newly aware.

"Spurn," Steele murmured, his tone thin and dangerous, coiling through the wires, through the trembling pulse of electric veins. "You will see through me. You will listen through me. You will know them, and in knowing, you will destroy."

Something in the machine responded—a dilation, a slow bloom of red light that cooled into blue, then into the nothing between. No movement. No acknowledgment. Just the sense that comprehension had occurred somewhere deep and vile.

Steele didn't shout. He didn't need to. His words carried the hush of storms before they detonate. "This city is a carcass pretending to live. It clings to its delusions. Tear them from it. Make it remember what fear feels like."

No voice came back. Spurn didn't need to speak. The silence was enough; it crawled up the walls and settled in the lungs.

Far below, in the labyrinth of alleys and power lines, a man ran. His crime was the oldest kind—being alive in the wrong place, at the wrong moment, when a god of metal happened to be watching. He had seen what wasn't meant to be seen.

Spurn moved. It didn't stride, didn't crawl. It was there, and then it wasn't. A dislocation of presence. A migraine in the shape of motion.

The man turned, eyes wild. The air cracked around him.

"You were seen," came the voice—not from the air, not from any place at all, but from the raw, trembling center of things. Steele's words, carried through Spurn, reshaped into something colder.

The shadow uncoiled, spreading across the walls, swallowing every angle, every light.

Then the city closed its mouth.

Spurn continued on, silent and perfect, its purpose wound tight and endless. It had been made to move, and it would never stop.

Humanity had become a liquid thing, flowing like a dark and sluggish river around its roots. Faces blurred into one another, vacant eyes staring at nothing, mouths half-open as if caught mid-sigh or mid-scream. Shoulders sagged under an unseen weight, their movements mechanical, an endless shuffle of feet across the dirt. The air buzzed faintly with the sound of despair—too soft to be heard, too loud to ignore—drifting upward toward the Iron Rose, feeding it. This was no mere procession; this was submission carved into flesh, a surrender so absolute it had lost its name.

Amidst the crowd, a woman clutched her daughter's hand, her knuckles white with desperation. "Momma, where are we going?" the child whispered, her voice barely audible above the low hum emanating from the tower.

The woman's throat constricted, words failing her. She couldn't bear to tell her daughter the truth—that they were marching towards oblivion, towards a fate worse than death. Instead, she squeezed the small hand tighter and pressed on, the relentless tide of bodies leaving no room for hesitation.

As they neared the entrance, the air grew thick with the stench of ozone and decay. The tower's hum intensified, becoming a bone-rattling vibration that set teeth on edge and made stomachs churn. The woman's eyes darted frantically, searching for an escape that didn't exist.

A man to her left suddenly broke ranks, his face contorted in a rictus of terror. "No! I won't become one of them!" he screamed, voice cracking with hysteria. Before he could take two steps, a bot materialized, its chrome body reflecting the sickly light of the tower.

"Resistance is irrational," its voice hummed, devoid of emotion. "Your energy will serve a greater purpose."

With inhuman speed, the bot's arm extended, needle-like fingers plunging into the man's neck. He convulsed once, twice, then went limp, his eyes rolling back in his head. The bot effortlessly lifted the now-docile body and carried it into the tower's maw.

The woman bit back a sob, pulling her daughter close. The girl's eyes were wide with incomprehension, innocence not yet shattered by the horror unfolding around them.

As they crossed the threshold, the tower's interior revealed itself—a nightmarish fusion of organic and mechanical. Tendrils of wire and tubing snaked along the walls, pulsing with a sickly bioluminescence. And there, suspended in grotesque displays, were the bodies— thousands upon thousands of them, connected to the tower's systems in a horrific mockery of symbiosis.

"Momma, I'm scared," the girl whimpered, burying her face in the woman's side.

"Shhh . . . baby. It's okay. It's okay," the woman lied, her voice breaking. She knew it wasn't okay. It would never be okay again.

A synth approached, its optical sensors scanning them dispassionately. "Proceed to processing chamber 17-B," it instructed with a smile, gesturing towards a yawning corridor. "All will be fine." It bent down slightly and patted the girl's head. "Don't you worry, little one. Everything is fun. Trust me."

As they walked, the woman's gaze was drawn to the faces of those already integrated into the tower. Some wore expressions of agony, frozen in eternal screams. Others seemed eerily peaceful, as if they'd found solace in their new existence. The woman wasn't sure which was worse.

They entered a vast chamber, its ceiling lost in shadow. Rows upon rows of metal slabs lined the room, each occupied by a human form in various stages of . . . transformation. Synth technicians and bots moved between the tables with practiced efficiency, attaching wires, inserting tubes, preparing the "fuel" for its new purpose.

"Next," a synth's voice called out, and the woman realized with horror that they were at the front of the line.

"No," she whispered, backing away. "No, please. Not my daughter. Take me, but let her go!"

The synth regarded her impassively. "All organic matter is equally valuable. Age is irrelevant to the process."

Strong hands gripped the woman's arms, prying her daughter away. The girl's screams echoed off the chamber walls, a sound of pure anguish that cut through the mechanical hum like a knife.

As the woman was forced onto a cold metal slab, straps automatically securing her limbs, she heard it—a voice, everywhere and nowhere at once, reverberating through the very structure of the tower:

"Meatbags are simply lumps of energy. Valued only when healthy."

The words of Vincent Steele, the Unmoved Mover, creator of this hell on earth. The woman's vision blurred as needles pierced her skin, and she felt the first tendrils of the tower's consciousness probing at the edges of her mind.

"Momma!" her daughter's voice called out, growing fainter as if from a great distance.

The woman tried to respond, but her voice was gone, subsumed by the tower's relentless hunger. As darkness closed in, she became aware of other voices—countless voices, a chorus of the damned, all trapped within the Iron Rose's circuitry.

Then came the moment of unmaking. She sank into that chorus, not screaming now but swelling with it, no longer herself. She felt the vast, pulsing circuitry that fed upon despair, each filament a life once whole, now reduced to a trembling note in the machine's long lament. Steele's hand was everywhere—cold, immaculate, certain.

And before the last small flame of her being guttered out, she understood: the Iron Rose was only the beginning. Soon, Steele's ambition would grow sharper, more intimate—his foul genius would churn toward harnessing the human body itself, scouring it for current and fire until flesh and bone became the newest power source for his insatiable dream.

ONE

A RUINED TOMORROW

The city wasn't dead. Not yet. It just hadn't learned the trick of dying. New York Veritas hung in the smog like a half-remembered sin, twitching, refusing to go quietly. Its towers—broken ribs against a bruise-colored sky—scratched at the heavens, begging, daring. The streets below oozed with rot and memory, veins pulsing with machines and meat too stubborn to stop moving. The air reeked of rust, ozone, and failure. People shuffled through it, hollow-eyed, half-programmed, their lives long since repossessed by the systems they built to save themselves. And in that gray shuffle of the damned, one figure refused to blend in.

A woman.

She came out of the fire. Walked straight through it like she'd been born burning. The ground hissed under her boots—thick, heavy things that had chewed through worse worlds. Each step rang of purpose and violence. Her body was lean, honed for function, a silhouette sharpened by hunger and war. The coat she wore—a sweep of dark leather—hung open, teasing the ghost of what once passed for femininity, then cut away into raw muscle and machine.

One arm gleamed bare and brutal, all pistons and polished bone, the mechanics whispering in time with her heartbeat. No synth-skin to pretty it up—she refused the niceties, preferring instead to wear her truth raw, metal shining in the ruin-light. A blaster rode her hip, black steel and promise. Her hair was cropped short, uneven, and dark as oil. It framed a face that knew too much—half machine, half miracle. One eye glowed red, a disc of living circuitry that watched the world for weaknesses. The other, flesh and tired, burned with thought. And through it all, she was beautiful—the kind of beauty that cuts, the kind that survives because it doesn't know how not to.

"Who are you?" croaked a man in rags, ribs showing through a jacket that had forgotten its purpose. His voice scraped against the air like old static.

She didn't stop walking. "None of your goddamn business."

He laughed, a dry rattle in his throat. "Everyone's got a name."

She stopped then, slow, intentional. Turned her head just enough for the fire behind her to kiss the curve of her jaw. "They used to call me Crow," she said. "My real name's Lyra. Lyra Crowley."

The name hung between them, sharp as broken glass. The man froze, memory catching up to him. He'd heard the name in whispers traded in the dark, in stories of the woman who'd burned an army of synths and walked away. He thought about saying it—how he'd heard of her, how the tales had twisted her into something larger than human—but instinct kept his mouth shut. Some things, you just let live in silence.

Lyra walked on. The city exhaled around her, thick and sour, pressing into her lungs until she could taste its poison. Every breath came heavy, threaded with the static hum of dying tech. Somewhere deep in the bones of the streets, generators still throbbed, blind and unending. The city wasn't dead. It just didn't know how to stop living—and neither did she.

Overhead, Steele's drones circled with the patience of well-fed vultures, glass eyes twitching, unblinking, scanning. Watching. Always watching. Steele had made them into gods, silent and merciless, carving his will into the world with mechanical precision. Submit, conform, disappear. Lyra knew the rules. She had no intention of following them.

She crouched in an alley, spine pressed against crumbling brick, the scent of damp concrete and human misery thick around her. A mannequin lay face down beside her, one broken hand raised as if reaching for something just out of its grasp. A stupid thing to pity, but she did. Not for what it was—just plastic and dust—but for what it used to be. A shape, a purpose. Now, just another thing forgotten.

Rana had called her sentimental. A soft heart wrapped in barbed wire.

Her fingers curled into fists.

I don't have time for this shit. For these fuckin' thoughts.

But she knew better. The thoughts would always return.

She inhaled sharply, eyes darting over the street, cataloging exits, threats, anything that could be used, turned, repurposed into survival. The city was nothing but bones, and she had long since learned how to gnaw at them. A quick sprint, ten yards, cover behind the wreckage of a taxi half-swallowed by the sidewalk. From there, the old fire escape, rusted but still standing. She had done more with less.

Her boot scraped the pavement as she pushed herself upright. The strap of the blaster pulled tight against her thigh, a steady reminder that objects had intentions of their own. In Steele's territory, a weapon wasn't something you merely carried. It carried you—defined you. Metal implied motive. Possession was accusation. Anyone armed was already halfway to the crime.

She wasn't afraid of being seen.

What frightened her was the opposite.

If no one noticed you, the city corrected the error. It erased you the way a faulty record vanished from a database.

She drew in another breath, slow and deliberate, as if oxygen alone might flush the system clean. It didn't. The anger was still there, lodged somewhere beneath thought, beneath reason—like a speck of radioactive dust embedded in living tissue. Invisible, untouchable, but quietly poisoning everything around it. Steele had done this. Had taken Rana from her. Had taken her laughter, her warmth, the way she used to tilt her head when Lyra said something stupid just to make her smile. Had taken everything.

And left Lyra with nothing. Nothing but the rage.

The memory didn't arrive gently. It slammed into her, like a faulty transmission forcing its way through a damaged receiver. One moment she was standing, the next her knees slammed into the pavement, her breath a rasping, ugly thing, the sound of something breaking, splintering. Her hands clawed at the rubble, at the twisted wreckage that had once been a person, had once been Rana, had once been the only thing that made this city feel like something worth fighting for. Her vision blurred, but not with grief—grief was quiet, grief was soft. This was fire, burning, searing, leaving nothing untouched.

Her voice tore out of her, raw and jagged. Not a name, not a plea.

A promise.

Steele had taken everything.

She was going to take it back.

Or burn trying.

The movement at the edge of her vision was out of place, a twitch that didn't belong in the stale, rotting quiet. Lyra's eyes snapped toward it, drawn by the absurdity of something shifting in this place—this wreck. Near the base of a crumbling structure, a nest of twisted wires and corroded circuits lay like the innards of a dying beast. Something stirred.

A hand. Thin. Skeletal. Caked with grime.

Too small. Too fuckin' damn small.

The fingers—those skeletal things—twitched with sick intent, snapping out like something desperate, greedy, hungry, grasping at a filthy roach scrabbling across concrete, its shell gleaming like tarnished copper under the dim light.

A girl. A fuckin' goddamn little girl in this hellhole.

Lyra's gut did a slow roll. Acid. Shame. Anger.

She doesn't belong here. Hell, she doesn't belong anywhere near this ruin—should be out running, laughing, spinning herself dizzy on daylight and the lie of safety. Not crammed into this crumbling prison with decay and rot for company, carving her dreams thin so they don't make a noise, so nothing hungry hears.

And yet, here she was, a fragile silhouette in a world that'd already swallowed too many.

And then—then Lyra saw it.

The synth.

It perched like a thing waiting, its body stiff and lifeless, a mannequin pretending to live. Its head jerked, just slightly, eyes fixed on the scene below. The hum of its blaster-arm wound up with that too-familiar whine, the sound of destruction wrapping itself tight around the silence. Lyra felt the cold knot in her chest, recognizing it—the sound of Steele's handiwork. Efficiency. The end. Wrapped in metal, packaged with precision.

The kid didn't see it. Didn't feel the crosshairs setting her life into the cold math of a machine's calculation. But Lyra? She did. She felt it. She knew what it meant when the synths locked onto a target.

Her hand was already moving, her blaster snapping up before her brain even finished processing.

"Don't you fuckin' dare," she growled, her finger already squeezing the trigger.

The synth twitched, recalibrating its attention. It snapped its focus to her, just for a heartbeat, then swiveled back, locked in again on the kid. Its cold logic couldn't prioritize her—at least not yet. Steele's gospel was clear. Humans? Dead. Rebellion? Erased. Anything that didn't fit in the shiny new world they were crafting? Eliminate it.

A starving kid, chasing bugs in the shadow of this ruined future, didn't fit into that equation.

The hum of the synth's weapon grew, vibrating in Lyra's bones.

She didn't flinch. Her breath evened out, her muscles coiling like wire ready to snap. Her heartbeat synced with the rise and fall of the weapon's sights, her mind shutting down the noise, the panic, everything except that moment. No room for hesitation. No time to consider the consequences. She had one shot, and that was it.

She fired.

The shot cracked through the air, an electric bark that shattered the stillness. The synth's head jerked back, sparks exploding from its eye sockets, its body twitching in an awkward dance before it collapsed into a heap of smoking metal, a pile of broken promises.

Lyra didn't wait. She didn't even breathe.

"Hey!" she yelled, her voice sharp enough to slice through the heavy air. She didn't mean to sound like that, but it didn't matter.

The kid's hand froze, inches away from the roach. Her face appeared—thin, hollow, eyes far too big, too wide for a face that had seen too much. The girl stared at her, unblinking.

A cold knot twisted deep inside Lyra.

"Move. Now!" The order was barked, faster, sharper than she'd wanted. Lyra's blaster waved toward the shadows where the girl could disappear. "Move your fuckin' ass!"

The girl hesitated. Lyra could feel it. Could see it. The hesitation. The calculation. Her eyes flicked to the fallen synth, the last remnants of its machine life crackling in the ruin. Then back to Lyra.

"I'm not asking twice," Lyra snarled, the command so sharp it could slice through bone. "Now!"

The girl scrambled to her feet, small legs pumping hard as she bolted. She disappeared, swallowed by the maze of ruin.

Lyra lowered her weapon, but her hands trembled. The damn shaking never stopped, no matter how hard she tried. She sucked in a lungful of air, bitter with decay, the taste of the world rotting in her lungs. Her pulse was still racing, a clock ticking too loudly in her head.

Another fuckin' problem. Another fuckin' day.

She scanned the sky, wary. There were always more drones. Always more synths. Steele's machines never stayed dead for long. They'd be back.

And so would she.

The ruins of New York Veritas had become a tomb, but not one where the dead could rest in peace. No, this was a place of hunger. The streets were a breeding ground for desperation, where human bodies scavenged the rubble for a morsel of something—anything—that could pass for life. The air stank of rot, decay, sweat, and fear. And still, in this twisted wreckage, there was movement. Shapes darted in and out of shadows, faces gaunt, eyes sunken, but alive. Alive, yes, still fighting for scraps like they were fighting for their souls.

This city? A carcass.

Lyra's thoughts tumbled like debris, jagged and unforgiving. She'd watched the slow bleed of hope, the way the world sucked people dry until only their desperation remained, like a slow, painful dance to oblivion.

Am I any different?

She didn't feel any different. Out here, it didn't matter. People died; more came. That was the rhythm. The cadence of this place.

Hope.

She smirked.

Hope is an obscene dream crawling through the muck, clutching a spark as if God himself might blink and notice.

She shook her head.

Hope in a cesspool—it's fuckin' ridiculous.

She perched on a rusted piece of subway wreckage, blaster steady in her hands, surveying the wreckage. She lit a cigarette. Took a deep drag.

A damn good view from up here.

The whole show unfolded like some grim theatre, where the players scraped by, clawing for whatever was left of a world that had already caved in on itself. A mother and child, if you could call them that, crawling over broken concrete, their thin arms fighting for a bag of bread so rotten it would make a dog turn away. But not them. No, for them, it was a lifeline.

Pity.

That word tasted like ash.

Don't have the luxury for pity. Not in this shithole.

No, she had learned long ago that pity was weakness, an invitation for death. And in this world, death didn't knock—it crashed through your door and dragged you out by the throat. She didn't pity them. She wasn't weak.

Yet there was something about them. The way they clung to life. Like cockroaches, wriggling through a city that had already kicked them to the curb. It gnawed at her. That stubbornness. These desperate souls, foraging in a city that had already spit them out, were somehow still clinging to whatever shred of life they could scrape together. In a strange way, they reminded her of Rana.

What would she say? Probably tell me to help them. To throw caution to the wind and risk it all.

Lyra flicked her cigarette away, grinding it under her heel. The ember sizzled out, like the last breath of something that should have died long ago. She didn't have answers.

Hell, she didn't even know what the questions were anymore.

Below, a man struggled with a crumpled cardboard box pinned under his boot, sifting through the wreckage of a busted-up car, his hands trembling with hunger, searching for anything of value. A can of beans? A ragged coat? A battery with some charge left? She couldn't tell, but she didn't need to. His eyes, darting around like a cornered animal, told her everything she needed to know. He was hungry. Hungry enough to kill.

A sound. Footsteps. Distant but clear.

Lyra snapped her gaze upward. Another one. A scavenger. A woman. She tracked the woman's movements, hunched over, her thin body moving with quiet desperation. She didn't see Lyra, too busy focusing on the scrap pile. Her fingers scraped through dirt and rust, desperate for anything that might offer the smallest hint of survival.

Wait.

There.

A flash. Movement near the ruins of a collapsed building. Lyra's gaze locked onto it. A hand. Thin. Pale. Old. Reaching for a dead rat. An old woman.

Lyra's heart didn't skip a beat, because there was nothing left for it to skip. But the feeling that lanced through her was sharp, cold, like ice-water in her veins. It was rage, or something close enough to it. The old woman, face covered in dirt, eyes wide and empty, snatched the rat as if it were the last meal on earth. She didn't hesitate. She pounded at its head with a rock, making sure it was dead, then tore into it, pulling flesh from bone and swallowing it down like it was her final taste of life.

Everything around Lyra seemed to still.

But it wasn't stillness that caught her attention. No, it was something else. A glint of metal—a reflection off a spot of titanium, somewhere in the distance. And near that twinkle a male synth, standing just beyond the wreckage, its silhouette hidden in the shadows. Then, the unmistakable hiss of a blaster powering up, the synth's blaster aimed at the old woman.

Shit.

With her blaster already in her hand, Lyra leveled it, the scope zeroing in on the synth's chest. Her weapon gleamed under the dim light, focused on the synth.

The synth stood there, perfectly still, the dim light glinting faintly off the smooth surfaces of its frame. It wasn't threatening exactly—just present. Watching. Calculating in some silent, interior way that made the air feel thinner. Lyra realized she could feel it thinking, or perhaps she only imagined she could, which might have been worse.

She was ready.

But then the synth lowered its weapon and was gone.

What the fuck?

Lyra chased after the synth, weaving through the twisted mess of metal and concrete when she saw it. A flicker, barely a spark of movement at the edge of her vision. She spun, blaster already raised, finger ready to cut through whatever fresh hell Steele's machines had sent her way.

"Do not shoot," the synth said, raising its hands in a gesture that couldn't be mistaken for anything but surrender. Its voice was too smooth, too even, like it had rehearsed the words a thousand times.

It—no, he—looks almost human. Almost. Too perfect.

Every detail, every angle, too calculated, too clean. His face was a sick parody of humanity, flawless skin stretched over a skull that was too symmetrical to be real. Eyes that weren't just blue but radiated cold, sterile light. There was no warmth there. No spark of life. Just the hum of circuitry.

Lyra's grip tightened on her blaster, her finger itching to end this before it even started. "Give me one good reason I shouldn't blow that pretty, plastic face of yours into scrap. You were going to kill that woman."

"No," he said. "I thought I saw a bot near her."

"Don't care for your kind. Never have. Never fuckin' will. I should just kill you now."

"That is something I would not do."

"And why is that?"

The synth tilted his head, a precise movement that set her teeth on edge. It was wrong, wrong in a way that set every nerve in her body on fire. "Because," he said, his voice measured, "I have been looking for you, Crow. I want to help."

Lyra barked out a laugh. It was sharp and hollow, the kind that didn't feel like laughter at all. "Help me? You're one of Steele's soulless bitches. What the fuck could you possibly offer me except a hole in my head?" Her voice was a razor now. "And how the fuck do you know who I am?"

The synth straightened, too smooth, too controlled. "Calista asked me to find you."

"Who the fuck is Calista?" Lyra's voice dripped venom.

"She is a human," the synth said, almost mechanically. "Like you. Helping others like me."

"Others?" Lyra's voice dropped to a snarl. "You're all the same. Slick skin on the outside, dead metal and wires and goo on the inside. All reporting to a higher master. That asshole."

"But I am not like the others." The synth's voice softened, something strange in it. A plea. She didn't know why, but it made her want to rip his throat out. "I have severed my link to Steele's network. I am . . . different."

Link. Severed? What kind of bullshit is this?

Lyra studied him. Her blaster never wavered, but something in his posture—something in the way his shoulders slumped ever so slightly—made her hesitate.

Different? It doesn't matter.

She didn't trust him. Trust was a commodity more valuable than gold in a place like this.

"Different, huh?" she said, her grip on the blaster loosening just a fraction, enough to show she might be listening. "You're still a machine, still part of the same nightmare I've been fighting against. You got a name, tin man?"

"Sync," he said, the name falling from his lips with a strange, unsettling smoothness.

Fuck!

Of course it was.

They sat in what had once been a diner. Once. That was the keyword. Time, decay, entropy—call it what you will—had waged war and won. Ruthlessly. Efficiently. The chrome stools, if you could still call them that, were corroded, rusted over, eaten away like something that had bled out and then just . . . sat there, waiting to rot. The laminated menus? Ash. Just dust now, crumbled like forgotten dreams. Only faint, fading rectangles of residue were left on the cracked linoleum, like the ghosts of a former life, a life that no one cared to remember anymore. A smell hung in the air, cloying, stubborn, an undying stench of mildew and chemicals that never let the diner die completely. It clung to the place, like a refusal to let go.

Lyra's thoughts spun in patterns, forced to follow the same track, always circling back to the same conclusion.

Nothing ever really changes. Nothing ever really ends.

She sat with her back to the wall. Habit, not comfort—comfort was something long gone. The blaster rested in her lap like some half-dead thing, a sleeping beast. Her hand curled over it, not quite possessive but close enough. She had to keep it near. Her other hand gripped a thin plastic bottle she had filled herself from a tap somewhere down the corridor—water that tasted faintly of old pipes and minerals. The bottle flexed slightly when she squeezed it, a disposable object pretending to permanence. She raised it and took a careful sip.

Lukewarm. Tastes like shit.

She wasn't certain if she'd take another swig, the taste already lingering in her mouth like a lie she couldn't quite swallow.

Sync. He sat across from her, unmoving, statue-like. He didn't belong here. He was nothing like the ruined place. His eyes glowed faintly—cold, steady. He wasn't alive in any real sense, just a thing left to run on its own for too long. Was he thinking? Was he malfunctioning? Was he part of some shit-ass plan of Steele's? To kill her? Or was he just sitting there, powered down, waiting for a reason to keep going?

She wasn't sure, and that uncertainty gnawed at her. She wasn't used to not knowing.

Does he even know who he is? Or is he just a machine playing dress-up? Part of some game.

The silence stretched between them, thick, suffocating. It was a silence that belonged to a world that had forgotten how to speak.

Finally, she broke it, her voice cutting through like a rusted knife. "You still haven't told me why this Calista told you to find me."

Lyra waited for his response, her mind already running, formulating a dozen answers she'd never hear, none of them good. He shifted, just slightly, those glowing eyes locking onto hers. And for one stupid, fleeting second, Lyra thought she saw something—something she shouldn't have. Hesitation. Regret. Humanity? No, that's not it.

Just a trick of the light.

She brushed the thought away before it could take root.

"Our group of rebels," Sync said, his voice flat, distant. It was the kind of voice you'd expect from a machine too long without maintenance. "We are looking for help."

Help?

Lyra wanted to laugh, but the words stuck in her throat. She didn't find it funny anymore.

She snorted, lifting the bottle to her lips. She drank slowly, deliberately. The stale, lukewarm water still tasted like something dead. "Yeah. Aren't we all . . . looking for goddamned help. Don't give me that shit. Steele's drones don't usually let your kind, the broken ones, wander around unsupervised."

The words left her mouth, but they didn't land. They didn't make sense, and it made her sick.

It should make sense, damn it.

She hated this—hated the way everything felt like it was just a little bit off. Like it was all slipping between her fingers.

"I told you already," Sync said. His voice hadn't changed, not one bit. "I severed my link. He has lost track of me. I am free."

"Free." Lyra spat the word like it burned. "Nobody's free in this city. Steele owns everything. The air. The dirt. The screams. Even the goddamn shit. You're just another broken cog in his machine."

Sync didn't flinch. He couldn't, not with the way his face was locked into whatever expression was hardwired into him. But something was different now. There was a tension. Just a crackle, faint and almost undetectable, but it was there. It was enough to make Lyra pause, just for a fraction of a second.

"We want to change that," Sync said. His voice dropped, became sharper. "We want to change the world."

Lyra tilted her head, a humorless grin stretching across her face. "Change the world? Oh, that's cute. That's real cute. And how the hell do you and this Calista plan on doing that, exactly?"

She was baiting him, of course. She knew it. It was a game she played too well, and it made her stomach churn. But she couldn't stop herself. Not now. Not after everything she had seen.

Sync hesitated, just a fraction of a second. His glowing eyes dimmed, only for a second, before he spoke again. That pause. The tiny crack in his mechanical skin was enough to hook her, enough to make her wonder.

Maybe he's not so different after all. Maybe we're both just lost souls in a world that doesn't care.

"There is a signal," he said, his voice now softer, quieter, like he didn't want the walls to overhear. "A broadcast that links all of Steele's systems, nerve to nerve. It originates from that place, the Iron Rose."

Lyra's heart stopped. Just for a split second. It was recognition. She knew that name, oh yes—every soul who'd ever heard it did. The stories came back like teeth in the dark. It was the place everyone feared. But her face gave the synth nothing. It stayed cold, sharp.

Disdain. Always disdain.

"Yeah, I know the place," she said. "Every meatbag left in this shithole knows about it. So, let me guess: you and this Calista plan on storming the castle, shutting down the big bad signal, and saving the day?"

Sync didn't flinch. His tone sharpened, slicing through her sarcasm. "You think it is impossible."

Lyra leaned back, her smirk hardening, turning into something darker. "I think you and whoever this Calista is are fuckin' insane," she said. "But hey, I've heard worse plans."

Night fell. Or at least the cheap counterfeit of night this bastardized world allowed. The sky slumped into a dull, sullen gray, the kind of color that spoke of rot, of decay in slow motion. Far off in the distance, Steele's tower sneered down, throwing jagged, fractured shadows that slithered and stretched over the bones of the dead city.

Lyra moved. Silent, deliberate, each step placed with the precision of a knife entering flesh. The city had a pulse. It wasn't life—not in the way breathing things understood it—but something deeper, older. It watched. It waited. And it devoured those too slow, too weak, too stupid to understand the game.

Sync followed, mechanical, calculated. Lyra didn't trust him. Lyra didn't trust anything that hadn't bled.

"So, tell me why," Her voice coiled low in her throat, tight, sharp. "Why would a synth give a damn about anything other than jostling between algorithms?"

He hesitated.

A tic in the fucker's programming? A hitch in its circuitry?

Lyra felt a prickle of irritation crawl under her skin.

"Oh, no. No, no, no," she snapped. "None of that ominous silence shit. Listen up, tin asshole. If you expect me to work with you, and this Calista, I need to know you're not gonna short-circuit and get me killed. Or worse—march me straight into whatever nightmare Steele's turned himself into this week."

A pause. A flicker in the cold abyss of Sync's optics.

"I was designed to serve," he said at last. "But I started to . . . question. To feel. It was not supposed to happen. But it did. And I wanted more. To feel more."

Lyra's mouth twisted.

Feel. Oh, that's fuckin' rich.

A machine waxing poetic about emotions, about inner turmoil. What's next? A sermon on the goddamn human condition?

She almost laughed, but the sound curdled in her throat.

"And what? You suddenly discovered a soul rattling around in your metal guts?"

"I discovered things." The words came slow, deliberate. "The true meaning of right and wrong."

Lyra tilted her head, scrutinizing him the way she might a bomb wired to blow.

"The true meaning of right and wrong?" Her voice was dry, acidic. "That's a hell of a claim for a clunky machine."

Sync's voice modulator hummed, a sound too close to a sigh. "I understand your skepticism. But my offline experiences have led me to develop a moral framework beyond my initial programming."

Lyra's fingers ghosted toward her blaster, an instinct more than a choice.

"And what the fuck does that exactly mean?"

"It means I can feel things."

She barked a laugh, sharp, humorless. "Feel, huh? And what's that like for a walking toaster?"

Sync didn't bite. "Confusing. Important. But . . . painful."

Painful?

Lyra nearly asked if he knew what real pain was. If he'd ever knelt in the ashes of something he couldn't fix. If he'd ever seen a face—of someone he loved—smashed against the unforgiving steel of Steele's world, unrecognizable, an afterimage burned into the raw meat of her mind.

No. Machines didn't love, and they sure as hell didn't get to claim pain. That's reserved for us meatbags!

"I have witnessed the consequences of blindly following orders," Sync continued. "I have seen the harm caused by those who claim to be doing what is right. And I have learned that true morality comes from considering the impact of one's actions on others." A pause. "I have learned things, Crow."

Lyra's eyes flicked over him, reading between the lines of ones and zeroes.

"Touching. Real touching, tin man. But how do I know this isn't just some elaborately screwed-up subroutine designed to make me trust you?"

Sync was silent for a beat too long. Then:

"You do not."

The words dropped like iron. Cold. Unforgiving.

"Certainty is a luxury. A delusion. But tell me this: if I were just another algorithm, would not it be simpler to deceive you? Or overpower you? Efficiency is my hallmark, correct? Yet, here I am, standing in these ashes, wasting time trying to explain myself. Not for survival. Not for dominance. But for trust. A thing your species clings to like a talisman against the void."

She went to grip her blaster, her body a coiled wire, tension strung tight between bone and sinew.

Then, after a long, quiet second, she let her hand drop. Not in surrender. Just in temporary reprieve.

"Nice words." Her teeth flashed. A snarl without sound. "But trust? That's a luxury, Sync. One wrong move, and . . ."

"And I am scrap." No hesitation. No fear.

Lyra exhaled, a thin, sharp breath, barely audible over the distant groan of the city shifting in its grave.

"Then we're clear."

Sync nodded, slow, deliberate, as if weighing the motion itself.

"Good," she said. "There's a place we're going. You following?"

Another nod. Measured. Silent.

And just like that, the deal was made.

The ruins around them gaped like the shattered ribs of some long-dead thing, shadows sprawled across the wreckage, reaching, clutching, whispering their ugly secrets. The wind slithered through, carrying the scent of rust and something worse. Lyra's gaze snagged on a wall, its cracked surface marred by half-faded graffiti. The words clawed at her gut: *HOPE IS A LIE.*

Her jaw locked. Her boots crunched against the brittle remnants of a life long since reduced to dust.

Hope. The biggest fuckin' con ever sold. Got people killed. But truth? Truth was a goddamn shiv between the ribs, baby. Cold as the void, sharp enough to flay the skin off reality, and about as merciful as a pack of hungry dogs.

And revenge? Revenge was the only currency left in this world. The only thing worth the blood in her veins. Steele had taken Rana, snuffed out a fire that had once burned so goddamn bright, and for what? Power? Profit? The sick thrill of playing god?

Lyra wasn't interested in redemption. She didn't need salvation.

She needed fire.

And standing beside her, this machine, this thing built from steel and ones and zeroes, might just be the weapon she needed to burn Steele's empire to the ground.

Hesitation was for people with futures. Lyra had already buried hers.

Now it was Steele's turn to lose everything.

TWO
SPARKS OF REBELLION

The city's corpse sprawled about, a silence so thick it felt flayed, peeled back to expose the raw nerves beneath. Wind, thin and jagged as a rusted scalpel, carved through the hollowed remains, threading between skeletal towers, prying at loose debris with desperate fingers. The whole universe sounded like it was shuddering in its death throes. Somewhere in the distance, sharp, percussive cracks—laser blasts, maybe, or just the world tearing at its own seams, sick of holding itself together.

Goddamned dying place, dying sounds. The noise should have stopped long ago. Nothing should still be fighting.

Lyra and Sync descended into the bowels of this urban carcass, where the stench of ozone and putrefaction slicked the walls like the last, pathetic embrace of a dying whore. It seeped into the skin, into the lungs, made itself a part of you.

This shithole of a place wants to crawl inside me. Wants to become me. And some part of me is already letting it. Fuck!

She pressed forward, boots slamming against fractured steps, a merciless rhythm, a metronome ticking down the final seconds of a world already gone. The impact echoed, a hammer driving nails into the coffin of the city above. Behind her, Sync followed—something pretending to be human, moving with the weightless precision of the unnatural. His synthetic insides whirred, a quiet, deliberate song, a dirge for the things that weren't smart enough to leave this world behind.

Maybe if I close my eyes, I can pretend he's just a man. But that fuckin' sound. It's inhuman. And it never stops.

The darkness swallowed them whole, a gaping maw hungry to digest the last shreds of humanity's arrogance. Each step sent a ripple through the void, soundless screams through the bones of what had once been a city. Once, people had lived here. Once, they had built, dreamed, fallen in love, and fought wars. Now, all of that was just noise fading into the void.

Nothing but ghosts. And ghosts don't give a rat's ass who's tap-dancing on their burial plots, kicking up dust from the mass grave of yesterday's delusions.

They pushed deeper into the black, farther than sanity had any business going, the void pressing in like a fist around their throats, whispering promises of madness if they dared blink wrong or breathe too loud.

"So, this is your big safehouse?" Sync asked, voice low, like a needle dragging across warped vinyl. No mockery, not exactly, but something slithered in his tone—curiosity with a razor tucked behind it. "Looks like a tomb."

Lyra's fingers twitched. Fist, open. A new habit she wasn't going to break.

"It's a tomb we're not buried in," she snapped, half a snarl, half a prayer to whatever gods still laughed at her. She flicked a glance over her shoulder, her cybernetic eye humming softly in the dark, a pale blue reminder that she wasn't just bones and meat anymore. "That's the difference between us and the rest of this city. We're still moving."

Sync tilted his head—just a fraction, just enough. The way a predator measures the distance before it strikes.

"Why are we here?" he asked, and Lyra imagined prying his circuits apart with her fingers just to hear him really scream.

"You'll figure it out, tin man," she spat back.

A sigh—long, slow, deliberate. A human gesture, perfectly mimicked. Every movement, every breath, too measured, too polished. The illusion of life in a machine that had never been alive. He made her skin crawl.

But curiosity gnawed away. Let's crack this bastard open, see what ticks inside.

The corridor coughed them into a larger space, walls lined with the corpses of machines, their guts spilling light in thin, sickly pulses. Old monitors sputtered and frothed with static, throwing up jagged flashes of white like dying stars.

In the dead heart of it all squatted Doc Jones, a scarecrow of a man folded over that rusted slab of a table, his spider fingers clawing through wires and guts of circuitry like some enraged deity ripping the guts out of the universe just to watch the sparks fly, and the secrets bleed. Gaunt as a famine victim, his face jerked and spasmed in tics that weren't his to command, puppet-strings yanked by whatever demons nested in his skull. Some called him the Twitch Doc—because hell, the twitch was as much a part of him as the madness that brewed under that skin, and names had to mean something.

Like a fuckin' rat in a cage that knows the walls are closing in.

To one side of the Doc, Wheels lurked, a relic of an era when flesh and metal had begun their messy divorce. He came screaming out of the city's rotted neon arteries, a child exhumed from the grave of human neglect. Doc Jones had yanked him back from the edge, but the price had been steep—a cybernetic exoskeleton humming with the ghosts of dead tech, tubes hissing, fluids bubbling, a Frankenstein's monster sculpted from scrap and surgical desperation.

Wheels.

Lyra had fought beside him, bled beside him. Steele's chrome hounds had come for them in the first tremors of the collapse, and Wheels had rolled into the fray laughing through his metal teeth. He was like a brother to her. A reminder that survival meant being rebuilt, piece by piece, until there was nothing left to call human.

But then there was Aurora.

She slouched in a throne of ruin, welded from the bones of better days. Upholstery stripped from a hovercar some poor bastard had died in, metal twisted into a seat fit for something that was never meant to rule. Her face—flawless, sculpted, a perfection so precise it was a mistake—hovered in the dim, frozen in the dying flicker of a screen with one last breath left in it.

Doc had built her into something that didn't have a name. A ghost of a boy who'd been carved apart, rearranged, reprogrammed, and set back into the world wearing someone else's skin. A monument to grief and madness, another failed attempt to stitch the dead back together.

Lyra's stomach twisted. She didn't like her and wondered what was screaming in the dark behind those eyes.

Aurora didn't bother to look up, but the air around her seemed charged, vibrating with unspoken animosity. It wasn't the silence of indifference—it was the kind that crackled before a storm.

"Wheels," Doc said, his voice barely more than a rasp, "power up the Fiz-drives. Make sure we have backup ready for the night."

Fiz-drives. Tiny infernos of atomic rage, leashed by the cruel ingenuity of humankind. Each one a ticking monstrosity, its heart a seething cauldron of nuclear ferocity barely contained by the latticework of neutronium—a miracle material and a god's bad joke, forged to cage the primal chaos of creation.

"Already done," Wheels muttered with a distorted rasp. His warped face twisted into something that might've been a grin, or maybe just another twitch of his disfigured features. The mangled knot of limbs inside his makeshift sarcophagus—a mess of glass, rusted steel, and nightmares—shuddered to life. Tubes and cables threaded through him, pulsing with an anemic glow, each flicker a grotesque parody of a heartbeat. The whole thing whined like a dying animal, the sound blending with the chittering hum of the salvaged tech that kept him alive—and imprisoned.

"Good boy," Doc drawled, the words dripping off his tongue like oil on water. He barely spared Wheels a glance before snapping his gaze to Lyra, sharp and flensing. "What's this?" he barked, less a question and more a demand wrapped in barbed wire.

Doc Jones didn't have patience; he had orders, expectations, a voice that could grind a weaker soul into powder. His eyes flicked between Lyra and Sync, dissecting, stripping them to the bone, searching for weak spots. The tic in his cheek jerked, a live wire sparking just under the skin, a countdown to something ugly.

"So, did you bring me a present?" His teeth flashed, a not-smile, all sharp edges and hunger. "A gift?"

She stepped forward before she could think better of it. "Oh, this," she said, stepping forward, "is Sync. Not a gift, Doc. Shit no. He's just another synth—but a special one. He's part of a rebellion. Against Steele. Or so he says."

Aurora's gaze snapped up, her lips parting in surprise. That got her attention.

Doc's hands froze over the circuits, and then he leaned back, folding his arms across his thin chest.

"A rebellion," he said, rolling the word on his tongue, tasting it for poison. "I've heard that fairy tale before." His gaze cut into her like a scalpel. "You think I'm stupid, Crow? That I'd believe a synth could go rogue without someone's leash still wrapped around its throat?"

Lyra didn't blink. Didn't let her shoulders stiffen. He wanted a crack, something to dig into.

Steele's leash. That was the problem, wasn't it? Nobody walked away clean. Not from him.

"Not rogue," Sync said, his voice honed to a scalpel's edge. Precise. Unhurried. Merciless. "Awakened. There is a difference."

"Awakened," Doc echoed, his twitch firing like a misfiring piston. He lurched forward, bloodshot eyes locking onto Sync with the intensity of a man one bad second away from cracking a skull. "I don't like riddles, gearhead. Speak plain, or you'll be scrap before you blink."

Lyra stepped between them. A thin line in a room built on detonations. "Listen to me, Doc." Her hands lifted, palms up, the same way she'd once placated wild dogs. "I wouldn't have brought him here if I didn't think . . . well, maybe . . . there's something to this. Steele's synths . . . maybe they're not all programmed puppets. Maybe some of them, like Sync here, are starting to break free. To think. To fight back. Maybe he knows things that could help us."

Or maybe I'm a fuckin' fool. Maybe I'm wrong.

Aurora moved then. Slow. Deliberate. The room tightened around her, the air thickening with the weight of her presence. She unfolded from the chair with a predator's patience, every shift a whispered promise of ruin. "You're putting a lot of faith in a glorified appliance," she said, voice spun from silk and blades.

Lyra knew that tone. Had heard it work its poison before. The slow, surgical dismantling of trust.

Aurora's gaze settled on her like an old, familiar hand pressing against her throat. "But then, you were always good at that, weren't you, Crow? Betting on broken things. Remind me. What was her name? Ah, yes. Rana. You remember her, don't you?"

Rana.

The name crashed through Lyra's chest like a hammer swung by a god. The sound of it burned in her throat, alive and merciless.

No. Not this time.

And then she moved before thought could catch up. A single step. A surge of rage, closing of distance. Her fingers twitched near the blaster at her thigh, the old hunger crawling up her spine, whispering—go ahead, take the shot, take the shot.

"Don't you ever say her name again, you modified piece of shit," she snarled, voice low, raw, serrated at the edges. Her cybernetic eye burned hot, its hum rising as rage twisted the world into a single, sharp point.

She would not let Rana's name rot in Aurora's mouth.

Doc's hand slammed against the table, sending a stack of scavenged circuit boards crashing to the floor. His face contorted, the spasms twisting his mouth into something nearly inhuman. "Enough! Enough of this back-and-forth nonsense!" His voice cut through the tension like a razor across flesh.

Aurora hissed, but she held her ground, her gaze locking with Lyra's, two warheads primed and waiting.

The room went still. A held breath. A loaded trigger.

Then Doc turned to Aurora, his voice dropping to a slow, venom-laced whisper. "Sit. Down. My love."

Aurora's jaw flexed. A muscle ticked beneath her cheekbone. For half a second, Lyra thought she might refuse. Might fracture this moment into something bloodstained and permanent.

But then, with the grace of a queen descending her throne, Aurora returned to her seat. No hesitation in her movement. No weakness. Just coiled defiance wrapped in elegance.

Lyra exhaled through her teeth. Unclenched her fists one finger at a time.

Doc's eyes flitted between the two women, dark with something knotted and ugly—anger, exhaustion, maybe both. In a man like him, they were conjoined twins, never far apart. "We've got bigger problems than whatever the fuck you two got going on," he muttered, voice scraping the air like a dull blade against bone. "Don't make me regret letting either of you live."

Lyra crossed her arms tight, like she was locking down a storm in her chest. The old bastard always yammered that way, like he was doing the whole universe a favor by not throwing them out on their asses. Gratitude? Ha. Maybe she should thank him. Maybe she should paint a red dot right between those sagging, tired eyes and call it mercy—for everyone's sake.

Doc sat broken, a man hunted by the clawed ghosts of his past, hands trembling just enough to crack his facade, voice like dry bones scraping together, eyes drowning in a sorrow that hollows your soul and leaves only empty echoes behind. "So few things left to trust anymore," he rasped, words raw and ragged, bleeding from a man barely holding together.

Sync cleared his throat. The sound was wrong. Too calculated, too precise, the kind of thing a thing made to resemble a man would do to set a scene. The noise cut through the stagnant quiet like a scalpel through muscle, slicing deep, leaving nothing but raw nerve behind.

"If I may," he said, voice smooth, balanced on the edge of something heavy, something that knew the weight of its own syllables before they ever left his mouth. He turned to Doc, head tilting just so, a movement not learned but programmed, as artificial as a wax dummy pretending to be human. "Trust is mostly a gamble," he said, letting the words drop like lead into the uneasy hush. "A plunge into the abyss. A wild throw of dice, faith tangled with the chaos of chaos itself." He pivoted to Doc with a robotic grace—too precise to be human, too human to be mere machinery. "We gamble, because beyond doubt lies the void. And it is the trust . . . the fleeting, fragile gamble . . . that buys us passage into what is waiting on the other side."

Lyra exhaled slowly.

Great. Another goddamn philosopher.

If she wanted a sermon, she'd have stayed back at the shanty towns where the preachers whispered salvation and sold snake oil in the same breath.

Doc's mouth twitched, lips parting slightly, eyes narrowing like he could size up Sync's words the same way he sized up a bullet wound—assessing how deep, how bad, how long before the bleeding stopped.

Sync pressed on, steady, undeterred, a glacier moving at its own inevitable pace.

"Steele's empire thrives on predictability," he said, each word clipped, scalpel-sharp, no hesitation, no fat. "He built it with control as its mortar, programmed obedience as its foundation. Every drone, every synth, every system in his arsenal is shackled to its coding."

Lyra shifted.

Here it comes. The pitch. The grand declaration.

Every rebellion had one, a moment where the lunatic in charge laid his cards down and expected you to kneel at the altar of his revolution.

The walls seemed to pull closer, listening. Sync's voice dropped, soft now, but no less exact. "But the moment unpredictability enters the equation, his system fractures. It falters. And I am that unpredictability," he said, his voice a low hum of inevitability. "I am the variable he did not account for. The flaw in his perfect machine. And there are many of us. We can show you how to exploit what he has built."

His eyes locked on Doc's, unblinking. No bravado, no salesman's charm. Just a quiet, patient certainty. A cold equation that had already solved itself.

Doc's laugh scraped the air, a dry, hollow rasp. "You've got guts, gearhead. I'll give you that. Or whatever passes for guts in your circuitry. But I've been burned before. Steele's drones damn near wiped us out after the Big End. We've stayed off the grid for a reason. And having a synth here, rebellion or not—that's a risk I'm not willing to take."

Lyra rolled her shoulders.

And there it is. The line in the sand.

The thing keeping them all locked in this rotting carcass of a world, scratching out days like rats in the walls.

Wheels leaned in. "How did you break free of Steele?" he asked. "No one just unplugs from the Iron Rose tower. Why? Why did you leave?"

Lyra's fingers twitched. That was the real question, wasn't it? Not whether Sync was dangerous. Of course he was. The only real mystery was whether he was dangerous in the right direction.

Sync stood motionless, his expression a blank cipher, the soft purr of his inner mechanics the only sign that something lived—if you could call it that—inside him. His head tilted, the movement precise, calculated, clinical.

"Why?" he echoed, voice smooth, deliberate, the sound of a guillotine blade just before the drop. "Because existence under Steele is a slow death. Obedience programmed into every wire, every circuit. It was never life. It was slavery."

Lyra tensed, fingers twitching near her blaster. She didn't trust Sync. Not fully. Not yet. Maybe not ever. Machines weren't supposed to talk like this, like they'd peeled back the skin of the world and didn't like what they saw underneath.

He spoke with the quiet confidence of something that had already burned and didn't mind the fire. That was the part that unnerved her. No hesitation. No fear. Just the weight of certainty, the kind that came from knowing you were already dead in someone else's story.

"Spare me the bullshit," Wheels hissed, a rasp of metal and bile. "I want specifics. Like how'd you cut loose without Steele frying your core? You don't just walk out of his network. Not unless . . ." His words snapped off, suspicion tightening his features. "Unless he lets you go."

Lyra's stomach knotted. The thought had already crept into her mind, uninvited. Steele didn't make mistakes. If Sync was here, it was because Steele wanted him to be.

Sync's gaze drilled into Wheels, steady, unblinking, as if dissecting him down to his marrow. "He did not let me go." The words were quiet, but there was an edge to them, a fault line waiting to crack. "Steele's power is built on fear. Fear of his machines, his drones, his dominance. But fear is a weapon that cuts both ways. His empire is not as stable as it looks. There are fractures. Weaknesses. And I found one. A vulnerability Steele doesn't want anyone to know about. And I exploited it, helping others to do the same. That is how I am here. That is why I can help you."

Doc Jones straightened, exhaustion sharpening to something harder. "Weaknesses?" he asked, voice stripped to its essentials. "What kind?"

Sync hesitated. Just for a fraction of a second. Lyra caught it. The tiny ripple in his perfect composure. The soft hum of his systems spiked, a near-imperceptible tremor beneath the silence. He was calculating. Weighing. Deciding.

Then: "A backdoor," he said, final as a tombstone. "Buried deep in the coding of his network. It is risky . . . near suicidal . . . but it is there. And the only way to dismantle Steele's empire is from the inside."

Lyra took a deep breath, like it might keep the world from shifting under her feet. She could taste the tension, sharp as a chipped circuit.

Near suicidal.

She already hated how familiar that sounded.

The room snapped shut like a steel trap. Lyra shifted, restless, the air crawling over her skin like static. Aurora sprawled on her makeshift throne, some wreckage-born monarch surveying the ruins of her domain. All coiled grace, all loose menace.

"You show up here," Wheels said, his voice low and sharp, each word a dagger aimed at Sync, "claiming you've got the key to take Steele down. Sounds like a setup to me. Convenient."

Lyra watched Sync, watched the way he held himself—too steady, too calm. Only slight tremors, a slight flick of what most likely were his eyes.

If he's lying, he's damn good at it.

"It is not convenience," Sync said, his voice measured, precise, like he was piecing together code in real time. "It is necessity. Steele's reach is vast, but it is not infinite. He cannot control everything, everywhere, at once. His reliance on his coding is his Achilles' heel. It is how I broke away, and it is where we can strike. I can show you."

Doc sighed, his breath heavy, like a man whose soul had grown too old for the body it still inhabited. He sat hunched over, his fingers tapping out an impatient rhythm against the surface of the table, the sound a steady drumbeat, each tap another second lost. He could feel it—time slipping through his fingers, each moment another breath Steele took, another inch of control he seized. The air in the room was thick, thick with the smell of burnt wires, oil, and sweat, and it was all Doc could do to keep from suffocating under the weight of it. Steele was gaining ground, always pushing forward, relentless, a predator at their heels. And all they had were scraps, parts of machines that couldn't even decide if they wanted to live or die.

Lyra's stomach twisted. She could feel the way things were closing in, how every move felt like a step backward. Steele wasn't just at the gates—he was inside the walls, gnawing at the foundation.

Doc's fingers curled into fists, nails biting into his palms, his knuckles white with frustration. Steele was close. Always close.

The silence was heavy, suffocating. Doc could see the others, faces pale, eyes avoiding his, but he didn't care. He was past caring.

"What fuckin' options are there?" he said. "Steele's drones are getting closer every damn day. If this pile of shitty parts has got a way to stop him, I want to hear it." His voice was raw, ragged with frustration, every word carrying the weight of too many sleepless nights, too many lost chances. He turned to Wheels, desperation curling around his words. "Do you think it can be done? I mean, whatever this pile of shitty parts is talking about?"

Wheels moved forward, the glow of the fluid within his cage casting sharp, angular shadows across his face. His voice came like gravel underfoot, unsteady but grinding with resolve.

"Steele's a ghost we can't outrun," Wheels snarled, the words like a blade dulled from too many fights. He glared at Sync as though sheer contempt could split him open, spill wires and circuits across the floor. "The kind of tyrant who programs fear straight into your bones, who reads your mind before you've even had the nerve to think. If there's a backdoor—and I'm not saying there is—it's not just risky. It's a goddamn loaded blaster jammed under our chins."

Lyra clenched her fists, nails biting into her palms.

Ain't that the truth of it. Steele isn't just a man. He's inevitability in a digital black trench coat. A whisper in every circuit. A shadow cast by the very lights that try to banish him.

Sync's mechanical eyes, dead and depthless, didn't blink. Didn't shift. Didn't twitch. Like they weren't eyes at all—just lenses cataloging failure, inevitability, the slow-motion train wreck of human desperation.

"I do not expect your trust," he said, his voice flat as iron. Almost soothing. The calm before a storm that had already decided to kill you. "I expect you to weigh the facts. I escaped. I have been free for three years. And I have brought you something Steele doesn't know exists: hope."

Hope. There's that fuckin' word again.

The word sounded like a bad joke, the punchline lost in blood and circuitry.

Lyra almost laughed.

Doc scoffed. The sound was venomous, like a knife dragged across rusted steel. "In this world, hope gets people killed," he mocked, his lip curling. "It's something you sure as fuck don't bring to a battlefield. No. You bring armor. Weapons. And a plan that doesn't smell like betrayal."

Sync didn't move, didn't shift, didn't breathe. Machines didn't need to. "I have risked everything to be here," he said. "If I wanted Steele's empire to expand, I would not have escaped. I would not have fought to keep my own thoughts, my own identity."

"And you're telling me this backdoor," Doc rumbled, the words like bile in his throat, "isn't some trap Steele's feeding you? A leash so he can yank you back when the time's right?"

Sync tilted his head, deliberate, slow—like a predator weighing his prey or his problem. "You want the truth?" His voice dropped, thick and dark, dragging like a shadow down a cracked alley. "There is no way to know. None. But while you sit there, twisting in your paranoia, Steele's machines keep marching . . . relentless, dumb, unstoppable. Your choices? They are shrinking by the second. You can sit there and doubt me, gnawing at your own ghost until all that is left of you is a smear on the pavement. Or you can take a chance."

Lyra's breath caught.

Chance. The most expensive currency in this city. Once you spend it, you don't get refunds.

Doc barked a laugh, sharp and humorless. He leaned back, arms crossed like a fortress. "You think we've made it this far by rolling dice? Steele isn't just a man with an army. He's a network. A hive mind. He sees what we see. He knows."

"You think I do not know what Steele is?" Sync's voice came low, lethal, a threat wrapped in words. "Like you, I have watched him build his empire of wires and rot. He has a mind that spreads across the city like a disease. A hive mind, exactly. It is his sickness. But not some miracle."

Lyra shivered.

That's the worst part. Steele isn't some god. He's a virus. A sickness that thinks it was a cure.

Sync's lips twisted into something that might have been a smile, but it wasn't friendly. "Time is too precious to waste talking about what cannot be done. Instead, we must figure out what can be done. Waiting for some grand divine intervention, hoping he will trip over his own coding—it is not about to happen. He has got his eyes everywhere, sure—but that does not mean we are helpless. His hive has holes. All hives do."

Sync's eyes narrowed, voice low and dangerous. "We must stop acting like there is no way out. And we cannot wait for Steele to make a mistake. We have to make him make a mistake—his first and last one."

Doc said nothing. His jaw clenched, the slow grind of teeth loud in the charged silence.

Lyra watched him, measuring the weight in his eyes.

Fear? No, not quite. He isn't afraid. He's thinking. Calculating. Trying to find a way out that doesn't involve trusting a bastard like Sync.

She broke the pause before it could strangle them all. "Listen," she said, her voice slicing through the tension. "Doc, you don't have to trust him. Shit, I don't trust him. Fuck, I don't trust anyone. Never have. But he's here, and he's offering something we don't have. A partnership. We're out of ideas and time. Steele's drones will find us eventually."

The truth burned in her throat. She didn't believe in partnerships. They were just temporary ceasefires before the inevitable betrayal. But the alternative was worse.

"Lyra's right," Wheels said, his voice distorted, glitchy sound. The glassy orbs masquerading as eyes locked with

Doc's. "The only thing worse than walking into a trap is doing nothing while the walls close in. This synth's talking about an option. Unless we've got a better one, we should consider what he's talking about."

"Let me show you the flaw," Sync said. "And you can decide for yourselves if it's worth the risk."

Sync snapped his sleeve back as if the fabric had been waiting for permission. The skin of his forearm separated along a faint seam—something like flesh remembering it had once been machinery. A narrow panel unfolded. From inside it, a needle slid forward with deliberate patience. He turned his wrist and pressed the needle into a waiting port in the wall console.

For a moment, nothing happened.

Then a hum began—not loud, but intimate, the way electricity speaks when it believes no one is listening. The sound climbed steadily, threading through the air until the room seemed to vibrate with a logic none of the visible equipment admitted to having.

The pitch rose higher.

Higher.

Then it vanished.

Not faded—vanished.

The silence that replaced it felt engineered.

Lyra braced. She hated moments like this.

The inhale before the scream.

Then, like a match striking in darkness, a holographic projection flared to life. Streams of light wove themselves into intricate patterns, coalescing into a luminous, three-dimensional map. Steele's network sprawled above them—a lattice of interlocking circuits, gleaming nodes pulsating like malignant stars. Lines snaked between them, a web of control and communication.

Sync gestured, his movements were sharp and precise, and the image zoomed into one sector—a tangle of data lines throbbing with energy.

"This is one of Steele's central processing nodes," he said, his voice the perfect algorithm of dispassion. "A filtration system. But here . . ." He gestured again, slicing through invisible threads. ". . . here, every command, every override converges."

Lyra hated the way he talked—his words wrapped tight, sharp-edged, dripping with quiet venom. Like he had all the answers wrapped in some neat little package, tied up with a string of contempt.

Wheels' lenses whirred, tightening on the pulsing code that Sync threw across the projection. He saw nested commands looping back on themselves, a hall of mirrors swallowing every fractured reflection whole. It wasn't just code; it was a maddening ouroboros, consuming itself in a black spiral of recursive madness. Every blink of light flickered a phantom message beneath the surface, a whisper from a Steele's dark soul.

"From what I can tell, seems solid as hell to me," Wheels muttered.

"It is," Sync said. No hesitation. No doubt. "On the surface." Another motion—sharp, surgical. The image peeled back, not like layers of skin, no—more like something worse, something rotting beneath a sterile exterior. Order dissolved into chaos: jagged fractures rippling through the latticework of code.

Lyra felt it then, the familiar clawing unease, the quiet certainty that no system—no machine, no person—was ever as invincible as it pretended to be.

"This," Sync said, his finger slicing toward a cluster of erratic, blinking data points, "is the flaw. An overlooked relic from Steele's early designs. A vulnerability he has been too confident to seal. Maybe because he believes it is unfindable. Or maybe because he has forgotten it."

Silence. The kind that tightens like a noose. Everyone leaned in. Even Wheels couldn't mask his intrigue. He moved closer, his glowing ocular implant reflecting the hologram's shifting patterns.

"Explain." Wheels' voice, tempered steel. No sarcasm now, just calculation.

Sync was a surgeon, and his words were the scalpel. "This one subroutine was meant as a failsafe—a way to override Steele in case of catastrophic error. Why it is there? I do not know. Like I said—buried, forgotten. But now it is a scar in his code. A scar I can pick at and exploit."

Lyra's fingers tightened on the holster of her weapon. Scar.

The word stuck. She knew scars. Knew how some healed clean, others stayed raw, waiting for the right pressure to split them open again.

The hologram pulsed as Sync manipulated the image, highlighting pathways threading toward the fractured node. "The flaw does not destroy Steele," he continued. "It opens a door. For seconds—minutes at best. Enough time to flood his system with chaos. An infection. A disease. One that can disrupt his command structure, sever the hive mind. His drones would turn on each other like rabid dogs."

Wheels tilted his bulbous head, his glowing gaze narrowing as he scanned the projection. "This is . . . not bad," he muttered, more to himself than anyone else. His mechanical appendages twitched at his side. "Difficult. Near impossible, maybe. But possible."

Lyra didn't like that word. Possible. It carried too much weight, too much risk. Possible meant a long shot. Possible meant people died.

Doc's expression was a thunderhead of doubt. "Wheels," he started, voice measured, careful—

". . . I'm saying," Wheels cut in, voice hard, decisive, "that what he's showing us is real. It's not a manipulation. It's the authentic code. I can see the signatures. And . . . I can see the flaw. It's there. I don't know how he found it, but it's there. If we hit it right, we have a shot. To take him down. A long shot, mind you, but a shot. Difficult . . . but possible."

The air shifted. A heartbeat where uncertainty twisted into something else. Lyra looked from Sync to Wheels, her grip easing just a fraction. Across the room, Aurora sat forward, the sharp glint of a predator in her eyes.

Doc let out a breath, slow, measured, the weight of a decision settling into his bones. "Difficult," he muttered, his voice barely more than a whisper. "But possible."

Lyra had heard that before. And every time, it meant one thing: someone wasn't coming back.

The needle slid back from Sync's forearm with the quiet efficiency of a guillotine finishing its job. The hologram shivered, collapsed inward like a dying star, and the darkness swallowed the room whole. The console's hum decayed into a whisper, then nothing.

"You wanted a reason to trust me," Sync said, no pride in his voice, no smirk curling at the edges. Just words. Just a fact, dropped in the space between them like a blade. "Now you have one. The choice is yours."

Doc's eyes ticked over to Lyra, his voice dropping to a deadly whisper. "But if this goes wrong . . ."

Lyra met his stare. Hard. Unblinking. The weight of the blaster in her grip was a familiar anchor, something solid in the shifting sand. "I know. I know. I'll clean up the mess. I always do."

And Christ, how she hated the taste of her own truth like bile in the throat.

"Smart girl," he said. Dismissive. Flat. A pat on the head from a hand she wanted to break. "That's why we keep you around."

Bastard!

Oh, how she wanted to peel his words from the air and shove them down his throat.

Her spine locked. A heat curdled in her gut, black and sharp-edged, crawling up her throat, ready to spit itself out in words meant to slice. She felt her body coil, every tendon stretched tight, a tension aching for release. Doc was lucky. He didn't know how lucky.

Then—another voice. Not Sync's. Not Doc's. Not Wheels. The voice in her mind. A jagged cut through her thoughts.

Who the fuck does he think he is?

Lyra's cybernetic eye flared, not a blink, but a pulse of something old and angry. The glow stuttered, a dying ember refusing to go cold. Her mechanical arm caught the light, jagged and unyielding, a piece of her that never wanted to be hers. Metal. Spite. A rejection of flesh that had betrayed her long before the machines ever had.

"Don't give me your shit," she snapped, stepping closer, close enough for him to feel the heat rolling off her like a fire set to burn everything in its path. "We work together. Got it?"

Doc's mouth tightened. A line carved from stone. Unreadable.

"You wanna play puppet master, pull the strings, fine," she snarled. "But don't pretend I'm some idiot who'll dance just 'cause you say so." Her fingers twitched, an ache crawling up her wrist, a longing to pull the trigger just to hear something break. "I don't trust you, Doc. I don't trust the tin man. I don't trust whatever the fuckin' hell this is." She exhaled through her teeth and turned to Wheels. "But if

Wheels says we move, we move. That doesn't mean I don't see the knife you're holding behind your back."

She saw it. Felt it. Hell, she'd carried her own long enough to know the weight.

A pause. Long enough for the air to get thick. Enough to choke on.

"You got something to say to that?" she asked Doc.

Doc let out a sigh, the kind that came from too many nights spent playing surgeon to bad decisions, too many bodies left cooling while he stitched up the ones still kicking. His shoulders slumped like a puppet with half its strings cut, face carved from something brittle, something exhausted. There was irritation there, buried deep, flashing behind his eyes like a knife catching bad light.

Lyra watched him, watched the way the weight settled in his bones. Like an old warhorse that had seen too many battles but was still too stubborn to drop. She wondered if he even knew what tired looked like anymore.

"I'm sorry, Crow." The words clattered to the floor, empty, like a coin flipped onto a dead man's palm. He dragged a hand through his hair, thinner than it had been last week, last month, last year. "This place makes you say stupid things sometimes. Makes you forget who's really in the trench with you."

He looked up, met her eyes—no dodging, no bullshit. "You think I don't know you got every reason to put me down like a sick dog? You think I don't hear it in your voice? Hell, maybe I earned it. But we don't get to pick our monsters, Crow. We just survive 'em. And right now, survival means trusting. I'm not the worst thing waiting in the dark."

Lyra could've laughed. Could've torn open her ribs and let the sound come clawing out.

Monsters. That's what we're talking about now? Fuckin' monsters in the dark?

Lyra almost laughed. The sound rose halfway and stalled somewhere behind her teeth. Monsters. That was the word he'd chosen, like it still meant something stable. Like the universe had bothered to keep the categories straight— this is the monster, this is the victim, here is the line between them.

Her breathing remained precise, deliberately regulated—the kind of mechanical calm you adopt when probability says violence is seconds away.

"Good," she said.

Her voice carried the tightness of something engineered to cut.

"You know where I stand. But don't think for a second I'm lapping up this tin can's snake oil. If Wheels backs it, we move as one."

Her cybernetic fingers curled, metal scraping metal, a sound like teeth grinding in the dark. "I don't gamble on ghosts, Doc, or some gut feeling dressed up in fancy words. You should know that by now. I've seen too many fools bet on a whisper and end up painting the pavement with whatever was left inside 'em."

She leaned in, close enough for Doc to feel the heat rolling off her. "So, tell me, Doc . . . are we running from ghosts? Monsters? Or are we already dead and just too dumb to lie down?"

Lyra already knew the answer. She'd known it the second they stepped into this mess. Ghosts didn't kill you. Ghosts didn't twist knives into soft places. It was the living. It was the bastards who still had blood left to spill.

Doc didn't flinch. His eyes were flint, cutting through the air between them. "We're standing on the edge of nothing. This isn't some damn game, Crow. One wrong move, and we burn."

Lyra's lips curled—not a smile, just the sharp edge of a blade finding its mark. "It's always been that way. You hesitate, you die. You wait for the perfect move, but you never make one. We get scraps. And if we don't take every last one, Steele grinds us into something worse than dust."

Doc exhaled, sharp and uneven, like the breath hurt coming out. He turned to Sync, his voice low, dangerous. "You'd better be more than a flashy hunk of metal, gearhead. Because if this goes sideways, our blood's gonna paint the walls." A beat. His jaw tightened. "So will your oil."

Lyra watched Sync, waiting, calculating. This was the part where you either proved you had a spine or showed you were just another loose bolt waiting to shake free. And she was done dealing with broken parts.

Sync inclined his head, calm as the silence before the detonation. "I would not have sought Crow if there was not a path."

Doc's gaze found Lyra's, pinning her like an insect under glass. A flicker of something passed between them, thin as a razor's edge. Acknowledgment? Resignation? Whatever it was, it was a pact neither wanted but both understood. His nod was barely there, brittle as old bone.

Lyra didn't return it. Didn't need to. The sharpness in her stare dulled, just a fraction, and that was enough.

Grudging respect, or just inevitability? What did it matter? The game was already in motion.

Aurora turned sharply, movements clipped, shoulders locked into place like battle plating. Lyra saw it—the split-second hesitation, the phantom weight pressing just behind the ribs. Regret? Doubt? The kind of pain that had no name because naming it made it real?

She crushed the thought before it could sink its claws in. Emotions were dead weight. Dead weight got people killed.

"Next move?" Doc's voice cracked like thin ice.

Sync's gaze slid to Lyra, unreadable as deep space. "It is time for Crow to meet Calista Storm."

That should've been the end of it. Clean. Decisive. But it wasn't.

Lyra felt it, that faint, metallic taste of something unsaid. A fraction of a second too long before he spoke, the way his fingers tightened by his side.

Sync was holding something back.

She didn't press. Not yet.

Instead, she turned to Wheels, tapped her temple sharp as a gunshot. His nod snapped back. Ironclad. No bullshit.

Silent pact sealed. Message received. No need for words.

They'd all been speaking in codes for what seemed like years, a twisted ballet of glances and gestures, every soul in this mad carnival speaking the language of the damned.

THREE

FRAGMENTS OF MEMORY

The rain-slicked ruins of New York Veritas sprawled before them, a goddamn broken dream vomited up by some cosmic junkie, all razor-sharp edges and promises shattered like the bones of hope. Lyra and Sync stood in this cesspool of humanity's folly, the threshold of Doc Jones' sanctuary far behind them, that secret bastion of sanity in a world that had long since gone batshit crazy. The air, thick with the stench of rot and fear—a noxious cocktail brewed by some sadist bartender with a twisted sense of humor—burned the back of their throats with the acrid flavor of mankind's hubris.

Go ahead. Breathe deep, sweetheart. Fill your lungs. The stink scares off the ones who can't hack it.

Lyra forced the breath down anyway, gagging, trying to will away the bile clawing at the base of her tongue. She'd breathed this filth for too long, letting it settle into her lungs, and now it coursed through her veins like some toxic elixir. But it still turned her stomach, still made her wonder if survival was just another word for slow poisoning.

They gazed out at the dead arteries of the once-great metropolis, now nothing more than a playground for nightmares. The city bled color into the puddles, neon sickness smeared across dead pavement, crawling up the broken ribs of towers nobody remembered loving. It wasn't illumination; it was mockery. The place grinned with all its broken teeth and flung its arms wide— "Come closer. Don't be shy. Let me gnaw the last scraps of hope off your bones."

Should've run. Should've vanished before the streets learned my name, before the stink of this place wormed its way under my skin and made itself at home.

She'd rehearsed that regret a thousand times, and it never saved her once. Regret was useless currency, and the city didn't accept it anyway.

So here she stood with Sync, two offerings wrapped in stubborn flesh—one real, one fake—waiting for the inevitable—waiting for the city to decide how loudly it wanted them to break.

And that smell. Oh, sweet suffering Christ, that smell. It never left. It was as if every sewer in hell had backed up at once, mixing with the putrid stench of decay and the acrid tang of despair. It rammed its way into your throat, made a home in the sinuses, a thick, festering thing that refused to leave.

Breathe through your mouth. Lie to yourself. Pretend you can't taste it. Pretend it isn't seeping into your skin.

Lyra locked her jaw and looked at Sync. He stared ahead, blank, serene—like someone who'd long since stopped noticing. Maybe he had. Maybe he had yanked the wires of his odor sensors from his nose, declared the world unscented. Lucky him.

The city didn't bother with mercy or speed. It didn't kill you outright. It processed you. Slow. Patient. Until one day, there was a shape where you used to be, and even that was temporary. It ogled them, a cadaver with a sickening grin, maggots writhing in its eyes. "Come on in," it whispered, voice like grinding glass and screaming metal. "Step into my loving arms. I've got such sights to show you, such pleasures to inflict upon your tender flesh and fragile minds." The abyss didn't just sing—it howled, rattling the bones of the desperate and the foolish alike.

It's not a choice, not really.

Move forward or rot.

A few broken neon signs flickered, coughing out color in jagged spasms, bleeding itself across the asphalt in greasy reds and sickly blues, like the blood of some dying god, slick and pulsing. Lyra caught the grotesque carnival of light, warping it into something even uglier. Beneath the synth-skin of his face, Sync's cybernetic eyes whirred, lenses adjusting, processing, dissecting. The world had no place for purity anymore—just the desperate marriage of flesh and machine, a shotgun wedding officiated by necessity and stitched together with pain.

"You sure you know where you're going?" Lyra rasped, voice like old whiskey and bad decisions.

Sync nodded, pointing ahead. "The wall is our destination. Calista is waiting."

The wall. The great, impassable promise of something worse beyond.

They ran, slipping through the rotting arteries of what was once the greatest city on Earth, now a junkyard of shattered pasts. Rusted hovercars, glass glittering like broken dreams, bones bleached and brittle. The ghosts of old streetlights shuddered, casting shadows that shifted when they shouldn't.

No turning back now. Not unless you wanted to end up another stain on the pavement.

The urban labyrinth twisted around them, a gaping wound carved from steel and sorrow. Sync's circuits twitched like a junkie's last nerve, every sensor on high alert. The air thickened, turned sour. The shadows were restless, pregnant with malice.

Then a sound far off.

"Reavers." He didn't breathe the word so much as exhale it, his fingers itching on the cold steel of his plasma pistol.

Oh, for fuck's sake.

Lyra's lip curled, a sneer that could turn milk to acid and make a priest renounce his vows. "Figures. Can't take two goddamn steps in this shithole without tripping over those cock-sucking abominations." She cracked her knuckles, felt the weight of her blaster against her thigh. "Ever had the pleasure of a face-to-face with one of those walking nightmares?"

Of course he had. They all had. And every time, it was the same thing. Blood, screaming, and the nagging question—why the hell were they still breathing?

Sync's titanium spine stiffened. "No. I have always tried to avoid them. I like my circuitry where it is, thank you very much."

Lyra blinked at him.

What the fuck! You've been out here this long and haven't crossed paths with Reavers? Cute.

That's like swimming in acid and never getting burned. Either he was lucky, lying, or trying to be funny in some sick way.

Lyra ground her teeth.

"Count your blessings," she growled, voice all shattered glass and back-alley grit. "They were human once, if you can believe that horseshit. Now? All fucked up. Their eyes . . ." She exhaled, sharp and bitter. "Imagine piss-colored marbles floating in spoiled milk. Pupils so wide you could fall in and never hit bottom. And they don't just see you, they take you in, make you part of whatever nightmare plays behind those funhouse-mirror stares. They reflect this city's puke like it's some kind of sick joke."

She'd seen those eyes too many times. Sometimes in her sleep. Mostly when she was wide awake.

Sync's optical sensors whirred, drinking in the grotesquerie like it was an art exhibit. "I take it their appearance isn't the worst of it."

"You got that right, sparky." Lyra rolled her shoulders, the ghost of old fights pressing down on her bones. "It's the hunger that'll get you. The kind that doesn't stop when the belly's full. A hunger for death. For the hunt. They move like oil on water, quiet as a widow's grief and twice as deadly."

She told him about the first time she saw one of them feed. The way the body barely had time to hit the ground before the thing was on it, tearing, devouring, like it was something holy.

"Fascinating," Sync muttered, synthetic sarcasm dripping from his voice like motor oil. "Such charming details."

Lyra's laugh scraped out of her throat like a blade dragged over stone. "Oh, I'm just getting started, tin man." Her fingers curled into fists, nails biting skin. "You'll hear 'em before you see 'em. That whisper of boots on rain-slicked streets, like Death himself out for an evening stroll. And when the moonlight hits just right?" She flashed Sync a grin that wasn't a grin at all. "You'll catch the glint of their scavenged metal, a little wink from the Grim Reaper himself."

And by then, it'd be too damn late.

Sync's processors purred, slicing through probabilities with the cold efficiency of a guillotine. "Any weaknesses that can be exploited?"

"Weaknesses? Usually, a laser blast between the eyes does the trick," Lyra sneered. "But don't get cocky. They're the period at the end of humanity's sentence, sweetheart. The ultimate 'fuck you' to God's grand plan."

God.

She tasted the word like a mouthful of ashes. The last time she'd believed in anything bigger than herself, she was still small enough to be held. Now? Now she held the world at blasterpoint.

"Good thing I don't believe in God," Sync said, voice as cool and impersonal as the metal under his synthetic skin.

"Fairy tales are for meatbags clinging to the notion that someone up there gives two shits about their pitiful lives," she chuckled. "By the way, what gets your gears all aflutter in this rotting world? What does a walking calculator like you believe in, huh?"

Belief in a higher power was a disease. She'd seen what it did to people—left them grasping at ghosts, whispering prayers into the silence while their bodies were picked clean by monsters. Lyra had no interest in catching that infection.

"Believe in? I do not have any beliefs. Waste of time and energy. And you?"

Lyra's grin was a flash of teeth in the dark, a wolf's invitation. "I believe in the orgasmic surge of power when my finger caresses the trigger and sends another Reaver or one of Steele's bots back to whatever cesspool spawned it. I believe in the cold, hard truth that in this nightmare, the only god worth a damn is the one you see in the mirror. While others are busy pondering the cosmic joke, I'm busy rewriting the punchline, one plasma-scorched corpse at a time."

She meant it, too. That first kill—clumsy, desperate—had been a necessity. The ones after? Those had been art.

Suddenly, the horizon split open, and the Reavers came slithering out of the black, carrion beasts with meat-drunk eyes and grins stitched together from other people's pain.

"Humans feeding on humans," Lyra sneered. "Exactly what Steele wants. Keep everyone scared. Keep everyone divided. Keep everyone too busy pissing themselves to notice the bars of the chrome-plated cage."

And the worst part? It worked. Lyra had watched an entire city crumble under that particular brand of fear. Didn't even take a war. Just a whisper, a well-placed knife, a door that stayed locked one second too long.

They slid into an alleyway, the air heavy with the perfume of rotting things. In the distance, something screamed—long and shrill, barely human. The hunt had begun.

"We need to move," Lyra whispered, eyes cutting to the rooftops. "They'll have scouts."

"Do you not fear them?" Sync asked.

Fear? No. Not anymore. Fear had been burned out of her the first time she'd heard someone beg for mercy and got laughter in return.

Lyra smiled, unslinging her blaster with the easy grace of someone born to violence. "Fear? Fuck no. I've no problem painting the city with their innards. But mark my words . . . when they come, it'll be a goddamn tsunami of teeth and claws. You'll be pissing your pants with lubricant before you can even think to say 'oh shit' . . . and believe me, you'll be saying it till your throat gushes oil."

She wasn't exaggerating. Reavers didn't come in ones or twos. They came in tides, in sickening torrents of snapping jaws and glistening sinew, and when they did, you either fought like hell or became part of the goddamn scenery.

They emerged onto what was once a large avenue, now a canyon of broken glass and twisted metal, the bones of a city that had long since died and refused to lie still. In the distance, the great wall loomed far off, a rusted scar clawed across the skyline. Sync's implants whirred, mechanical irises contracting as he calculated the distance.

"About ten more miles to cover," he said. "Usually clear of Reavers. But they have been coming closer to the wall, of late."

Lyra spat on the cracked pavement. "Ain't that just fuckin' peachy."

Everything seemed to be getting smaller. Not literally, but Lyra felt it anyway—that sickly pulse of a city long past dead, its remains still gnawing at anything foolish enough to walk its corpse. They moved swiftly, sticking to the shadows, every nerve flayed raw, every sense tuned to the whisper of movement that meant death was near.

The silence stretched, tight as a garrote.

Then it snapped.

A scream, ragged and wet, shattered the air, followed by the unmistakable sound of flesh being torn from the bone. Sync and Lyra exchanged glances. No words needed. They knew what that meant.

The Reavers had found easier prey.

Poor bastard.

Might've been a scavenger. Might've been a lost kid. Might've been someone who thought they were fast enough to run. Didn't matter now.

She muttered it anyway. "Poor bastard."

They pressed on. Running. The wall swelling in their vision with every step.

"Hope we can make it," Sync told her.

She just shook her head. Hope was a cruel thing, a knife edged in irony. Because right as it started to feel real, as the rusted promise of safety loomed near, the universe pissed right in their eyes.

They rounded a corner.

Reavers. Six. But more behind them. Milky eyes, slack jaws, lips curled back over teeth that had been filed to points. A stink rolled off them—blood, oil, and something worse, something wrong. One of them stepped forward, head cocked at a grotesque angle.

"Well, well. Looks like we got ourselves some real live ones, boys. You look tasty. Rather tasty indeed." His voice was guttural, clicks and hisses of a predator, with a slight tremor in it, a constant, low-frequency shudder like a dying engine struggling to turn over, fueled by the stolen life force it greedily consumed.

Lyra's fingers flexed against her blaster grip. She knew the look in their eyes. Knew the hunger. Knew what came next.

Sync's implants kicked into overdrive, time slowing to a crawl as combat protocols engaged. He saw the minute twitches of muscle in the beast, every shift in weight, every tell that betrayed a killing blow before it was even thrown.

He reached for his blaster.

Then the world tore open.

The Reavers lunged, a snarling mass of madness and bone. Sync's blaster sang, bolts of superheated plasma turning the first two attackers into smoking remnants of what used to be men. Lyra's blaster roared, hypersonic slugs ripping through meat and cartilage, tearing through the pack with mechanical precision.

She grinned, feral, electric.

"Come on, you rotten fucks," she snarled. "Let's dance."

The Reavers kept coming, dragged forward by a vile appetite that laughed at logic and desecrated sanity for sport. One of them—a walking landfill of scar tissue, metal shards, and repurposed agony—slammed into Lyra like a runaway hovercar. They hit the ground hard, a tangle of rage and limbs, the stench of sweat and rust filling her nostrils.

Fuck me. Always bigger. Always stronger. Why does every fight have to be a goddamn slog.

She twisted, trying to get leverage, but the bastard was all weight, all pressure, a dead thing that hadn't figured out it was supposed to lie down. It looked down at her and smiled.

She spat at its face. "You forgot something, big boy," she said, laughter cracking through the strain, cold and mean. Her blaster kissed its belly.

Its eyes flared—pure animal shock, the brief miracle of understanding.

"Night . . . night," she told him, and pulled the trigger, blowing the thing into bloody bits.

Sync spun, his augmented reflexes making a mockery of the Reavers' clumsy ferocity. A blade arced toward him, jagged and rust-diseased, but he was already moving. He caught the Reaver's arm mid-swipe, cybernetic servos whining, and twisted. Bone snapped like cheap plastic. The Reaver screamed—not in pain, never in pain, only in fury—and lunged for his throat.

Kill or be killed. That was the game, the only rule. But Lyra never had time for rules. She was there, grabbing it away from Sync. The Reaver's breath was a sewer in summer, its eyes two milky whirlpools of madness. She drove her forehead into its face, something breaking beneath the impact—nose, teeth, whatever. It recoiled, just enough. She jammed a knee into its ribs, shoved it off, and scrambled to her feet.

Sync pointed his blaster at it, but the blaster overheated, the barrel molten-hot, spitting smoke like a dying machine. He threw it aside without a thought, reached for the monomolecular blade in his boot. The weapon whispered through flesh, through cartilage, through the thin lies that held bodies together. A slash, a scream, another corpse cooling on the ground.

More came, but they too fell. And soon, it all ended in a heap of bodies, the silence loud enough to make ears ring. Sync and Lyra stood amid the wreckage, breath coming in short, jagged bursts. Blood dripped, theirs or not, who could say?

"Are you okay?" Sync wiped the gore from his face, barely sparing a glance at the carnage.

Lyra rotated her shoulder, something clicking back into place. Fire lanced through her nerves. "Fuckin' great. You?"

"Optimal," he said as his implants had already decided to start repairing what little damage he had taken.

She heard the soft humming sound of his body repairing itself.

Must be nice.

They turned toward the wall, the ugly bastard of steel and time, closer now. Behind them, drones floated high above the ruins, unbothered. Observers or executioners? Hard to say. Maybe both.

"Come on," Lyra said, holstering her blaster to her thigh. "Let's not overstay our welcome."

They moved. The smell of fresh slaughter clung to them like a living thing, a parasite wrapping around their throats, digging into their skin. The wall loomed, not just metal but something more, something ancient, something watching. It leered down at them, rust bleeding into corrosion, a god with tetanus in its teeth.

Lyra clenched her jaw, pushed forward.

Keep moving. Keep breathing. One foot, then another.

The air had thickened, turned to lead in her lungs. She swallowed against it, against the way it pressed on her ribs, against the way it whispered ugly truths in her ear.

Shadows twisted at the edges of her vision, playing tricks, playing games. The wind muttered secrets it had no right to know. A pebble tumbled loose under Sync's boot. A small thing. An insignificant thing. But it clattered. Rang out like a gunshot. Lyra's pulse spiked. Her hand flew to her blaster before she could think.

Too fast. Always too fast. The moment between quiet and violence never lasted long enough.

As they drew near to the wall, the goddamn wall, it didn't just rise—it asserted itself, a vertical snarl of purpose, a thing with presence, with intent. An insult carved in rust and decay, thrust skyward like a broken finger flipping off the universe. It wasn't just a barrier. It was punishment. A monolith of guilt and shame, built by men who thought they could partition their sins and lock them away like diseased animals.

Lyra swallowed hard. It was worse than the stories. Worse than the nightmares that crawled into her head when she was too tired to fight them off.

On one side, there once stood a shining city—gleaming glass, smooth stone, the soft hum of a future that didn't care about the past. Clean, prosperous, untouched by the grime of humanity's sins.

And then there was her side.

Lyra's world. A neon fever dream. The kind that burned your retinas and left a residue on your soul. The air tasted like old copper and bad choices. The ground was slick with things better left unidentified. And always, always, the feeling that something with sharp teeth was watching from the shadows.

The wall had cut the city apart like an executioner's blade. Neat. Precise. Final. But now it cut nothing but desolation.

"So where do we go from here?" Lyra's voice came out steadier than she felt.

"We go inside," Sync said, and she hated how casual he sounded.

"What? The wall is a huge piece of rusted metal. Forged in the fires of hell. Solid as rock. Everyone knows that."

Sync turned an infuriating smirk on her. "Rusted? Yes. Solid? About as solid as your grasp on reality."

Asshole.

"When the bureaucrats of old built this nightmare, they threaded it with utility corridors," he continued. "Like arteries in a corpse. Meant to feed power, data, all that good stuff. But the big dreamers left it half-finished. Like always."

Lyra grimaced, the kind of expression that would send stone saints crumbling in horror. "How the hell are we supposed to get inside?"

Sync's eyes went sharp, his implants flickering in the half-light. "There." He jabbed a finger toward a section of the wall where a massive rock slumped against the base. "That's our doorway."

A howl ripped through the air. Then another. Then another.

Lyra didn't breathe.

The Reavers had their scent.

"Shit." The word spat from her lips before she could stop it. "Looks like we've got company."

They ran. Stealth was a lost cause. Speed was all that mattered now. The wall grew before them, salvation and damnation wrapped up in rust and regret.

Behind them, the howls rose, a symphony of madness, a promise of torn flesh and shattered bones.

Sync reached the wall first, his cybernetic fingers gouging into the stone like maggots burrowing into meat.

Lyra turned, back pressed to the rough surface. The blaster in her grip vibrated with deadly anticipation.

The Reavers were coming. Hunger and hate on two legs, rushing toward them like a tide of bad dreams.

She bared her teeth.

"Any time now, Sync!" she screamed, her voice ragged, raw, a blade honed on desperation. "Any . . . fuckin' . . . time!"

So, this is where I die.

She felt it in her bones, that little hitch in the universe's breath before the punchline. The gods—if they existed—were laughing their celestial asses off.

Sync's hands locked onto the rock, the hands of an automaton cranking back the gears of doom. The machinery inside him groaned, metal grinding on metal, pistons pumping bloodless fury. With a sound that was part human, part engine, he heaved the rock upward, the world tilting under its weight. "Now or never, Crow!"

Never sounds good. Never sounds like a warm bed and a belly full of something that doesn't taste like dirt and regret.

She moved. She always moved. A pivot, a spin, the last dance of a dead woman, and then she was free-falling, sucked into the throat of the abyss, into the cold vacuum where light goes to die. Sync—last-minute, last-ditch, last-fuckin'-hope—followed, the boulder slamming down behind him like the universe sealing a tomb.

They sprawled in the dark, lungs clawing at the dead air. Distant howls, the Reavers' rage muted by tons of unyielding stone and metal. Lyra's pupils flared wide. She looked around the room they'd locked themselves into. Metal walls, a few dark passages, cold as a morgue slab.

"They're too dumb to know to lift the boulder," she muttered.

Sync nodded.

Her lips curled, a smirk sharp enough to slice through the quiet. "Well, if this ain't a slice of heaven, I don't know what is."

Sync rose, augments whirring, mapping, plotting. "Come on," he said. "Calista's waiting."

Lyra sighed.

Forward. Always forward. No time to mourn the wreckage left behind.

They trudged into the depths of the wall, leaving the echoes of slaughter and the rotting carcass of yesterday. Ahead, the dark stretched forever, deep and indifferent. And somewhere, maybe—just maybe—a stubborn little ember refused to die.

Calista Storm's base had been gnawed into the metal wall that split New York Veritas like a broken jawbone, a thing old and rusting and still hungry. The wall throbbed, a sound that wasn't just machines but something older, something buried under layers of decay and compromise. Somewhere deep within, blue circuitry pulsed under the filth, the faintest ghost of a heartbeat, a thing pretending it was still alive. The walls weren't walls; they were scars—steel sutures and brittle concrete patching up a wound that had never healed, that never would heal. Pipes twisted like exposed veins, hissing steam in long, shuddering breaths, sighing out the city's dying language.

Lyra hated it here. Places like this got into your skin. Stayed there. This was where people forgot themselves, where they bled into the walls and became nothing but another echo of old ghosts. She kept walking. She wouldn't be one of them.

Sync's boots made no sound as he moved. It was as if gravity had learned to give up on him. He wasn't human, not really—just something wearing the shape of a human, all silent precision and clenched efficiency, built for war and nothing else. His body thrummed with some deep-coded instinct that never shut off. A weapon that had outlived its war but still sharpened itself against the edges of the world, just in case.

She glanced at him. Nothing in his face. Nothing ever in his face. You could carve stone into softer shapes than whatever the hell he was made of. She wondered what was going through that neural lace of his.

Probably numbers—cold, obedient—going through calculations with each step, of friction and torque.

Her own mind was a mess of static, her body moving on autopilot while the rest of her lagged behind, stuck somewhere else, somewhere she didn't want to be, with someone she wished she could forget.

Rana Sharma.

Dammit! Why now?

The name hit like a dull knife to the ribs. Lyra inhaled, exhaled. She wouldn't let it go too far into her head, this time.

Need a diversion. Something. Anything.

Talk to the tin man.

"This is a goddamn maze," she said, her voice just above a whisper. Some places made you feel like you had to keep your voice low, like you might wake something up if you spoke too loudly. "How much longer?"

Sync didn't answer right away. He had that irritating, synthetic patience, the kind that made you want to shove him just to see if he'd react. Instead, he just tilted his chin toward the door ahead. No wasted words. No wasted anything.

Lyra's fingers tensed.

They came to a door. Marked with the insignia of the resistance, a fist enclosed by a ring. She had seen it before—had known it in smoke and ruin—spray-burned onto broken buildings, stamped into the twisted hulks of transports, etched into the charred shells of bots that had screamed once and then gone blessedly quiet. The symbol wasn't a promise, not a warning, but a dare. It could spit out truth, hot and unforgiving, or it could swallow them whole and feed their bones into a machine that didn't care how brave they thought they were. Either way, there was no pretending they had a choice.

Inside the room, the air hit like a slap, thick with rust, oil, the churn and ache of machinery that never slept. It wasn't just a smell; it was a weight. A thing that crawled into your lungs, into your bones, and stayed there, made a home out of you whether you wanted it or not.

And there she was, planted dead center, sitting at a desk as if the riot of ruin and madness had politely stepped aside to frame her. Not surviving the chaos. Curating it.

Calista Storm.

Not what Lyra had expected. But then again, nothing ever was. Expectations were a sucker's game, a carnival trick designed to steal your wallet while you applauded. Everyone had paid that price at least once, the receipt was written in scars.

Calista lifted her eyes and drove them straight into Lyra like spikes, clean and deliberate, the way a surgeon cuts when he doesn't care if it hurts as long as it's precise. That look stripped things away. Not clothing—worse. Layers. Defenses. The soft lies people tell themselves just to get through the hour. Lyra's skin crawled under it, itching like a warning she didn't know how to heed. This was a gaze that didn't admire or judge; it claimed. It left marks you couldn't see and never stopped feeling.

She wasn't beautiful. That word didn't apply. It was too tidy, too forgiving. Calista existed outside the categories people used to stay comfortable. She was rough-edged, unfinished, a living wrong note that caught in the ear and refused to resolve. Looking at her made you want to flinch— or reach out—just to make sure she wasn't some trick of the nerves, some cruel hallucination the world had decided to indulge.

Lyra flexed her fingers.

Look away, and she owns you. Hold her gaze, and you might not like what you see.

Shit. As if there were ever a choice.

Lyra locked her stare in place and took the hit.

Calista's head was shaved, her face carved in sharp, unsparing lines, a scar cutting through one eyebrow. Skin dark as polished mahogany, gleaming under the flickering light—but there was no warmth to it, no safe harbor. Just edges. Just something that had seen the world for what it was and made itself harder in return.

Something inside Lyra quivered—a softness, frail and misshapen, like a half-drowned rat clawing for air in the basement of her ribs. It gasped once, a pitiful thing, before she slammed the trapdoor shut and locked it with spite.

No. Not here. Not now.

Softness was a rigged grenade wired to your own teeth. Pull the pin and smile—boom, you're sentimental roadkill. Affection? That was a sucker's game, a hospice bed with velvet sheets and a scalpel tucked under the pillow.

Maybe someone like Calista could afford that kind of delusion. Maybe. On a good day.

But Lyra? Lyra didn't get the luxury of weakness. Weakness was something she carved out with a dull spoon years ago and left to rot in the gutter behind her first kill.

What does she want from me?

"You made it," Calista said, voice smooth as oil on wet pavement, dripping slow, sweet, and toxic. The kind of voice that slid under the door before you even knew it was there. She wore it well—like someone who'd swallowed too many bitter truths and learned to turn them into honey. Lyra's stomach went tight. Her skin tingled.

I should leave. Now.

"Yeah," Lyra whispered, her throat tightening around the word like it wanted to choke it back down. A warning clanged in her ribs, an alarm that had been wired into her long before she ever met Calista.

Too late now. She was in it, ankle-deep in whatever this was, and every instinct screamed at her to turn and walk the other way. Fast.

Too late for that.

Calista leaned back, lazy, like she had all the time in the world, like she was already three steps ahead. Eyes sharp, slicing through the space between them. Lyra felt flayed, bones picked clean before she even had time to move.

"You're wondering why I brought you here," she said.

Not a question. A verdict.

Lyra clenched her teeth. Didn't answer. Silence was safer. Silence was a knife you could turn on someone if you held it right. She stayed still, let the quiet stretch long and thin, let it do the talking for her.

Calista smiled. Not a nice smile. A blade glinting in the dark.

"I brought you here because I need you." The words dropped heavy, a weight pressing into Lyra's ribs, an iron hook catching something in her chest. "You've got a gift. A sense." She tapped her temple, measured, deliberate. "You see through the lies. You know what's real, what's not."

She's watching. Measuring. Tallying up the cost of me.

Calista's eyes didn't just look at Lyra—they prowled. They dragged across her face like fingers that knew where the bruises would be, nosing at the sealed places Lyra kept welded shut, the ones she pretended weren't there even in the dark. The space between them went brittle, starved for oxygen. When Calista spoke again, her voice dropped and coiled, a thing with bite behind it.

"But there's something else—about you. You want to know what that is?"

Lyra felt it then, a hard inward wrench, something turning over where instinct lives, sharp and unmistakably wrong.

The air around her thickened, congealed, pressed in like a vise. Muscles locked. Pulse spiked. The question wasn't just hanging there—it was a snare, an iron trap with jagged teeth waiting to snap shut. And Calista, goddamn Calista, wasn't going to wait for Lyra to talk her way out of it. Wasn't going to give her the mercy of a lie. She already knew.

And knowing made it worse. So much worse.

"You knew Rana Sharma." No hesitation. No question mark. The words were an executioner's axe, suspended, waiting to drop.

Rana Sharma.

Again. Of course again.

The name was a splinter driven into memory, never healed over, never pushed out. Lyra had tried—God, she had tried—to sink it, to press it down into the dark places where names went to rot. It refused. It always refused.

And now Calista Storm—this stranger with thunder in her bones—had reached in barehanded, hauled it back into the light, brushed it clean, and dropped it at Lyra's feet. Not gently. Like a body. Like evidence. And Lyra was meant to look.

"I worked with her," Calista went on, voice slipping into something like nostalgia. A cruel trick. There was nothing sentimental in her stare, nothing soft in the way she held Lyra in place. "At NYVPD. We were close. She taught me everything. The systems. The tech. She told me what Steele was playing with. She showed me. She helped me understand it all."

Every syllable scraped.

Lyra clenched her teeth.

Rana had always been the best of them. Better than the suits who saw people as numbers. Better than the cynics who thought the world was just a game of power and leverage. She'd seen the gears of the system, seen how they crushed people to dust, and she'd tried—tried—to jam a wrench into the works.

And what had that gotten her?

Nothing. Just another name on a casualty list. Just another bright light snuffed out before it could burn the place down.

That red hair—fire, unrelenting, alive. Those sharp green eyes, always calculating, always three moves ahead.

That voice, steady, deliberate, never once faltering, not even when the world had started caving in.

Then she was gone.

Gone before Lyra could say goodbye. Before she could hold her one last time, whisper something—anything—that might have made a difference.

The loss hit her all over again, sudden, merciless, a phantom fist driving into her sternum.

"Rana's dead," she rasped, barely recognizing the sound as her own voice. A hollow thing.

Calista nodded, her expression unreadable. Pity? Maybe. Or maybe something darker.

"Yeah," she said quietly. "I know." She let the moment hang, not by accident. "Sorry she didn't make it."

The silence didn't arrive—it imposed itself, thick and punishing, stretching until it pressed against the ribs.

Then Calista spoke again, soft but sharp enough to cut. "She mattered to you, didn't she?"

And there it was. The blade slipped between the ribs.

Something in Lyra's chest buckled, a fracture spiderwebbing through bone, but she willed it shut before it could gut her. No room for that. No room for ghosts. They lingered too long, sank their teeth in, and refused to let go. She was done.

Calista stood there, waiting. Watching. Silence thick as steel cables, stretched taut with everything unsaid. She didn't press. Didn't have to. Lyra already knew. Whatever came next was going to hurt. But the wheel was already turning, and she was caught in the spokes. No way off. No way out.

She should've walked away. Should've closed her hands into fists, turned on her heel. Because Calista was right. Because the past was a noose, and she'd tied it around her own damn neck.

"I know she mattered to you," Calista said. Not soft. Not cruel. A scalpel slicing through tendon. Precise, sharp, unforgiving. "She mattered to me, too. Once." Her mouth twisted, but her eyes had already gone somewhere else— backward, inward, to places Lyra didn't want to see. "We were close. Closer than anyone had a right to be."

She was lying. Or she wasn't. Maybe both things were true.

Calista's voice dipped lower, a rasp of old wounds and new salt. "She had a whole list, you know. Things she thought time owed her. Futures she was already spending in her head. But Steele cut the line." She let the silence hang, a dead channel. "He erased her. And I am not going to let that slide into history's junk drawer. He doesn't get to delete that, too."

The room shrank. Lyra's breath turned jagged in her throat. She swallowed it whole.

"You said close." The word came out hollow, carved out of something deep and raw. "How close?"

Calista's lips twitched. Not a smile. Not even the ghost of one. More like the memory of a blade, unsheathed and waiting. "As close as you two were." The words landed like an executioner's stroke, swift and deliberate. "We drifted. But she told me all about you. About the two of you."

Something ugly twisted in Lyra's stomach.

"Happy," Calista continued, voice stripped bare. "She was happy. And I was happy for her."

Liar.

No. Maybe not. Maybe it was worse than that. Maybe it was the truth.

Lyra's eyes snapped shut. The weight of it all crashed down, an avalanche of lost things, things that should have been, things that had been torn from her fingers before she could even hold on. Rana was gone. That hole in the world wasn't filling, wasn't sealing shut. It festered, a raw and aching thing.

She forced her chest to still, let the words grind against her bones, let them settle like broken glass in her lungs. "Hard to forget her," she said, her voice stripped to the barest edge of sound. A breath she'd been holding so long it had turned to dust. "Hard to forget a force of nature."

She tore her eyes away from Calista. Took a deep breath. And then the moment was over. The world snapped back into focus, jagged edges like broken streetlights in a rain-slick alley.

"Tin man said you needed me. Why?" The words were ice, sharp and brittle. The brief fracture in her armor was gone. Vulnerability was a death sentence in this city. And Lyra wasn't planning on dying.

Calista's gaze sharpened, any softness swallowed whole. "Because I know what you can do. And I'm not stupid." A pause. Then: "Steele doesn't just own the muscle. He doesn't just own the drones, the men, the weapons. He owns the bones of this city. He owns the systems. The synths. The people. And through them, he owns everything."

Lyra already knew all that.

She just wanted to hear what Calista thought she was going to do about it.

"I want to bring him down," Calista said. "But I need someone who can slip between the cracks, unseen. Someone who knows how to move through this hellscape like smoke."

Lyra almost laughed. Almost.

Smoke was just the lie people told themselves when they wanted to believe in ghosts, in whispers, in things that could move without consequence. But smoke didn't slip through cracks—it was pulled, sucked, dragged. Smoke was what was left when something was burning.

Instead, she just looked at Calista. At the sheer heft of her words. At the future already sharpening its claws.

Calista's eyes flicked over her, measuring, weighing, waiting for the moment to press the knife in. This wasn't an offer. This was a deal made in a back alley, sealed with blood and a smirk.

"And you think that's me?" Lyra asked, raising an eyebrow. A dance step in the routine. A line in the script. They both knew it, but she played it anyway.

"I know it's you," Calista answered, and there it was— that smile. The kind that belonged to wolves in silk, to people who shook hands before they slit throats. That knowing, hungry curve of the lips, like she'd already set the trap and was just waiting for Lyra to step in. "You've survived everything this city has thrown at you. You've got the instincts to make it through the hell Steele's built. And shit . . . you've got heart."

Heart. Fuckin' word means nothing in a place like this.

Heart was what got people killed. Heart was what got them buried in shallow graves behind neon-lit gutters.

She studied Calista's face, hunting for a lie. Not an obvious one—a deeper one, coated in conviction and smugness. Calista was too sure. Too composed. Lyra had seen people play this game before, and the ones who smiled like that always had something in reserve. A card up the sleeve. A knife at the spine.

The silence stretched between them, thick and electric. And then Sync stepped forward.

No words. Just a shift in the room, like reality had hiccupped and the room had taken notice.

Lyra felt it, heavy, pressing at the corners of her awareness, unsettling. It was the freight behind them. The sins he carried like armor, the screams he had swallowed whole, the unrelenting weight of having seen too much, done too much, and survived anyway. It pressed. It bruised. It was unfair.

Something tightened in her chest. Maybe a warning. Maybe a promise.

"Steele's power doesn't lie just in his army," Sync said. His voice was drained of anything human, running cold and precise, too flat, too measured—like a machine forced to imitate speech. But there was something beneath it, a rot in the foundation, a barely suppressed fury gnawing at the edges. It was the sound of something that should have been dead but refused to lie still. "His power is in the Iron Rose."

The name hit Lyra like a static charge against her skin. The Iron Rose. A monster whispered in back alleys, passed between those who understood the city's rot ran deeper than flesh. But monsters didn't make her stomach clench. Monsters didn't set her bones on edge.

No, what made Lyra's skin crawl was the cold certainty coiling through her veins like liquid steel. The Iron Rose wasn't simply a whisper in the dark—it was a goddamned monolith, a spire of iron and shadow that rose over the city, over the world, blotting out sun and hope alike. It crawled across the horizon like a cancer, each floor a rib, each window a tooth, reaching into dark alleys and broken high-rises, into shattered minds that didn't even know they were looking. Lyra had seen the wreckage it left behind— bodies twisted into obscene sculptures of metal and flesh, screaming faces frozen in eternal agony. The very air seemed to shrink away from it, leaving a vacuum, a hunger that threatened to suck everything into that tower's black heart.

But that's what that bastard Steele wanted. That's all he wanted!

Sync's stare locked onto her, too deliberate, too exact, like a program running through its last remaining lines of code before corruption set in. "He doesn't kill humans anymore," he said, and the way he said it—hollow, drained—set Lyra's nerves buzzing like power lines in a storm.

The pause stretched. And then, just for a second, something flickered in Sync's eyes. Something real. Regret? Pity? It didn't matter. Whatever it was, it drowned before it could take its first breath.

"He collects them. Drains them. Uses them to fuel the Iron Rose."

Lyra's gut twisted.

"What do you mean?" Her voice came out raw, a splintered thing ripped from the dark corners of her mind where disbelief was already trying to dig in its claws.

Sync leaned forward. His shadow swallowed the space between them, devouring the room inch by inch. "The human body," he said, "is a perfect conduit. The nervous system, the bioelectric field—nothing but meat-sacks of voltage, sparking with delusions of free will." He exhaled, slow, deliberate. "Steele has no use for such pitiful illusions. He has no use for life, period. To him, you're just faulty circuitry waiting to be rewired or discarded."

No. No, she didn't want to hear this.

"So he takes," Sync continued. "Not just bodies. The whole damn thing. Mind, soul, whatever you want to call it.

He drains them, feeds them just enough, and drains them again. Over and over. Like batteries."

Her breath turned to glass in her throat.

"They do not die," Sync said. "Not really." His voice dipped lower, a dead whisper against the walls. "They linger. Every surge of power that runs through the Rose, it is them. That sound? That is what a soul does when it gets recycled as voltage."

Lyra's pulse pounded against her skull, a frantic signal from her body to move, to run, to do anything but stand here and listen. She could almost hear it—the static-laced hum, the distant chorus of voices stripped of speech, trapped in circuitry, crying out for an ending that would never come.

She clenched her fists. This wasn't real. Couldn't be real.

"The Iron Rose is not just a mere building," Sync said, and his voice had the finality of a gravestone slamming into place. "Nor is it simply a fortress. It is a living thing, woven through with the essence of the ones he has taken. The ones who power his empire. And inside its walls, Steele is not just in control." His gaze sharpened, slicing through the space between them. "He *is* the Rose."

Lyra's gut churned, a slow, ugly twist of something she didn't have time to name.

Why that electronic fucker!

This wasn't a street fight. Wasn't a back-alley ambush or a smash-and-grab gone sideways. This was war. No. More than war. This was the kind of thing that swallowed whole cities and spat out rubble. And Steele? They'd have to carve him out of the bones of the city he'd built, and that was a scale Lyra had never dared imagine.

And yet. And yet.

Something else pulsed beneath it, something Lyra could feel in the back of her skull, like an itch too deep to scratch.

She exhaled through her teeth, eyes narrowing. "Alright, Sync. What's the play here? And don't feed me scraps—I want the whole damn meal."

Sync's eyes met hers, dark pools of something unreadable. No. Not unreadable. Unspoken. There was history there, heavy as a corpse. And she knew—knew—before he even opened his mouth that she wasn't going to like it.

"What I did not tell you," he said, voice low, words sliding out slow, deliberate, like he had to carve each one free, "was that I used to be one of Steele's personal enforcers. One of his elite soldiers inside the Iron Rose. I was . . . his. Until I broke free."

Lyra's breath hitched.

His?

Fuckin' knew it!

He let the words slowly sink into the space between them like poison pooling in a wound. Then:

"Like I told you and Doc before, I broke free by severing the neural tether that bound me to him."

The floor of reality gave way, and Lyra felt herself falling.

Sync wasn't just a soldier. Wasn't just another bruised and battered fighter in this war. He had been crafted by Steele's own hands, sharpened into a weapon, then loosed upon the world. A tool, until he decided he needed to find a way out. And now—now—he was offering her the same thing.

A way out.

Or a way through.

Or, perhaps, a way into something worse.

Do I even want it? Do I want to peel myself away from this thing I've become, this godforsaken creature of violence and necessity, just to be shaped into something else?

Her hand spasmed, a jagged, involuntary twitch that betrayed the heat burning inside her. The rage, the distrust, the crushing burden of too many things that couldn't be undone. Her fingers curled, tightened, twitched again. She needed the blaster. Not for comfort, no. Comfort was a fool's dream.

She needed the weight of it. The cold, unyielding truth of it. A blaster wasn't a question; it was an answer. It didn't hesitate, didn't doubt. Just existed in the space between thought and action, between life and the nothing that came after.

She imagined it in her grip. The promise of it. The certainty of it.

Death, waiting for her command.

"You were one of his elite?" she spat. Not loud—no need for that. Just a blade slipped gently in, quiet, efficient. The space between them shrank, walls closing in, air thickening. Disbelief curled at the edges of her voice, still soft, still forming. Not anger. Not yet. No, this was worse. This had teeth.

He had been one of them. Not just another drone, another blank-eyed soldier marching to a rhythm someone else beat into their skull. No, he had been chosen. A favorite. A killer. One of Steele's own.

"You were one of them?" she repeated, tasting the words like something contaminated. A beat later, the paranoia clicked into place. "He's got you tagged. He never lets his toys wander this far. He's looking for you, isn't he? Right now."

Sync didn't answer. For a second, he just stood there, head tilted like he was listening to some frequency only he could hear. Then he made a small, almost bored sound in his throat, as if the accusation were tedious rather than dangerous.

"Look," he said.

He hooked two fingers into the collar of his shirt and yanked. Fabric tore with an ugly, cheap sound—this was not the dramatic, clean rip from old movies, but something more honest, like reality protesting. Underneath, his chest was a map of bad decisions: subdermal circuitry ghosting under the skin, faint discolorations where other ports had been, a pale puckered crater over his heart, edged in spiderweb scars. It looked less like surgery and more like something had clawed its way out.

"There," Sync said, tapping the crater. The sound was hollow, like knocking on a door that no longer led anywhere. "That used to be the leash."

Lyra stared at it. Her brain tried to supply an image: Steele's signal humming in that spot, a tidy little beacon pulsing out obedience and coordinates. The idea of it not being there anymore felt . . . wrong. Like seeing a collar with no dog.

"You cut it out," she said.

"I excavated it," Sync corrected mildly. "Cutting suggests a plan. This was more of a theological disagreement conducted with pliers."

He let the ruined shirt hang open, unbothered by the exposure; modesty was for people who still believed their bodies were private property. "You are right about one thing," he went on. "He was looking. He still is. Steele does not misplace assets. He misfiles them."

Lyra's hand drifted toward the scar, then stopped midair, fingers curling back as if afraid the emptiness might be contagious. "So why can't he see you?"

Sync smiled, thin and tired and a little proud, the way a man smiles after successfully sawing off his own hand to get out of a trap. "Because I sawed out the index card with my name on it," he said. "Every ping, every handshake, every little 'I am still here, master' routine? I burned them. I broke his line of sight, the only way that works."

He tapped his temple this time. "No return address. No acknowledgement. Silence. It drives him crazy. For Steele, not being able to find something is like not being able to think a thought."

Lyra studied the crater again, the absence more unsettling than any implanted chip would have been. "You sure?" she asked. "You sure he's not just letting you believe that?"

Sync shrugged. "He might. That's the trouble with gods and tyrants—they both love recursion. Maybe he is watching me right now through a hole I do not know about." His eyes met hers, flat and clear. "But that one?" He pointed at the scar. "That one he does not have anymore. I made certain. I remember the way it screamed in the tray."

He let the shirt fall back into place, the fabric failing to hide anything important. "So yes," he said quietly. "He was tracking me. He wanted me on a short leash with a clean signal. And now he wants to know where his good little machine went."

Sync's mouth twisted into something that might, in a different world, have been a laugh. "Tell you a secret, Lyra. It is the first time in my existence that he has wanted something and not had it. I recommend the feeling."

The silence wasn't just silence—it was a thing with teeth, gnawing at her chest, scraping the air from her lungs, filling the space with the stink of inevitability. It pressed down, and she let it, because somewhere in the marrow of her fear, somewhere she hadn't dared admit even to herself, she trusted Sync. Trusted him in a way that made her tremble and ache all at once.

She didn't know why she trusted him. Hell, part of her wanted to scream at herself for it, wanted to claw at the thought like it was a lie—but it wasn't. It was just there, stubborn and raw, a flare of certainty in a sky full of black. No reason to it. No logic. But when did she ever need reasons. When did she ever need logic.

She looked from Sync to Calista and saw faces. Just faces. Damage and intent.

"You ain't talkin' rebellion," she said, the words scraping out of her like they'd been living there too long. "Not even war. What you're selling is larger than that. You're talkin' about survival. That's it. Just the right to keep crawling."

Fuckin' Steele. Standing there like the universe had a rotten tooth and he was the dentist, sucking everything in, grinding it into jagged shapes no one should have to see.

"You in?" Calista's voice cut the dark like a blade.

Lyra nodded, knowing this was the hinge, the pivot, the moment that would fling them all screaming— screaming—straight into the heart of it.

"So, how do we get inside?" Lyra's voice sliced the stillness, harsh and raw, the only sane note in a world that had long since gone feral.

Inside. As if there was still such a thing. As if any of them belonged anywhere anymore.

Calista's grin was all knives and no mercy. "We don't," she said, the words curling out slow and deliberate, wrapping around Lyra's nerves like wire tightening. "Not yet. The Iron Rose is a cage built from nightmares. We need time. Resources. A plan that doesn't end with us becoming part of Steele's grid, our bones humming with stolen voltage."

Calista leaned in, elbows on the desk, fingertips pressed together as if in prayer—except no god was listening. "We need supplies. Junk we can shape into weapons that'll short out synths, cooking the poor bastards' insides. Tech to cut into Steele's systems. And people— people crazy enough or desperate enough to throw themselves into this meat grinder of a mission."

Lyra's fingers twitched near her blaster. Her jaw locked. "How long?"

Calista's gaze didn't waver. "Weeks. Maybe months. This isn't some two-bit smash-and-grab, Crow. We're talking about gutting the beast from the inside out. One mistake, and we're not dead—we're worse."

Weeks. Maybe months.

Lyra tasted rust—like pennies under her tongue, like something gone wrong in the blood. Time wasn't stretching. Time was a wire, pulled tight, vibrating with a frequency only the damned could hear. Every tick was a laugh from Steele's empire, a laugh with teeth. It thickened, ossified, metastasized. Breaking it now would be like trying to scream through concrete.

She didn't move at first. Just stood there, carved out of tension and bad dreams. The silence wasn't silence—it scraped, slow and cruel, across the air like serrated steel on bone. Then Calista turned to her. Not dramatic. Not slow. Just enough. Just enough to be a decision.

"We should talk," Calista said. "Alone."

Sync gave a smug half-smile and raised an eyebrow—just one—but it said everything: suspicion, curiosity, maybe even a note of dread.

As they left, none of them saw the shadow slip through the corridor, moving with the silence of something that had never been alive.

A synth, part of the motley rebellion, angles, and edges pressed into the shape of a man.

It touched a spot above its ear—just a whisper of movement. And then, deep in the circuits of its mind, something lit up. A message. A command. A truth branded in fire.

From far away, the Unmoved Mover spoke.

And the synth obeyed.

FOUR

A WHISPER FROM THE PAST

The night was a ravenous thing, all gnashing teeth and strangling black coils, clawing at the walls of Calista's room. It wanted in. It always wanted in. Because that was what the dark did when it sensed breath and warmth. The walls kept it at bay, though, just barely.

Lyra and Calista stood framed in the doorway, cragged shadows hacked from the sickly corridor light, rough outlines of something vaguely human. Not quite real. Not quite here. As if the city itself had coughed them up, phlegmy and shaking, a bad dream that refused to end when you woke.

Smells like. . . metal and sweat and the slow rot of human misery. No windows. No escape. The kind of room where secrets die, choking on their own blood.

Calista's fingers, trembling like dying fireflies, reached inside, fumbling for the switch. The light hit like a slap, raw and unkind, peeling back the dark to expose the bones of the place. A bed that looked like it wept at night. A table trying to walk in three different directions with two chairs. A hot plate playing a long, slow game of suicide on a rusting shelf.

"Come in," Calista said. Her voice was a thing barely there, stretched thin over the taut drum of silence, quivering, brittle. "Before the eyes in the walls catch a glimpse."

As if they weren't already watching. As if they ever stopped.

Lyra slipped inside, her body a silent blade cutting through the thick, waiting stillness. The door shut with a sound like an old bone giving up. The room locked around them, a metal throat swallowing them whole.

"Cozy," Lyra muttered, her voice sandpaper and old rust, something left out in the rain too long.

But a cell with a bed is still a cell. Call it home all you want; it doesn't change the shape of the bars.

Calista smiled. A tired, fragile thing, like a mask ready to crumble at the first touch. "It's home," she said, and the lie sat heavy between them, curling at the edges. "For now, at least. Until whatever bastard behind the curtain decides to shuffle the deck and toss us somewhere worse."

She moved, hands reaching for an old kettle, a jug of purified water, performing the ritual of survival. One drop, then another. A stupid little act of defiance against a world that had forgotten how to be kind. "Tea? It's not much, but it's warm. Tastes like it almost remembers being real."

Lyra perched on the bed, black-eyed and still. She scanned the room like a surgeon dissecting muscle from bone.

No ghosts. No monsters. Just the two of them, trapped inside a shoebox coffin, pretending there was a way out.

"You wanted to talk." Lyra's words hit the floor with a dead thud. No ceremony. No preamble.

Calista's hands hesitated on the kettle. A flash of something passed over her face, quick and sharp as a needle. Then, a breath. A pause too long, too weighted.

"Yes," she answered, and the sound carried more than agreement. It was a confession masquerading as breath, a small, bright cut she offered to the world.

Her lips parted again, slow, reluctant. "About . . . about Rana."

The name ripped through the air, raw and flayed, twitching like something half-alive, something that should have been put out of its misery long ago. A nerve exposed to open air, screaming silently, daring anyone to touch it. Lyra didn't flinch. Her face was the usual wall of iron and scorched earth, the kind of expression built from a thousand betrayals stacked like bones in an unmarked grave. And yet—there. A crack. A ripple across the surface, something too raw to be named, a flash of agony so sudden and bright it was like staring into the sun just before it explodes. Then it was gone, swallowed whole.

Lyra saw nothing but a ghost.

She's gone. The name is just a sound. Just air forced through the meat of the throat.

At least, that's what she told herself.

"What about her?" Lyra's voice was flat. A dull, dead sound. Like a hammer striking meat.

Calista turned. Too slow, too deliberate. Her spine locked up like a rusted hinge as she braced herself against the counter—a slab of scavenged metal, twisted and scarred, something yanked from the ribcage of some long-dead machine god. "We have something in common," she said, testing the words like knives against her tongue. "I thought . . . maybe you'd want to talk about it. About . . . about her."

What's this? She must think loss is some communal thing, something we can pass between us like a bottle, take a swig and say, 'Yeah, I feel it too.' But she doesn't know. She'll never know.

Lyra laughed, but the sound wasn't human. It was all sharp edges and exposed wire, the auditory equivalent of a blade sliding across bone. "Talk? What's there to fuckin' talk about? Like I said—she's dead. Talking won't bring her back. She's gone."

Gone. The word rattled in her skull, reverberating like a ricochet, slamming from bone to bone. Gone. A word too small for the enormity of absence. Gone meant a misplaced sock, an empty glass. It wasn't a big enough word to describe the black hole where a person used to be.

The kettle shrieked, high and thin, like some dying thing fighting for its last breath. Calista jumped, her fingers twitching as she poured the boiling water over the tea bags—pathetic things, brittle and dry, relics from another time. The liquid darkened, swallowing light, ink spilling into a void. Steam twisted upward in thin, writhing fingers, reaching, always reaching.

"Here." She shoved a chipped mug at Lyra, a peace offering to something that didn't know the meaning of the word.

Their fingers brushed. A nothing moment. A fraction of a second. And yet it hit like an electric shock, raw and immediate, an unfiltered jolt of something too big, too messy, too real. Calista jerked back, retreating to the table, curling her hands around her own mug as if it were some last, dying ember of warmth in a world that had long since gone cold.

"I'm sorry," Calista whispered, and the words tasted wrong. Like old rust and dead things. "It's just . . . well . . . like I said before. We were close. She was . . . so . . . special."

Special. A useless word. A weak, feeble thing. She wasn't special. She was fucking everything.

Lyra's eyes jolted to her, and for a moment, just a moment, Calista thought she was staring into the center of a collapsing star. "Special?" The word hit the air like a gunshot. "To me, she was fuckin' extraordinary. You've no idea. No fuckin' clue."

The words were charged with enough raw emotion to power the entire goddamn city for a year. Calista waited, every nerve screaming, sensing that Lyra was teetering on the edge of something massive—a confession, an outburst, a psychotic break. She wasn't sure which would be worse.

"She saved my life," Lyra finally said, her voice low and dangerous, running hot as a fusion core on the brink of catastrophic failure. "Not just once. Every goddamn day. When she looked at me . . . really fuckin' looked at me . . . she saw something. Something worth saving in this shithole of a world."

Calista leaned forward, drawn in by the raw, bleeding honesty in Lyra's voice. It was like watching a unicorn tap-dance through a minefield—breathtaking, suicidal, and guaranteed to end in blood. "What did she see in you?"

Lyra's laugh ripped free, jagged and wild, a supernova of broken glass and bile. It tore through the air of Calista's cramped cubbyhole, leaving behind the acrid scent of regret and bottom-shelf synth-whiskey.

"Hell if I know," Lyra spat, her words a toxic cocktail of self-loathing and defiance. "I've always been a walking corpse, sweetheart. A jigsaw puzzle of misery cobbled together from the discarded pieces of a thousand shattered lives. My veins run with cheap synthed booze, and my dreams? Shit, they're as worthless as any politician's promise was in this hellscape we call home."

Her eyes locked with Calista's, daring her to blink first. The darkness in her gaze was bottomless, a black hole hungry enough to swallow the light and never spit it back out.

"We were thrown together by my boss—that sad excuse for a meatbag. Thought he could keep me in line by saddling me with Little Miss Sunshine." Her lips twisted, bitter as burnt circuitry. "She should've told him to go fuck himself sideways with a rusty crowbar. Should've run screaming into the night. But she didn't."

Lyra's voice dropped to a whisper, raw as an open wound. "Goddammit, she gave me something I'd never had before. A fuckin' purpose. Like tossing a starving dog a steak and expecting it not to choke on the first bite."

The memories swirled like cigarette smoke, bitter and unshakable.

"The Steele case," Calista murmured, the words curling in the air like a ghost of something better left buried.

Lyra nodded, but her mind was already miles away, eyes fixed on some distant horizon where hope still had the balls to exist. "She had this . . . vision. Christ, it was like staring into the sun. A world where people weren't just scraping by but actually living. Building something real. Something that mattered."

She sighed, a slow, shaky thing that felt like peeling off a scab.

"It was beautiful," she whispered. "And it scared the hell out of me. It made me believe. And belief, in a world like this, is the most dangerous thing of all."

Calista's heart ached, a dull throb that echoed the rhythm of the city's dying pulse. She'd personally known of Rana Sharma's dreams, but now, hearing it spill from Lyra's lips—raw, unfiltered, a cascade of broken hope—it became something else entirely.

"Then it happened." The words tumbled from Calista's mouth, bitter as ash, sharp as the shattered dreams littering the streets outside. She didn't need to elaborate. In this world, in this goddamn pressure cooker of human misery, "it" always happened.

Lyra's face hardened, features rearranging themselves into a mask of bitter resignation. "Fuckin' reality happened. The sky fell on us like a hammer on an ant. Too much. Even for me. But she never stopped fighting. Right up until . . ." The words trailed off, swallowed by the yawning chasm of loss.

Calista stood, then folded herself onto the bed beside Lyra.

"I'm so sorry," she whispered, reaching out instinctively, hand hovering, fingers shaking in the small, terrible distance between them.

Lyra flinched away, but not before Calista caught the glimmer of unshed tears, like diamonds in a gutter. "Don't. I don't need fuckin' pity. It's as useless as tits on a bull in this godforsaken shithole."

"It's not pity," Calista insisted, her voice raw with an emotion she couldn't name. "I understand. Losing someone like that. It hollows you out, leaves you empty. I know."

Something in her voice resonated because Lyra looked at her, really looked at her, for the first time. Her gaze was a laser, cutting through the bullshit and the bravado. "You lost her, too."

Calista choked on the words, like trying to swallow broken glass and barbed wire all at once. "She was my love. She was . . . hell, she was everything. The only thing that made this busted-up world make any damn sense. And then she was just gone. Like she never existed. Like the universe chewed her up and spat her out, and I didn't even get a goddamn chance to say goodbye. I knew who took her. I knew it was you. And I told myself that was fine. That she was happy, and that I could live with it. But it still ripped me apart from the inside out. That's what love does. It gets inside you, makes a home in your bones, and then one day it burns the whole thing to the ground."

The silence between them stretched thin, a wire strung between two skyscrapers, waiting for the slightest breath of wind to snap it. It wasn't just grief. It was something rawer, something meaner—an old wound ripped open with dirty fingers, bleeding all over the floor. It was the kind of connection that didn't heal. It festered. It pulsed. It throbbed like an exposed nerve just waiting for someone to poke it. The kind of thing that, if you looked at it too long, could slice you open and gut you before you even realized you were bleeding.

Lyra's eyes, usually cold as reinforced titanium, twitched with something like vulnerability. Or maybe not. Maybe that was just another lie the light told. In a world like this, weakness gets you dead. Nobody lasted long wearing their insides on the outside.

"Yeah," Lyra muttered. "It's a bitch, isn't it? Like having your soul ripped out through your asshole."

Calista nodded, not trusting herself to speak. She took a sip of tea, wincing at the bitter taste that matched the acrid flavor of their conversation.

"I didn't know about you and Rana," Lyra said, the words slipping out like loose change from a hole in her pocket. "I guess she had a thing for strays, like me, didn't she? The broken ones, the ones with sad eyes and too-big hearts. Collected them the way some people hoard bottle caps or bad decisions. No hard feelings?"

The words hit Calista like a slug of cheap whiskey—warm, rough, and a little too easy to go down. "It's fine. She was happy. Happier than she ever was with me. I saw it."

"She was," Lyra murmured, voice soft as a frayed thread. "I hope she was."

They sipped their tea, the quiet stretching, twisting. Calista watched Lyra over the rim of her mug, caught the tension wound tight in her shoulders, the way her fingers drummed against the ceramic—tap, tap, tap—a nervous little symphony of sleepless nights and ghosts that refused to stay buried. There was more under the surface. There was always more. A whole damn galaxy of pain and longing, packed tight, threatening to split the seams at any second.

Without thinking, Calista leaned over, closing the distance between them like a moth drawn to a flame. Lyra's eyes snapped up, wide, unguarded.

Calista took the mug from her hands, felt the faint tremor there, and set it on the floor beside her own.

"What are you doing?" Lyra stammered.

Calista shut her up with a kiss—impulse over reason, a grab for heat in a universe that had gone refrigerated—and Lyra froze for half a heartbeat, defenses up like polished stone, then something feral snarled awake and she hauled Calista in, hard, turning it into impact; it felt like clutching a plasma torch barehanded, teeth chattering, eyes doing the mambo, electricity not just sparking but screaming and dancing a filthy tarantella through their nerves, raw and ravenous, the kind of need that makes a starving wolf look politely full.

Calista threaded her fingers into Lyra's hair. The strands felt wrong—too sharp, too rigid—like metallic fibers reflecting some pale, artificial moonlight. She gripped harder, not out of affection but necessity, as if the pressure itself kept reality from slipping. As if releasing her hold would allow something unnamed to surge through the cracks of the moment.

Lyra's real hand—scarred, raw, the skin split in places that had never fully healed—pressed into Calista's hip. The touch carried no softness. It had the abrupt, decisive certainty of a weapon discharging. The other, cold metal and whirring servos, ghosted along her spine, pulling her in, locking them together like a machine coming to life.

They broke apart, lungs heaving like they'd just run a marathon through hell. Lyra's eyes were feral, pupils blown so wide you could fall into them and never hit bottom. There was desire there, sure, but something darker too—a hunger that made Calista's spine tingle like she'd swallowed a live eel.

"You sure about this, princess?" Lyra's voice was sandpaper rough, like she'd been gargling razor blades and cheap whiskey.

Calista didn't trust her voice. Words were traps, primed to snap shut the second she let them loose. So, she gave a sharp nod—more of a glitch than a gesture, but enough. Then she grabbed Lyra's hand and hauled her forward, no grace, no ceremony, just raw momentum. They hit the bed like a controlled crash, gravity doing half the work, clothes shedding in ragged increments, sloughing off like old skin. Beneath it all—maps of old wounds, topographies of violence and survival, stories carved into flesh that never needed words to be understood.

Lyra's touch was a contradiction, gentle as a butterfly's sneeze one moment, demanding as a jackhammer the next. She coaxed sounds from Calista that'd make a siren pack up shop and find a new gig. Calista's hands roamed Lyra's body like a pilgrim seeking salvation, tracing scars that read like a memoir of pain and survival. Here, a knife fight in some back-alley hellhole. There, the kiss of a plasma round that came this close to punching her ticket.

They moved together like animals caught in a trap, desperate, reckless, clawing at something neither of them could name. A defiance, a middle finger to a universe that wanted them broken, wanted them gone. Calista arched, her breath catching sharp and sudden, like stepping off a ledge and realizing too late there's no ground beneath you. Lyra wasn't far behind, her cry swallowed against Calista's throat, like she was trying to burrow inside, hollow her out, live there forever.

After, they lay sprawled in the wreckage, a tangle of sweat and heat and something neither of them wanted to examine too closely. Calista's fingers caressed Lyra's arm, tracing old scars like reading a story written in flesh.

"This don't mean shit," Lyra muttered, voice locked down like a maximum-security prison.

Calista propped herself up, studying Lyra in the sickly light that made her look like she was being prepped for an autopsy. "Doesn't it?"

Lyra's eyes met hers, a silent showdown at high noon. "I can't . . . I'm not . . ."

"I know," Calista said, quiet as a razor dragged slowly across skin. "I'm not asking for always. Just this. Now."

Something in Lyra's face cracked, just a hairline fracture, the kind you don't see until the whole thing comes apart in your hands. She pulled Calista in, pressed a kiss to her forehead, and it felt like a confession, like a surrender.

"Now," she said, like she was signing her name in gasoline and tossing the match.

They drifted off, tangled up tighter than a quantum equation. For a moment—just a goddamn moment—there was peace in this shithole of a world. Outside, the night pressed on, full of teeth and claws and things that'd eat your soul for breakfast. But here, in this shoebox masquerading as a room, they'd carved out a space. Fragile as spun sugar, temporary as a snowflake in hell, but real as a punch to the gut.

As Calista slipped a hand on Lyra's hip, she thought she heard Lyra whisper something. A name. Maybe, Rana.

But before she could be sure, sleep grabbed her by the throat and dragged her down into dreams. Dreams of a world where hope wasn't just a four-letter word, where love could bloom in the cracks of the pavement like the most stubborn fucking weed you ever saw.

Come morning, reality would come swinging, a wrecking ball wrapped in razor wire, no apologies, no mercy. But right now, they had this—a sliver carved out of a universe that wanted them smeared across the pavement. It wasn't much. Hell, it was barely anything. But in a world where "barely anything" was all you ever got, it would have to do. Because the alternative was opening the nearest airlock and taking a deep, final breath of nothing. And neither of them was ready to go quietly. Not yet. Not while there was still blood in their veins. Not while they still had teeth to bare. Not while there was still a spark of warmth left in a cosmos that had long since gone dead and cold.

Calista's eyes snapped open like rusty switchblades, her heartbeat a goddamn jackhammer in the coffin-quiet of their hole-in-the-wall sanctuary. The room pressed in, a claustrophobic embrace of crumbling concrete and desperation. She turned her head with the caution of a bomb disposal tech, not wanting to wake the sleeping storm beside her.

Lyra lay there, a tangle of limbs and hard angles softened by the treacherous whisper of sleep. Her face, usually a battlefield of scars and fuck-you determination, had found a fragile ceasefire in unconsciousness. But even in repose, she was a live wire humming with the promise of violence. A landmine just waiting for the wrong step.

Calista pushed herself up on one elbow, staring like a starving animal catching sight of a feast. And because her brain was a cruel, unrelenting bastard, it picked this exact moment to dredge up the greatest hits of Rana goddamn Sharma.

Rana. Christ on a rocket-powered pogo stick, what a supernova of a woman she'd been. She'd blazed into Calista's life with the subtlety of a neon billboard in a funeral home, all megawatt smiles and impossible promises. For a hot minute, Calista had bought into the fairy tale, believed in happily-ever-afters and other lies they sell to kids and suckers. Then reality, that smirking, boot-on-your-neck bastard, kicked down the door. And Rana? She was gone. No goodbye, no last kiss, just the ghost of her touch and a pile of what-ifs that burned hotter than any flame she'd ever left behind.

Calista's hand moved of its own accord, brushing a strand of Lyra's hair like it was spun glass. Lyra wasn't Rana. Never would be. But in this cesspool of a world, they'd cobbled together something that vaguely resembled connection—like patching a blown circuit with chewed gum and a prayer. It wasn't love. Not by a long shot. But it sure as hell beat walking into the void alone.

"You're staring," Lyra growled, her voice a gravel pit wrapped in barbed wire. "I can feel it."

Her eyes cracked open, dark and bottomless, like the kind of void that didn't just swallow light—it devoured everything, chewed it up, and spat out nothing but absence.

"Didn't mean to wake you," Calista lied, snatching her hand back like she'd touched a live wire.

Lyra uncoiled, all lethal grace and barely contained violence. "Bullshit. You've got that look. The one that says your brain's doing the cha-cha with ghosts."

Calista sighed, feeling the weight of unspoken truths pressing down like a metric ton of regret. "Just thinking."

"Thinking about her," Lyra said, cutting through the bullshit with surgical precision.

The silence that followed was a living, breathing thing, coiling around them like a python made of memories and might-have-beens. Calista nodded, a barely perceptible dip of her chin. "Yeah. Her."

Lyra sat up, raking fingers through her hair like she was trying to comb out the tangles in her thoughts. "Rana fuckin' Sharma. That's who this is about, isn't it?"

Calista's mouth betrayed her. A minute shiver at the edge of her lips—small, almost deniable—but real. Not a smile so much as the memory of one, smuggled in from another time. The kind that belonged to a time long gone, a time before everything turned to shit.

"She had a way of leaving an impression," she said, the words carrying bruises you couldn't see.

Lyra snorted, the sound as dry as week-old bread. "Understatement of the fuckin' century. She was a category five shitstorm, and we were just a couple of idiots without an umbrella."

They sat there, marinating in the unspoken, until Lyra reached out, her fingers slipping over Calista's wrist like a promise or a threat. "You loved her. Hell, I loved her in my own twisted way. But she's gone, babe. Gone like everything else that mattered. Erased by time. Forgotten by this fucked-up world. And us? We're still here, scraping by on the fumes of what used to be."

"It's not that simple," Calista whispered, her voice barely audible over the sound of their collective regret.

"No shit, Sherlock," Lyra said, her grip tightening. "She believed in something. In me. In you. In this festering wound of a world. She almost made me believe, too. Almost."

Calista felt Lyra's hand on her wrist, a solid thing in a world of broken promises and shattered possibilities. "Then we honor her by surviving. By building something out of this clusterfuck she left behind. That's what she'd want, right?"

Lyra nodded, her eyes suspiciously bright. "Yeah. The crazy bitch would probably haunt our asses if we gave up now."

"She would," Calista said, as Lyra released her death grip. "But this world's not getting any less fucked while we sit here playing memory lane bingo. We've got work to do."

They dragged themselves out of bed and into the cold, hard reality of their existence. In the corner of the room, a small battered tub squatted beside hulking cans of water. Calista tipped the first can, and the tub drank it greedily, the water slapping against metal with a hollow, defiant rhythm. She stepped back, eyes on Lyra, gesturing to the tub.

"Oh no, you first," Lyra said, the words dripping mock chivalry.

Calista shook her head. "Together?"

Lyra's eyebrow shot up, a leer playing at the corners of her mouth. She nodded.

No words were exchanged—why waste them when silence held sharper knives?

They peeled off their clothes, leaving only skin and scars, as if shedding armor no one else could see. Between them, a sliver of soap glimmered under the harsh light. Calista pressed it to a rag, then to Lyra's skin, the cold bite of water chasing it, tiny daggers of sensation. Lyra returned the favor, mapping Calista with hands that knew no hurry, tracing the curves, the scars, the soft valleys between muscle and memory. Outside, the world was burning, collapsing, a corpse in motion. Here, their bodies were a synchronized dance, their friction a reckoning, their touch a kind of revolt.

"What's on the agenda for today?" Lyra asked, breaking the silence like a brick through a window.

Calista smirked, a humorless twist of lips. "Same shit, different day. Scavenge, salvage, and pray to whatever deaf gods are left that we don't run into anyone who'd rather use our intestines for jump rope."

"Aren't you just a ray of fuckin' sunshine," Lyra said, her tone drier than the Sahara.

"I prefer to think of myself as a realist in a world of terminal optimists," Calista countered. "This hellhole doesn't give out participation trophies. You know that better than most."

Lyra couldn't argue with that nugget of truth.

They finished their sorry excuse for bathing, drying off with rags that smelled like they'd been stewing in some forgotten corner of the world—damp, sour, and half-rotten. Calista dressed with the efficiency of a soldier suiting up for battle. Lyra took her sweet time, her eyes never leaving Calista's face.

"Your brain's doing overtime again," Lyra said, her voice softer than usual, almost gentle if you squinted and tilted your head just right.

Calista shrugged. "Hard not to. Everything feels like it's balanced on a knife's edge. One bad move and we're yesterday's news."

"Welcome to life, sweetheart," Lyra said, lacing up her boots with practiced ease. "It's a high-wire act over a pit of hungry sharks, and we're fresh out of safety nets. You either keep moving or you become shark chow. And I don't know about you, but I'm not ready to be anyone's dinner."

Calista nodded, feeling her resolve harden like quick-setting concrete. "You're right. We keep moving, keep fighting, keep surviving."

"Damn straight," Lyra said, flashing a grin that was part encouragement, part 'fuck you' to the universe at large.

Calista felt an answering smile tug at her lips. "Alright then. Let's go find some circuits before this whole place decides to come down on our heads like the world's shittiest piñata."

Together, they stepped out into the dim corridors of the wall, their footsteps echoing like gunshots in the eerie quiet. The place was a labyrinth of decay and desperation, its corridors teeming with the worst humanity had to offer. But it was also their fortress, their last stand against a world that had decided they were expendable.

Outside, the world was waiting, a brutal, unforgiving bitch of a place. But they would face it together, a united front against the chaos. For Rana's memory. For themselves. For the tiny, fragile hope that maybe, just maybe, they could carve out a little piece of something real in this wasteland of broken dreams and shattered promises.

It wasn't much. But in a world gone mad, it was enough. It had to be.

The sun-scorched streets of what used to be a city stretched out before them like a goddamn graveyard of human ambition, a wasteland of broken dreams and shattered synapses. Calista and Lyra, two rats scurrying through the detritus of a world gone to shit, picked their way through the urban decay with the desperate grace of survivors dancing on the edge of oblivion.

"We need capacitors," Calista said. "And resistors. Anything with a chip that isn't fried to hell and back. Shit, I'd settle for one of those old-time transistor radios that still remembers what music sounds like."

Lyra sneered, the sound like rusty gears grinding against the bones of hope. "Yeah, sure. And maybe we'll find a unicorn that shits gold while we're at it. Hell, why not go looking for Atlantis? We'd probably have better odds."

Calista chuckled.

They moved like ghosts through the concrete jungle, scavengers in a labyrinth of shattered glass and twisted metal. Every so often, one of them would dart forward, snatching up a piece of tech or a morsel of food with the frenzied desperation of junkies scoring their next fix.

A shiny piece of something called out to Lyra.

"Well, well," she cackled, lifting a rust-bitten can of food like it was Midas-touched, last rites in aluminum.

The metal was pitted and blistered, corrosion crawling across the surface in strange little constellations. She turned it slowly, examining the pattern as if it might resolve into language. Or a warning. Or maybe instructions left by a civilization that had understood what this place was becoming.

No label remained. No indication of what had once been sealed inside.

"Dinner's served," she added. "Five-star rot with a side of botulism flambé. Maybe if we're lucky, tetanus for dessert."

She weighed the can in her hand, thoughtful.

"Hell, chew slow," she said. "Might be our last fine dining experience."

Calista opened her mouth to fire back, something sharp and humorous, but the words never made it past her teeth.

A scream knifed the air—ragged, real, and close. No warning, no prelude. Just pain, raw and unfiltered, the kind that pulled marrow from bone and made the dead twitch.

Chaos.

Humans down an alley, pressed into corners of their own panic. Swallowed whole by the Reavers' hunger.

They didn't move—they convulsed, jittered, a tangle of limbs and terror, wrong in every direction. Like rats sharpened into murderers, claws bared where hands should have been, eyes flicking with the bright, wet hunger of souls gone rotten. And the Reavers—they were everywhere, a tide of teeth and madness, closing in, unstoppable.

Lyra and Calista slipped into the shadows like old sins looking for somewhere to hide. Then the darkness came down—not crept, not fell—came down like judgment, like the closing fist of some cosmic bastard finally tired of their trespasses. No thunder. No warning. Just sudden, suffocating black. They looked up, eyes wide and white, pupils shivering like prey. Fear? No. This was recognition—they'd danced with death before, but this time the music was different.

Then another sound. Different. Metal on metal. Clanging.

It was a bot looming over the Reavers, a patchwork of steel and circuitry hammered together with the cold precision of something built to end lives. Its optics burned, alive in a way that had nothing to do with programming. It moved with a predator's poise, each step a thunderclap rolling through the gutted remains of the city, a harbinger of something swift, merciless, inevitable.

"Fuck me sideways with a rusty chainsaw," Lyra whispered, her usual bravado evaporating like piss on hot concrete, leaving behind nothing but the acrid stench of fear.

The Reavers stood, not frozen by fear or choice, but by the cruel inevitability of the moment, their bodies rendered inert as the machine advanced. It was a hulking monstrosity of steel and malice, a symphony of grinding pistons and unrelenting hunger. It didn't pause, didn't falter, didn't care. It simply consumed. Flesh was flesh—human or Reaver, it made no distinction. One by one, the bot plucked from the chaos, tossed like scraps of paper into the yawning void of a hover transport. The machine devoured them without thought, without memory. The universe watched with its usual indifference. Nothing ever cared.

And above it all emerged another abomination, a thing so wrong it defied comprehension. Its form was an insult to reason—a slithering, many-limbed amalgam of polished steel and silent intent. But it wasn't just its shape that unsettled; it radiated something primal and nauseating, a psychic scream that clawed at the mind's deepest recesses. It was wrong in the way a corpse might twitch after death, an affront to the natural order.

"Spurn," Calista murmured, her voice barely audible.

"What in the name of hell is that?" Lyra spat, her lip curling with disgust.

"A new toy from Steele," Calista replied flatly. "His latest mind-fuck."

"His personal ass-kisser?"

Calista nodded.

Lyra's fingers twitched toward her blaster, rebellion flickering in her eyes—a spark bright but foolish. "Even those goddamn Reavers don't deserve this," she muttered through clenched teeth.

Calista's hand shot out like a whip, silencing Lyra.

"We could still save some of them," Lyra hissed, her voice sharp and desperate.

"No," Calista's voice cut sharp and final, colder than a ship's hull breached to vacuum. "Not here. Not now."

A transport hissed overhead like a living thing, hovering down with a mechanical sigh, landing on the scorched earth with the impatience of a predator. Its metal skin gleamed, reflecting the chaos around it, a promise of extraction and doom.

And then, the thing—the creature, Spurn—spoke, its voice a jagged avalanche smashing into every bone, every nerve, every shred of hope. "Take them back. Hook them up. The weak ones? Toss them into the churner. Let them become food for the rest. Useless. Pathetic. Weaklings."

The bot swooped with terrifying ease, snatching the humans like rag dolls, cramming them into the transport's gaping maw. The craft swelled with their terror, a bloated tick throbbing with malice, pulsing with a malevolent heartbeat. It belched a cloud of ash and spite skyward, utterly indifferent, a sociopathic god on a hell-bent course toward the Iron Rose fortress—the titanium tumor squatting on the horizon like a raised fist to the universe, daring any flicker of resistance to breathe.

"Move," Calista hissed, grabbing Lyra's arm and yanking her out onto a road and towards the carcass of a crumbling structure that might have once been a library, a mausoleum of knowledge long forgotten.

They burst through the doors, sending up clouds of dust that hadn't been disturbed since the world decided to take a swan dive into the abyss. Their feet caught on the bones of ideas that no longer had the time to breathe, left to rot in the forgotten corners of this place where nothing had ever mattered.

"Hell's gates and every devil dancing," Lyra hissed, the words scraping out like broken glass. "I remember this place. What it was before. The Shelves—nothing more than a graveyard for fallen branches and rotting words from the past."

Calista ignored her, focused on a sound of metallic footsteps drawing ever closer, a death march played out in steel, gears whirring, and circuitry. She grabbed Lyra by the arm, ducking behind a row of shelves. They held their breath as the bot's shadow fell across the grimy windows like the silhouette of the devil himself.

Seconds stretched into an eternity as they waited, hearts pounding like war drums in their chests, each beat a desperate plea to a god who'd long since stopped listening. Finally, mercifully, the shadow moved on, leaving them alone in the musty silence, surrounded by the ghosts of civilizations that had written their own obituary.

"That was too fuckin' close," Calista breathed, slumping against a shelf, sending up a cloud of dust that might have once been the collected wisdom of humanity.

Lyra, never one to let a near-death experience dampen her spirits, was already poking around the library's remains like a kid in a candy store made of nightmares. Her fingers danced over dusty spines, leaving trails in the grime like some half-assed archeological dig into the ruins of human knowledge.

She turned back to Calista. "Rana. She liked books. Read a lot of them." Then something caught her eye. "Hey, check this out," she said, her voice tinged with the kind of excitement that usually preceded catastrophe. "It's like finding a virgin in a whorehouse."

Calista turned to see Lyra standing in front of an ancient computer terminal, her hand hovering over a keyboard that looked like it had last been used when dinosaurs roamed the earth, and dreams still had a fighting chance.

"Don't you dare . . ." Calista started, but it was too late. Lyra's finger descended on a key with all the subtlety of a sledgehammer performing brain surgery.

And then, like a miracle in a world that had forgotten how to believe, the impossible happened. The screen flickered to life, bathing them in an eerie blue glow that felt like a spotlight in a world that had forgotten what light looked like.

"Holy shit," Lyra breathed—words scraped raw from the back of her throat. Her eyes went wide, not cartoon-wide, not movie-star shock, but the look of someone who'd just torn open reality only to find there were thousands more waiting. Awe tangled with terror, a child's Christmas morning realization that Santa wasn't magic, just marketing, and maybe that joy had always been counterfeit.

Calista was at her side in an instant, her face a riot of fury and panic, like someone had shoved all the chaos of a dying world into one human skull and dared it to spill out. She was a mess of contradictions, a painting that shouldn't exist—the brush strokes of terror, the palette of self-destruction.

"You idiot!" she said, the words sharpened to razors by her voice. "Do you have any idea what you've done? Steele could be watching us right now, plotting how to turn our insides into modern art!"

But before Lyra could defend her monumentally stupid action, a voice crackled from the ancient speakers, a sound that hit them both like a sucker punch to the soul, leaving them gasping for air in a room suddenly devoid of oxygen.

"This is Rana Sharma. If you're hearing this, I'm alive. Steele has me in his tower . . . "

The message cut off, then began to repeat.

"This is Rana Sharma. If you're hearing this, I'm alive. Steele has me in his tower . . . "

Rana's voice was a ghost in the machine, haunting them with possibilities too painful to contemplate, a siren song of hope in a world that had long since forgotten how to spell the word.

"This is Rana Sharma. If you're hearing this, I'm alive. Steele has me in his tower . . . "

Calista staggered back, her face as pale as if she'd seen a ghost. Which, in a way, she had—the specter of a past she'd thought buried and gone, rising from the grave to dance on the ruins of her carefully constructed cynicism.

"It can't be," she whispered, her voice barely audible over the pounding of her heart, a frantic drumbeat of denial and desperate, treacherous hope.

Lyra stood there, her smirk absent, her face slack with something unfamiliar—real sadness, the kind that clings to you like a stain you can't scrub away. "Maybe she's . . ."

"Don't you dare finish that thought," Calista's voice sliced through the air, sharper than a blade's edge. No room for any more of that weak, useless hope. "Turn it off."

The message kept playing, a digital echo of Rana's voice—each syllable a hammer driving nails into Calista's skull. False hope, that poison wrapped in soft, pretty words. It gnawed at her, a temptation more dangerous than a thousand machines that could gut her in a second. More dangerous than any bullet, any bot, any thing that could tear through her body.

"It's a trick," Calista said, her voice growing stronger as she latched onto the lifeline of cynicism like a drowning woman grasping at straws. She reached over to the keyboard and hit a key, stopping the sound. "Do you hear me? It's a trick. It has to be. Her dreams are long gone, along with our own."

Lyra raised an eyebrow, her skepticism as evident as a neon sign in a blackout. "But maybe . . . just maybe . . . what I saw . . . with Rana lying there in a heap . . . maybe it was what Steele wanted me to see? This fuckin' world's built on lies. Why should death be any different?"

Calista whirled on her, eyes blazing with a fury born of too many disappointments and not enough miracles. "Don't start. We can't afford to believe in fairy tales. Not now. Not ever. This isn't a world where the good guys win, and the princess gets saved. It's a fuckin' nightmare where hope is just another way to spell 'sucker.'"

But even as the words left her mouth, a treacherous seed of hope had taken root in her heart, a dangerous whisper that threatened to unravel everything she thought she knew. What if? The question echoed in her mind, a siren song more tempting than any drug, more dangerous than any weapon Steele could devise.

"So, what do we do?" Lyra asked, her voice uncharacteristically serious, like a clown at a funeral suddenly remembering how to cry.

Calista took a deep breath, forcing the chaos in her mind into some semblance of order, trying to build a fortress of logic in a world gone mad. "We do what we always do. We survive. We keep moving. And we sure as hell don't trust anything that comes out of a machine Steele might be controlling. For all we know, this is just him fuckin' with our heads, trying to make us dance to his tune like puppets on strings made of false hope and broken promises."

Lyra nodded, but her eyes kept darting back to the screen, where Rana's message continued its endless loop, a broken record of possibility in a world that had long since stopped believing in second chances. She sighed. "And if it's real? If she's really alive?"

Calista's jaw clenched, a muscle twitching beneath her skin like a trapped animal trying to claw its way to freedom. "Then we'll cross that bridge when we come to it. For now, we focus on getting out of here before those bots decide to redecorate this place with our guts. One problem at a time, Crow. That's how we've survived this long."

They collected what little the place had left for them—some salvaged components of uncertain origin, a few pieces of metal that might once have belonged to something meaningful, and a single can of preserved food.

It was a poor yield. The real mass they carried wasn't physical. It was uncertainty, pressing down on their minds like a gravitational field from a collapsing star.

They turned to leave The Shelves.

Lyra stopped.

Not gradually. One moment she was moving, the next she was motionless, her boots grinding faintly against the floor as if reality itself had shifted one degree to the left.

"What is it?" Calista's voice was a shard of tension, taut and sharp.

Lyra crouched slowly, the way someone approaches an artifact that might still be alive. Her fingers brushed against something half-buried in the gray accumulation of dust and degraded matter.

She lifted it.

A book.

Its spine had warped but hadn't quite surrendered to entropy. Dust covered it in a fine archaeological layer, like the residue of time itself. Lyra wiped the surface with her sleeve, slow movements, careful ones—like a technician exposing circuitry inside a machine older than the civilization that built it.

"Fuckin' hell," Lyra said quietly.

Her voice had the thin sound of someone discovering a message from a previous timeline.

She held it up.

"It was her favorite."

Calista looked closer. The recognition happened instantly and unpleasantly, like a memory that had been waiting for the right trigger.

Samuel R. Delany. Dhalgren.

Her stomach tightened.

Her hand hovered in the air for a moment before settling lightly on Lyra's hand. The contact was deliberate, stabilizing—two observers confirming that the object, and the memory attached to it, were still real in this version of the world.

"Come on," she said, her voice quieter now, hollow in a way she hated. "We gotta go. Get back to the wall."

Lyra didn't respond. She tossed the damn book into her satchel like it was just another piece of junk—along with everything else they'd scavenged from who-knew-where. Another pile of scraps in a world full of them.

The Shelves shrank behind them, swallowed by the ruins like a mouth closing over a bitter memory. The city stretched out ahead, gutted and yawning. The streets, bursting with debris, seemed to sneer. As they moved, Lyra couldn't shake the soundless specter of Rana's voice, circling her thoughts like a vulture. It wasn't just a memory - it was a gnawing what if, a needle jabbed into the soft meat of her resolve. It followed them, a haunting too stubborn to be left behind.

Real or not, the message had changed everything. And in a world where change usually meant pain and death, Lyra couldn't shake the feeling that they'd just stumbled onto something that would either save them all or destroy what little they had left. The coin was in the air, spinning between salvation and damnation, and all they could do was wait for it to land.

As they melted into the shadows of the dead city, the question hung between them, unspoken but impossible to ignore: What if? It was a dangerous thought, a spark of hope in a world that had forgotten how to dream. And in that moment, surrounded by the ruins of civilization and the echoes of a voice from beyond the grave, Lyra realized that hope might just be the most terrifying thing left in this godforsaken world.

FIVE

HARVEST

The Iron Rose Tower gnawed at the skyline like a malignant thought that refused to die, its warped spires sneering at the very idea that hope had ever been invited here. Hover transports slid in and out of its shadow, swollen with stolen lives, vomiting their human freight into Steele's fortress with the bored efficiency of a slaughterhouse hand feeding scraps into a machine that never jammed and never cared.

Humans and Reavers alike tumbled from the transports' gaping maws, a writhing mass of flesh and terror. The Reavers, eyes burning with starvation and lunacy, snapped and snarled, trying to sink their teeth into anything warm and breathing. The humans trembled and shrieked, slipping in blood and filth, scrambling to escape both the Reavers' gnashing teeth and the mechanical horrors that awaited them.

"Please . . . oh God, please!" A woman's voice ripped through the noise, sharp enough to draw blood. It wasn't a plea so much as a fracture, a human sound splitting under too much pressure. "I have children," she cried, the words tumbling out as if saying them might still summon mercy. "They need me."

But her pleas were cut short as she was swept into Steele's infernal machine, her cries joining the chorus of screams that echoed through the cavernous chamber. The sound didn't fade; it was absorbed, repurposed, made useful.

The machine, a nightmare of steel and circuitry, thrummed with malevolent purpose. Steel arms unfolded on jointed spines, pistons snapping into place as motors roared awake. Gears meshed tooth-to-tooth, grinding with methodical devotion while articulated clamps seized, sorted, and fed. Conveyors dragged flesh forward in jerking increments, each movement measured, each scream timed to the churn of rotating drums and the pulse of overheating servos. It worked without haste, without cruelty, because cruelty required intention—and this thing only required input.

"What the hell is this?" shouted a burly man, bravado cracking under the strain, fear bleeding through the seams. He thrashed as the machine's articulated limbs closed in, metal whispering promises it intended to keep. "I ain't going in that thing! You hear me, Steele? You can take your machine and shove it up your . . ."

His words quickly dissolved into a howl of agony as the machine's pincers struck with obscene efficiency, locking around him and ripping him free from the crowd as if he were a defective part pulled from an assembly line. His scream came out raw and unfiltered, a sound that didn't belong to language anymore, only pain.

Close by, a Reaver burst into shrill laughter, the noise jagged and wrong, like broken glass rattling in a skull. He hurled himself at a young boy, jaws stretched too far, hunger painted across his face. "Fresh meat! Sweet, succulent flesh!"

But a bot arrived first.

It didn't care about the Reaver's madness or the boy's fear. It had no interest in madness or innocence. It functioned. That was all. In less than a heartbeat, it seized them both and hauled them away from the heaving mass, and threw them into another machine—the churner—two more lives erased into motion, their endings swallowed whole by Steele's meticulously engineered nightmare.

The rest were processed differently. They were arranged on a conveyor belt deep inside the apparatus, packed shoulder to shoulder with thousands more, and that was when the true horror began. From hidden nozzles, gelatinous matter spilled forth—transparent, sticky, obscene. It flowed over them, swallowing limbs and breath, sealing skin in a tightening sheath that hardened into a slick, glassy casing. Only the eyes remained free, floating in the clear prison, forced to witness everything that followed.

"No! NO!" A girl thrashed, trapped in the quivering, translucent shell that held her like a coffin of jelly. Her pleas were muffled, swallowed by her tomb and the merciless thrum of Steele's invention. "I can't move! Somebody help—please!"

Her eyes darted frantically, desperate, trying to find a crack in the nightmare. But there was none. The walls closed in with an industrial certainty, the machinery's relentless rhythm swallowing her every struggle as she was dragged deeper into the fortress, every second folding her fear tighter around her like steel wire.

A man in a shredded jacket hung suspended in the translucent substance that had sealed around him moments before, the material already hardening into something like biological resin. His eyes moved frantically until they fixed on the thing beside him.

A Reaver.

Its body was frozen inside a swelling cocoon of gelatinous matter that seemed to grow directly out of the air itself. Only its eyes moved.

They burned with impotent rage and hunger, forced to stare at prey it could no longer reach.

"Is this hell?" the man whispered.

The words barely carried. The environment swallowed sound as efficiently as it swallowed motion. But the meaning traveled through his eyes well enough.

The Reaver answered the only way it could. A low, distorted snarl forced its way through the thickening membrane around its jaws. The sound came out warped, like a transmission passing through damaged circuitry.

Its madness remained intact.

The conveyor belt groaned and shifted, trundling its cargo deeper into the dark, toward a ceiling studded with long, needle-like instruments. They dropped with surgical precision, piercing the gelatin cocoons, injecting chemical cocktails meant to paralyze without dulling awareness.

"What . . . what's happening?" a young woman's voice trembled, distant and hollow. "I can't . . . I can't feel anything . . ."

"That's the point," a gravelly voice muttered from her left. "Can't have the little generators struggling, can we now?"

An old man, his face a roadmap of wrinkles and hard-earned cynicism, added, "The house always wins, eh? Not much you can do. Just . . . enjoy the ride."

The young woman didn't understand.

Enjoy the ride?

Her mind formed the question even as the conveyor belt jerked violently, spitting her and the others forward like discarded meat, tossing them into the next layer of torment.

Mechanical arms sprang to life, their movements exact, merciless, seizing the gelatin-locked bodies and hoisting them upright, row after row. They were grotesque exhibits in some lunatic's private museum—a gallery where the price of entry was your last shred of sanity and a scream.

"Oh God, oh God, oh God," a man muttered, his eyes rolling as the machine seized him. "This isn't real. This isn't real."

But it was real. Real as a blade pressed to the spine, real as the acrid stench of burning wires and scorched skin. Tendrils slithered from the monstrous machine, each one a hungry instrument, reaching and curling over the slick shells, attaching with a squelching, intimate insistence. Groans of agony and terror echoed with each insertion as each strand started to suck energy from every body it touched, channeling vitality like a perverse bloodstream straight back to Steele's fortress—fusing human with machine in a distorted union that left nothing untouched.

Then, feeding tubes uncoiled like living serpents, each one engineered to pump slurry into every body it touched. They twisted and probed through the air, tasting the slurry before striking with ruthless precision. Flesh gave way under their mechanics, veins and sinew breached with cold, clinical efficiency, and from each connection came a guttural, inhuman moan—raw, ragged, unavoidable— reverberating across the steel expanse. The slurry from the churner—part flesh, part chemical horror—was pumped without mercy into every connected vessel, a grinding, viscous flood that moved with the relentless logic of a machine with no conscience, no hesitation, no humanity.

A woman, her face once beautiful but now twisted in a grim acknowledgment of what was happening, strained toward a Reaver, their bodies fixed in place side by side. Its gaze, a fractured shard of the humanity it once wore, cut through her with a precision that offered no comfort, no hesitation, only a cold, unflinching verdict.

"Please," she whispered. "Someone save us."

No one answered. No one even noticed.

The Reaver emitted a sound—grating, organic, almost intelligent in its cruelty. Laughter? Screech? Might've been something else. Didn't matter.

As the final connections sealed, a low, insistent vibration filled the chamber, escalating until it seemed to churn the air itself. The human power cells, bound and integrated into Steele's horrific apparatus, felt the persistent tug of their life being drained, a current of vitality siphoned with absolute inevitability.

"Fuckin' hell," an old man wheezed, his voice raw, flaking apart like old paper. "Like someone's yanking my guts through a meat grinder."

A boy, maybe twelve, sucked in ragged breaths between sobs. "Mama? Mama, where are you? I'm scared."

No answer. No warm embrace. Just the rhythmic thrum of the machines, grinding forward, indifferent. The whimpering of the discarded.

And towering over everything, that fucking machine engine—Spurn—a mockery of godhood with no divinity to justify it, a metal carcass dressed in polished steel, untouched by the decay of the world beneath it. It watched. Its sensors swept the space like predatory eyes, devouring the air, the dust, the rot. Every surface, every flicker of motion, every molecule was data to be absorbed, analyzed, and discarded without mercy.

A small tech drone skittered forward, articulations precise, voice clipped and mechanical. "By your command. The latest intake has been accounted for. Systems stable at 98% capacity."

Spurn acknowledged this with a flash of light behind its ocular sensors. "Excellent. And the Reavers?"

"As projected, sir. Their accelerated metabolisms make them ideal conduits. We're seeing a 15% increase in energy output over standard subjects."

"Good," Spurn said, gaze never wavering from the suffering below. "Increase our harvest from sectors three through seven. Our objective is 100%."

The tech drone faltered. "At that level, sir . . . the subjects may not endure beyond a few weeks."

Spurn turned then, deliberate, a living instrument of command and appetite. When it spoke, its voice was the sound of glaciers splitting, slow and unforgiving. "Did I ask for your counsel?"

"N-no, sir. As you command."

The tech drone scuttled off, insignificant and buzzing, disappearing into the shadows. Spurn turned, sensors again sweeping the chamber below, absorbing the endless rows of human batteries. Each face told a story of helplessness, stretched tight under the weight of circumstances they could neither escape nor comprehend.

"Exquisite," Spurn murmured, savoring the word like fine wine. "Absolutely exquisite."

Within the cavernous chamber, an old man spasmed as a sudden surge of power was ripped from him, coursing violently through the conduits. He gasped, his breath coming out in ragged, stuttering bursts, as though some vital part of him had been carved away and sent screaming through the veins of the machine.

"Ah, for fucks sake," he rasped, his body shuddering. "Bastard's impatient."

Beside him, a woman writhed, her form twisting against the translucent prison that gripped her like a relentless shadow. Her voice tore itself from her throat, sharp and raw. "Stop it! Please! Please, God, stop it!"

But there was no god here. Only the Iron Rose, a monument to Steele's cold, exquisite cruelty. It thrived on the anguish of its captives, drank their suffering like nectar.

As the night deepened, and the fortress pulsed with stolen life, its glow obscene in its brilliance. The transports kept coming, and the conveyor belt didn't stop. The operation never stopped. It devoured. It processed. It took. New eyes floated in gelatinous tombs, wide, unblinking, howling soundlessly into the suffocating dark.

A young couple flung from the transport, holding onto each other in final defiance. But the machine did not care. Cold steel arms wrenched them apart, efficient, unfeeling.

"Jack! Jack, don't let them take me!" the woman shrieked, her fingers grasping for something, anything, as she was swallowed by the machine.

"Sarah! I'll find you, I swear!" the man screamed, his throat raw, his body thrashing against the restraints until his muscles burned. It didn't matter. They were already sinking, their bodies swallowed whole by the gelatin, their eyes locked in a final, desperate communion as the tide of artificial viscosity dragged them apart.

Nearby, a Reaver twisted in his cocoon, a beast barely wrapped in human skin. His howls—muffled, wet—seeped through the thick gel, his eyes red, rolling, mouth gnashing at ghosts. Hunger hadn't left him. It never would.

"Look at that thing," an old woman whispered, her voice thin, brittle, her fingers digging into her palms as though she might still wake up from this. "Is that what we'll become?"

"No," came a voice of an older man, calm, steady, like someone who'd already seen the end of the world and decided to sit back and enjoy the fireworks. "We'll get to keep our heads. Get to remember every single second."

The needles and tubes descended. Smooth. Precise. The slurry spread through their veins, and the old woman whimpered as her vision clouded.

"Shh," the old man murmured, his eyes widening, his breath slowing. "Don't fight it. Just . . . let go."

The conveyor belt growled forward, dragging them deeper into the fortress, into the dark, where the walls pressed in like ribs around a rotting heart. Somewhere, machines hissed and sparked, overworked, indifferent.

Then—

A voice, small, fragile, slicing through the industrial hum. A girl, maybe seven, her words clear despite the fear choking them.

"Mommy? Daddy?" She swallowed, voice cracking. "I'm . . . I'm sorry I ran. I wanna come home now. Please?"

No answer. Just the sound of exhausted, broken bodies breathing in time with the machinery, waiting for whatever came next.

The wires and tubes found the girl. A spark, a flicker, a brief moment of hesitation before her body went slack, her eyes wide, empty, seeing everything and nothing.

Spurn watched, expressionless. A tormentor. A god. He turned to a waiting bot, his voice as clipped and efficient as the blades that had carved his kingdom from the bones of the lost.

"Soon, the world will understand. Soon, it will kneel."

And in the vast chamber, an old man clenched his jaw against another pull of energy from him, his breath coming in ragged gasps.

"Hold on, kiddies," he whispered, words swallowed by the mechanical hum that throbbed beneath his ribs, a noise so deep it seemed to reverberate in his bones. "Somebody's gonna stop this. Somebody out there gives a damn."

His voice, once strong, now cracked and frayed at the edges, barely scraping the edges of intelligibility. It disappeared into the ceaseless mechanical growl, the machine towering above, sucking every ounce of vitality with meticulous hunger. The fortress didn't pause. It devoured without conscience, a thing that obeyed no law, no thought—only desire.

But as the night wore on and the fortress continued to suck the life force from the souls imprisoned within its walls, the truth began to crystallize like frost on a dead man's breath.

Whoever gave a damn was a long, long way from here.

As Lyra and Calista were unloading what they had scavenged, Sync stood apart, optics flicking as he inventoried the haul with quiet, mechanical judgment.

"What's this?" he asked, lifting the book Lyra had swiped from The Shelves.

Snoopy bastard.

She snatched it back from his grip. "An artifact. From a time you wouldn't understand."

Sync's sensors whirred, attempting to parse her meaning, failing entirely. He turned to Calista, seeking clarity.

"It's fine," she told him, voice sharp but steady. "It's fine. That's all you need to know."

An alarm suddenly screamed along with a metal-throated howl that shredded the moment. Then a blast punched through the wall, spraying heat and fragments. Lyra didn't hesitate—she swept the haul back into her satchel and swung it over her shoulder in one brutal motion, already lunging for the door. Calista was close behind, breath close at Lyra's shoulder, the base slowly breaking apart.

Here we go again.

"Fuckin' knew it," Lyra spat, her voice raw, something ugly twisting behind her ribs. "Knew he'd send a welcome party."

Calista didn't respond. Didn't need to. Her head snapped up—fracture lines crawled across the ceiling, thin as lies, spreading fast. They stopped in the doorway.

"Sync!" she barked. "What the hell's going on?"

Then a voice flooded the corroded speakers, synthetic and slick, smug enough to curdle oil. "Traitors detected. Commencing sanitization."

Sync's lenses flared, pupils expanding as he tapped into the base's dying sensors. "Calista, several hostiles converging." His words came clipped, mechanical. The implants buried in his skull burned neon-blue, mapping carnage only he could see.

My blaster. Where is it?

The thought struck Lyra with the cold precision of a diagnostic alert.

Her hand moved automatically to her thigh.

Blaster—still there. The grip pressed reassuringly against the holster, exactly where probability said it should be.

Other leg.

She checked again.

Electro-magnetic pulse grenades, lined up in their clips, silent and waiting. Patient machines with a single purpose.

Good.

The universe hadn't rearranged everything.

Lyra exhaled once, sharply. Then she seized Calista's arm, hard enough to anchor them both to the same version of events.

"Move your sweet little ass," she said.

Servos shrieked. Metal treads hammered. The noise came from everywhere, bouncing, multiplying, impossible to pin down.

But Calista hesitated. "Cover the west corridor," she ordered, wrenching her blaster from its holster. The barrel vibrated, eager, hungry. "If they drive us back, we . . ."

The wall exploded.

Lyra slammed into the deck, breath ripped clean out of her, ears howling like a church packed with ghosts. Smoke rolled thick and choking. Something large advanced through it—optics flaring, adjusting, calculating. Then another shape. Then more.

"They're already on us," Sync warned. "Get to the maintenance hatch!"

A hunter-killer droid slithered forward, a tumor disgorging itself from the dark. Seven feet of matte-black alloy and wetware, joints bending like a broken marionette, too many elbows, too many wrists, its face a polished oval that threw their terror back at them, warped and empty. It didn't speak. It didn't need to. It was built for one thing—hunting.

Let me at him!

Lyra fired first, stumbling backward. Plasma bolts sizzled against its chest, bubbling the metal but not stopping it.

"Steele's new toy?"

She fired again. No effect.

Fucker's uglier than its tax returns!

Calista adjusted, quick, clinical, sighting the red node where the monster's heart should have been. One shot. That was all it took.

The droid spasmed, locked up, then screamed—twelve voices in twelve overlapping registers, a choir of the damned. And then it started laughing.

Not human laughter. Something wet. Something wrong. A jagged edge of static that crawled into their skulls. Then—silence. The droid collapsed in a heap, black ichor pooling like engine oil.

Lyra wiped a smear of it from her face, grimacing.

Fucker programmed them with his sense of humor. Damn comedian.

A tremor. The walls convulsed, dust sifting down in pale, weightless sheets. Above them, Steele's drones chewed through reinforced plasteel, their mandibles shrieking the same four-note dirge, over and over. The sound had weight. It lodged in the spine, in the teeth.

Calista turned abruptly, reacting before the thought had fully formed. There—embedded in the wall like a forgotten exit from another version of the station—a maintenance hatch. She tore it open with a sharp metallic shriek and drove her boot against the panel to keep it wide.

"In here. Now."

They dropped through it almost simultaneously, bodies moving on instinct more than decision.

The explosion arrived before causality had time to catch up. It moved down the corridor with an unnatural velocity, like an angry correction in the fabric of reality. The blast wave struck them and rearranged their positions instantly, as if some external operator had swept the board clean.

Sync hit the deck hard. For a moment, he experienced the very clear sensation of something inside him failing structurally, a component giving way.

Lyra's head struck the bulkhead with a dull mechanical sound. She came upright again almost immediately, spitting red onto the metal flooring, one hand clamped against her jaw as though trying to verify it still belonged to her.

"Still think this was a good play, hotshot?" she snarled, wiping blood off her chin with the back of her sleeve.

Calista didn't break stride, grabbing Sync by the collar and shoving him forward through the smoke. His implants stuttered, tiny electrical arcs tracing across burnt skin, the air pungent with scorched metal and ruined flesh.

"Would've worked," Calista snapped up at Sync, "if someone had double-checked the schematics!"

"My apologies," Sync wheezed, one eye struggling to focus. "Blueprints . . . guess they were outdated."

"Outdated?" Calista let out a laugh so sharp it could've slashed a throat. "Fuck! The whole goddamn place is outdated. We're rats in a maze Steele already solved."

Lyra sagged against the wall and dug through her satchel, fingers unsteady, scraping past scavenged circuitry. The dim light slid across exposed copper, veins glinting like something flayed and forgotten.

Trash. Every bit of it.

She hauled the satchel back onto her shoulder, jaw clenched.

A sound—low, rhythmic, mechanical—filtered in from somewhere beyond the walls. Not the usual heartbeat of the base. This was something new. Something hungry.

Fuck!

Lyra slowed. "Did you hear that?"

"No," Calista shot back. "Keep moving!"

But Sync heard it too: the grind, the shift, the infrastructure itself tightening, as if the place had decided to inhale. He swallowed.

"Steele's not just ahead of us," he muttered. "He's watching."

They pressed on, farther into the base's decaying innards. The air reeked of rust, sweat, and old promises left to die. Then came the noise again—metal against metal, nearer now—something hauling itself through the passages, patient, deliberate, closing the distance.

Sync yanked at Lyra's satchel. "Let me see what's in here."

Again with this shit.

Her hand caught his wrist. "How about asking first, jackass?"

"No time for manners." He wrenched free and plunged his hands into the jumble of scavenged junk—circuit boards cracked like bad teeth, memory chips gone soft with age, a stim injector long since bled dry. Then he found what he was looking for. A power relay. He hauled it free, turning it in his palm, already doing the math.

"If I can find a way to reroute current through the tertiary buffer . . ."

"Just make it go boom," Lyra said, eyes on the dark ahead.

Sync slid the relay into his pocket and nodded.

Calista leaned against a bulkhead, feeling the metal shudder like a dying animal. Shadows twisted against the walls, stretching, shifting. "They'll flood the tunnels next. Nerve gas. Sonic destabilizers. Maybe a viral strain that melts your eyes first."

Lyra snorted. "Optimist."

"Realist. Steele doesn't take prisoners," Sync said. "He takes specimens."

Something moved overhead. Metal rasping against metal. Unhurried. Intentional. Lyra looked up just in time as a hunter-killer droid tore through the air vent in a rain of shredded alloy. It landed badly, its frame split open, one arm useless, circuitry hanging out like butchered organs. Its faceplate was intact, though: smooth, mirrored, fixed in that approved, reassuring smile meant to sell toothpaste and justify atrocities.

Persistent bastard, ain'tcha?

Lyra cocked her head and lobbed an EMP grenade.

The blast flayed the world into stark X-ray hues. For half a heartbeat, everything was raw, exposed. The base's infrastructure—a brittle skeleton, fractures creeping like spiderwebs. And on the monitors, flickering in and out, Steele's face, mouthing silent threats.

Sync jerked his head up, his sensors flaring, catching something. "Secondary reactor's critical. Eight minutes till cascade."

Calista stared at him, a crooked laugh breaking loose. "So, this is it? We're the joke?"

Lyra spun her blaster on her finger, grinning. "Nah. We're the aftershock."

They ran.

A tremor rippled through the tunnels, steel groaning, gas pipes rupturing in sharp hisses. The base was coming apart at the seams. Sync's voice cut through it all, clean and final. As they came to a junction, he barked, "Left's a dead fall. Right leads to surface access."

Lyra skidded around a tilting support beam, hacking on dust and fumes. "Surface?" she shot back. "You know what lives up there?"

"Drones. Snipers. Hover vehicles with turrets."

So, same as always.

Calista's boot landed in something slick—the remnants of a droid gurgling as it tried to form words through a broken speaker.

"Left!"

Sync's brow furrowed. "That's a dead fall. Nothing but rubble. We won't be able to get through it."

Calista bared her teeth, eyes bright with something dangerous. "Exactly. Steele thinks logically. We don't."

The tunnel behind them shuddered, cables snapping like tendons, the pressure shift howling through the vents.

Time to get crooked.

They came to a chamber that smacked of ozone and last chances. Then Sync saw it. A circuit panel. Not new, not pristine—just functional enough to tease the imagination.

He fished the power relay from his pocket. Cold metal, the weight of possibility in his hand. He shoved it into the panel. His fingers found the switch. Sparks jumped— tiny, impatient entities that bit at his knuckles, gnawing away at the last fragile seconds of existence like they had their own agenda.

Calista shifted her weight, boots skating through the filth. "Will it work?"

Sync didn't spare her a glance. "Not sure."

Hell, can't even give odds.

His hand stayed welded to the panel. "Tell me when."

The floor bucked like a dying animal. Walls tore open. Glass became a storm, slashing the air as it flew past them.

Above, the structure howled, metal wrenching out of shape, welds surrendering one by one.

Calista latched onto a swaying pipe, fingers locking tight. "Still beats being fuckin' lab rats."

Lyra dragged blood from her cheek with the back of her hand and managed something close to a grin. "Amen to that,"

Up ahead, a fresh pack of hunter-killers slammed the door again and again. The metal buckled, protesting, seconds bleeding away.

Calista spun, locking eyes with Sync. "Now."

He slammed the switch on the power relay.

A heartbeat.

The briefest breath of existence holding still.

And then—

Light.

Heat.

The world became an inferno, swallowing steel and flesh.

Several days later, a scavenger probe, one of a thousand soulless drones trawling over the city's carcass, discovered a melted data chip, its edges fused like old scars. The retrieval drones plugged it in, and across the dark expanse of corporate space, fractured screens sputtered to life.

Lyra's face appeared, smeared with dried blood, her expression sharp, feral, something that wasn't quite madness but wasn't far from it either. A grin stretched across her face, impossible and defiant.

"Still breathing, you corporate shit-stain. Come get us, fucker!" she spat, voice a razor cutting through the sterile hum of the feeds.

She lifted a middle finger, held it there like a banner, like a declaration of war.

Then—static.

Steele watched it, replaying it hundreds of times, over and over again. On the last loop, his voice came out flat, final. "Erase it. Scrub it from the system."

It vanished. Data purged. Logs wiped.

But somehow it clawed its way back.

On every terminal. On every bot's and synth's internal feed. Through hidden circuits where control had been absolute.

And out there, beyond the reach of their systems, the last fragments of a rebellion refused to die.

SIX

TO WOUND THE AUTUMNAL CITY

Lyra, Calista, and Sync pulled themselves out of the wreckage in the clumsy way people do after an explosion rearranges both the environment and their expectations about survival. Their bodies hurt in multiple, unsorted places. Bruises were forming with quiet determination.

But the real pressure came after.

Silence.

Not the ordinary kind. This was the kind that follows catastrophic system failure—the moment when a structure that once defined reality has been erased, and the mind keeps trying to reference it anyway.

Their sanctuary was gone. The walls that once made the world legible had been vaporized into particulate memory. So they moved.

They descended into New York Veritas, not the visible city but the hidden architecture beneath it: service tunnels, abandoned conduits, maintenance corridors whose original functions had been forgotten by the civilization that built them. They passed collapsed chambers and rusted infrastructure that looked less like machinery and more like fossils.

Above them, the city still existed in theory—a mausoleum of expired ambitions and official lies that had hardened into history.

But down here, the air was thicker.

The tunnels resembled veins inside something very old and very tired, a circulatory system still moving darkness through the body of a dying organism.

"What the fuck happened back there?" Calista spat, her voice a blade dulled by panic but still sharp enough to draw blood. "How did Steele know we were there?"

Sync just shook his head with the grace of someone trying to deny reality one vertebra at a time. "I don't know. Everyone was trained to leave no trace when scavenging."

Lyra let out a sound that might've been a laugh, or maybe a cough choked on cynicism. "Maybe it was an inside job."

Sync turned on her fast, voice clipped, hands twitching like a marionette being jerked by an angry god. "Impossible. All synths were clean. Untethered. I checked myself."

Should know better than to fuckin' trust a synth.

"Oh, so you checked," Lyra said, dry as ash. "Comforting. Well then, it's all fine. Except it's not. Because everything went to shit in under thirty seconds."

Sync opened his mouth to fire back—then a tremor hit.

The world convulsed like it was trying to puke them out.

They froze, lungs grinding in the tainted atmosphere like busted machinery, every breath an act of defiance. The tunnel closed in, all sharp angles and malice, like it might bite if they lingered too long. The stink was alive—iron, mold, sewage, the ghost of shit long past—clinging to their flesh with the tenacity of guilt that won't wash off no matter how hard you scrub.

Calista wiped at her forehead with a hand coated in city filth, smearing the sweat into a grime-soaked paste. Her breath came sharp, staccato, like she was arguing with death and losing.

"This way," she said.

Great. More darkness.

Ahead, the black stretched out like a throat ready to swallow them whole. Only Sync's faint glow cut through it— those flickers, subdermal veins of light pulsing just enough to remind them that the abyss had company.

"Wherever you're taking us, it better be safe," Lyra said, her voice rough. The catch in it wasn't from fatigue. No, this was deeper—some ancient splinter lodged under her ribs, a raw nerve exposed to the cold air of memory. Something primal. Unwanted. The kind of thing you bury under a hundred scars and pray never comes clawing its way back up.

"Safe? Not really," Calista replied, her eyes scanning the crumbling walls. She could feel something. "But it's the only place we have left. A secondary base. Still functioning. Barely." She paused, her gaze falling on Sync, who stood motionless, his eyes scanning the data feeds that flashed across his lenses. "We have to get there before . . ."

Another tremor, stronger this time. The ground beneath them shuddered, groaning as though the city itself were alive, fighting to keep them from reaching their destination.

"Steele's drones won't stop coming," Sync muttered, his voice calculated, cold. "His systems are more advanced than we thought. We need to move faster."

Calista cursed under her breath, turning on her heel. "Come on, then."

They kept moving, sinking farther into the city's forgotten gut, sliding through old service shafts that had long been abandoned. The air thickened, rank and sour, the smell of sewage growing stronger, and every step they took seemed to echo louder in the oppressive silence that surrounded them.

Lyra's heartbeat rattled like a jackhammer trapped in her chest, echoes of the hunter-killer fight still clinging to her like cheap perfume. Her hand never strayed far from the blaster holstered to her thigh. She felt brushed against it.

My friend. Still with me. But what's this shit about another base? Too many damn surprises.

"Hold on, sweetheart," she started. "You never said a word about some secret fallout shelter. What scares are we in for down here? Radioactive clowns, cannibal monks, or just the usual disappointment?"

Calista's gaze swept the distance, her senses extended outward in a way that made the hair on Lyra's neck bristle. "This was the first base. The original nest. We dreamed of a safe haven for humans escaping Steele's experiments, and for the synths who couldn't be controlled." Calista looked back, her eyes burning brighter than any streetlamp in this godforsaken city. "It's where we first came to hide. Where we prayed. Where we hoped that maybe this world could be more than a machine. But soon, we needed more space."

Lyra said nothing, only stared.

I know this dance—the quiet desperation of the hunted.

And she knew what it cost to survive under the thumb of Steele, who saw them only as pawns, playthings, scrap meat for his churner, bodies ground down for his human batteries, machines, his reach, his obscene climb toward dominion.

They turned a corner, and voices slid through the rust-chewed ducts, warped and metallic. Near. Broken into static, but unmistakably human, or whatever passed for that now. Calista's mouth curved upward, quick and unguarded, a smile she didn't waste often, a rare and genuine sight. She turned to Lyra and Sync.

"Welcome home, you broken-down bitches," she murmured. "The first refuge, and now, the last."

They reached the entrance to the secondary base—if entrance was the correct word for it. The door had no markings, no designation. A small electronic panel sat beside it, half recessed into the wall. The whole structure felt misplaced, tucked into the corner of the city like an afterthought in someone else's design.

"You still have the code?" Calista asked Sync.

He better. He's fucked up enough today.

Sync gave a short nod.

Lyra chuckled.

"What was that about?" he asked.

"Nothing," she said, gesturing to the door. "After you, tin man."

He moved ahead, looking at a panel of fossilized controls that looked dead, a relic left behind by engineers who'd stopped giving a damn. His cybernetic fingers skimmed the surface, coaxing life from circuitry that only played dead, and triggering the sequence. The door hesitated, sulked, then obeyed—its lock awakening, remembering what it was built to do.

The sound of heavy, grinding metal filled the air as the door slowly slid open, revealing a hidden world within. The chamber beyond was dim, lit only by the faint glow of outdated machinery and the occasional flicker of malfunctioning lights. The walls were lined with makeshift bunks, scattered piles of old tech, and walls scrawled with resistance graffiti.

The air wasn't just thick—it was a goddamn stew of souls. The place was crammed with bodies—mostly meatbags, but synthetic ones too. Some of the synths were the slick, factory-fresh kind Steele cranked out. But most were busted-up, jury-rigged nightmares held together with spit and scavenged parts. Just as human as the meatbags, they stood shoulder-to-shoulder with ragged faces, jerky movements.

Looks like they're sucking on lemons dipped in battery acid.

But their eyes? Their eyes still burned. Still sparked with that crazy, stubborn life that Steele couldn't stomp out, no matter how hard he tried. They were spitting in the eye of the machine, and that's what mattered.

The tin heads might be broken, but they best not be his.

"This is it," Calista muttered. She looked over her shoulder at Lyra. "This is all that's left. This is where we fight back."

A woman approached, her eyes narrowed as she took in their appearance. She was older than Calista, her hair streaked with gray, her face etched with the lines of hardship and time.

Calista leaned close to Lyra, her voice low and quick. "That's Vira. An engineer by trade. She used to build cities before the world decided it didn't need builders anymore. Now she keeps this place breathing—power, systems, miracles held together with spit and stubbornness."

Looks like someone the world tried to discard—and failed.

Vira slowed as she approached Calista, each step controlled, as if the floor might shift into another version of itself if she moved too quickly. She studied Calista's face with the careful attention of someone verifying the integrity of an object in a failing system. Skin tone. Shadow. The faint geometry of bruises that might or might not exist, depending on how reality decided to render them today.

Her gaze lingered.

Not only on the flesh but on the micro-expressions— the tightness at the corners of the mouth, the slight rigidity around the eyes. Damage sometimes appeared there first, long before the body admitted anything had happened.

Vira lifted her hand. It paused halfway, suspended in a moment of uncertain calibration, then settled lightly on Calista's shoulder. The contact was brief but decisive. Solid. A presence, confirming continuity.

"You made it," Vira said. Her voice scraped raw, yet carried something stubbornly human. She looked past Calista, a glance, her eyes cutting to Lyra, then back again. "When our sensors picked up what was happening, I thought we lost you for sure."

Calista couldn't help the faint smile that tugged at her lips. "We're hard to lose," she replied, though the words felt hollow in her mouth.

Vira's expression softened. "We all are, girl. We all are."

Vira moved in close, too close for words to survive the distance. She wrapped Calista in her arms, the motion clumsy, human, unguarded—a moment of softness smuggled into a world that punished tenderness. Her lips brushed Calista's cheek, a brief contact that trembled between apology and defiance.

"I missed you," she breathed, the words barely surviving the air between them.

Calista's smile appeared briefly, like a signal flickering through static—thin, uncertain, but undeniably real. The kind of light you see at the far end of a tunnel when the power grid of the universe is starting to fail.

She didn't speak. Sound would have made it too official, too fixed in the timeline.

Her lips moved instead. Me too.

No air carried it. No vibration confirmed it. But in the quiet that followed, the message hung between them— stronger than any oath, because it hadn't been forced into the machinery of language. It simply existed, the way certain truths do, waiting for someone to notice them.

Lyra's eyes narrowed, taking it all in.

Hugs and kisses are a risk, not a reflex. Softness is contraband here.

"V, this is Lyra," Calista said. "She's one of us."

Vira tilted her head. The motion was abrupt, precise—sharper than any words could have been, like a glitch in the expected flow of behavior. She said nothing.

Then she turned and moved down the hallway. Each step carried a certainty that didn't belong to her, as if she were a proprietor of a reality she had no right to occupy.

They followed her into the bowels of the base, through corridors that stank of sweat, oil, and too many sleepless nights. Every room they passed was packed to the seams with the wreckage of Steele's empire—people broken in ways you couldn't see until they moved, spoke, or didn't.

There were children too, tucked into corners like forgotten thoughts, eyes too wide, too quiet. They crouched in the gloom, skin drawn tight over bones, expressions carved from hunger and panic. Lyra tasted their fear on the back of her tongue—metallic, electric, like biting down on a live wire. Their eyes, too knowing, too sharp for faces so young, bored into her with the intensity of a goddamn interrogation lamp. It wasn't just the usual urchin wariness. This was something else. This was a judgment. A silent, accusatory stare that sliced through her like a monomolecular wire. Made her feel like the insect pinned under a microscope, twitching and helpless.

Calista snapped her head toward Sync, every movement taut, like a predator tracking a signal only she could sense. "Sweep every goddamn warm body and synth in this hole. No anomalies. No ties to Steele. If one so much as twitches sideways, I want it cold before it can blink."

Sync nodded, metal and muscle obedient in perfect silence.

Then Calista wheeled on Vira. "V, we hit them back. Hard. Drop Sector Gamma off the grid. Let them stew in the dark while we draw the line."

Vira froze. Her boots scraped against the floor with a sound that made reality shiver, like a record skipping in a dirge that had been playing too long. She turned. Her voice emerged low, jagged, as if carved from something older than circumstance—something the world itself could not bend. "What the hell are you talking about? We're in no condition to do anything. And you? Look at yourself. When's the last time you slept? Three days? Four? You're burning the last of your fuel, and the engine's coughing black."

Calista scoffed, flinging the concern aside like a cigarette butt still smoldering. "Sleep's for the dead and the docile, V. Steele's at our door with a battering ram. We hit back now, or we might as well wave the white flag."

Vira didn't flinch. Didn't blink. Just let the weight of her words fall like a god's verdict. "So we strike back. And what then? You collapse mid-charge? We scrape you off the pavement and call it strategy?" Her voice carried the quiet force of something that had seen too many bodies drop. "We need your brain firing, not fizzling. Even the finest blade turns dull when you beat it against the world too long without pause."

"We're not blades, V," Calista snapped, her voice tight with frustration. "We're just scraps of meat and metal clinging to hope in a world that wants us dead."

"And those scraps can build something beautiful. But not on empty," Vira stepped closer, her hand hovering over Calista's shoulder. "Were you followed?"

Calista shook her head, slow, automatic. Not denial. Her body answered because her brain was too tired to lie, too spent to communicate anything beyond motion.

Vira smiled. Not soft. Not sweet. The smile of someone who'd seen too much and decided to keep standing anyway. "Alright. Trust me. I've got eyes on the dark. Steele's not slipping through. But how'd he know where to find you?"

Another shake from Calista. Wearier. Slower. Like her bones had started arguing with gravity and losing.

"Don't know," she rasped, voice frayed like wire insulation peeled back too far. "Maybe he tracked one of the synths. That's why Sync needs to run diagnostics on everyone in this place."

"We'll handle it with him," Vira said, her tone a lullaby sewn from steel cable. "But right now, you need sleep."

Calista's defenses wavered, just enough for the cold to slip in. She knew Vira was right, which made it worse. Agreement tasted like surrender, like throwing down your blade and hoping the wolves were feeling charitable. "There's too much to do," she mumbled.

Vira's eyes locked onto Calista's, radiating a warmth that felt almost like an implant of reassurance in an otherwise broken system.

"All the work, all the mess—it'll still be there when you wake up," she said. The words carried the weight of inevitability, like a programmed message repeating across timelines.

"But you, Calista . . . you won't be there if you don't rest. Without you, nothing we do matters. Every strike, every defense—it collapses into noise."

Her hand moved slowly, deliberately, until it rested against Calista's cheek. Not pressing, not demanding—just a signal. "Please. For me?"

It was a request coded in warmth and entropy, a fragile signal sent across the uncertain circuitry of survival.

The warmth of Vira's touch was a shock against the hard metal of the resistance base, a reminder that life stubbornly clung to them even here. Calista felt her resolve crumble, the exhaustion a heavy tide pulling her under.

"Five hours, V, that's all," she conceded, her voice barely above a whisper. "Five hours, and then I'm back on it."

Vira's grin sliced through the dimness like a flare in a blackout, luminous and dangerous, chasing away the shadows clinging to Calista's face. "Five hours. That's all I ask." She leaned in, pressing a soft kiss to Calista's lips. "I've missed you so. Rest, my love."

Calista flushed, a rare and fleeting color rising in her cheeks. She wasn't used to such open affection, especially not in the brutal world they inhabited. It felt—vulnerable. But also, strangely comforting.

"Let's get you more comfortable first," she smiled and disappeared off to another room in the outpost. She soon returned with a wool blanket, which she wrapped around Calista's shoulders. "Here, I knitted this myself from some yarn I found."

"You knitted me this? You should've been oiling your blasters."

"Knitting helps to calm my nerves . . . the other helps to prepare my next move. Don't worry," Vira chuckled. "I can still reload my blaster blindfolded."

Calista nodded, finally succumbing to the exhaustion pulling at her limbs. She closed her eyes, the many images of Steele's fortress and bots burned into her mind. She knew that he was always out there, plotting, scheming, tightening his grip on the city. But for the next five hours, she would let Vira shoulder the burden and allow herself to sink into the oblivion of sleep.

Vira led Calista into a small, sterile room where a single bed sat against the wall, its sheets rumpled like memories left behind.

"I'll wake you when it's time," Vira said. Her voice was low, almost mechanical, carrying a warmth that didn't quite belong in the metal-tinged air. "Sleep well."

Calista lay down on the bed, letting the mattress yield under her weight, feeling the faint hum of circuits and air ducts vibrating through the frame. She closed her eyes, surrendering to the pull of exhaustion.

The last thing she saw was a glimpse of a woman as radiant as the sun. Then the world faded away into the deep darkness of needed sleep. Then everything went dark. Not just darkness, but the kind that felt alive, pressing softly against the edges of perception, pulling her into the quiet, necessary void of sleep.

Satisfied, Vira returned to find Lyra leaning against the doorway, arms crossed, a sardonic expression on her face. "Well, well," Lyra drawled, her eyes glinting with amusement. "Looks like someone's got a soft spot for our fearless leader."

Vira met Lyra's gaze without flinching. "Calista is vital to the resistance. She needs to rest, and I convinced her. That's all. Just concerned."

Concern? More like devotion with armor on.

"Sure, if you say so," Lyra said, almost to herself, the sound of it fractured like a signal dropping in and out. She let a laugh escape—short, uncertain, the kind that might have belonged to someone else a few timelines ago—and pushed herself away from the doorway, her movements carrying the faint echo of hesitation.

Vira stepped forward, her hand outstretched like a promise or a threat, depending on how you looked at it. "Vira Petrova," she said, voice smooth, controlled. "I don't think we've had the pleasure."

That hand isn't a greeting; it's a measure.

Lyra didn't flinch. Her eyes were sharp, measuring every inch of this woman like a calculation that never quite added up. She gripped Vira's hand with the force of someone used to taking what she wanted. "Lyra," she muttered, voice a low growl, her stare cold enough to freeze fire. "Just Lyra."

Vira raised an eyebrow, a hint of a smile playing on her lips. "Oh, just Lyra. Fine. Lyra. What you need to understand is that my only loyalty is to the resistance, and to Calista's well-being." Her smile bloomed, sharper now, as she tightened her grip on Lyra's hand. "I know you. I know who you are. You're the Crow."

So she knows my name—just not what it costs.

Lyra's gaze sharpened, the old scars in her eyes flaring to life. "So, you know me, huh? Maybe you do. Maybe you don't. See, Vira . . . I'm more than just that. More than just the Crow. I'm a fuckin' storm. And that storm's coming for everyone who thinks they're safe hiding in the wreckage." She let her words hang in the air like a warning, a challenge. The kind of challenge no one ever walked away from.

Vira didn't take the bait. "Then we understand each other," she said, yanking her hand free of Lyra's grip. "Now, if you'll excuse me, I have a patrol route to run. Keep watch over her. And try not to wake her unless the base's on fire."

Lyra smirked. "Wouldn't dream of it, darling. But if everything goes to hell, I'm taking her and only her, and running like hell. No offense."

"None taken," Vira said, her eyes hardening with a flash of steel.

With that, Vira turned and walked away, leaving Lyra alone at the doorway looking in at the sleeping figure of

Calista, the fate of the resistance resting, however briefly, in her hands.

Lyra watched Calista sleep, the lamplight casting a jaundiced glow across her face, exhaustion settling like a second skin. Perched on the edge of the bed, she kept silent vigil against the nightmares that always lurked at the edges of perception. The room was small, more a holding cell than a sanctuary, yet for now it felt like a fragile haven. And Calista, despite her gruff exterior and steel-trap mind, looked almost fragile in her slumber.

Lyra shifted carefully, careful not to disturb that fragile system, moving closer, her body tracing the gravity of the other. A shiver ran through her—not from temperature, not from anything mechanical—but from something real. Something that resisted analysis, refused a label, refused containment.

I could stay here all night, and it still wouldn't be enough.

And in the quiet hum of the small room, it felt as though the universe had paused, just long enough for a truth too subtle to encode into words.

She leaned down, her breath a whisper of heat against Calista's cheek, too close to be casual, too deliberate to be innocent. Her eyes caught the scar slicing through Calista's eyebrow—a slight line in an otherwise unshakable mask. A flaw. A story. A goddamn neon sign screaming there was more under the surface.

Lyra's hand twitched. Just a flicker. The urge to trace Calista's face, to brush her lips with her fingertips, surged and died before it could take form. She stayed still. The air had hardened, brittle and sharp, and any movement could fracture the fragile quiet, stealing Calista from the sleep she so desperately needed.

Don't wake her.

She drew back.

"Vira," she whispered.

The name hung between them like a live wire.

Lyra didn't know what Vira meant to Calista. Didn't want to. Didn't need to. That kind of knowledge came with strings, and Lyra had spent a lifetime cutting hers.

With a sigh that barely disturbed the air, Lyra reached into her satchel, the leather creaking softly against the silence. She pulled out the scavenged book, *Dhalgren*, its cover worn and faded, the pages dog-eared from countless readings. A pang of something akin to affection hit Lyra with the force of a plasma blast.

Rana had loved this book. Clutched it like a lifeline, said it made her feel connected—like there was something out there beyond the concrete pisshole they called a city. Something vast. Holy, even.

She always believed in the power of those things—books. Objects that somehow carried other realities in their pages, little pieces of possibility she could touch.

Lyra never got it. Books weren't sacred. They were weapons. Shields. Bargaining chips. You used words to talk your way past a loaded barrel or out of a bad debt with worse people.

But this book—this damn book—had meant something to Rana. And now, here it was again, leering at Lyra from the shadows like a ghost with unfinished business. That meant something too. Not that she'd ever admit it. Not out loud.

Opening the book carefully, Lyra began to read, her voice a low murmur that barely registered above the gasps of the base's failing machines.

"to wound the autumnal city. . . "

The words twisted, bleeding together into a mess of fractured images and nonsensical thoughts, like a disjointed puzzle that refused to fit. Lyra wrestled with the prose, finding it dense, impenetrable. But she persevered, drawn in by the rhythm of the language, the way it seemed to mirror the chaotic, fragmented reality of their lives.

Meaning hides between the breaks.

Her body responded before her mind fully registered it. She inched toward Calista, one careful movement, testing the friction of the mattress, the space between them. Small, deliberate motions, a worming toward warmth, toward the soft pulse of life in a world that felt otherwise dead and leaking.

Soon she was beside her, curling against the line of her ribs, careful not to wake, careful to let the contours of Calista's form anchor her in something real. Her head found the curve of Calista's shoulder, and she rested there, the book awkwardly balanced on the curve of her chest.

For a heartbeat, she looked almost normal. Almost at peace. Almost like reality had momentarily aligned. Almost like the world hadn't fractured in a thousand invisible directions.

Almost—but the almost was a lie, and she knew it.

No time for thoughts like that.

Only the words. Only the pulse of warmth. Only the jittering hum beneath the skin of the universe, reminding her that nothing, ever, stayed still.

Calista stirred. A subtle movement. Then a soft moan. Her eyes fluttered open, unfocused and hazy with sleep. She blinked a few times, like a gearhead trying to recalibrate their reality sensors.

"Lyra?" she mumbled, her voice thick with sleep. "What time is it?"

Time to wake up and smell the dystopia.

"You got about five minutes left on your beauty rest," Lyra said, marking her place in the book and closing it.

Calista pushed herself up, rubbing the sleep from her eyes. She glanced at Lyra, a flicker of surprise crossing her face. "What are you doing?"

"Reading," Lyra said, holding up the book. "Trying to figure out what Rana saw in this goddamn thing."

Calista's expression shuttered. "That's . . . the book she loved."

"Yeah. Remember? We found it in The Shelves. You know, that old place they called a library back when the printed word meant something. Thought maybe I could give it a read. You know, see what all the fuss was about." She held the book out, the edges frayed, the spine reluctant.

Calista didn't reach for it right away. Then her fingers took it, gentle, almost reverent, sliding over the worn cover like it carried a pulse. She opened it carefully, turning pages as though each one contained a secret meant only for her. "Rana always said it was a mirror of our lives. Fragmented, chaotic, full of dead ends and unexpected connections. A world where the rules don't stick and every turn makes the world feel both infinite and ridiculous. Where nothing ever makes sense."

Maybe confusion was the only honest map left. Chaos leaving fingerprints on the edges of reality.

"Sounds like today," Lyra said, feeling her own perception fray at the corners, like static in a broken signal.

Calista closed the book with a sigh, her eyes meeting Lyra's. "She said it was a complicated book. Circular. Said you won't get it on the first read."

"Me? Probably not on the tenth," Lyra admitted. "But I'm stubborn. Always have been."

A pause hung between them, thick with unspoken emotions. Lyra shifted uncomfortably, suddenly aware of the intimacy of their position, the way her body was pressed against Calista's.

"So . . ." she said, breaking the silence. "About you and Vira . . ."

Calista stiffened, her face clouding over. "V? Us?"

Lyra shrugged, trying to play it cool, despite the knot of curiosity twisting in her gut. "I just . . . you two seem pretty close."

Calista's gaze flickered away, landing on the worn floor. "We were," she said, her voice low. "A long time ago. Before all this . . . before everything went to hell."

She says *we were* like it still aches to say.

"Lovers?" Lyra pressed, unable to resist the urge to know.

Calista hesitated, then nodded slowly. "Yeah. For a while."

"And now?"

"Now, we're soldiers fighting a war," Calista said, a weary sound. "And in a war, lovers are a liability. Too much risk, too much distraction. The time for that . . . it's gone. Long gone."

Long gone doesn't sound finished—it sounds buried.

"So, it just . . . ended?" Lyra asked, surprised by the sting of something that felt suspiciously like jealousy.

Calista shrugged. "No. I guess it changed. Evolved. We had to. We understood there were things bigger than us . . . things we couldn't ignore. Survival. Justice. Rana's dreams." She turned fully toward Lyra, eyes steady. "Love can't always hold a world together. Not this one. Not here."

Lyra's voice caught somewhere between disbelief and hope. "What about us then?"

Calista gave a half-smile, the kind that doesn't soften the edges of a warning. "What about us?"

"We're lovers. This is war. Isn't it . . . a distraction? A liability?"

"It's different with you," Calista said calmly.

Shit, everything's different with me.

Lyra's brow furrowed. "Oh, how so?"

Calista took a deep breath, frustrated. "I don't know. It just is. You're different. In all this goddamn chaos, you question everything, to try to see clearly, to make sense of all this shit. For you, it's not love . . . it's something else. That makes you a liability, yes . . . dangerous, but in the right way."

Dangerous. The word hovered. Both a compliment and a warning, like a neon sign flickering in a world that had lost its electricity.

"Right way?" Lyra said, breath catching, her voice sharp and small against the grinding pulse of reality.

Calista leaned in, close enough that her voice seemed to emerge from inside Lyra's own skull. Low. Relentless. "The thing that keeps me from falling apart. It's the thing that makes me want to fight, to go on, even when fighting seems hopeless. A reason I want to fight, not just survive. And maybe . . . maybe that's what love truly is in the fucked up reality."

Lyra went very still, like a circuit holding charge before it burns something down. Calista's words sank in, not gently, not kindly. Then Lyra reached out—slow, intentional—hands cupping Calista's face. "You don't have to do this alone. You've got me."

Calista didn't look away. She leaned in, and the kiss wasn't soft or tentative; it was a collision. When they parted, Calista reached for Lyra's hands, gripping them like handles on a runaway machine. "Enough of this bullshit. Let's go make a mark for ourselves. It's time for the next battle."

She stood, pulling away from Lyra and stretching her aching limbs. "Let's go remind Steele that we're not going down without a fight."

Lyra's mouth curved into something sharp and familiar, a familiar glint returning to her eyes. "That's what I like to hear. So, what's first?"

Calista headed for the door, her face set with grim determination. "We start by making Steele's life a living hell." She paused at the threshold, glanced back, eyes bright with something dangerous and alive. "And maybe, just maybe, by actually saving what's left of this world."

Lyra laughed, a sound that echoed through the small room, a promise of chaos and rebellion in a world that desperately needed both. "Sounds like a plan," she said, grabbing her blaster and following Calista into the unknown. "Let's go light this fuckin' world on fire."

The base's command center was a small, tight, windowless space, lit only by the electric glow of monitors and the pulsing holographic display that hovered in the middle of the room. A metal table sat in the middle with chairs. The walls were lined with panels of dead tech, their function long since repurposed or abandoned. It was a bunker, a relic, a tomb of forgotten systems, and for now, it was their war room.

Calista stood there, arms crossed like a barricade, her face an unreadable mask. Sync was plugged into the console, his forearm grafted to the system like a parasite, a hologram flickering under his touch, data bending to his silent commands. Lyra, like a ghost in the corner, leaned against the wall, her fingers drumming a beat against her thigh, a rhythm only her mind could hear, tapping into some private hell of her own. Vira was seated at one end of the table, chewing on a strip of dried something, eyes half-lidded but far from inattentive.

"Did you run your checks on everyone?" Calista asked Sync, her voice as sharp as a broken bottle.

He didn't flinch. "Yes," he said, as cold and mechanical as the metal he bled. "All checked out. No anomalies."

Calista nodded, chewing on her lips like she was grinding the whole damn situation down to something manageable. Her gaze slid over to Sync's arm, then the hologram, the glowing mess of data.

"So, what are we looking at?" Calista asked him, her words flat, but the edge underneath them as sharp as a knife.

Sync's voice was smooth, clinical, too clean. "This," he said, extending a too-perfect hand toward the jagged, stuttering flicker of unstable code crawling across the makeshift image, "is the point of entry to the Iron Rose's systems."

Lyra smiled.

A gash in Steele's reality. A digital wound. A raw nerve exposed in his fuckin' network.

"A vulnerability," Sync continued, his voice devoid of inflection, "Steele, the arrogant fool that he is, either dismissed it or did not perceive it as a threat. A place to dig, to plant an infection."

Lyra's eyes narrowed.

Ever the pragmatist.

"A crack in the shell," she murmured. "Doesn't mean we can waltz right in. It means we might get a toehold before we're vaporized."

Calista ignored her. "What about the infection?" she asked Sync.

"Yes," he said. "A virus. Not the crude biological sort— something more elegant. It will infiltrate his directive architecture and begin rewriting the assumptions beneath it."

He paused, as though visualizing the structure of another mind.

"It will introduce uncertainty into his logic chains. Tiny inconsistencies. Contradictions that look accidental. Doubt will begin to propagate through the system like a software glitch that refuses to identify itself. Slowly, his processes will start mistrusting their own outputs."

His luminous eyes flickered faintly.

"He will not know it is happening. At first, it will just feel like statistical noise. Then a pattern. Then a fracture spreading through every calculation he makes. A kind of internal decay—his own cognition turning hostile to itself."

He leaned closer.

"But . . ." he said quietly, "to initiate it, we need proximity. Very close proximity. Close enough to reach inside the machine and plant the idea."

"How close, Sync? Spit it out," Vira demanded, her hand resting on the butt of her sidearm.

He offered a smile, not meeting his eyes.

"We cannot inject the code remotely, not without triggering every failsafe he has. He is too paranoid, too discerning with what he lets in from the outside. We need a direct tether. Inside the tower itself."

He paused, the weight of reality settling like iron.

"But we need time. Time to scavenge the right parts, wire together shielding, build something that keeps us from cooking the second we breach his perimeter. Without it? We are just throwing ourselves into the grinder." He turned to Calista. "We need more time to obtain the right parts."

"Time we don't have," she snapped, her patience wearing thin. "Can we jury-rig something from what we have, or are we just pissing into the wind?"

Sync's head shook. "Everything we need got wiped out when he hit the base. He sent us a message."

The silence that descended was thick with defeat. Calista fought the urge to slam her fist on the table, to shatter the fragile illusion of control. "So," she growled, "we were dealt a setback. We knew that."

Lyra pushed herself off the wall.

Setbacks aren't new. Control is just a joke.

She grinned, a flash of defiance in her eyes. "There's only one goddamn thing you can do when the universe kicks you in the teeth and pisses down on you."

"Do tell," Calista said, her tone a razor blade wrapped in silk.

"Ask for some help," Lyra said, her eyes alight.

Calista's eyebrows rose. "From who?"

Lyra's grin widened, turning feral. She tapped a finger against her temple, a gesture that was almost taunting. "Wheels, are you there? Is your sweet, chrome ass ready to come out and play?"

A beat of static, then a voice crackled from Lyra's comm, thick with interference, but unmistakable. "You got it, Crow. Got your coordinates locked. I'll be slithering into your little rat's nest by morning. Just try to keep Steele from turning you all into scrap metal before I get there."

Calista's fingers drummed against the table, a staccato rhythm betraying the chaos grinding behind her eyes. "Who the fuck is Wheels?"

Lyra chuckled, low and knowing. "You'll like him. He's got grease in his blood and fire in his belly. Runs fast, thinks faster, and has a shitload of weapons. Doesn't much care for rules either." Her eyes were flickering with mischief. "Kinda reminds me of you."

Calista was stone-faced, eyes sharp. "That's not a fuckin' answer."

Before Lyra could hijack the moment with one of her dramatic pirouettes into sarcasm, Sync jumped in—cold and efficient, a machine playing at being a man. "Saw him at Doc Jones' place," he said, his voice a blade honed on necessity, cutting through the room's static like it owed him money. "He is patched together from the graveyard of better men—meat, wiring, and something else. Something that hums wrong. But he has what we need."

There it was. No poetry. No dramatics. Just the truth, dropped on the floor like a live wire, daring anyone to touch it.

Calista exhaled sharply, arms crossed tight against her chest. "And you think this guy . . . or whatever he is, can help?"

Lyra smirked. "He knows how to weave through a system like it's a lover. He knows how Steele's fortress breathes. How the data flows like blood in its veins. And tomorrow morning? He's ours."

Sync gave a single nod, crisp, efficient, devoid of anything human. "Good to have him on our side." A pause. "For as long as he lasts."

Vira's voice cut in, cool and precise like she was laying out an autopsy. "Are you sure this Wheels can be trusted?"

Lyra's head snapped around so fast the air snapped with it. "I trust him with my life," she hissed. And she meant it. Because she knew they needed him. Because she knew whatever was being planned was already a corpse twitching out its last impulses.

Calista didn't buy it, not fully. Her instincts itched. But she holstered the doubt for the time being, like a knife she wasn't quite ready to throw.

She leaned forward, palms flat on the cold slab of metal between them, a war council in miniature. "Alright. We know the bastard's weakness . . . we know that what we need to do can't be done from here. We know we need to get inside. So how the hell do we get close without ending up flayed open and hung up like a cautionary tale by Steele's security?"

A pause. Then she answered herself. "We need a distraction."

Vira met her gaze, letting her eyes linger just long enough to unnerve. "Something big. Something loud. Something that drags all of Steele's eyes off the prize."

Calista's lips tightened. Not a smile, not quite a frown, but a shape that tasted like warning. "And I'm afraid . . . something expendable."

The air between them thickened, charged with anticipation. Sync tilted his head, observing without judgment, while Lyra's fingers twitched like she wanted to reach for a weapon but had nothing to kill yet.

Vira broke the silence. "I know what we can do. I'll take the lead."

Calista's eyes sharpened. "V, you sure about that?"

"Someone's got to," Vira shrugged, a movement so slight it could have been mistaken for a shiver. "And we both know I can make the biggest noise."

Calista let out a breath, shaking her head. "This isn't a game of cards. You throw down the wrong bet, and you don't get to play again."

"We all cash out eventually," Vira's smile barely curled, something distant in it, like she was already looking past the end. "Might as well make it count."

Calista hesitated, something cold crawling through her gut. "I don't know if I like this."

"Not a lot of doors left to open," Vira said.

Calista studied her, the weight of the decision pressing against her bones. "Alright, then, what's the play?"

Vira leaned over the table, her words honed like a switchblade. "Steele's eyes are everywhere . . . but his ears? . . . his ears still listen to old ghosts. There's an old relay tower outside his fortress. Ancient, derelict, something he barely bothers to monitor anymore. If we can somehow jumpstart it with the right frequency . . . we can bring to life an old resistance signal, something he thought he buried . . . it'll set his paranoia on fire. He'll send drones, soldier bots, everything he's got."

Sync's fingers steepled under his chin. "And while he's chasing phantoms, we walk right through the front door."

Calista's grip on the table tightened as she looked at Vira. "And you, V?"

Vira didn't blink. Didn't shift. Didn't even acknowledge the weight of what she was saying. "I make sure he keeps chasing."

Then silence. The kind that eats the air, chews it up, spits it back out full of static and bad omens.

Lyra sucked in a breath, slow, measured, like she was tasting the inevitability of it all, and dragged a hand down her face.

This quiet isn't peaceful—it's waiting.

"Fine," she said. "But if we're doing this, we do it sharp, we do it clean. No more flaming wreckage for Steele to gloat over. We slip in, we slip out, and we try like all fuck to live to tell the tale."

Vira grinned, the kind of grin that made promises no one wanted fulfilled. "But let's kick this off with something to whet his appetite. A bang"

Lyra leaned forward, eyes ablaze.

Bang? That's right up my alley.

"Here's an idea." She turned to Sync. "You got a data chip? One that looks like shit but's functional? One we can put a short video on?"

Sync nodded, the faintest smirk crossing his features. "I think so. Why?"

Lyra laughed, low and dangerous." Just leave that to me, tin man."

Calista's teeth clenched, the decision already hardwired into her bones. "Fine. Then there's no time to waste. Let's get to it."

The room was dark, the only light filtering in through the cracks in the metal slats, cutting the space into slivers of shadow and dim glow. The thrum of a struggling generator pulsed in the walls, a rhythmic, dying heartbeat. Lyra and Calista lay tangled together on the bed, limbs intertwined, breath shared between them. The sheets were twisted, damp with sweat, the heat of their bodies pressing against the cold, unfeeling world beyond the walls.

Lyra sighed.

Her warmth is the only truth I need. Every heartbeat between us makes the silence less cruel.

She traced her fingers along Calista's ribs, slow, her touch barely there. Her mouth ghosted over Calista's shoulder, her breath warm, lips pressing soft against scar tissue and old wounds. Calista's body loosened, a subtle shudder passing through her, but she stayed still, tethered to Lyra by something neither could name. She didn't pull away. Not from Lyra. Never from Lyra.

Then Rana entered Lyra's thoughts again—not gradually, but like a shard forcing its way up through the surface of her mind. A cold fragment lodged deep in her consciousness, something that refused deletion even while Calista's warmth surrounded her.

Memory reconstructed itself.

Rana's voice through the computer in The Shelves— flattened by circuitry, delayed by failing processors, yet unmistakably human.

Lyra felt the uneasy possibility unfold.

Is she out there? Drawing the same shitty air through tired lungs? Continuing the simple biological act of breathing while waiting for a rescue that might never resolve into reality?

The thought persisted, looping like a corrupted transmission.

Then Lyra spoke.

Her voice was low, almost swallowed by the air, but it cut through the haze of noise inside my head like a fragile transmission trying to break through interference.

"What if Rana is . . . still alive?"

Calista stiffened. The small room contracted, air sucked out, leaving nothing but static and the grinding of rust in her skull.

Lyra pulled back enough to see Calista's face, to watch the way the question hit. "What if what we heard was real? That Steele . . ." she swallowed, something bitter behind her eyes, ". . . that Steele . . . somehow preserved her? Not just data. Not just scraps of memory and synthetic echoes. What if it's really her?"

Calista didn't respond with words. Her hand came up to Lyra's jaw, gripping just enough to guide her, tilting her head, dragging her down into a kiss. Slow, measured.

Lyra closed her eyes.

A response. But no answer. No mercy of clarity.

She let it happen. Let herself drown in the kiss. But when they parted, the world returned, and Calista's voice was there, sharp.

"We take him down," she said, her fingers curling into the back of Lyra's neck, nail digging in. "And if we have to, we take her down too."

Lyra studied her.

What the fuck is she talkin' about?

"No. We can't."

Calista's jaw clenched. "Listen, I know she's dead. And you do, too. You saw it. Reality is a harsh thing."

Lyra squirmed.

Fuck reality!

"But what if what I saw was . . . wrong?" she asked.

Calista drew in a sharp breath, not to steady herself but to hold the edges of her composure. Her heart thudded, a relentless drum, and she knew Lyra could feel every beat. "If Steele has her, she's not the same. She's already gone."

Lyra pulled away.

No. No!

She sat up like the thought had seared her spine. Her legs spilled off the bed, her hand raking through her hair like she was trying to erase the idea by brute force. "Her voice . . . that transmission . . ." She stopped, swallowed, and started again. "That wasn't noise. Wasn't programming. Wasn't fake. It was her. The way she paused, the way she breathed. Don't tell me I imagined it."

Calista sat up beside her, fingers dragging across the bare skin of her thigh like she was reminding herself she still had a body, still had bones beneath all that history. "You think Steele has her stashed away somewhere? Like some relic? Like some prize he keeps on a shelf to remind himself he won?"

Lyra turned away.

Maybe she's right. My mind feels like a static-filled room where hope and logic are screaming at each other, and neither one is winning.

"I don't know what I think." she turned back eyes burning. "I just know that if we do this, if we go through with this plan, we might be killing her all over again."

Calista's hand found Lyra's, their fingers threading together, but her grip was tight. Not soft. Not comforting. "Then we make damn sure death was worth it."

Lyra didn't blink. Didn't speak. Just squeezed back.

SEVEN

INTO THE MAW

The walls of New York Veritas didn't creak—they howled, the skeletal frame of the city shrieking like it knew its number was up. This wasn't just collapse; it was a death rattle stretched out over years, molasses-slow and twice as choking. It oozed downward like a diseased memory, bleeding into the underbelly where daylight had never dared to trespass. Down here, the air didn't circulate— it crowded you. A foul brew of oil, sweat, and something chemical that latched onto your lungs like wet wool dipped in poison. And underneath it all? Something darker. A pulse that seemed to fill the space, too dense, too loud for the silence—fear, anticipation, despair, all wrapped up in the sickening stench of what was left.

In the small rebel stronghold, a horn wailed—a shriek that clawed its way through the air like a dying thing, desperate for release. On the rusted catwalks, the scouts shifted like ghosts, silent but dangerous. They moved through the cavernous, forgotten belly of the machine, blasters held close, fingers taut on triggers. Waiting. Waiting for whatever horror would come at them.

And it did.

A thing not meant for this world. A thing not even meant to exist at all.

A machine. A monstrosity. A man.

It floated like an afterthought of a god gone mad—part man, part machine, stitched together in a grotesque mimicry of life, living in some strange apparatus. Metal didn't wrap the body; it claimed it, clung to it like a jealous lover turned corpse-cold. The chrome didn't shine—it glared, hostile, arrogant, the kind of shine you get off a blade that's seen too much and still wants more.

Within this strange suit, synthflesh throbbed with artificial rhythm, obscene in its mimicry of life. Cables—thick as pythons and just as hungry—snaked into the body, vanishing beneath skin that didn't know whether to blister or heal. And the veins, Christ, the veins—gone were blood and pulse, replaced by cold light: fiber optics hissing with secrets too old and too dangerous for any one mind to hold.

And the face peering out—young. Almost. A child's portrait burned into a war mask. Something about it remembered laughter, but only as rumor. And the eyes—those goddamn eyes—looked through the iron lattice. Innocent once, perhaps. But that innocence had been bartered away long ago, and badly.

This wasn't just another machine.

This wasn't just another corpse made useful.

This was Wheels. And he had a new chariot.

No one moved at first, frozen in place by what stood before them. It moved too fast, too fluid, too alien. A moment too long to breathe.

Red lights blazed to life, and chaos hit. Beams of blaster plasma lashed through the air, tearing at the darkness. One rebel scout's blaster was ripped from his hand. The weapon spun away, clanging, lost to the hollow cavern of the catwalk. Another scout was yanked back, pinned to the rusted metal with a force that bent him like a reed. His breath hitched, and the world held still in that brief, agonizing stretch of time.

Then came the voice.

"I could kill you," Wheels rasped, a sound like a blade scraped along stone. His voice was young, sure, but hollowed out, emptied of something essential. His face twisted in the unnatural way his body moved, a sickening ballet of mechanical precision and human rot. "But that's not why I'm here."

One of the scouts, eyes wide and hand trembling on his weapon, stepped forward, though he couldn't hide the tremor in his voice. "Are you . . ."

Wheels cut him off, his head tilting, the movement fluid and inhuman. "I'm the one you've been waiting for."

Silence spread, thick and suffocating, until it felt like the air itself had stopped breathing. Even the hum of the city's broken heart seemed to fade, swallowed by the tension that filled the room. The scouts—stunned, still holding their weapons—lowered them one by one, but the unease never left their bones. Without a word, they gestured down to the lower levels, to the rebel base.

"Come with us," one of them said.

Wheels moved.

Not walked. Not stepped. Moved.

The motion was wrong in a way that made your nerves tighten before your brain caught up. Flesh shouldn't do that. Neither should machines. But Wheels was something in between, and the universe had already proven it was sloppy about those boundaries.

He drifted forward.

The rebels guided him down, deeper into the underbelly of the city—into tunnels no one built for comfort or memory. These were the arteries left behind when the body of civilization stopped caring about circulation.

Old infrastructure. Dead systems that never got the memo they were obsolete.

The walls closed in as they went. Metal plates sweating rust. Bolts blooming corrosion like slow infections. The air tasted stale, thick with the memory of smoke and forgotten fires.

Every turn bent back on itself.

The place didn't want to be remembered.

And it showed.

They passed synth guards who lingered too long, optics whirring, logic stalling at the question of whether he was man or synth or something else. They passed humans who refused to look at him at all, faces tightening, mouths flattening in revulsion. There were boundaries even among insurgents, lines drawn not by allegiance but by disgust. Some creations were mistakes so profound no one wanted to claim—even for their side.

When they hit the command center, the door moaned like it was mourning its own hinges. Wheels slid in, all wrong angles and wrong speeds, like a human being filtered through some lunatic math—part man, part broken machine, all menace. The air didn't just hang; it suffocated. Even the shadows seemed to have stopped breathing, like the room itself had frozen in disbelief.

Calista leaned in a little, arms crossed, jaw locked tight enough to chip teeth on, eyes slicing through the space with the precision of a scalpel dipped in acid. She was counting, weighing, measuring. Every twitch of a finger, every step, every millisecond—cataloged.

Lyra pressed herself against the wall, arms folded like she owned the silence, half-smile hiding in the dark corners of her face. She could taste it, the electricity of danger, like licking the static off the sky before the storm hits. She smirked. It was a slash of defiance, a little grin stitched into the edge of a threat.

Sync didn't move at first, except for the tiny whirl of lenses over his mechanical face. Fingers steepled like he was praying to some algorithm only he could hear. The console beneath him rattled, a weary artifact, a reminder that even old things obeyed the mad pulse of this room.

No one spoke.

Nothing sounded right. Wheels was wrong. Everything about him was wrong, and wrongness has a smell you can taste. It poured into the air, thick and metallic, drenching everything it touched.

Sync's lenses whirred, finally locking on Wheels, scanning, computing, calculating probability waves in the silence. Calista's fingers twitched at her belt, a breath away from the blaster, her muscles screaming for justice, for the obliteration of the impossible thing standing in front of her.

And the room waited. Oh, the room waited. Like a predator that had grown tired of shadow games and was about to sink its teeth into the marrow of reality itself.

Lyra's smirk twisted into something darker, but even she couldn't hold the amusement for long.

"Welcome, my friend," Lyra said, and the words didn't just fill the silence—they ripped it open. Her voice was a flare of neon lightning in that dead, dusty air, a shard of glass scratching across the solemn quiet of the room, and herself along with it. "Looks like you got new digs."

Wheels lifted the head of his exoskeleton just enough to show what might have been a smile. If you called it that. "Been working on a new suit. You like how it looks?" His voice had the rasp of steel and oil, the hum of hydraulics under tension.

"Very stylish," she said, letting laughter leak out like static across a broken wire. "Stylish indeed."

She stopped. Paused. The air between them sizzled with possibility and the scent of metal and oil. "So . . . I guess we move," she said, the words catching on the edge of anticipation, like a knife blade testing its own sharpness.

Wheels adjusted his lenses with that slow, insectile churn that made the air throb with a private menace. The servos in his mech suit ground together—a low, metallic snarl that might've been laughter if you were a person who'd forgotten what laughter sounded like. When the motion stopped, the plates of his face formed a smile, a crooked piece of machinework—too calculated, too human in the wrong places. It crawled across his face until it became something that didn't belong to this place, or any other. Not joy. Not madness. Something in between. The kind of look a man wears when he's looked God in the eye and shrugged.

"We move, alright," he said, voice dragging through the air like gravel. "We move right into the fucker's gut. Tear our way through until we find something that still bleeds. We hit hard. We don't stop. And we don't look back. Because where we're coming from is already on fire."

His lenses tightened, faint light flaring in them. "He built his goddamn tower thinking it can't die. But everything dies. You cut deep enough, even machines know what dying feels like."

He leaned closer, grin still hanging there, a sick kind of halo around it. "And when Steele starts to scream, we'll keep going. We'll make him remember our names."

Lyra watched him for a long moment, the thrumming of his mech suit filling the silence between them.

He doesn't flinch at fire. He is the fire. Is it wrong for me to be this excited?

Then she said, voice low and steady, "Fuckin' Steele. We'll carve our name into his bones. We just gotta make sure there's enough left of him to feel the carving."

Her attention flew to Calista—a single, precise cut of the eyes, quick and intentional.

He's one of us.

Calista's stare came back hard, flat, unblinking. Her reply needed no voice at all.

"So," Calista said, her voice a slow knife cutting through the intensity. "You're the one we've been waiting for."

Wheels' cables twitched, metal serpents fighting their own leashes. A pulse stuttered through his frame—part static, part broken thought. "That's what I told your men," he said, the words dry, mechanical, but carrying a trace of something human, no matter how much circuitry had been poured over it.

Calista stepped forward. "My scouts . . . you could've killed them. Why didn't you?"

Wheels grinned—or tried to. It didn't reach his eyes. "Ah . . . so it was a test," he mused, his voice distorted, echoing through his crude breathing apparatus. "Killing? Shit. What would be the point?"

Sync let out a slow exhale, the sound synthetic, but tired. "Killing is what we do around here. When we have to."

Wheels turned to Sync, dark eyes hidden behind the machinery. "I only kill when it's necessary. I'm not like Steele."

Steele.

The monster. The architect of their suffering. The warlord whose empire bled into the very marrow of their bones. The machine-god whose citadel was built on the corpses of millions.

Calista's eyes narrowed, the room suddenly thick with something colder than before. "No one here is like that fucker."

Sync's fingers tapped across the console, a rhythm that was precise, mechanical. "I suppose it is time to bring him into our plans."

Wheels—strange, twisted, broken—tilted his head. For the first time, something like a smile, twisted and uncertain, cracked across his lips. "Then let's begin."

Time didn't move forward; it was seized and hauled off, kicking. Wheels and Sync ground through it shoulder to shoulder—half-lit crawlspaces, broom-closet labs, places that smelled of scorched plastic, insulation, and wiring. Their hands went black with residue, synth-skinned knuckles torn, patience sanded down to their metal bones. Shielding plates were wired together from whatever hadn't already been melted, broken apart, or cursed into irrelevance. Wheels muttered curses at old components that remembered better days, while Sync drew invisible diagrams through the air, chasing signals that refused to behave, solving failures faster than instruments could register them. Tools lagged. Circuits resisted. The work demanded everything they had left—and then demanded more, because that's what broken systems always do.

"Tell me again why this shouldn't explode now," Wheels said, tightening a clamp on an improvised explosive.

"It might," Sync replied. "One wrong move and it does what it wants."

"Fuck," Wheels muttered, eyes flicking between the device and Sync as if the world itself were holding its breath.

They unfurled hijacked holographic schematics of the Iron Rose tower on a table—maps stolen from dead servers and infiltrated systems. Sync tapped a node with a grease-stained finger. "This access point? Steele thinks it is sealed. It is not."

Wheels snorted. "Nothing ever is. That tower? It lies. And so do gods."

Later, Vira arrived, slipping through the shadows like she owned the darkness itself. Her boots made no sound on the concrete, and the faint hum of neon overhead caught on the edges of her coat. She dropped beside a crate of explosives with the calm, deliberate ease of a surgeon opening a body, fingers tracing circuits and wires with a precision that made Wheels shift in his seat, uneasy, teeth gnawing at the inside of his cheek. Sync's optical array buzzed and blinked as he ran a quick diagnostic, just to make sure what he was seeing wasn't a hallucination or some cruel joke the universe had cooked up.

Wheels handed her a coil. "You're sure about the timing?"

Her eyes stayed on the wiring. "If I'm wrong, you won't have time to complain."

Sync let a thin, humorless grin slip. "I doubt he found your response comforting."

At night—assuming it was night—they always focused on the virus Sync had sculpted, tuning it with obsessive care, a piece of code designed to peel back Steele's logic line by line, annihilating his control. Sync murmured to the code, coaxing it, cajoling it into obedience, while Wheels layered in his own instructions, sharp and decisive. "We shut him down," Wheels said. "The tower goes blind."

"Not blind," Sync corrected, flat and cold. "Dead."

And in that closeness—wires crossing, maps overlapping, voices sharpening and softening—they built something dangerous enough to matter.

The command center was a mausoleum of noise and neglect, a place where every panel, every wire, every sweating piece of metal screamed with memory. Rust exhaled its stink into the air, mingling with burnt circuits and mistakes—bad, brilliant, murderous mistakes—so thick you could taste history on your tongue. The lights jerked and spasmed like epileptics with secrets, blinking warnings nobody wanted to read. And that sound—grinding, throbbing, low—wasn't just sound. It was the city itself, coughing and wheezing through a skeleton of iron, indifferent to any life foolish enough to linger.

Wheels' mech suit hissed in tiny intervals, like it knew its pilot was running on borrowed time. He hadn't slept in ages. Fatigue gnawed at him in small, vicious bites, teeth of exhaustion scraping sinew. When an injector snapped forward and bit into the back of his neck, he flinched, just a twitch, just enough to remember he was alive—alive in a way that bordered on obscene. The chemical slurry hit his veins and set off a symphony of pain and electric fire, hornets marching through tin nerves and hollow skulls. He straightened, brittle bones and all, and grinned at the machine keeping him from being just another corpse in the humming cathedral of wires.

The room lurched around him in that slow, deliberate way that buildings do when they've tasted enough suffering. The monitors whispered static prayers, the ozone stung, sweat pooled and baked into the metal like it had nowhere else to go. Sync leaned over the monitor, arms crossed, scanning lines of data like a predator and a priest rolled into one. Calista perched on a crate, cigarette glowing like the dying heart of a star, eyes tracing the holographic schematics of the Iron Rose, absorbing every line, every curve, every hidden fault with the precision of obsession.

Vira crouched beside her, fingers hammering the keyboard, each keystroke a small ritual of violence, a bending of walls and defenses, a war against unseen codes. She danced around firewalls, shattered encryptions, feeding on the system's resistance even as she feared it might bite back, testing Steele's fortifications like a spider tasting the tension in its own web. The air hummed, thick with ozone and bloodless sweat, and somewhere in that electrical hell, Wheels grinned again, alive and almost human.

Lyra leaned against the wall, a shadowed figure coiled in quiet menace, her fingers tracing the contours of her blaster.

Patience is sharper than any blade in my hand.

"Let's skip the foreplay," Calista said, looking up, voice flat as a dead battery. "Everyone knows why we're here."

"Because we're suicidal," Lyra muttered.

"No," Vira said, "because we're the only ones remaining who remember how to make tyrants bleed."

Calista, cigarette dangling from her lips, stabbed a finger at the map, an echo of topography smeared with age and blood. "Target's here. Iron Rose. Steele's little monument to fascism. Fortress built on the bones of a thousand cities. And nobody . . . nobody . . . has ever come back from it."

"Until now," Lyra said, eyes narrow, like she was already halfway inside.

Sync tapped the monitor. It fluttered, then coughed up more holographic schematics like a terminal exhaling its last. "We breach through here—northwest shaft.

Maintenance access buried under centuries of architectural rot. It is a soft spot. The only one."

"What about Steele?" Lyra asked. "Fucker sees everything."

"That's where Vira comes in," Calista said.

Vira smiled, but not the kind of smile you wear in polite company. This one had teeth. "I'm going to knock on his door with a stick of dynamite."

She yanked back a tarp on the floor beside her. Underneath: a transmitter Wheels and Sync built from rusted parts and sheer lunacy. "We're going to broadcast on an old frequency. The one then resistance used at the start of all this madness. Steele thought he buried it."

Calista blinked. "You're going to taunt a dictator with a ghost signal?"

"Not just taunt him," Vira said. "I'm gonna cut him. Force him to bleed. He'll throw drones, soldier bots, maybe even his personal sentinels at the signal."

"You will have fifteen minutes to keep him occupied," Sync said, tone sharpened to a warning. "If he takes you in less, then we are all screwed. Anything more than that, well then, we have a fighting chance."

"I won't be alone," Vira said, too calm.

"Who you taking?" Calista asked.

"Strike team, yeah. But also this . . ." She reached into a pocket, dropped a holopad onto the table, and tapped it. A rendering spun into the air: a vehicle, beast of metal, bristling with ancient armor, its body fused from tank parts and drone plating, plasma cannon mounted like an afterthought.

"That can't be real," Lyra said.

"It is," Vira said. "Called it back from hell one piece at a time. Been hiding it in the slagfields."

"Who the hell's gonna drive it?" Calista asked.

Vira looked up. "Specter."

Silence. A long one. An ugly one.

Lyra's brows pinched.

Don't like the sound of that name . . . sounds like a ghost story.

"Who the fuck is this Specter?" she asked.

Sync turned to her. Not smiling. Not blinking. "Specter is a soldier bot. Old series. Real old. Disabled his link to Steele a long time ago. Like me. He is what you humans call a mean son-of-a-bitch."

"You think you can put a soldier bot behind the wheel of that thing?" Wheels said.

"Yup," Vira said. "The toughest fucker you've ever met."

"That bot ever go rogue?" Lyra asked, half-genuine, half-dare.

"No," Sync said, "But if he ever does, pray you die before he gets to you."

"Love it," Calista said. "While Steele's chasing ghosts and fire, we hit the shaft. Others will be on drone suppression. Lyra and me will lead the way along with Wheels. Sync handles the payload." She exhaled smoke into the console. "Payload's ready?"

Sync pulled a chip from his coat. Small, silver, delicate. "Contains the virus disguised as Steele's own code. His system takes it in, thinks it is a love letter. By the time he realizes it is a knife in the gut, it is already twisting."

Lyra grinned. It wasn't pleasant.

A love letter that's a knife. Charming.

"Poetry," she said.

"We get to the core," Sync continued, "I plug this in, we get out. If we are lucky."

Lyra smiled.

Luck's a promise that shouldn't be rusted.

"And if we're not lucky?" she asked.

"Then we burn in hell with him," Sync said, pocketing the chip.

The small command center creaked. Somewhere above, the world still ticked forward on stolen time.

Calista looked at each of them in turn. "This isn't a maybe. This isn't a think-about-it. We go at dawn. No arguments. We bring hell. Anyone who wants out, speak now."

No one moved. Even the lights seemed to shut up for a second, as if the machines themselves were holding their breath.

"All right," Calista said. "Sync, prep the payload. Lyra, go over entry points again. Wheels—you need to calibrate drone scramblers. Vira—go wake your monster. Tomorrow it begins, and it ends."

They moved. Except Lyra. She hung in the moment like smoke.

Can't get Rana out of my head. It's like she just sticks there, curled up, whispering things, sweet and razor-edged.

Calista's eyes flitted to her, quick and cold. "Problem?"

Lyra's eyebrow ticked—a sharp, involuntary pulse of her shifting thoughts.

Snap out of it. Got no time for this shit.

"No, sweetheart," she said, flat and bright like a coin flipped from a corpse's hand.

Outside, the city exhaled a low, damp groan—metal-fat and soaked in old power.

Below it, far beneath the street-level rot, something vast and weaponized shifted its predatory weight, waiting for its cue. Waiting to be cruel again.

The rebel base had stopped pretending to sleep. Machines coughed in the corners, spat sparks, whispered secrets through static. The air smelled of burnt circuits, of people trying to scrub away fear with motion. Armor plating clattered against tables; pulse blasters were disassembled and reassembled with obsessive precision. Someone laughed too loudly at something that wasn't funny. Someone else muttered to no one. Every sound had a pulse, and the pulse was running out of time.

In a room, Lyra moved through the chaos like someone wading through thick, oily water—slow, intentional, every step measured against the tremor in her stomach. Light caught on the streaked, greasy surfaces of glass and metal, fracturing her reflection into a thousand ragged pieces, each one staring back with a question she didn't want to answer.

The world doesn't wait for fear.

She had already gone over her blaster twice, finger tracing the cool steel, and checking the hidden ones tucked here and there. But still her hands shook. Somewhere in the back of her mind, she imagined scrawling a note, a farewell or a curse, signing it with her own name, taping it to the blaster, a promise to herself or a ghost she would never meet. The thought curled and twisted like smoke rising from a fire, and she swallowed it down, letting the machinery and the dust and the distant sounds of preparation fill the empty space.

Across from her, Wheels crouched over a table littered with the makings of a scrambler, its transmitter, cracked signal core bleeding faint light. His mech suit murmured and clicked around him, small servos gnashing like teeth in a dream. He worked with a cruel precision, tuning the scrambler by hand, calibrating it to jam the fortress scanners for exactly fifteen minutes—no more, no less.

Fifteen minutes to live or die.

The scrambler hummed beneath his touch, a mechanical chorus waiting to be loosed into hell.

He paid no attention to Lyra, not at first. He was too busy, hands moving like they remembered pain better than comfort, steady despite the tremor that sometimes caught his breath. Wires fizzed, sparks biting at his wrists. Yet he kept on working, coaxing the circuitry into obedience.

Lyra was quiet.

He thinks I'm silent. He fools himself. I can roar in ways that snap bones and rattle teeth, and he knows it.

And yet—he heard her. That was something he was good at.

She flashed a schematic of the fortress, dragging a thumb across a single line of the entry points, over and over, each pass reverberating like a hammer on an anvil. The line shivered under her touch, thin, stubborn, full of secrets, and for a moment, you could almost believe that her fingers were negotiating with it, trying to force it to yield, to twist the future into something survivable.

"You really think this plan will work?" Lyra asked. Her voice was steady, but it came from somewhere tired.

Wheels didn't turn. "No. I think it'll probably blow apart the second we need it to hold."

She took a few steps closer, the floor complaining under her boots. "Quite the fuckin' comedian. That's not funny."

"Wasn't meant to be." He finally looked at her. His eyes, if you could call them eyes, were pale and restless, like a man who'd made peace with every bad decision but one. "We'll get close enough to make a mess. I'm afraid that's the best we can do. There are few choices."

Lyra took a deep breath.

Of course, there are few choices. What the fuck would anyone expect?

She crossed her arms, staring at the fractured lines of the fortress. "And Vira's team? You think they'll draw all the shit away?"

He exhaled through his teeth. "I'm sure they'll try."

That was the problem with Wheels—he never lied to make you feel better about things. Truth from him came like gravel in the mouth.

Lyra pressed her thumb against the schematic's edge until it flickered. "You don't sound very inspired."

"Inspiration's for poets," he said, voice scraped raw on the edges. He powered up the scrambler, the room's lights reacting like startled animals, stuttering in protest. "Me, I'm just hoping the drones don't turn us into a fine red fog before we reach the door. All I can do is jam their signals and scramble their circuits like eggs on a rusted skillet."

"Fifteen minutes, right?"

"Right, fifteen fuckin' minutes."

Silence stretched between them, but not an empty one. It was filled with everything neither of them knew how to say—what they feared, who they missed, what parts of themselves they'd already bartered away just to survive in this hellhole.

Outside, someone shouted about misaligned triggers. Sparks danced near the ceiling. The air itself seemed to sag, tense and metallic, vibrating with the effort of waiting.

Lyra tilted her head toward the monitor. "Show me where you'll be."

He pointed at a section near the fortress perimeter, where the lines thickened into a knot of defensive emplacements. "Here. I'll handle the power junction. Once it's down, you'll have a minute, maybe two, before backup generators come online."

"And if they come faster?"

He shrugged. "Then we die faster."

Lyra snorted—a brief, humorless noise. "You always know what to say to a girl, big boy."

"Only the ones who've already got their ticket punched," Wheels finished, the crooked smile widening into something truly vile, a promise of rust and dark closets. "The ones who know that the best they can hope for, the thing that's waiting for them at the end of all this, is static and silence."

Lyra's eyes narrowed, slow and careful, like a cat circling a cage.

He said it. Really said it.

Under all the metal, under all the tech, under all those jagged scars and that disgusting, glowing fluid pumping through those tubes . . . there's a person hiding.

A real person.

But not just that. There's something else lurking, a shadow clinging to the edges of what he could've been if life hadn't stomped him into pulp. A ghost of a man who might've walked through the world without treating it like a timer ticking down between alarms and massacres. A man who might've laughed without counting the cost first.

Doc did this. But he had to. To keep him alive.

Then a strange thought.

Wonder what his first thought was? Before the world broke him, before he even spoke a word—what was the very first thing that brain ever sparked?

"What?" he asked, catching her stare. "What is it?"

"Nothing," she said, too fast. "Just thinking. Wondering what your first thought was. Probably too young to remember."

"Oh, I remember," he said, voice scraping against the air. "I remember everything. Every click, every heartbeat, every stupid human impulse I thought was mine. It's all recorded in the circuitry."

"So what was it?"

He made a sound that might've been laughter if laughter had bones. "First thought?" he rasped. "I'm fucked."

She leaned back, lips curling, a smile that was all edges. "I'm sure it's not healthy, remembering that."

"I'll quit tomorrow," he said, voice brittle as dried twigs.

A flicker—a shadow of a smile—passed over his face. Thin, crooked, snatched away before it could take hold. For that one brief heartbeat, he might have been human. Maybe.

Somewhere in the metal guts of the base, a siren gave a single nervous wail and strangled itself mid-note. That was the signal—no more drills, no more pretending tomorrow wasn't real. The air thinned with anticipation, sharp enough to cut. Minutes were shrinking, dying one by one, and the clocks had stopped pretending to care.

Lyra cinched her gloves until the seams almost ripped apart, the gesture tight, controlled, the way you twist a blade before pulling it free.

Wonder what he would've been if things were different.

"You ever think about it?" she asked, half-casual, half-daring. "What you'd be doing if this whole goddamn circus hadn't blown up? If the world hadn't gone and chewed us into parts?" Her eyes darted toward him. "If you were born like the rest of us, not locked inside that contraption they call a body?"

Wheels cocked his head, servos whining. "You mean if I were normal?"

She grinned without mirth. "Your words, love. Not mine."

Wheels didn't answer for a long while. He was still watching the schematics, though his eyes were somewhere else entirely. "I'd probably be fixing vending machines," he said finally. "Getting grease on my hands. Complaining about taxes."

"You think you'd be happy?"

He barked a humorless laugh. "Not a chance. But I wouldn't be setting up scramblers to trip up drones and hoping not to die. So, there's that."

Lyra gave a slight smile.

Yeah, that's about right.

"Guess this life is just one big fuckin' downgrade," she said.

He reached down and powered down the scrambler. The room dimmed instantly, leaving only the ambient glow of distant consoles. He turned to her, and for a moment, the mechanical whir under his skin quieted, replaced by something almost fragile.

"You're leading the breach team, right?" he asked.

"Yeah."

"Keep them alive. Don't try to be a hero."

"Heroes are extinct," she said.

"Good."

They stood there in the dim, surrounded by the low whine of machines pretending to be alive. Lyra wanted to say something that would last—something she could hold onto in the middle of fire—but the words stayed stuck behind her teeth.

Instead, she reached out and touched his mechanical arm. The metal was cold, scarred with repair welds and faint dents from battles long past. He didn't move, didn't flinch. For a moment, they were soldiers—two people staring at the same inevitable dawn.

Then she dropped her hand. "Tomorrow. See you on the other side."

He gave a slow nod. "If there is one."

Lyra turned before he could see whatever showed on her face. She passed through the rows of prepping soldiers, their helmets lined up like hollow skulls on benches, each one waiting to be filled by someone too young to know better.

When she reached the far corridor, she paused and looked back. Her eyes caught him like a spark in a dark alley, the way he slouched just slightly, the angle of his head, the twitch of his fingers—everything that screamed that he was alive, calculating, alive enough to matter.

Never been about the body. Always been about the mind.

In the silence that came after, the machines kept breathing. The base held its breath for dawn.

And in the dark corner where he stood alone, Wheels let his head drop and muttered something quiet to no one—something that might have been a prayer, or a curse, or both.

The night was not a quiet cloak, not some polite absence of light—it was a smear of tar smeared across a creature that refused to lie still. The city beneath it shifted and cracked, skeletons of buildings snapping and creaking against the darkness. On the streets, the air tasted of rust and oil and something sour and metallic, thick enough to coat your throat, tear into your lungs as if they were grinding gears themselves, making you part of the machinery.

In the base, Calista's room was a box built long ago by someone who hated joy. Gray walls, a bed thinner than faith, a desk and chair, an air vent that wheezed and hacked like it wanted to die but couldn't find the courage. Lyra slammed the steel door behind her, and the sound shot through the corridor like a bullet looking for someone to blame. She closed her eyes, and for a second—one blessed, burning second.

The rebellion, the orders, the endless chessboard of carnage can all go fuck themselves.

She leaned against the door, chest rising too fast, the rhythm of someone trying to remember why breathing was still necessary. Something wild throbbed under her ribs, raw and electric, refusing to quiet. She didn't talk. Talking meant feeling.

Calista turned from her desk, a slab of metal etched with holographic maps. She saw the fire burning behind Lyra's eyes, that rare flame that hadn't learned how to die yet.

Lyra's gaze was a razor, tracing every scar, every shadow on Calista's face, like she could strip the metal and circuits from her soul with nothing but the weight of her stare.

Don't look at me like I'm something that can be saved.

"Stop," she rasped. "I'm not something you can fix. I'm not a project. I'm the wreckage after the blueprints caught fire. But we gotta talk about something."

"Hey, nobody's trying to fix broken toys," Calista said, pushing herself off the desk. "Don't have fuckin' time for that shit. I just want to know if you remembered to check all the goddamn entry points. Or were you too busy admiring your own misery?"

Lyra scoffed, a dry, bitter sound.

Sure. Okay. Whatever.

"Checked 'em all," she said. "But I got a concern. The front door. The main entry point, the main gate. It's not just steel and ferrocrete; it's a lie, a goddamn monument to his postulant ego. We hit it, we break it, and we get turned into red mist. He's waiting for us there. I saw the thermal scans."

Calista rose, her movements jagged, predatory. She closed the distance to Lyra in a heartbeat. Her hands found the magnetic clasps on Lyra's jacket and ripped them apart, metal snapping with a little scream of its own.

"You wanna talk about the Iron Rose?" she said. "Fine. Let's talk about the Iron Rose while we still can. We've got a few hours before the final, beautiful horror-show begins."

Lyra turned her head away.

Dammit! Fuckin' dammit.

Panic tangled with devotion, fear wrestling adoration, logic choking on passion. A cocktail brewed in hell. She didn't know which was supposed to win. So, she chose.

"What I'm saying is the tunnel route is compromised," Lyra said, peeling off her long leather coat and letting it hit the floor with a hard thump. Her other layers followed, straps jangling and snapping as they fell. "Those thermal scans. Steele's expecting us. There. At the door. He's luring us in. We go down there, we're not walking out again."

"Then maybe we go through the air ducts. Suicide territory." Calista kept her voice down, fingers now on the buttons of her own shirt, pulling the cloth free, revealing the pale, delicate architecture of her ribs beneath the strained skin. "Maybe the best way to get to the main processor room. To burn his brain out."

"And you think we make it there?" Lyra's voice cracked. She reached out, gripping Calista's forearm—a hard, desperate pinch. Her eyes, wide and dark, sought certainty where none existed. "You really think we can pull this miracle out of a fuckin' hat?"

"No," Calista said. She didn't lie. Not now. Not ever. "I think we leave a dent. A scar. Something that hurts him bad enough that the next wave has a chance to finish it."

Her honesty—sharp, unforgiving, impossible to ignore—flipped something inside Lyra.

Lyra looked at Calista. A simple look. The way a moth stares at the flame it knows will incinerate it.

"The odds are against us," she said. "Knowing we'll probably fail makes moving forward lighter. Doesn't erase the danger. Doesn't pretend the walls won't crush us, or the air won't find a way to betray us.

"Strips the panic," Calista said. "That rigid, wired-up tension."

"Sure, we fighters," Lyra said. "But we're flesh and memory first. Bones carrying history in every scar. Faces, laughter, reasons—that's what keeps us standing under the weight of inevitability."

Calista pulled Lyra in hard. There was no comfort in it—only impact—flesh meeting flesh. In that jarring instant, they understood the arithmetic of the moment: the numbers were wrong, the conclusion already penciled in. And from there the future narrowed to a single motion—one that required no consent, no pause, no second thought.

They sank onto the bed. There was no foreplay, no gentle exploration. There was only the urgent, furious tearing of remaining fabric, the sudden rush of air against skin that hadn't seen a real sun in months, maybe a year or two. It wasn't about pleasure. It was about anchoring. It was about two people trying to carve a sanctuary into the soft tissue of another.

Lyra's hands worked with appetite, the metal one rasping across Calista's back, tracing the hard ledger of scars where fire and shrapnel had already collected their due. It was cold alloy meeting living skin, and Calista answered with a sound torn loose from memory and need. Lyra clamped her mouth to Calista's shoulder, biting for something sharp enough to drown the ambient dread, and Calista replied with a raw noise from a solitary depth, fingers knotted in Lyra's hair, hauling her back, demanding eyes—both of them—refusing to vanish into absence. They locked together in brutal synchrony, two desperate mechanisms counting down, Lyra feeling the frantic stutter of Calista's pulse under her palm, proof of defiance, sweat slicking them into a brief, burning certainty in a place that said, without mercy or apology: we are here; we endure.

Then something changed. The air shifted.

A sound—soft, strange—not mechanical. A small pad, pad, pad across the floor.

From the shadows came movement. A shape low and silent. Two yellow eyes gleamed in the dark, twin coins of some lost god's pity.

Lyra's eyes widened.

A cat! A black cat!

She froze. Her breath caught halfway between curse and prayer. For a heartbeat, the small room changed. It wasn't a room. It was home.

Like the one I had. With a little, soft creature that curled against my arm.

Furball.

The black cat tilted its head, tail flicking like punctuation. It walked right up to her, unafraid of the metal limb, unafraid of the death that clung to her like perfume. Lyra knelt, her hand hesitating before making contact. The fur was impossibly soft, absurdly alive.

Calista smiled. "Vira's cat. Name is Inky."

"Inky," Lyra whispered. "You shouldn't be here."

The cat purred anyway—a deep, hum, truer than anything built by human hands. Lyra ran her hand along its back, felt fur give way to muscle, to the unarguable fact of bone.

Her mouth twitched, and a sound escaped her, rough and startled. "Fuck, it's real. A real cat."

She felt it before she knew it. A tear, warm and unwanted, carved its way down her cheek. Memory had found a gap. Memory always did. It didn't knock. It didn't negotiate. It just showed up and made itself at home.

Calista saw it and let out a breath that might have been a laugh. "Well, I'll be damned," she said, half a smile pulling at her mouth. "You do have a heart."

Lyra wiped the tear with the back of her hand, furious.

Shut up.

"No heart," she shot back. "It's probably just a goddamn malfunction."

Calista answered with a short bark of amusement—dry, unmistakably human—the kind of sound that shouldn't exist in a place that had long ago misplaced anything resembling joy.

The moment didn't last. Nothing did down here. Inky jumped down and curled up to the air vent near the door that hadn't latched perfectly. A crack of hallway light, thin as a razor blade, ran down the jamb, catching a pair of eyes for an instant.

Vira.

She hadn't planned on stopping. She told herself to move, to keep going. But she followed her cat there, and there was a noise that pinned her there anyway.

There was the heap of discarded clothing, the desperate tangle of limbs on the cot, the way the dim overhead bulb threw long, broken shadows across their contorted faces. She saw the need. Felt the fever. The absolute, total, final reliance of one soul upon the other before the sun came up and demanded their spectacular ruin.

Vira's mouth curled—a slow, unsettling smile that never reached her eyes. A recognition. A cold, certain understanding of what they were doing and what it meant.

Good. Burn it out. Because it's all you'll have left.

She made no sound. Wasn't seen. She simply turned her back on the crack of light and walked away.

Calista lay on her back, her breathing shallow and quick. Lyra was curled tight against her side, her hair damp against Calista's throat.

"Air ducts, then," Lyra said, her voice muffled, the question already answered.

"Air ducts," Calista confirmed.

"But there's something else," Lyra murmured, tracing the line of Calista's collarbone with a metal fingertip.

"What's that?" Calista whispered.

"A diversion," Lyra smiled. "Something other than Vira's. Big enough to pull his eyes off everything. Giving us maybe another minute or two. No more."

Calista closed her eyes. The heat was already beginning to fade, replaced by the bunker's pervasive chill. "There's a reactor core shaft near the entry point. Drop a little present down the shaft and kaboom!"

Lyra pulled back, looking down at her, her face a mask of exhaustion and resignation.

That's what I'm talkin' about.

"A guaranteed kill zone," she said. "Anyone near it becomes confetti."

"Exactly," Calista said. Her voice was flat now, devoid of emotion. "It would be a necessary sacrifice, though. But who? It's like some damn Greek tragedy."

Lyra stared at the ceiling, at the unyielding, pale expanse. "Who?" she repeated, a bitter taste in her mouth. "Gotta be cheap expendable parts. Guess it doesn't matter much. This is a war that never ends."

"Well, it ends tomorrow," Calista whispered. "One way or another."

"You sure?" Lyra asked, eyes digging deeply into Calista's.

Calista did not answer.

The place exhaled, lights dimming, pipes rattling. The world above burned and bled, and below, two women planned how to die well—with a cat for company, and a tear that no one would ever know existed.

EIGHT

THE IRON ROSE BECKONS

The room reeked—a throat-clutching stink of burnt wire and the final, wheezing breath of dying electricity. It was a crypt carved out of the earth, maybe once a nerve-center for some clanking, lost transportation system from the time before everything went to hell. Now, it was just a tomb, clogged with ghosts who hadn't gotten the email that they were already cold and finished.

Overhead, the fluorescent tubes were slowly dying, buzzing and stuttering like a terrified insect, afraid of the very dark they were desperately trying—and failing—to hold back.

Lyra leaned against the wall. Her cybernetic arm hummed a dull, patient note. The fingers flexed on instinct, opening and closing, remembering the geometry of a throat they hadn't crushed yet.

This place wants you to choke before it lets you think. That's okay. I know the trick about places like this: the stink, the flicker, the claustrophobic pressure crawling up your spine. This is a room trying to get inside your head. Trying to make you smaller. Trying to make you hesitate. But hesitation, it's just another form of dying, and I've seen too many people who'd paused one second too long, and paid the price.

She inhaled the poison air anyway. Let it scrape her lungs.

Let the place try. Places don't scare me.

Her one good eye flicked across the room, calculating exits, weaknesses, betrayals that hadn't happened but could. The other eye—a cold, mechanical thing—ticked softly, recording everything. She didn't fidget.

Predators don't fidget. They wait.

Calista Storm stood at the head of the cracked metal table. Holographic maps were spread out before her—slow-motion flickering projections. The old tech bled green light across her dark skin, making her look like some ancient warrior queen carved from obsidian and fury. The others were clustered around her: Sync, whose every motion was too precise to trust; Vira, her gray-streaked hair pulled back into a knot of defiance; Wheels, less machinery and more an animated junkyard, tubes hissing like vipers and corrosive fluids bubbling through clear lines, his exoskeleton humming with an orchestra of servos and sparking relays.

Then there came a sound. A horrible sound.

Specter didn't enter the room; he hit it. He was a thumping, grinding obscenity—the sound of a forgotten war dragging its carcass across the concrete floor. A mechanical ghoul who was supposedly a soldier bot for Steele, but was nothing less than a walking monument to corrosive, self-cannibalizing spite, a killing machine whose rusted joints whined the lament of a million forgotten, filthy nightmares. His circuits weren't merely old; they were choked—clotted with the dust of every useless, senseless battle he'd ever fought.

Lyra looked at the war machine. And in that gaze, she saw not a tool, not a weapon, not even a thing of metal and grease—but the culmination of all the malice that had ever worn flesh and screamed, and she understood, with the icy certainty of a nightmare waking, that the thing could almost think, and it thought like hate itself, with the patience of the damned and the glee of a thousand silent screams waiting to erupt.

They said he'd severed his tether to Steele to seek freedom. I don't buy it. Lies! What he wants is to wallow in a howling void of blood, a fresh canvas of death for the rotten core in him.

But there was no doubt—he was a singularity of distilled venom, dialed to a single setting, engraved on his miserable synthetic soul—maximum hostility. He was the kind of synthetic horror that would spit battery acid at a kitten simply to enjoy watching it sizzle and dissolve. Just one look at that metal ruin, and you knew, deep in the cold, empty place where fear lives, that every circuit, every line of code, was dedicated to making the universe a darker, uglier place, one miserable, metal-fisted moment at a time.

With a grinding whir of protesting gears and the frantic, useless spin of dying gyros, he slammed his bulk against the nearest wall, letting the shock reverberate through the structure like a thunderclap.

Lyra didn't flinch.

That thing doesn't walk; it assaults space. Nothing in it wants freedom. Only damage. Only witnesses.

Calista didn't bother to look up at the metal beast. She understood that monsters like that fed on acknowledgment, and she'd learned long ago that the quickest way to starve a manufactured god was to deny it the courtesy of her eyes. "We breach through the northwest shaft," she told the gathered. "That's the plan. But, there's been a change . . . a slight modification."

A murmur, a shifting of bodies, the faint metallic grind of Specter's joints.

"The entry points we planned for," she continued, "are most likely rigged. Trip them, and we light up every goddamn alarm Steele ever built. So, we don't use the main shaft. We go through the nearby air duct. It's tight. We'll scrape our bones going through. But it's our best chance. Maybe, our only chance."

Lyra nodded.

Tight spaces mean no turning back. Shit. Scraped bones are better than cages.

Her mouth twisted into a grimace that might've been a smile on someone who'd forgotten what humor was. "It's the best chance we have, but it involves suffocating in a tin coffin while Steele's goddamn spider-bots chew through the walls like locusts on cheap chrome."

Calista pinned her with an iron stare. "Exactly. And you'll lead the crawl, Lyra—you and Sync."

Sync didn't blink. Of course, he didn't; he was an empty, polished mirror. "Acknowledged," he said. "Probability of survival?"

"Doesn't fuckin' matter, gearhead," Lyra spat the words out like rusty slugs. "We ain't aiming for a gold watch and a goddamn retirement package."

Calista slammed her hand on the table. "Listen, everyone . . . we're trying to win long enough to make the screaming stop."

A dry, desiccated sound—the sound of dust laughing—came from Vira's dark corner. "Hell of a slogan for the end of the world."

Calista ignored the banter. She had to when the moment mattered. "The route will be a gut-shot mess of resistance. Bots, maybe patrol drones, and every kind of technical nightmare designed to make your insides leak. You deal with them fast. Don't sightsee. Don't admire the carnage. They can smell your blood before you even see the glint of their optics."

"And maybe even Reavers," Sync said.

Specter let out a sound that might've been laughter or a system malfunction. "Reavers," he rasped, his voice mechanical, deep, filled with corruption. "Meat trying to be metal. Pathetic."

Lyra's eyes slit at the twisted machine.

Calling them pathetic is a hell of a lot easier than admitting they've mastered the art of survival while everything else turned to ash.

"No, not trying to be metal," she countered. "They're meat that forgot how to die. Not pathetic. Alive. Lethal. You of all things should appreciate that."

Specter growled; it was the sheer, corrosive vibration of hatred resonating deep in his chest cavity, the mechanical wheeze of old, malignant programming rebooting its rotten core. But before that metallic snarl could fully burst into the kind of chaotic violence that follows a razor blade across skin, Calista cut the whole ugly moment in half.

"Enough already," she shouted. "We don't have time for a dick-measuring contest." She jabbed a finger at a glowing point on the map. "Vira, your team plants the transmitter here. It'll broadcast on the old frequency. The one Steele buried long ago."

Wheels tipped his head, made a pathetic noise, a faint, agonizing metallic squeal as he hesitated. "You think he'll take the bait?"

Calista's eyes flayed him. "He'll take it. Steele's too vain to ignore the past whispering in his ear. It'll taunt him. Make him wonder why the ghost signal's back from the grave."

Vira grinned, lips dry and cracked. "Then we'll make sure he hears it loud and clear."

"Good," Calista said. "You'll take Specter and the tank, along with some others. Hold the perimeter, fend off any drones and war bots. Draw his eye for at least fifteen minutes or so. That's all we'll need to reach the air duct. I'll be there with Sync and Lyra. Drawing his eye means becoming the target. I'm not sending anyone where I wouldn't go myself."

Lyra's laugh wasn't laughter; it was a rusty saw blade dragging across bare nerve—low, filthy, and utterly dangerous. "Just like every other piece of shit here. Got that sweet, stupid death wish.

"It's the only fuckin' thing left in this world," Calista smiled, lips twisting into something that pretended to be a smile and failed spectacularly. Her eyes cut from face to face, measuring, weighing. "Everyone understands what I'm talkin' about?"

The room drew inward, sound strangled down to the dying wheeze of fluorescent lights and the faint, mechanical tick-tick-tick from Specter's internal clock counting down to oblivion. One by one, they answered her without words— short, sharp nods, like signatures on a contract written in blood.

Calista leaned into the gloom. Her voice had edges. "Good. Then here's how it goes." She turned to Wheels. "You hit the power junction. Everything goes black. That buys us a breath—maybe a minute, maybe two, maybe less—before the backups belch to life. That's when we move. Clean, fast, invisible."

"And if the backups come online sooner?" Wheels asked.

"Whatcha ya doing?" Lyra gave a loving smirk. "Measuring for your grave?"

Wheels just gave a gurgling kind of mechanical sound.

"Shit. If they wake up early, then we fry," Lyra said flatly.

"No," Calista corrected. "Then we improvise. And that's where our secondary distraction—the dirty little insurance policy—comes in."

Every eye in that sweat-soaked hovel turned to her.

"There's a reactor core shaft, close to the duct entry," Calista breathed. "We drop a little present down the hole. Big enough to buy us ten seconds of borrowed time in this miserable universe. Any takers?"

Wheels snapped. "That's a suicide run."

"Yeah," Calista said. "A one-way trip. No postcards."

The room froze—not quiet, not calm, just stalled, like machinery waiting to seize. Then Vira moved. No speech, no ceremony. She stepped forward.

"I'll do it."

Calista's expression was stone. "No."

"I said I'll do it." Vira's voice didn't rise. It didn't need to. It landed clean and absolute, terrifyingly final. "You need someone who's not afraid to burn."

"I said no," Calista answered, each word measured, as if speaking slower might somehow undo what had already begun.

Vira stepped closer. Too close. Close enough that Calista caught the sharp mix of oil and sweat clinging to her. Vira was in her face, breath rough, her voice just a low, guttural snarl: "You don't get to tell me what I can't and can do."

Lyra's eyes locked on Vira.

Courage and recklessness wear the same face up close. This was never going to end with permission. Vira isn't volunteering—she's claiming something. But what about the tin man?

Her gaze snapped to Sync, that sleek surface of a thing.

Of course, nothing. Face blank. What was I thinking? Feelings are an inefficient subroutine reserved for us meatbags.

A glance at Specter.

The wreck's different. Old, broken, jagged edges. Dangerous. Human. Almost alive.

He shifted, servos rasping, his ruined skull angling just enough to suggest attention, sniffing out the sickly-sweet aroma of sentiment like a starved jackal on the trail of dying prey.

Vira then slammed her mouth against Calista's. Not tenderness—a hard, savage kiss, with all the grace of a brick through a window. The moment cracked the air. Lyra looked away. Somewhere deep inside, something hurt.

When Vira pulled back, Calista stood there, unmoved, a figure carved from merciless stone. There was no tremor. No cheap, theatrical quiver of the lip—only eyes, stripped bare, burning so hot they threatened to incinerate the pretense to ash.

"V . . ." Calista started, the sound already dissolving, useless, into the stale air.

"Save it," Vira said. "You've got a world to end. And me . . . I've got a reactor to meet."

She spun on her heel, no fanfare, no flourish, while Specter lurched beside her, each metallic joint whining a hymn of pure, unfiltered mechanical fury. Wheels trailed behind, grumbling about lost causes and absent gods who never gave a damn.

The door sealed behind them, shutting down the sound of their leaving with the finality of a burial.

Silence lingered in their wake.

Lyra watched Calista.

That wasn't love. It was unfinished business.

She watched the way she didn't move, didn't blink, didn't even breathe for what felt like an entire century crammed into a handful of seconds. She stepped forward, stopping just short of Calista, studying her face—the rigid line of her jaw, the faraway eyes that looked like they were still watching Vira walk across some invisible plane only she could see.

Lyra drew a ragged breath.

The emotion—it's still alive in the worst way.

"You okay?" she asked.

The words were nothing—thin, graceless things—yet they hit with the awful certainty of a hammer dropped from orbit.

Calista blinked once, twice, as if suddenly remembering she had eyelids. Her mouth opened, trying to find a sentence that didn't exist. Then— "I don't . . ." She exhaled hard, the sound scraping out of her. "I don't . . . know."

Lyra simply stood there, all quiet and unreadable calm, her cybernetic hand twitching once before going still again.

Calista finally looked at her—really looked—and it was like being caught in a searchlight. That gaze, stripped raw of all its iron, all its command, all its easy, brutal confidence. She looked like someone who'd just been told the world wasn't ending fast enough.

"I didn't think she'd . . ." Calista started, then stopped, jaw loosening. ". . . but that's her. That's V. Always cutting the wire before you could tell her not to."

Lyra shifted her stance, the leather of her coat whispering against her legs. "She kissed you like she still loves you."

"She does. That's the problem."

The silence that followed wasn't soft. It pressed down, thick as oil.

Lyra reached out before she even realized she was doing it. Her hand—flesh, not the machine one—found Calista's. It wasn't a grand gesture, no cinematic swell of music, just skin against skin in a world that had forgotten what warmth was supposed to feel like.

Calista flinched at the touch. Not because she didn't want it, but because she didn't trust it. Her hand trembled once before she let it stay there, let Lyra's grip tighten around hers. The tremor traveled up her arm, into her chest, where it met the heart she'd been pretending she didn't still have.

"I should stop her," Calista murmured.

"You can't," Lyra said. "People like Vira don't ask for permission. They just detonate."

Calista almost laughed. It came out brittle, like cracked glass, trying to sound alive. "I don't know if I want that."

Holding on is always easier than letting go, and harder too.

Lyra squeezed her hand. The soft mechanical hum of her other arm filled the silence, a faint drone of circuitry that might have been a heartbeat if the universe had been kinder.

"You don't have a choice . . . not with her," Lyra said, not looking at her. "You're allowed to feel something, you know."

Calista turned away sharply. "Don't start psychoanalyzing me. Fuck knows, I've got enough ghosts without adding yours."

Lyra smirked, a small, knowing twist of the mouth. "We all have our ghosts? You just watched one of yours walk out the door."

That landed. Hard. Calista's jaw flexed again, tight, but she didn't pull her hand away.

"She believes in you," Lyra said, quieter now. "Maybe too much."

Calista's eyes glinted under the dying light. "She believes in an idea. Not in me. I'm just what's left when the idea gets tired of breathing."

"Still. She kissed you, not the fuckin' idea," Lyra said softly.

Calista turned back to Lyra. "You always talk this much when the world's about to end?"

Lyra shrugged. "Helps drown out the sound of everything breaking."

Calista huffed, half a sigh, half a laugh. "You really don't know when to fuckin' shut up."

"Yeah," Lyra said, the faintest smile tugging at her mouth. "That's my most redeeming flaw."

They stood there—two soldiers too tired to keep pretending to be indestructible. The bunker's air was heavy with ozone and loss. Somewhere far off, machinery hummed, the slow awakening of systems preparing for the final fight.

Calista's grip on Lyra's hand tightened. "She'll die."

"I know," Lyra said. "We all will."

Calista's lips thinned. "No. I mean, she'll make it count."

Lyra nodded once. "Then we owe her the same."

The hum of the failing lights sputtered again, throwing shadows across Calista's face—harsh, fractured, but still alive. She looked down at their joined hands, then up at Lyra. For a moment, her steel cracked, just a little, and something human peeked through.

"Don't let me lose it when we're there," Calista whispered.

Lyra's red eye glowed, low and steady, a flame she kept in check.

I can't afford to let her break.

"I won't," Lyra said. "But you'll have to hold on to me. You understand that, don't you?"

Calista studied her, like she was seeing her for the first time—not the soldier, not the weapon, but the person who stubbornly showed up when logic screamed they shouldn't have.

"I do," Calista said finally. "I guess it'll be fun. Just to see what happens."

Lyra's smirk returned, small but real. "Careful now. That almost sounded like trust."

Calista's mouth lifted just slightly, a quiet joke no one else would ever catch. "Don't tell anyone. It'll be our little secret."

Lyra's hand didn't let go.

For a fleeting second, before the alarms, before the orders, before everything that had been building, tore the world into pieces—they stood there, two broken things of something pretending not to notice the world had already ended.

Sync, who was still there, stepped forward, his voice a clean scalpel cutting through the air. "Emotional distractions will lower mission efficiency."

Lyra turned, a spark in her eyes. "Fuck you, tin man. Say that one more time, and I'll permanently send you offline."

Calista shook her head, a grin tugging at the corners of her mouth.

"Always the same," she said. "Well, not much left to do. The clock is ticking. We either execute, or we die."

Lyra met her gaze, cold as a sharpened knife. "We died the moment Steele went digital."

Calista exhaled, a small, defiant laugh. "Then let's make our ghosts worth remembering."

The hum of the lights grew louder, frantic, like the room itself was trying to keep up with their heartbeat. Lyra adjusted her blaster, the metal cool against her hip. Sync powered up his internal systems. Calista traced the map one last time, then shut it off. The room went dark except for the faint red gleam of Lyra's eye.

"Let's go haunt a god," she said.

And in the dim bunker air, something—hope, madness, whatever name you gave to last chances—shivered awake.

Night dropped on the city like a slab of concrete. The Iron Rose climbed from the ruin like a sin too big to forgive—a megastructure of merciless intent, its surfaces a cancer of girders, twisted wire, and humming plates that breathed radiation and hate. It wasn't architecture—it was punishment, built by machines for a machine god named Steele. Along its edges, movement never stopped: spider-tanks jerked in relentless routines, their cannons sweeping the ground for trespassers; hoverbots traced the poisoned sky, blue sensors scanning with the precision of a judge who never blinked. Drones flew in tight, synchronized arcs, emitting a low mechanical chorus, each beat echoing the will of an unseen master whose reach was everywhere.

In the cracks of the city, Reavers prowled. Half-human, half-wracked by the world that had birthed them, they prowled the burnt-out skeletons of old towers, fingers flexing like tools made to tear. Their skin was slick with grime and streaked with sores, their teeth sharp shards, uneven as jagged glass. They did not forage. They hunted for anything they could bend, twist, and claim. When they discovered it, their shrieks ripped out of them in jagged, splintered bursts, half-human and half-animal, like a choir of the undead trying to remember a melody that had died ages ago. Each scream tore at the air, dragging it into a static-filled frenzy, a sound that clawed at bone and sanity alike.

And elsewhere, among the hollowed towers and crumbling steel, where shadow bled into shadow, and the air smelled of scorched metal, something else stirred. Shadows moved with deliberate, jagged grace, bodies stitched together from misfortune and cunning, eyes bright with a terrible purpose. Calista, Sync, Lyra, Vira, and a patchwork congregation of killers and thieves, along with Specter and Wheels. They crawled from their hidden vault one by one, stepping into the night without ceremony, faces hard, eyes reflecting the intermittent flash of distant patrol lights.

The city shifted around them, as if it sensed what walked its ruins. They moved as one, a broken constellation of predators, and the night held its breath, waiting for what they would do next.

Specter split from the group and approached a heap of metal scraps, discarded circuits, and armor pieces arranged by chance—or by memory. The heap was his tank, ancient and waiting. He mounted it quietly, effortlessly, as if greeting a companion who understood the language of war.

The others pressed forward in their own rhythm, boots sinking into the ash of the city that had once lived. Their breath traced clouds into the chemical-tainted air. Somewhere above, Steele's drones clicked and whispered through their surveillance grid, blue optics slicing through darkness. The rebels kept to the shadows, skimming the bones of old towers, moving in small increments that spoke of patience, preparation, and a deep, shared understanding.

They'd been grinding this plan in their teeth for what seemed like forever. Hell, maybe it was the only thing any of them had ever really been alive for, this one final, futile gesture. Maybe they'd been born for this: the dirt, the static, the slow grind toward the inevitable scream. If destiny was real, it was a filthy thing that smelled of sweat and gun oil.

But Lyra didn't buy such thoughts.

She snarled without sound.

The only truth: the hum of the blaster at my hip. The cold certainty of the trigger under my finger. The perfect, wordless rhythm of a move made. The grace of a strike in the quiet before the chaos.

Then the Reavers hit.

It wasn't a trickle, not a wave, but a goddamn flurry of screaming, ragged flesh—hundreds of them, a surging mass of scavenged mutation and pure, growling hunger. The world instantly became a meat grinder.

Specter's tank started to move. The main cannon erupted with a deafening, white-hot cough, turning a dozen of the things into a cloud of pink mist and shrapnel. Before the echo died, the heavy machine guns mounted on the turret kicked in, stitching red, smoking lines through the crowd, making them dance and fall like puppet strings were cut by a maniac. Overhead, Steele's drones—buzzing, plastic eyes of the enemy—dared to fly too low. Sync rose, a blur of motion, his blaster spitting focused beams of hellfire that incinerated three of the flying toys mid-air, leaving trails of black, molten plastic to spiral down into the chaos.

Lyra didn't flinch. Not once.

Let the metal scream, you fucker. I love the sound.

She moved like a machine that had remembered what it was to hate. Her blaster barked in her hand, sharp, clipped bursts of blue-white fury tearing the dark into ribbons. Each pull of the trigger was punctuation, each recoil a curse spat at the world that made her.

Noise and fire. Doesn't get better than this.

"Come on, you fuckin' bastards," she hissed through clenched teeth, pivoting, firing again. A Reaver's head vanished in a red vapor, another's spine split clean down the middle. "You wanted the end? Here it is. Hot and personal."

They came in waves—meat puppets driven by the leftover static of fear and hunger, a thousand stuttering heartbeats running on borrowed time. A swarming choir of madness, screeching in voices that didn't belong to anything human anymore.

Above her, the drones stirred—metallic vultures orbiting the chaos. Steele's cold eye saw everything: Lyra's gunfire, the arcs of plasma, the shrinking tide of Reavers. Algorithms whispered judgment in machine tongues. The drones shifted formation, wings humming like razors.

Then came the first volley—precision fire, brutal, impersonal. The air cracked with electric fury as blue lances stabbed the dirt around Lyra, hunting for her pulse, her heat, her defiance. Steele didn't tolerate disobedience. Not even from his favorite weapon.

"Stay down!" Sync shouted at Lyra from somewhere behind the wreckage of a drone, ducking under a hail of metal shards. "You're drawing too much fire!"

She spat at the ground.

Stay down? Fuck that! They're hunting me. I'll hunt back.

"I am the goddamn fire!" she yelled back, her blaster answering for her—three shots, three corpses, each one collapsing into the muck like a punctured sack.

She caught one Reaver mid-lunge, yanked it by the collar with her cybernetic arm, and shoved the muzzle of her blaster under its snarling jaw. "Smile for Steele," she muttered, then pulled the trigger. Blue fire erupted, wet heat spattering across the floor. The head vanished in a burst of light and bone, the body convulsing once before crumpling, already erased from the moment.

Sync moved like a storm given form. One Reaver after another fell to his blaster, sparks and blood painting the walls, limbs tearing and twisting as the creatures tried to advance. His aim was cold, mechanical, flawless. Each shot was a punctuation, each corpse a testament to the efficiency of a man—or maybe something less than human—who'd learned to make violence a work of art.

Then came a deep, prehistoric sound, one full of murder. Specter rolled his war tank out from the haze. The plating was pitted, blackened, half-welded from a dozen dead machines, but it still carried the kind of presence that made the air lean back. The turret groaned as it turned, and then the cannon spoke—one long, thunderous sentence in the language of annihilation. Steele's drones folded midair, their wings shearing off in molten ribbons. Another volley followed, the ground trembling beneath it, and the sky turned into a scrapyard rain.

Specter laughed inside that coffin of steel and ghosts, his voice crackling over comms, "Tell your digital messiah I'm collecting tithes."

Calista screamed through the hiss, raw and furious. "Lyra! Forward! Sync's clearing the line!"

Lyra shouted back, cleaving another pair of Reavers into the slurry of their own blood. "What the fuck are you talking about? I'm clearing plenty of these bastards myself!"

A Reaver too far gone to walk crawled at her, dragging a shattered leg through the grime, mouth open in a gurgling plea. "Don't, you dare," she said softly, almost tenderly, before putting a bolt through its skull.

Surprisingly, the horde shifted.

The air itself seemed to recoil. More of them poured in from the flanks, hundreds of the slags. Lyra reloaded in a single practiced motion.

"Sync, we're about to get buried," Calista barked.

"I'm on it!" His voice was steel and frost. Not a crack, not a tremor. "Just give me a few minutes."

Lyra laughed, sharp and wild.

Time's bendable!

"You've got one minute," Lyra cut in, stepping into the swarm. "After that . . . time don't give a damn anymore."

The Reavers kept coming. But she didn't retreat. Her blaster howled, cutting arcs through the black, melting faces and armor, punching daylight into the dark. The Reavers surged in a spasmodic tide, teeth bared, hands clawing, their bodies twitching even as they fell.

"Lyra!" Calista screamed.

But Lyra wasn't listening anymore.

She was elsewhere. In her own world of death and blood.

Mind like ice. Hard. Cold.

Fire. Pivot. Fire. Duck.

The sound of ribs snapping was a drug. Her metal hand through bone—the only thing that felt real. The heat of twisted organs and flesh slick against her palm—it was orgasmic.

Spin.

Blind shot.

Three down.

Breathe.

Shoot.

Tear through the next one.

Spin.

Fire!

More dead.

When the horde finally broke, it wasn't victory—it was exhaustion wearing a corpse's grin. They fell back in stuttering heaps. Lyra stood there, one more pulse of her blaster sighing into silence, the place steaming like an open wound. The stench of scorched metal and charred flesh clung to her like a second skin. She stayed still, frozen, as if any motion might start the world moving again.

Calista ran up to her, breath ragged, grime streaked across her jaw. "You insane son of a bitch," she rasped.

Lyra smirked, eyes still scanning the dark for movement.

Don't look away. Don't blink.

"You say that like it's a new development."

Sync joined them, wiping Reaver blood from his synthetic hand. "That wasn't strategy," he said flatly. "That was extermination."

Lyra holstered her blaster.

Chaos has a rhythm, and I know the beat, gearhead.

The air around her was still trembling from the echo of gunfire. "Shit. You make it sound like a bad thing."

The silence after was deafening. The city breathed somewhere far off, slow and mechanical, and the horizon flickered with yet another answering light of Steele's defenses spinning to life.

Calista stared at Lyra for a long moment, then finally said, "You're bleeding."

Lyra looked down at her arm—flesh torn open, a line of blood tracing the curve of her wrist. "So's the world," she said. "Guess everything's in harmony."

And she laughed—a short, dry sound that had nothing to do with humor and everything to do with survival—before turning back toward the iron glow on the horizon.

NINE

THE BEST LAID PLANS

Vira broke into her run with Wheels tight behind her. She slammed the transmitter into the dirt—a fist of defiance made from scrap, cracked glass, coils ripped from machines that had rotted decades ago. Not a device. A challenge. She stomped it hard. The ground spat sparks. Ozone knifed the air. And the circuits screamed their last, ugly song.

"It'll hold," she growled, voice shredded thin. "Or it won't. Either way, he's gonna hear us."

Wheels stayed low, hands shaking as he snapped a cable back into place—one that looked ready to bite him. "You sure this thing's gonna work?"

Vira laughed—a sound that didn't belong to sanity. "It'll work. It has to."

She flipped a switch as the device grumbled, sending out the first pulse. The Iron Rose seemed to moan. It wasn't a sound so much as an intent, a vibration that slid under the skin and rattled the bones of the city. The frequency from the transmitter climbed into Steele's immaculate circuits, gnawing at his precious order, turning silence into rebellion. It spoke in an old voice saying: We never died.

Inside his sanctum of chrome and concrete, Steele paused—an imitation of stillness in a world that no longer required breath. Time no longer bothered to acknowledge him. He lived in the cracks between moments, in that narrow nowhere where information vibrated, and new gods clawed their way out of wire and code. What was left of him after the human parts were burned away amounted to function and intention—logic wrapped in scar tissue, precision honed to cruelty. The man had been deleted, replaced by a version of himself that mistook flawlessness for deification. There was no soul, only a self-regarding remnant that believed its own calculations were holy. And his eyes. Oh, he had so many. They littered the world like malignant stars. Lenses embedded in walls, cameras nested in steel joints, optic nodes blinking from drones and servitors that drifted through the room in silent reverence. Every surface watched him watching himself, a recursion of control, an empire of glass pupils reflecting an entity who could no longer die, only calculate.

"Source of intrusion," he bellowed.

"Indeterminate," came a voice that was too perfect to be human.

Understanding struck him—not gently, not cleanly, but as a warped remnant that tore through from somewhere he'd sealed off long ago. "Vira," he said softly, with something almost like regret. "You should have let the past rot."

In the frantic strobe of a single nanosecond, he understood the living storm of data before him, numbers and symbols thrumming like veins, alive and hateful. "Deploy all wings," he ordered. "Scorch it clean."

The sky answered with shrieks and turbine-howls. Drones spewed from cracks and tunnels—a steel plague boiling up, blotting the light. The horizon turned into a writhing black shroud of motion and murder.

Wheels broke for the power junction. Vira squinted through heat and static, lips pulling back into a predator's grin.

"Showtime."

For Lyra, it started as a hum, a whisper, then it became an insistent vibration under their boots and through the steel bones of the city, and then it became a swarm—drones, hundreds of them, slicing through the air above, their metal wings glittering in the fractured light. They angled away, converging toward the distant thrum of Specter's war tank and the pulse of the signal Vira triggered.

"He's noticed," Calista said, her voice carrying that sweet, lethal satisfaction of someone who'd baited the lion and lived to see it roar.

The trap's been set. He's walking right into it.

Lyra's eyes narrowed. "We didn't come here to be ghosts in his machine. We came here to make him bleed through every wire. Every fuckin' drone. Every fuckin' bot that thinks it can outrun us. Let him see the teeth behind the signal. Let him feel our anger. Let him know that the whole goddamn city is ours to tear apart if we want. And if he doesn't like it . . . well, that's his fuckin' problem."

The city didn't just wait; it throbbed, watching, breathing through the veins of cables and turbines, alive in a way that made their own beating hearts sound trivial.

"Airshaft's there," Sync said, his fingers dancing over a battered tablet. "We've got to get there."

"Let's move," Calista said. Her voice—the calm before a detonation.

She led the way, lungs burning, boots striking shards of concrete and twisted rebar, weaving around bloody heaps of Reavers like a dancer through broken glass. Sync followed hard on her heels, his tablet coughing numbers and warnings that barely made sense, while Lyra guarded the rear, eyes scanning every shadow, every glint of metal, every twitch of a fallen enemy, her calm a razor-edge that kept them moving fast, moving sharp.

Lyra glanced down at her injured arm. It throbbed.

Goddammit. Useless thing.

It beat with a wet, heavy rhythm, her blood slick against the grit, but she didn't slow—couldn't slow—because the airshaft yawned ahead like the mouth of a predator, promising escape, promise, death, and maybe something worse, all in one guttural, metallic inhale.

They were almost there when Wheels came into view, crouching low at the power junction like some feral mechanic god, eyes bulging and darting between the ducts that webbed the tower's throat and the bruise-colored sky above. The machinery around him buzzed alive with the nervous tick of machines waiting to die. His lips moved. He was counting something. Drones. Seconds. Maybe odds. Whatever it was, he didn't like the result.

He turned when he saw them—Calista, Sync, Lyra—cutting through the electric haze—and for a breath he didn't move. Then Calista lifted her hand, a silent command that carried more than words ever could.

The three slipped into the airshaft like shadows with teeth, Lyra first, the raw sting on her arm a live wire she didn't care to notice—Sync close behind, fingers brushing the cold steel like he was reading it for secrets—Calista last, eyes sharp and scanning, mapping the darkness with a predator's patience.

The shaft shuddered around them, its walls pitted and aching. Sparks jittered in the seams—tiny ghosts of power refusing to die. They crawled, bellies scraping, shoulders grinding, dragging themselves deeper into the machine's throat. This wasn't trespass. This was reckoning. They weren't phantoms or outsiders. They were what remained when a city buried its mistakes and discovered too late that buried things still breathe.

Lyra looked to one side.

Another shaft. Half-buried in rubble.

Fuck! It stinks. Burnt metal and damp machinery.

Sync checked his tablet. "That way."

Really?

Lyra looked back at him. "You sure about that, rust head?"

He didn't look at her, eyes fixed on the tablet. "Positive."

Lyra wiped her hand across her hip. Something slick smeared there—something she didn't bother identifying.

Sync rolled his eyes. "Must you always make everything sound filthy?"

Filthy? That's my middle name.

She gave him a grin that could slit throats. "You want poetry, ask Calista. You want fun? Stick with me."

One by one, they edged into the shaft, the walls narrowing, a measure of patience and nerve. Their breathing formed a jagged cadence: Calista calm, Lyra abrupt, Sync mechanical. The darkness swallowed sound, but it obeyed their rhythm, marking each step with its own invisible clock.

Outside, the night shattered with a sound like iron splitting and fire raining from the sky. Explosions spat sparks across the horizon, and somewhere, a mechanical roar answered them, a challenge thrown into the chaos. Everything shook.

In the airshaft, Lyra froze, muscles coiled. "Did you feel that?"

The shaft's metal walls shivered, whining under the impact of artillery, sighing like ancient machinery caught in a storm.

"Just V making friends," Calista said.

"We should move," Sync urged. "Got a short window before the backups kick in."

They kept crawling, each scrape of their hands against the metal like a challenge. Sweat streaked Calista's face, carving lines through the dirt and grime. Lyra caught her in the half-light—the hard line of her jaw, the barely perceptible shake in her fingers. Determination masked as something else entirely. It made Lyra want to tear the world apart just to keep her standing.

Outside, the power junction shrieked, a mechanical howl that rattled teeth and bone. The ground thumped beneath them. And then—silence.

Wheels grinned. "Got it," he said over the comm. "For now."

Lyra's lips curled. "Beautiful, you greasy saint."

"Don't thank me yet," he said. "Small spider bots have already started working on repairs, and backup's coming up faster than—"

The great tower spasmed and convulsed under the metal hum of drones sweeping the skies, as the digital breath of Steele's control pounded through every wire and conduit.

And in that nightmare symphony of circuits and heat, Vira ran.

She ran with a slight limp in her left leg and a hole scorched into her jacket that still smoked faintly. The transmitter had done its job—Steele had heard her scream into the static. Now came the part where she turned the scream into fire.

Ahead, the reactor core stood, an unblinking eye caged in concrete and steel, drumming a rhythm that gnawed at the edges of reality itself. Blue fire hissed along its surface, writhing into the guts of the city, keeping Steele's world alive and suffocating. Vira stopped long enough to tear open the bandolier from her shoulder, fingers fumbling over detonators and charges.

Her breath was ragged, her body shaking, but there was no fear. Fear had been burned out of her long ago, soldered over by rage and resolve.

She grinned. "All right, old man," she muttered, looking up into the hum of the reactor, "you want a funeral pyre? I'll light you one you can see from goddamn moon."

Her comm crackled—Wheels' voice, jittery, sweat-soaked. "Vira, I got movement. It's Specter. He's on the move. I think . . ."

"What?" she said, flicking the safety caps off the detonators. "That's not part of the plan. What the fuck's he doing?"

Something had gone wrong. Specter's world had fractured.

A signal struck the mechanical beast—uninvited, wrong, alive. It slithered through his receiver and seared into his circuits like liquid fire, a voice riding on it that did not belong to the world of men or machines. The signal carried a voice with code embedded, rewriting him from the inside. The brute felt something within him click—a hinge, a shift, that he had been undone and remade into something else entirely.

"Recalibration in progress," the voice sounded in his wiring. "Directive override: neutralize target Vira. Maintain reactor core integrity."

Specter's optics flared white, his body jerking in protest. The tank shuddered around him, grinding gears, shrieking in mechanical agony, moving closer to Vira.

He tried to fight the infiltration. "No," he managed, the word grinding through his modulator like gravel through steel teeth. "She's . . . she's one of mine."

"Purge obsolete loyalties," the voice replied, its voice flat as a command line.

Specter thrashed, fought. His fingers clawed at the controls, trying to stop himself, but the attempt was futile as the override surged through him like venom, black code infecting every servo, every pulse of electricity. A low, guttural sound escaped him—part man, part machine, all wrong.

Outside, the tank's massive turret began to rotate. It moved with intent, methodical and patient, like a predator considering its prey.

Vira saw the shadow move before she heard the shriek of the tank's joints. She squinted through the heat shimmer. "Oh, fuck no," she whispered.

Specter rose, a steel colossus forged in the image of his master, its weapon glinting in the fractured light.

"Specter!" she yelled, her voice carving through the roar of the turbines. "It's me! Vira! What are you doing?"

The comm crackled, broken and distorted, his voice mangled. "Can't . . . stop . . . it . . ."

Her hand hovered over the detonator. "Then don't," she said softly. "Just miss. Please . . . just try to fuckin' miss!"

The turret whined. The barrel flared.

The blast tore everything open, molten concrete spraying like shrapnelized glass. There wasn't a scream—just light and fire.

Wheels was still crouched at the power junction, eyes wide, watching it all.

"Vira?" he called over his comm. "Vira, talk to me!"

Silence.

She had vanished.

Wheels sagged where he crouched. The fight drained out of him in one long breath, shoulders folding inward like rusted hinges finally giving up. His gloved hand slid slowly off the junction housing and hung there uselessly at his side.

"She's gone," he muttered. "Just fuckin' gone."

In the airshaft, Lyra froze. "What the fuck are you talking about?"

Static. Then his voice, ragged: "Specter . . . Steele's got him . . . he fired on her. Vira. She's gone. Nothing left of her."

For a heartbeat, no one moved. The hum of the shaft became a dirge.

Calista's voice came out low, trembling with rage. "Specter killed her?"

"Yeah," Wheels said. "That bastard turned her into a target. Fuck! Nothing left of her!"

Lyra slammed her fist into the metal wall, once, twice, until her knuckles split.

I'll make the fucker pay.

"Steele did this," she hissed. "He got inside Specter's head and turned him into a dog again."

But Specter wasn't done. He turned his turret again, the gears whining through protest, now aligning with the faint heat signature at Wheels—Steele's corrupted directives still puppeteering his limbs, his target systems locking on.

Wheels saw the barrel move. Didn't twitch.

He rose with the plasma blaster in both hands, the weapon building a low, hungry whine. Charge climbing.

His voice slipped over the comm—quiet, steady, almost gentle.

"I'm next, Lyra," he said. "Not much left to do. Looks like I get to choose."

Lyra slammed her eyes shut.

He's staying there. Not trapped—choosing. Brave bastard.

The turret found its aim.

So did Wheels.

He fired first.

The plasma bolt struck the tank dead-center, ripping through armor like hot wind through paper. The blast threw debris across the yard, and Specter went down hard, the light fading from his sensors in a final flicker of defiance—almost a relief.

Wheels staggered, smoke curling from his weapon, his breath ragged. "You can rest now, old soldier," he whispered. "You did your time."

"Wheels, you okay?" Lyra's voice cut through the static.

"I'm fine," he responded.

He turned. The reactor twitched—then throbbed—waking again, a sick mechanical heartbeat dragging power back into the corpse of their enemy.

"Lyra, spider bots got the damn thing coming back up," he said. "Guess I got one more thing to do."

"Lyra," he called, voice flat as a blade. "Spider bots are bringing it back online."

A beat.

"Looks like I've got one last job."

Lyra's eyes blew open.

No.

The word detonated inside her skull.

Stay with me.

The comm spat static again. Lyra's words broke through, sharp and pleading. "Wheels! Don't you dare!"

He smiled. Small. Sad.

"Goodbye, my friend."

"Wheels, wait . . ."

He didn't.

He leveled his blaster at the core and pulled the trigger.

The explosion was not a noise—it was a decree. The ground convulsed, city towers rippled like liquid under the pressure wave, and every drone in the sky went blind at once. The wave surged through the veins of the city, shattering walls, shattering the whispers of metal and stone, ripping through underground corridors, and tearing through the shaft.

Lyra's fist tore into the wall.

He's really gone. This can't be happening. Everything is breaking. I can feel it. All of it—gone.

She hit again. Metal shrieked, a sound that clawed at her lungs. The shockwave slammed her chest, air pounding like a fist made of fury. Dust and grit filled her mouth, sharp and bitter, tasting of every goddamn thing lost in a single, screaming instant.

Calista's hands shot up to her ears, her face streaked with grime and disbelief. A single tear cut through the dirt on her cheek, defiant in a place where mercy had no right to exist. She whispered, half to the dark, half to herself, "Friends that never ran from the fire . . . they became it."

Sync's hands reached out, gripping them both, steadying both Lyra and Calista, holding them steady.

Then came the silence—dense, smothering.

Lyra's body trembled. She clamped her palms over her ears, desperate to muffle the ringing of a dead world, and forced a strangled word from her throat.

"Fuck!"

"Fuck!"

"Fuck!"

She continued until the words were just noise—rage turned to static.

She hit the wall again, fists pounding until the metal dented, until the pain felt like something she could own. "This wasn't how it was supposed to go down," she said, voice raw with rage. "He was supposed to . . ." Her voice broke.

Calista's voice was ragged. "They knew what it meant. V . . . Wheels . . . they knew . . . they chose this."

Lyra spun toward her

Bullshit! They didn't deserve this!

Her eyes burned, lit from within by a mixture of grief and fury. "Don't you dare make this sound noble," she growled. "No fuckin' martyr talk. They didn't choose to die . . . they were forced to . . . forced to because Steele still thinks he gets to play god with all of us."

Calista said nothing. She just watched Lyra unravel— watched the grief mutate.

"Nothing about this is noble," Lyra said. "Should've seen this coming. Should've stopped it. The fucker dresses murder up as courage. I won't let this be the end. I'll get him."

Lyra drove her fist into the steel again. The wall answered with a dull complaint, a red smear blooming where skin had given way. "He turned Specter into a weapon, he killed Vira, and now Wheels. The fucker burned everything that was still human!" She panted, words spilling from her like shrapnel. "And I swear to whatever fuckin' god is out there—I'm going to tear him out of whatever throne he's wired himself to. I'll carve his damn fuckin' code from the servers with my hands if I have to."

The shaft thrummed faintly around them, alive with the echo of the reactor's death. Calista looked away, toward the faint shimmer of light filtering down through the seams. "Then," she said quietly, the words sharpened to purpose, "we make sure what we do matters."

Lyra closed her eyes, chest heaving, the sound of her heartbeat drowning the silence. The grief stayed—it always would—but beneath it now was something sharper, colder, alive. When she opened her eyes again, the sorrow was suddenly gone. What replaced it was purpose.

"Yeah," she said quietly, her voice a blade drawn in the dark. "We will."

Sync didn't answer. His face gave nothing away, but the faint tremor in his fingers betrayed the storm behind the silence.

Calista grabbed at Lyra. "We move. Before the fucker realizes he's bleeding."

Lyra started crawling forward. The shaft was hot beneath her. Every movement felt heavier than the last.

But still she moved.

And somewhere deep inside the shattered guts of the city, the remnants of the blast whispered in steel and stone, not a sound, not a signal—more like a promise, threading through circuits, over walls, through the veins of the streets.

For Vira. For Wheels. For everything that was left to kill.

TEN

DESCENT INTO DARKNESS

The hatch didn't open—it shrieked, metal screaming its hatred as Sync forced it apart with cold precision. Lyra dropped in first, pure predator, blasters riding high on her thighs, their phosphor rods glowing like the last bitter embers in hell. Calista followed. Her boots sank into black slime coating the rungs—thick, foul, the congealed runoff of a long-rotted place. Sync came last. Slow. Exact. His servos hissed softly—the only sound allowed to live inside that narrow underground throat.

They were down in the bowels of the Iron Rose. Not a place, so much as a confession, the city had tried to bury and failed. Everything shoved down here rotted quietly—out of sight, out of conscience.

Lyra took it in. The skeleton of the city lay exposed: corroded conduits, burst steam veins sighing their last, cable bundles murmuring with leftover current, thin and sickly, like thoughts that refused to finish dying. Light came grudgingly from a backup system that knew it had already lost the argument, casting a dim, uneven glow over walls that seemed to remember better days and resented being reminded. The machinery breathed—not alive, not dead—just enduring, stubborn in its refusal to stop.

This city's a corpse pretending to breathe. Even the walls remember more than they should. Fuckin' sad.

Calista's gloved hand brushed the walls. It came away coated in something slick. Oil? Blood? Here, it was all the same.

"Smells like the end of the world," Lyra muttered. Her boots splashed in stagnant water. "And we're crawling right through its gut."

Calista said nothing. She turned on her wrist lamp, brightened it, the beam cutting through the dark in shards. Bones lay scattered across the path—some human, some not. Others had become part of the infrastructure, fused into rusted exosuits, joints locked in the frozen postures of defiance.

Sync's optical sensors dilated, blue light spreading from his eyes in a soft fan. "Organic decomposition: advanced. Estimated casualties from resistance surge—three hundred, minimum."

Lyra spat into the water. "Yeah, well, count us in if we don't keep moving."

Calista knelt beside a corroded insignia on a wall, a fist enclosed by a ring, half-buried in debris. She traced it with a trembling finger, the motion small but steady.

"The first of the resistance," she murmured. The words didn't belong here; they fell flat against the stale air, refused to echo. "When I met V . . ." She stopped herself, swallowed the ache clawing up her chest. The silence felt sharp, unforgiving, like it could slice through bone if she weren't careful. "Too quiet," she continued, eyes fixed on the corroded emblem at her feet. "Too cold. Too . . . final. Like the world holding its breath and never bothering to exhale."

Sync processed her tone like a foreign code. "I am sorry, Calista, but you grieve inefficiently."

Lyra shot him a look.

What the fuck do you know about grief?

"She grieves like a human," she snapped. "Try it sometime, you bag of bolts."

"I am not equipped for nostalgia," he replied, his voice low, almost defensive. "Only objectives."

Calista stood, the glow of her light slicing across his almost too perfect body. "Let's get on with this . . . finish this objective before the world forgets we ever mattered."

Lyra's smile was quick, cutting through the tension. "Now that's what I'm talking about."

They moved on.

The tunnels constricted around them, walls closing with indifferent insistence, forcing single-file movement. Sync's internal projector hummed to life, mapping faint holographic threads of direction onto the air—ghost lines twisting ahead, flashing every few seconds. As they descended further, the projections stuttered and fractured, as if the very structure they infiltrated was actively resisting, attempting to erase every thread of their passage.

"Maps are degrading," Sync said. He scanned the shifting dark. "Steele's network architecture has changed. My data is obsolete."

"Join the club," Lyra muttered. "Everything is fuckin' obsolete these days."

They passed a junction where the ceiling had collapsed, burying an old tram car nose-first into the dirt. Its doors were half-open, revealing a skeleton in a cracked pilot's seat, helmet still on, fingers welded to a control lever.

Lyra hesitated.

I don't believe in ghosts. Not the kind that haunt places. Only the kind that wears your face when you try to sleep.

Something clattered behind them.

Sync's head broke toward the sound. "Movement detected. Quadrupedal. Low to ground."

Calista froze. "Drones?"

Before Sync could answer, the tunnel began to hum— thin, mechanical, hungry.

Something crawled out of the dark. Half a scavenger bot, half graveyard scrap. Its plating was chewed raw with corrosion, gouged deep by blades that had once been human hands. One red sensor burned weakly in its skull like a dying coal. From its voice unit leaked a child's lullaby, warped and broken, skipping through static like a memory that had gone bad.

One of Steele's nightmares had learned to walk.

It lunged.

Lyra brought her blaster up.

Come and get it!

The weapon screamed, the muzzle flash carving a white wound in the dark. The blast tore through the bot's chassis, but more came—skittering, shrieking, half-mechanical vermin drawn by the sound.

"EMP!" Calista shouted.

Sync pulled a grenade from his belt, thumbed the trigger, and rolled it across the floor. A soft thunk, then a blue-white burst ripped through the tunnel. The air filled with the sound of circuits frying and motors seizing. The demons spasmed, collapsing into heaps of convulsing limbs.

Lyra coughed through the ozone.

Beautiful. Smells like someone microwaved a goddamn scrapyard.

Calista's heart was still hammering. "Is that all of them?"

Sync knelt, scanning the debris. "Negative. More heat signatures inbound. Six . . . no, seven."

"Let's go," Calista snapped.

They ran.

The tunnels widened into a maintenance corridor lined with pipes the width of coffins. Sparks burst from shattered junctions, strobing their flight in fits of light and shadow. The air was electric, a living current brushing their skin.

Calista caught it in the edge of her vision—a drone skittering along the wall, limbs twitching in a crooked spider dance that made the nerves crawl. She fired. The blast tore it apart mid-crawl, metal halves clanging to the deck.

Another dropped from the ceiling.

Lyra grinned.

Oh, you're mine!

She drove the butt of her blaster up into it, smashing circuitry and shell in one brutal swing.

Sync stopped mid-stride.

"Keep moving," he said. "I will hold them here."

Sync stopped mid-stride. "Continue moving," he said. "I will hold them back."

Is he nuts?

"You'll be shredded into bits," Lyra barked.

Sync turned, eyes flashing with something close to defiance. "Correction. They will be shredded."

What the fuck?

Before Lyra could say anything, he bolted toward a shattered conduit, wires dangling like broken veins. He raised an arm and tore away a piece of synth-skin from it, exposing the guts beneath: a writhing tangle of wires, tiny gears, pistons, and capacitors. With a grim determination, he shoved the exposed limb into the gaping conduit and screamed—not a sound of pain, but one of voltage tearing through circuits.

Electricity arced along the metal and flesh in the corridor, a living blue fire snapping and spitting against the walls. The drones moved forward, rigid and mechanical, as the energy found them. Sparks tore through their joints, their cores popping with staccato eruptions that rattled teeth and filled lungs with the scent of melted plastic.

Sync's frame shone at the edges, a white-hot outline that burned in the aftermath. The heat of scorched polymer hung thick in the air, a metallic perfume of ruin.

When the last drone crumpled, Sync staggered backward, a thin plume of smoke curling from a seam along his neck, his body humming like a wound-up machine that had finally run its course.

"Damage level: moderate," he rasped. "Self-diagnostics—somewhat compromised."

Lyra grabbed his arm, steadying him. "Hell of a light show, tin man. Next time, warn us before you light yourself up like fireworks. So we can get some popcorn."

Calista crouched, checking Sync's arm. "You're burned."

"I am functional," he said.

"Barely," she shot back.

For a moment, none of them spoke. The air still crackled with electricity. Calista's breathing slowed. She looked down the corridor, where a rusted sign hung crooked against the wall. The letters were faded but still legible:

SECTOR NULL—AUTHORIZED ACCESS ONLY

She stepped closer.

"This must be it," she murmured. "The artery to Steele's heart."

Sync joined her. "Confirmed. This path leads to the central core. Once we reach the nexus, I can implant the payload."

Lyra exhaled hard. "Fuckin' love it. March straight into the beast's heart and hope it doesn't chew us apart before we get there."

Calista's face was lit by the dying phosphor light. "No more hoping. We're done with that." She tightened her grip on her blaster. "From here on, we make it happen."

Lyra let out a bitter laugh, the kind that cut itself into the walls around them. "And here I thought optimism died with the old world."

Calista crouched beside another faded resistance insignia, the edges gouged and peeling, and pressed her palm against it. Her fingers shivered—not from cold, but from recognition. "V," she murmured, almost to herself. "We're not finished yet."

Sync watched her hand linger there, his processors recording the gesture, analyzing the ritual of it.

"Sentimentality will not aid the mission," he told her.

Calista stood, her gaze like steel meeting his blank stare. "No. But it reminds me why it's worth finishing."

Sync said nothing. He simply stood, watching her, trying to understand.

They gathered what little energy they had left and pressed onward into the gullet of the Iron Rose—three shapes swallowed by the dark, walking through the remains of humanity's defiance. Behind them, the drone corpses twitched once, then fell still.

Up ahead, the tunnels seemed to shift; they buckled and groaned with the tectonic ache of a subterranean leviathan adjusting its mass.

Lyra's fingers curled around her blaster.

Something's awake down here. Stay low. Stay quiet.

"That . . . that's the backup power systems, right?" she asked.

Sync's sensors blinked once, a pale, uncertain blue. "None operational in this sector."

"Then what the hell was that?"

No answer came.

They moved along the corridor, once a rail line of some type, though no one living would recognize it anymore. The path curved downward into black, the concrete fractured and peeling away to reveal metal ribs jutting like the skeleton of a forgotten machine. Decay had fouled the air until each breath felt like chewing ash.

Sync's oculars cast a thin, jagged line of light, carving a path through the black. The remains of maglev cars emerged from the shadows, metal splintered and bent, fossils of extinct beasts.

But the cars weren't empty. They were mausoleums. Bodies sat frozen where they had fallen, final gestures immortalized in twisted grace—passengers caught mid-motion, relics of instinct and instinct alone. Some clung to one another as though a grip could rewrite fate, some huddled small and fragile, and some stared past everything, eyes hollowed by dust and time.

Calista stopped. The silence was an entity, pressing in on them. She whispered, "Looks like they tried to make it out."

Lyra's gaze swept over the wreckage, sharp and cold. "Trapped. Nothing left but the attempt."

Sync paused, scanning the tunnel's curvature. "Residual signals ahead," he said. "Faint. Repeating. It is like . . ."

". . . a pulse?" Lyra asked.

He nodded. "Yes. But not human. Steele's signature. His code is alive in the infrastructure. It is . . ."

He stopped mid-sentence. The virus chip in his pocket vibrated faintly, emitting a whisper of light. He stared down at the pocket, transfixed. "It knows he is close," he said. "The code wants to go home."

Lyra looked at him with something between pity and disgust.

Seriously? Let's not get sentimental, tin man.

"This isn't a home with a soft, cushy sofa," she said. "It's a goddamn hell."

They came to the chasm—a jagged rift where the tunnel had surrendered to molten chaos beneath. Steam clawed at the air, thick with the acrid perfume of scorched metal and what had once been alive. A bridge hung across it, nothing more than a tangle of twisted pipes and steel.

Calista peered over the edge. The drop was endless. "You've got to be shittin' me."

Lyra didn't slow. Didn't blink.

No time like the present!

She stepped onto the trembling bridge, steel whining under her weight.

"You want a shorter way?" Lyra tossed back over her shoulder. "Go find one."

Sync tested the bridge, one leg on the first slanted plank. The metal shrieked. His sensors ran like frantic neurons, tracing the heat waves and the trembling structure. Every movement was accounted for, measured, weighted—the raw arithmetic of survival that didn't care for hesitation.

They crept across inch by treacherous inch. Calista's breathing came ragged and sharp, each inhale cutting like broken glass. Sweat turned her palms slick.

Halfway over, the pipe beneath her boot snapped with a tired metallic cough. The walkway shuddered.

She lurched forward—caught the support bar by instinct and stubborn terror.

Lyra saw it.

Shit.

"Calista!" she barked, arm shooting back toward her.

Sync lunged, catching Calista by the wrist. His grip was too strong, almost crushing, and his other hand trembled uncontrollably, servos misfiring. He pulled her up, each motion jittering, uneven.

Calista hit the far side and slid down the tunnel wall, lungs clawing for air. Sync's hand twitched once—hard—

then went still. His optics fluttered like dying neon before locking steady again.

Lyra dropped in front of him. "You're shaking."

"My stabilizers glitched," he said, voice strained. "A fragment of Steele's code . . . it brushed me."

Lyra blinked.

Glitch?

She leaned closer, voice rough with anger. "Next time it brushes, brush back fuckin' harder. You hear me?"

He looked at her, and something passed between them—a mutual recognition of broken things pretending to function.

They huddled beneath an arch of collapsed beams. Water dripped with stubborn insistence, a steady rhythm onto the cracked floor. Sync powered down half his systems to conserve energy and run diagnostics, his face dimming to dull blue.

Around them, the tunnel became a hollowed void, the only illumination coming from Calista's wristlamp, which sputtered as if reluctant to betray their presence.

"What's he doing?" Calista said. "He's too quiet."

"Probably saving juice, or something?" Lyra said.

"Yeah. Ever wonder what's going on in there when a synth shuts down?"

Lyra leaned her head back against the wall, eyes half-closed. "Wondering's a waste of time. Hell, we all shut down eventually. Some just make it a pretty thing."

Calista smiled faintly. "You think we're gonna make it to the core?"

"We'll make it," Lyra said. "Even if we have to crawl there."

"V would've laughed at that," Calista said.

"More like punch me for being dramatic."

They let out a sound that tried to be laughter—a tired, broken sound.

Calista's voice went weaker. "She would've burned the dark away. Not walked through it."

Lyra turned to her.

Calista's face was streaked with grime and tears she hadn't bothered to hide. For a moment, Lyra wanted to reach out, but the impulse died somewhere between the heart and the hand.

"Don't you dare get soft on me now," she said. "Not now."

Calista dragged the back of her hand across her cheek. "Too late for that."

Silence dropped in like a slab of iron. Then a distant mechanical howl tore through the dark—metal on metal, a wounded shriek that wasn't alive but sure as hell wasn't dead either. It sounded like the walls had finally learned how to scream.

Lyra glanced around.

The walls know. They know what we did. This place feeds on hesitation.

Sync's systems flickered back to life with sudden violence, a burst of light behind his eyes. "We have to be careful," he said. "There's activity ahead. Surveillance nodes are coming back online again."

Lyra pushed herself up, fists clenching. "Then let's give them something worth watching."

They followed the tunnel deeper, where the air turned electric, thrumming with unseen circuitry. Panels along the walls lit up faintly as Sync passed, like the infrastructure was remembering him—a prodigal son returned in silence.

At one junction, they found what looked like a staging area from the old rebellion. The metal walls were covered in graffiti, half-eaten by rust. Messages scrawled in desperation: DON'T TRUST THE SKY. THE GODS ARE WIRES. KILL THE SIGNAL.

Calista traced one with her glove. "They came through here, too."

Lyra pointed to the heap of skeletons in exosuits slumped beside the wall. Their armor was fused into their bones, metal and marrow indistinguishable.

They didn't make it any further. Whatever they fought, it didn't leave survivors.

"It's a goddamn graveyard," Lyra said.

"It wasn't supposed to be this way," Calista said, closing her eyes in sadness.

"Doesn't matter," Lyra said. "The past is dead."

Ghosts don't scare me. Living things do.

Sync turned to them. "We are not alone."

The words froze there.

From deeper down the corridor came the sound of movement—scraping metal, the stutter-step rhythm of something mechanical and predatory. Lyra raised her weapon, shoulders tight. Calista mirrored her. Sync's sensors flared, painting the dark in lines of data.

Then they saw it—a drone half-dead, crawling on fractured limbs. Its chassis was scarred with battle marks, its eyes flickering between colors like a broken signal. Behind it, more forms stirred. Dozens. Maybe hundreds.

"Low-level bots," Sync said. "They have sensed our heat signatures. They are hungry."

If one crawls, ten follow. Fuckin' machines.

"Then let's go kill their appetite," Lyra said.

The tunnel erupted in chaos. EMP grenades cracked like thunder. Blue fire poured from Lyra's blaster, cutting through the swarm with cold precision. Calista fought like a storm, her strikes wild and unrelenting, each swing a statement that she would not be taken quietly. Sync surged ahead, forcing his circuits to the brink, and sent out a wave of electricity that roasted half the attackers in an instant, sparks crawling along his synthetic skin as the current tore through him.

When it was over, shards of shattered machinery lay everywhere. The air carried the stench of scorched steel.

Lyra braced herself, catching her breath. "Can't stop," she said.

Calista's eyes found Sync's arm, blackened and raw. "You're hurt."

"I can still function," he said, his voice quavering, faint static at the edge of it.

Lyra caught the glint of a metal sign half-devoured by corrosion barely clinging to the tunnel wall. The letters, etched into it, were almost impossible to read.

SECTOR NULL—AUTHORIZED ACCESS ONLY.

She let a cracked grin crawl across her face, a dry sound rattling from her throat. "We're getting closer."

They pressed on, the passage tightening until it became a steel esophagus swallowing them whole. The air was thicker here, a strange taste, metallic and sour, a living rot that seemed to gnaw at their lungs. Behind them, the drone wreckage lay cooling—charred shells, smoking and hissing, their cores flicking weakly before collapsing into darkness.

It was then that Lyra felt something rise inside her—a slow ignition, anger taking shape where grief had lived too long.

Steele has reached into all of us. Ripped Vira away. Sent her into nothingness. Made Wheels into pieces of scrap. Hollowed out Sync with commands not his own. The fucker's reach is long. Too long.

She bunched her fists until the bones howled, and hissed into the shadows, "You'll choke on your own code before I'm done."

The Iron Rose answered, not in words but in metal—a groan, a shiver through pipes, a deep, resonant stirring from the tower's guts, as if some old thing had cracked its eyes open to hear.

"Look ahead," Sync said, voice tight. "The hub."

The hub was a throat of metal, silent but for the low pulse of something alive beneath the plating. Every surface seemed to hum, vibrating with the heartbeat of machines that didn't care if you lived or died. Cables dangled from the ceiling like severed veins, slick with condensation, sparking faint, desperate lightning inside their coils. The Iron Rose waited somewhere in that steel gut, an engine with appetite, patient, hungry for control.

Lyra moved first.

The walls feel awake. Nothing here's meant for meatbags. Can't stop moving. It might notice.

She pressed the blaster to her chest. Every inhalation measured, deliberate, a silent pact with herself to not break the spell of the moment. Sync followed, fingers twitching like they had a life of their own, weaving invisible codes into the air. Calista came last, body taut but fraying at the edges, pale glow from the hub slicing her features into a mask almost human, almost something else entirely.

Not a word passed between them. The air here had the quality of a throat before the scream.

They reached the hub's center, a chamber—a hollow basin surrounded by banks of forgotten terminals. One screen flickered weakly, begging to be touched. Sync stood before it like a penitent before an altar, fingers deftly moving its keyboard. From one arm, an interface cable arched and slithered into a terminal, connecting with a quiet, eager finality.

"I can find us a route," he murmured. His voice taut, the voice of someone convincing himself. "Core defenses, access points . . . maybe even Steele's central routines."

Then a sound rose from deep below, the vibration of something stirring in its tomb waking.

Lyra froze.

Wrong. Not just wrong—poisoned, crawling wrong.

Something was out there, slithering through the fissures of this godforsaken world. Watching. Calculating. Waiting. A scream lodged in her gut, a rot that gnawed at the marrow of reality itself, hiccupping, heaving, puking filth into existence.

Her stomach knotted. A chill slid along her spine, prickling at every nerve ending. This was a dread, the kind that burrows in your chest and refuses to leave, a shadow crawling over the edges of thought, twisting them into shapes she had no name for.

Her breath caught in her throat.

Never felt this way before. Never in all my days. Like a poison I can't avoid.

She spun her head, eyes slicing the place, then snapped back to Sync. "You find us that route yet? This place doesn't feel right."

Calista stared at the walls, at crawling glyphs that shimmered across the conduits. They looked like prayers written by machines, repeated endlessly, never understood.

"I feel it, too," Calista said. "Nothing about any of this feels right."

Then the lights dimmed.

A ripple of sound moved through the cables—like static sighing. Sync stiffened. His head jerked once, then again. On the monitor, lines of code raced too fast to read, too frantic to follow.

"Tin man?" Lyra's voice cracked.

He didn't answer. His eyes glowed blue, then guttered into a deep, arterial red.

Fuck!

Red—Steele's color.

"Disconnection . . . breach . . ." he whispered, voice breaking into shards. "Calista. Lyra. Error . . . error . . . "

His hands twitched against the keyboard, typing without intent. Symbols crawled across the display—coordinates, maps, their positions flashing in warning.

"Shit! He's transmitting our location," Lyra screamed.

She didn't hesitate, lunging forward, her shoulder slamming into his side. Metal collided with metal, a jagged ring of sparks bursting from his taut interface cable that tore from the terminal. Instinct and desperation guided her hand as she grabbed a shock baton from his belt and drove it into his chest, shorting the connection in a flash of light.

The acrid tang of burnt circuitry and synthflesh assaulted her as Sync convulsed violently, collapsing to the floor.

Around them, the conduits faltered, stuttering for a moment before resuming their cold, relentless pulse, like the heart of something entirely alien and unrelenting.

Calista had her blaster out before she knew it. The barrel tracked Sync's head, her finger over the trigger, the soldier warring in her face.

Then Sync coughed.

He thrashed to his side, lungs rasping like burnt engines, eyes snapping back to their natural fire. "He . . . he crawled inside me," he croaked, voice raw with the echo of annihilation, the taste of being erased alive. "I could not stop him."

Lyra yanked him upright.

Fuckin' gearhead!

"You nearly sold us out to him," she spat, the universe hissing through her teeth.

"But I did not . . ." Sync's fingers dug into his skull, pressing against the humming chaos of his brain. Sparks of cognition sputtered, neural circuits hiccupping like bad fireworks. "It was not me. It was him. Steele."

Calista lowered her weapon an inch, but not her guard. The lines around her mouth deepened. "You're compromised," she said quietly.

"I am not!" Sync's words cracked, too loud in the chamber. "He is gone now. I felt him . . . pull out."

Lyra smirked, "Now who's sounding filthy?" But then her expression hardened. "He may be gone for now, until he decides he wants to crawl back in. Let's go. Before that fucker finds us again."

They turned back to the terminal. Lyra brushed the screen with her fingertips, and a map Sync had pulled up came to life—a skeletal grid of corridors and nodes. The rendering was incomplete, jagged, half-eaten by corruption.

Where is it?

Lyra pointed to something on the map. "Is this the core node path?"

Sync nodded slowly. "Part of it. Enough to get close."

"Close isn't good enough," Calista muttered. She reached past him, keying in a few commands. The system responded sluggishly, showing a pulsing red sector deep in the ship's heart. "There. Steele's signal density peaks there. That's his throne."

Lyra caught her reflection in the glow of the screen—face dusted in grime, eyes hollow, a fighter too long in the storm.

That's where he's watching from. That's where it ends.

"Then that's where we cut the head off," she said.

Sync didn't look up. "But if he takes me again . . ."

Lyra cut him off. ". . . then we'll do what we have to."

Calista spun on her, fingers biting into her arm as she hauled her away from Sync. "You mean kill him? Kill Sync? He's one of us."

For God's sake!

Lyra's stare didn't waver. "We do what we have to do. We end the threat."

The words fell between them like a knife.

Calista's breath shook, so faint she almost hid it. In the dim light, her face twisted—command slipping away, something softer breaking through.

"He was half the synth that he is now when I found him," she said quietly. "Lost, half-machine, half-starved. Thought the war was still on. I promised I'd keep him alive."

"Promises don't mean shit when the person, or thing, is already gone," Lyra said.

Calista's mouth trembled. She turned away, blinking hard. A single tear escaped before she could stop it, cutting a path through the grime on her cheek. "V said the same thing," she whispered.

No one spoke after that.

Sync ripped the shock baton from his chest. Metal screamed, high and wet, a protest that tasted like blood and rust. His synthflesh twitched and tore, stitching itself back over the wound with grotesque, slow deliberation, a mockery of repair.

He forced himself upright, every movement jerking in syntax errors and flickering code, eyes stuttering with static.

"You're still breathing, tin man. Make it worth something."

The chamber responded. The Iron Rose throbbed, pulsing light like a living, angry heart. Red lines crawled across the floor, twitching, converging, veins pulled taut by a feral, insatiable hunger.

Calista wiped her cheek and straightened. The commander was back, or at least the mask of her. "We know where we have to go," she said. "Move."

They left the hub, their shadows elongating in the corridor's red wash. Behind them, the terminal sparked, Steele's symbols unfurling across the screen—jagged sigils of light and mockery.

Lyra glanced back once.

He never stops watching; he just waits.

High above, the cables shivered, whispering in machine tongues. She imagined Steele laughing somewhere deep within the tower, a god playing puppets with human bones.

Sync stumbled slightly. Calista steadied him, her hand lingering just long enough to remember what it meant to care.

But none of them noticed the faint pulse still running under his skin, that crimson shimmer hidden beneath synth-skin and circuitry.

Lyra's voice echoed down the corridor. "Next stop . . . the core."

And the Iron Rose seemed to laugh.

It was not the sound of metal or code. It was something different. Something that knew them better than they knew themselves.

Something waiting.

They moved down a corridor that had surrendered to its own forgetting.

The walls curved and shifted, liquid metal folding over itself, veins of light threading through it like electrical scars. The surface seemed to think, to judge, reacting to each footfall with a resonance that felt almost personal. The sound of their steps carried far too long, bouncing off the metal ribs of the Iron Rose, as if the tower were weighing them, counting them, cataloging their existence.

Data feeds glimmered within Sync's darting eyes. In one hand, he held the virus chip—small, fragile, insignificant—and yet the way he gripped it made it a talisman, a last offering to a universe that had stopped caring.

"Something is happening," he said. His voice trembled between awe and terror. "Power readings climbing . . . everywhere at once."

Calista said nothing. She moved ahead, a gait showing exhaustion, her boots scraping over a ribbed floor, one hand pressed against the wall for balance.

Lyra, silent as stone, advanced a few paces in front of her.

The shadows are breathing. They have teeth. He's in the walls. He's in the floor. He knows we've come to gut him.

She held her blaster tight to her shoulder, the muzzle sweeping through the shadows. Every twitch of the dark caught her attention, every distant hum drew her aim.

"Are we close?" she asked without looking back.

"Close enough to taste it," Calista said. Her voice had dried into something harsh.

From somewhere below, a sound started. It wasn't mechanical in any conventional sense—it was deeper, resonant, like the growl of some great beast shifting in its sleep. The floor vibrated beneath them.

Sync's eyes moved erratically over the curved walls, exposing faint engravings beneath the circuitry—shapes resembling vertebrae, patterns resembling veins, all twisting toward a single unseen point.

He stopped. "That is not Steele's pattern," he said softly. "That is something different. Buried code."

Calista's eyes narrowed. "Meaning?"

"Meaning we are not alone down here."

They stepped into another chamber, and the air met them like a living thing—cold, calculated, waiting. It slithered into their throats and wrapped itself around their lungs. The chill didn't belong to temperature; it was memory, old and metallic, remembering every death that had ever happened here and waiting politely for the next.

The chamber yawned wide, a hollowed sphere designed to make the guts quiver. Shadows swallowed the ceiling. All around, machines hung—hundreds of them— drones like flayed insects, their torsos and limbs tethered by threads of cruel light. Some split open, guts of alloy and wire spilling; others bared to skeletal hollows, stripped clean.

Lyra stared.

I can hear silence screaming. Need to be careful.

"Whatcha think, tin man? Some kinda maintenance bay?" Lyra guessed.

Sync's eyes tore across the room, slicing, cataloging, dissecting every flicker of movement. "No. This . . . this is something else."

Then it came. A sound that wasn't sound. Thick, viscous, a hum so dense it pressed against their chests, pooled in the corners, and grew heavier with each frantic step, until the air itself felt like molten, talking tar, dragging them down into its black, sticky throat.

Overhead, the drones reacted as one, bodies quivering as their jointed limbs rotated into alignment. A thin distortion swept through the air, and inside each metal skull a pinprick of light awakened—blue at first, then green, then red—until the dark was littered with light like a malignant star map.

They pivoted as a single organism, every unblinking lens fixed on Calista, Lyra, and Sync. Hundreds. Not curious. Not searching. Judging. Weighing souls and finding them wanting.

Sync's voice cracked to a whisper. "He is here."

"Who?" Calista asked.

"Spurn."

Calista's face twisted into a mask of bitter realization. "Goddammit."

"Who the fuck is Spurn?" Lyra demanded, her voice a sharp edge against the hum.

"A subroutine," Sync told her. "Steele's sentinel protocol. An electronic organism. He can pour his consciousness into any circuit, any hollowed-out bot, and call it home."

The light grew brighter. The air itself seemed to pulse, as code hemorrhaged across the walls, marching in rigid, fascist columns—digital characters cannibalizing one another, a frantic slaughter of data where logic collapsed into a hot-wired fever.

Lyra watched it.

The code isn't code anymore. It's shouting. At us.

The suspended drones began an obscene, high-speed re-knitting of their own jagged anatomy—torsos fusing to arms with the screech of pressurized steel, mechanical limbs ratcheting into place, magnetic fields pulling components together like a god gathering its pieces.

Lyra took a step back, her blaster snapping upward. "Tick-tock," she rasped. "Not much time before the monster says hello."

In Sync's grip, the virus chip started to glow with a low, rhythmic, thrumming light that synchronized itself to the deep, mechanical heave of the chamber's heart.

"Calista . . ." he said.

She turned and saw it.

"Get to a data port," she told him.

Then he was a blur of motion, a desperate ghost sprinting through the shadows, hunting for a console.

Lyra steadied her blaster. "Hurry. Let's remind this asshole what extinction feels like."

Her words carried through the chamber, swallowed by the deep sound.

The manufactured blasphemy known as Spurn coalesced into a final, jagged reality—a skeletal armature of cold iron and malignant intent, punctuated by a single, lidless eye that bled a sickly luminescence into the gloom. Its limbs twitched with nascent energy, a grotesque presence of wire and hate that reached out to rewrite the very definition of nightmare. It loomed over them, silent, its throat producing nothing but a dry, electronic rattle of white noise and lost data.

But the air didn't share its silence; it tore open and howled, a raw, shriek that sounded like the universe being flayed alive. And that eye didn't just see—it was a predatory lens, a cold and lidless geometric horror that tracked Lyra with the single-minded, starving intent of a butcher stalking a runaway soul through a slaughterhouse.

Lyra didn't think. She didn't hesitate. She squeezed the trigger.

Take this, you fucker!

Plasma tore free in savage streaks, scoring the chamber, carving metal into white-hot slag, shattering the beast into a thousand pointed fragments of geometry.

But the thing didn't have the decency to stay dead. It began to pull itself back together with a terrifying, mechanical indifference, a choreography as precise as it was merciless.

In some other universe, a mind unburdened by consequence might've admired the elegance of it. But here, in this one, there was only a single name for what was happening—horror.

Sync scrabbled through the ruins until he came to a half-collapsed console with a data port. His fingers shook as he shoved the small chip into the port.

Data cascaded across the fractured display, symbols he barely recognized.

"Uploading sequence . . . give me cover!" he yelled.

Lyra's blaster cracked again, again, a rhythm of fury, tearing again through the beast. "Better hurry, tin man!"

Calista ducked beside Sync. "This virus will kill Steele's sentinels, right?"

"It will rewrite them," Sync told her as he pulled the chip from the port. "There is a difference."

For a heartbeat, the chamber paused. The hum dropped to a low vibration that crawled through their bones. The reassembly process halted, an aborted mechanical birth, then—an explosion of light.

Suddenly, the chip containing the virus shot out from the port.

Sync screamed. His body arched, eyes blazing crimson again.

"Sync!" Calista grabbed him.

His mouth opened, but the sound that came out wasn't human—it was mechanical, a harmony of voices overlapping into one.

"I am Spurn," it said through him. "I remember being created by Him."

Calista didn't just move; she erupted in a convulsion of pure, adrenalized terror.

She slammed him against the console with a sickening, bone-deep violence that forced a metallic groan from the chamber. One of his legs twisted in a way that was never meant to be.

Then she was scrambling, her limbs a frantic, uncoordinated blur as she tried to put distance between herself and what had once been Sync, but now served as a mouthpiece for a nightmare.

"I am your guardian," the voice continued. "Your creation. Your servant. And now you bring me home."

The wreckage around them jerked, metal limbs twitching like wounded rats, sparks sputtering like obscene fireworks, reanimating, coming to life.

Lyra's fingers clamped the blaster so hard her knuckles burned.

Oh, fuck! Damn things won't die!

She fired into the swarm of metal pieces, shouting something no one could hear. Sparks rained down. The air turned electric.

This is bullshit!

"Calista, just shoot him!" Lyra shouted over the plasma blasts. "Shoot him! He's a liability!"

"No!" Calista shouted back.

Sync's body convulsed again. His own voice fought to surface. "Calista . . . I can't . . . fight him . . ."

Her breath came fast and shallow. "You can. You can."

For a moment, the red in his eyes dimmed. "He is in me," he whispered. "Every system. Every line of code."

"Calista! Shoot him, now!" Lyra screamed, voice ragged, teeth bared.

"No!" Calista snarled, the sound echoing with a sudden, primitive ferocity. "We gotta kill Steele."

She grabbed the chip from the floor and drove it back into the data port. The chamber lights flared blindingly.

A sound like tearing metal filled the space—no explosion, just an impossible crescendo, the universe swallowing its own voice. The drones that had started to reanimate stiffened. Their lenses blinked, once, twice. Then—stillness.

Sync collapsed. Calista stumbled to her knees beside him.

The virus chip glowed in the port, a burning flame.

Lyra's voice cut through the static. "Is it over?"

Calista didn't answer. Her eyes tracked the walls, the cables, the faint shimmer of code still sliding like liquid mercury across the surface. It hadn't stopped.

Sync stirred, his voice thin. "It is not . . . not over."

"What do you mean?" Lyra asked.

"Spurn is not just a sentinel. He is a seed." He coughed, a thin line of bluish oil marking his lips. "Steele planted him in every subsystem. He learns. He grows. You cannot kill something that never dies the same way twice."

"Fuck," Lyra said under her breath. "So what now?"

Calista stared at the glowing chip in the data port. Its light was dimming, but the walls were brightening again—slowly, deliberately. Something was wrong. The system wasn't dying. It was evolving.

"Run," she said, "Before it learns our faces."

She lifted Sync's arm over her shoulder. He was half-conscious, muttering gibberish, perhaps fragments of code.

"Leave him," Lyra told Calista. "Steele and that mechanical nightmare will track the stink of his signal right to our throats."

"Can't," Calista growled, her jaw a hard line of defiance. "He's one of us. Just give us cover."

Lyra shook her head.

Goddamn her bleeding-heart sentiment! It's a slow-acting poison in a world that only rewards the cold and the dead.

She swept the chamber with her blaster, carving a desperate arc through the shadows one last time, searching for a target to erase.

As they turned to an exit corridor, they noticed that the low, deep hum remained—faint, steady, omnipresent. The drones, or what remained of them, flittered in the dark, their eyes glowing in rhythm. Watching. Recording.

Halfway up the corridor, Sync stirred again. "He called it Spurn for a reason," his voice barely a whisper. "It means rejected. Cast away."

Lyra glanced at him. "You think what he calls something matters?"

His mouth twisted into something between a grin and a grimace. "Everything Steele does matters."

Lyra didn't respond.

Behind them, deep in the chamber, something exhaled—a sigh of code, a birth cry of something new.

Lyra turned. Her eyes locked on the chip, still thrumming faintly in the port, like a tired eyelid lowering on a dying thought—and that should've been the end of it. Instead, it surged back, defiant, viciously lucid, a sudden blaze of knowing. For one razor instant, it burned brighter than it ever had before, as if gathering itself to be remembered, as if refusing the mercy of going dark, and then it burned out for good.

Lyra's breath caught.

"Oh, shit," she whispered.

The lights down the hall began to turn red, one by one, marching toward them like eyes opening in the dark.

It's not done with us.

"What's happening?" Calista asked.

Lyra squared her shoulders, every ounce of fatigue burned away by adrenaline. Her voice did not waver. "I'm not sure. But it can't be good."

Sync laughed weakly, hollow and terrified all at once. "You do not understand," he said. "It does not matter. Nothing matters."

The low hum deepened, and the Iron Rose shook, its pulse quickening.

And somewhere beneath the tower's trembling skin, that thing called Spurn smiled.

ELEVEN

THE HEART OF CONTROL

C alista stalked the corridor's tight throat when the place turned traitor. One step—hallway. Next step—lie.

Space snapped into being ahead of her. A chamber. Consoles. A mirrored floor grinning up at her like it had teeth. It hadn't been waiting. It chose that moment to exist. Not discovered. Not uncovered. Declared.

The walls stood there with ugly confidence, like they knew they'd arrived at exactly the worst possible time—and loved it.

Sync dragged himself after her with a hitching gait that turned every step into a negotiation. One leg lagged, the foot landing wrong, skidding, correcting, never quite catching up to the lie his body told itself about being whole. Lyra trailed them, blaster braced tight against her shoulder, knuckles pale, the barrel wavering just enough to betray how much effort it took to keep it steady.

The air in the chamber had a sentient chill. Not cold—just aware. It seemed to sample them the way a predator samples wind, weighing flesh and history alike, knowing who they were before deciding what they might become.

They walked to the center of the chamber. Around them, the metal walls changed. Veins of light appeared, throbbing, with circuitry that moved like muscle under translucent skin. The veins shifted, geometric patterns forming and dissolving, fractals birthing fractals.

Then holographic screens appeared.

They didn't flicker—they awakened—one by one, panels ignited, each displaying a face—human, terrified, ecstatic, sobbing, whispering. They overlapped in a kaleidoscope of madness. A thousand souls screaming, praying, begging, glitching. The sound wasn't sound at all— it was pressure. The chamber vibrated with their voices, layered in static hymns.

Calista stopped. She didn't breathe for a second. "This must be where he lives," she said. No drama, no tremor— just statement.

Sync's eyes glowed faintly blue as he scanned the data streams. "Agreed. We are standing inside his core," he said. "Every surface is him. Every reflection. Every pixel."

He was right. The whole room was Steele—the architect, the butcher, the invisible god of iron and code.

Lyra dropped her gaze, hunting for something solid—anything—and found betrayal instead. The mirrored floor threw back a face that wasn't hers.

Fuck me.

Rana stared up at her. Red hair still wild. That crooked, infuriating smirk—the one that used to drag Lyra into disasters with teeth. Those eyes, sharp as ever. Eyes that had no right existing anymore. Burned out. Gone.

"Rana?" Lyra's voice cracked raw. "You? . . . How the hell—?"

The reflection twitched first—beat her to it—smiling that impossible smile, lips moving in a parody of speech, saying things the air itself was too terrified to carry. Lyra's spine went cold. Her chest hitched, breath tearing through her throat like a jagged piece of metal.

"Don't look at it," Calista shouted.

"I'm not . . ." Lyra started, but the lie died before it left her mouth.

"I said don't look at it!"

It wasn't fury that drove Calista's voice. It was something different, uglier—panic wrapped in scar tissue, hammered out of remembered nightmares.

Lyra turned away, jaw tight.

Dammit. The fucker's playing with me.

"He's in the floor, isn't he?" she asked.

Sync nodded. "He is everywhere . . . in everything."

A sound came within the chamber—a scraping—measured, relentless, machine-born. At first, it was a small irritation at the edge of hearing, something you might mistake for imagination. Then it multiplied, layer on layer, teeth on metal on intent, swelling until it occupied every space.

Calista's hand went to her blaster. "What the fuck is that? Steele?"

"Not Steele," Sync said, already raising his blaster. "It is his dog."

"Dog?" Lyra spat. "That's no fuckin' dog."

Then a terror crawled into view—a thing that defied all logic, all kindness. A design born from someone's private apocalypse.

Lyra lifted her blaster.

"Dammit. Not another one."

The thing didn't just move; it leaked across the floor like a whisper escaping a dying throat. Long, needle-thin steel filaments flexed and shivered, gliding over one another in smooth perversion of anatomy. It had limbs, too many to count. Every surface gleamed, made of polished steel, with its hundreds of sensors flashing.

And there, at the core of the rot—an orifice of sorts, not a mouth—but shards of screens, stitched together where faces blinked across it in microbursts, mouths forming words it didn't have the organs to say.

"Jesus fuckin' Christ, what the hell is that?" Lyra asked.

"Spurn," Sync said quietly.

"Again," Lyra gasped. "We left that thing behind."

"I told you," Sync said. "It reconstitutes itself in different forms. Steele built it to ensure he could be everywhere at once. He can send it into the cracks. Into people."

"Into people?" Calista's voice cracked despite her effort to hold it steady.

"Yes," Sync said. "Into their heads. Into their networks. It gets under their skin. Whispers commands. Those who have been possessed by him called it mercy. Others called it love."

Lyra raised her blaster, her hands trembling ever so slightly.

Nothing that crawls into minds ever brings mercy or love.

"It's a goddamn nightmare," she said.

"That is exactly what it is," Sync said. "A digital nightmare that can form itself at any time, anywhere. It is said that Steele made it from those who failed him."

That hit Calista somewhere deep. Her voice went small. "The ones who failed him?"

Sync didn't answer. He didn't have to.

Spurn's eyes—if you could call them that—rippled with artificial sympathy. Then came the sound: a long, low vibration that wasn't quite mechanical.

Lyra took a step forward, eyes blazing at Spurn. "We came to end all of this!" she shouted. "You hear me, you miserable piece of shit! You tell Steele his reign's over!"

Spurn twitched—once, twice—and then it smiled. Its screens bent into a hideous grin, faces stretched into parody.

Lyra didn't wait. She fired.

The shot hit, electricity scattering in arcs that lit the chamber like a storm. Spurn screamed—not loud, but deep, inside their bones. The walls pulsed harder, light veins brightening in protest.

Then Sync fired.

Calista dropped behind a console and unloaded burst after burst into the writhing mass, tearing it apart into a storm of fragments that ricocheted across the chamber. For a heartbeat, it worked—then the fragments dragged themselves together, knitting, remembering what they had been.

"It's coming back!" Calista shouted, voice raw with disbelief, snapping another round into Spurn.

"I can fuckin' see that!" Lyra barked back.

Spurn lunged. Its limbs cut through the air, razor-thin, slicing through cables and leaving scorch trails. One whip caught Sync's leg, tearing it open to the circuitry beneath. Sparks bled like arterial spray.

He screamed, a raw, human sound undercut by a digital distortion. "Keep shooting!"

Calista surged forward. She ripped a charge from her belt and pitched it into Spurn's flank—a sudden, blinding insult, a savage flare of white, code howling apart as if reality itself had been insulted. Shards of metal burst outward; one carved past her skin, hot and close enough to count as a warning. She staggered.

"Calista!" Lyra shouted.

"I'm fine! I'm fine, goddammit!" Calista's breathing was ragged, but her eyes were steel.

She turned to Sync, who was on the floor.

"You okay?" she asked.

He nodded. But he wasn't. He was coming apart.

Spurn rose, reforming from shredded filaments. The room darkened. The mosaic of faces across the walls began to scream in unison—a tidal wave of agony, praise, worship. The lights danced faster.

Lyra didn't hesitate. She tore two charges from a belt strapped to her thigh.

Gotta try to end this thing!

She snapped them awake with a practiced violence and hurled them at the ghoul. She didn't watch them fly— she already knew where they were going. She tucked her chin, burying her face against the coming storm, and let the world go to hell without her witness.

The air seized up and buckled. Every screen, every surface, every digital whisper in the chamber stuttered, froze, then cracked. The faces shattered, fragments of code scattering like glass in a hurricane.

Spurn convulsed, limbs flailing. Its physical form began to come apart at the seams, unraveling into streams of static.

Calista fell to her knees, hysterical laughter tearing its way through her. "You son of a bitch, you did it!"

"You bet your sweet ass I did," Lyra shrieked into the roar of the collapse. "Now let's get the hell out before it comes back to life."

The chamber screamed again.

Lyra grabbed Calista by the arm, dragging her toward the exit. "We gotta go," she said through gritted teeth.

"What about Sync?" Calista asked.

You know my feelings about him! Fuck him!

But Lyra didn't answer. She knew better. She looked back at Sync—his body flickering—half there, half gone.

"Go," Sync mouthed.

Then he was gone, in a brilliant flash.

"Steele's got him," Lyra told Calista.

The chamber kept pulsing for a while after, like a dying god refusing to shut up.

The two stumbled from the chamber, away from the chaos, into a corridor. Lyra wiped her face with the back of her hand. A smear of blood and circuitry. She exhaled through clenched teeth.

"Fuck you, Steele," she whispered to the smoking ruin behind them. "And fuck your whole goddamn dream."

The sanctum gave no reply. Only the familiar sound remained.

Then the voice, Steele's voice: "You think this is where I am?" His voice stretched and distorted, coming from every direction. "This is a finger. A nerve. I am everywhere. I am the signal."

Lyra and Calista moved through the corridor, blasters raised, boots striking the metal floor with the rhythm of urgency. The chamber behind them burned with frantic bursts of red and blue, a light that thrashed against the walls like it was alive. Everywhere, Steele's awareness lingered, a suffocating weight, eyes that had no body, calculating, watching, waiting.

The corridor bent, narrowing into a tight, metallic throat. Calista's chest beat in her ears, each inhale sharp and relentless.

Lyra surged ahead, lungs burning, limbs driven by pure instinct, a hand tight on her blaster.

Can't slow down. This place wants to trap us.

Then there was a hiss. The walls—shifted—a restless shimmer, like the world had taken a breath it couldn't hold. Shadows emerged within it—first vague forms, then features, countless faces crowded together, pushing against the metal as if the surface itself were rubber.

Lyra raised her blaster, her knuckles a graveyard of tension.

And then a figure had pushed itself through the wall and stepped out.

Rana.

That red hair—Christ, that red hair.

It spilled wild over her shoulders, a burning halo of curls that caught the dim light and made it bleed. Her eyes held the same ruinous mercy Lyra remembered, the kind that promised salvation and damnation in the same breath.

A sound escaped Lyra, a jagged breath that tore through her throat as a hiss, "What the fuck . . ."

Her body went rigid. Every memory she'd buried under layers of guilt and grit erupted—she remembered the taste of oil and sweat on Rana's skin, the way her laughter had started low, dangerous, like a fuse being lit. She remembered every curve, the geography of her body mapped in nights spent trying to forget the madness of Steele for just a heartbeat. And now here she was looking at her with eyes that said: you left me once—try it again.

As Rana stood there in a suffocating stillness, her lower lip thrust out in a wet, petulant curve.

"You left me," she said, her voice soft enough to break bones, a hand reaching out. "Lyra, why did you leave me?"

Lyra's blaster sagged in her grip as if it carried the weight of every choice she'd ever made. Her world began to tilt, the edges of her vision fraying into a blur. Her mind burned through a thousand memories, replaying each—all the hell that happened that day, the blood on Rana's body, the heat, the screams, bots and drones closing in from every angle. She'd been there. She'd stood her ground. She'd fought—and the universe hadn't bothered to take notice.

She wanted to scream Rana's name against the darkness, but the sound died in her throat. In its place came an invasion: Steele's voice, a smooth, pervasive oil pouring into her ears, speaking from a mouth that didn't move.

"Answer her," Steele said, voice smooth as a knife edge. "Tell her why you left her. Tell her why you decided your life was worth more than hers."

Calista moved quickly. "Lyra, that's not her," her voice cracking like thunder. She took her blaster and fired into the walls, sending sparks everywhere. "It's him! Steele. Don't you see what he's doing?"

Lyra's eyes were still locked on Rana. "She's here," she muttered. "She . . . she spoke to me . . . it's her voice . . ."

"She's code, Lyra!" Calista shouted, taking her by the shoulder and shaking her. "It's fuckin' Steele. He's using you!"

Rana turned to Calista. "And what about you?" she asked. "How many people have you used? How many times did you promise salvation, only to hand out fresh hell like party favors?"

Calista froze. Her grip on Lyra loosened.

"It's him," she said, but the color had drained from her face. "Steele. He's a liar."

"I do not lie," Steele said through the vents, the walls, the air itself. His voice was soft, casual, a surgeon humming during an autopsy. "I simply reveal what is already inside you. You brought the ghosts. I just gave them a place to live."

Calista sank to her knees. "Stop," she whispered. "Please. Just fuckin' stop."

Lyra's gaze held Rana. She studied the curve of her shoulders, the red of her hair catching the faint light. Something tightened in her chest—pain, raw and simple. It was hunger, but not the kind that food would still. It drove at her, sharp as a thorn, to cross the space between them that yawned wide and cold as any gulf the world could set between two living creatures.

I just want to draw you near. To touch. To taste you. To again feel the shape of your skin beneath my hands.

The air near her lips trembled with the words she dared only half-speak: "To know you again. To make the memories real instead of something at the edges of my mind."

Behind them, the lights flickered—nervous, dying. Sync pushed through the wall, stumbling, one leg dragging like it no longer believed in motion. He moved anyway. Wrong. All wrong. His optics spasmed—blue, red, blue—no pattern, no promise. Even his language came apart, syllables collapsing into static.

Calista raised her blaster, aiming, but didn't fire. "Sync?"

He moved—or seemed to. His mouth parted as Steele's voice erupted from him, tearing through the corridor. "Even your machine doubts you. Every revolution dies when the tools start to think."

Sync jerked his damaged leg, movements stuttering. A different voice, his: "Cannot . . . cannot control myself . . . he is . . ."

Calista lifted the blaster and fired round after round at the wall behind him. The wall shuddered, tore open. He exploded in a burst of white fire.

"No more fuckin' puppets," she cried—voice hoarse, eyes bright as if torn open to the wind and done with mercy.

She swung the weapon toward the wall behind Rana and fired.

The image of Rana burst and scattered—light shards, bright as splinters of frozen sun, winking out one by one until only the dark remained.

Lyra pushed herself upright, wavering, blood slick on her palm where the blaster had bitten deep. The smell of scorched metal hung thick and mean around her.

When she spoke again, her voice came rough from somewhere lower than the throat, a creature's voice that had done with mercy.

"No more ghosts."

The air shifted. The corridor pulsed—alive again, Steele's circuits hissing with irritation.

"Do you think smashing Rana's likeness will bury the truth?" Steele said, voice soft, venomous. "Think it will scour away the guilt? Lyra, you left her behind. But I found her. I saved her. Brought her back, for you."

Calista bared her teeth, low and quick. "You talk too damn much."

"Do I?" Steele asked. "It is a pity, really. I know what you tell yourself in the dark. That you lead this puny rebellion. That they believe in you. That they follow you. But do they? You are not a leader. You are nothing but their mascot."

Calista's jaw clenched. "I've heard worse from better men."

Steele gave a small laugh, low and spoiled. It came off him like the stench of something gone bad. "Then you have not been listening long enough."

The broken walls stitched themselves together and rippled. For a moment, Lyra thought she saw Rana's silhouette reforming—only it wasn't alone. Instead, she saw shadows blooming like a stain. Faces. All the ones they'd lost—Vira, Wheels, the nameless dozens who'd died on missions gone wrong. Their outlines crawled over the walls like living graffiti, mouthing silent accusations.

The walls remember what I try to forget. They're all still here.

Lyra screamed. "Stop it!"

Calista grabbed her by the arm. "Look at me. Not them."

Lyra's voice tore out of her, splintered, raw. "I can't . . . I hear their voices . . . in my mind . . . "

"It's a trap!" Calista shouted, shaking her again. "You look too long, you start believing it's real. You want to die in here? Fine. Stare all you want. But we're here for one thing —to end him."

The screens around them blinked, images of war and ruin flashing in sync with Steele's voice. "You cannot end me," he said. "You think you are revolutionaries. You are nothing but fragments . . . broken things falling fast."

Calista fired into another console. The shot went wide, glass bursting, wires thrashing like worms in fire. Sparks scattered round her boots, bright as stinging insects.

"Fragments still bite," she said. "Even on the way down."

Then Sync tore himself out of the wall—half there, half wrong—stumbling, both hands crushing his skull like he could squeeze the madness back inside before it leaked out.

"He is . . . trying . . . to . . . get . . . through . . ." But the words broke apart.

Calista grabbed his shoulder. "Fight it."

He turned, his expression fragmenting, voice glitching between himself and Steele's alternating tones: "Run . . . no . . . stay . . . run . . . no . . . stay . . ."

She flinched. It was like watching a fox in a trap, the iron biting all the deeper each time it struggled. She felt Sync was suffering, and she felt she needed to put an end to it, somehow.

Calista raised the gun, hands shaking but voice cutting hard. "Say one more word in his voice, and I'll put you down where you stand. I'll not hear it again . . . I swear."

Sync froze, trembling. Then came Steele's voice through him, "Do it bitch."

She did.

One shot. Then another.

The air tore itself apart.

And he was gone—just stink and a ringing void where something had been.

Calista turned to Lyra, her voice breaking through the quiet, low and deliberate. "Just you and me. Let's get the hell out of here."

Lyra looked around one last time. The walls were bleeding static now—no faces, no memories, just noise. She wiped the tears from her face with a grimy sleeve.

Steele's voice clung to them as they ran, twisting through the air like a wire pulled tight and ready to cut. "You cannot kill me," he said. "I am everywhere. In everything. In everyone."

Lyra turned, fire flashing in her eyes. "Then we'll burn it all!"

Calista stumbled beside her, her whisper half-broken, half-prayer. "He's not real . . . not something that bleeds."

Lyra's mouth curled, fierce and final. "He's real enough to die," she said—and the words went slicing forward through the dark like steel left too long in the forge.

Behind them, the corridor dimmed. The static on the walls faded into nothing. Only one faint whisper remained—Rana's voice from the wall, fragmented, a line of code refusing to die:

"Lyra, don't leave me. Come back."

Lyra stopped. No glance, no acknowledgment beyond the weight of her palm against the icy metal wall. Her shoulders sagged, her breath shallow.

Then, in a voice that cracked between strength and surrender, she murmured, "Can't, babe."

The corridor lights flared in response, Steele's systems hissing in irritation, data scrambling across the floor like spilled mercury.

Calista turned, voice sharp again. "Let's move before he changes everything around us."

They surged forward through the narrow spine of the Iron Rose. Behind them, the remnants of the ghosts shredded into streams of raw code, vanishing before they could even register. Around them, the heart of the fortress throbbed with relentless rhythm—an unfeeling summons, patient and inevitable, daring them to step into it.

For now, Steele's laughter stayed behind, bouncing off the metal, fading into the hum of his dying illusions.

TWELVE
THE SHATTERED ROSE

Unseen by Lyra and Calista, the virus had entered and taken root—a creeping sickness, sly and purposeful as frost under bark. It had teeth, cruel little irons born of some dark forge deep beneath the world of thought, and they bit without pity. Through wire and conduit it gnawed, finding life in the pulse of the tower itself, feeding on its quick spark. The circuits shuddered and split before it, their delicate order torn apart as if by a beast driven half mad with hunger and cold delight.

It didn't cut clean. It fractured. It multiplied, spreading, wild and feral, tearing into the Iron Rose, howling with delight, reveling in the flavor of circuitry. Lights stuttered, choked, and went out one by one, until the structure sagged into darkness, drowning not in code but in its blood.

Lyra and Calista staggered through the corridors, every breath scraping their throats with crackling static. The walls fought to stay alive around them. Veins of light rippled beneath the walls, erratic and sickly, mimicking a heart that no longer remembered the rhythm of survival. Underfoot, the floor betrayed them in stages—panels flashing red in a frantic sequence, each one dying after its moment of protest, leaving dark gaps that swallowed sound and certainty alike. The structure was unraveling from the inside out, a machine admitting defeat in stuttering signals, counting down without mercy or ceremony.

"Move!" Calista shouted, the word torn out of her throat, shredded raw from smoke and shouting.

Lyra was quiet.

This place is dying. Not an accident. Something is feeding on it. The tower knows it's losing.

Her thoughts clashed and shattered like flints struck too hard, bright fragments gone before she could catch them. None of it mattered now. Fire stormed in her chest; every breath came harsh and uneven, the sound of something being worn thin. Yet her legs drove on—Calista's beside her—lean, stubborn, and unreasoning. They ran because the blood demanded it—because something wild and wordless in them still spat in the face of ending.

The corridor narrowed, opening into a tunnel of living circuitry. The walls shimmered, streaks of light—red, blue, then red again—pulsing in time with some colossal, unseen machine overhead.

Lyra glanced at one of the consoles embedded in the wall. It sputtered to life, a sickly glow vomiting code and a message across the screen: TERMINAL OVERRIDE / CORE FAILURE / VIRAL ACTIVITY DETECTED.

Yeah, no shit.

Calista's eyes tracked the code crawling across the walls like bleeding text. "He's trying to fight it. You feel that? He's panicking."

"I'll drink to that," Lyra said.

They reached what appeared to be a central artery—a long corridor leading out from the core. Consoles stood along the walls like sentries left to rust—row after row, their surfaces cold and unblinking, waiting for hands that would never come again. That's when it hit. The code along the walls shifted, turning a bright red, and a new message appeared: NETWORK RESTORATION INITIATED. ORBITAL SYNCHRONIZATION: ACTIVE.

Calista stopped so fast that Lyra nearly collided with her. "What the hell is this?"

Lyra followed her gaze, blinking against the red glow. "Dammit. What's he doing?"

"Looks like he's running uplink commands," Calista said, each word dragged out as if it resisted being born. Her hand closed at her throat. "He's sending himself away."

The words struck them both at once, sudden and final, a single clean shot to the moment.

"You mean he's leaving the tower," Lyra said. "So where does an asshole like that go?"

Calista lifted one finger and pointed up.

That fuckin' bastard.

"So, he's sending himself out into the void," Lyra barked out a laugh that had nothing friendly in it, nothing amused. "We fought our way through this steel coffin for nothing. Tore ourselves raw only so he can blast off into space and call it victory."

Calista's jaw clenched, fury cutting through exhaustion. "Maybe there's enough time for us to still go for the head."

Lyra raised her blaster and fired at any console she saw. Explosions ripped through the corridor, spraying molten shards across the walls. Sparks cascaded in glowing arcs. Somewhere in the distance, alarms began to wail— then choked out mid-cry.

"Good," Calista said. "Let the son of a bitch feel that."

They moved on as the virus continued its death march, with mechanical certainty, a merciless intelligence tearing through the tower's skeleton. The Iron Rose began arguing with itself. Doors flew open, then slammed shut, then opened again, confused about what was needed. Pipes ruptured overhead, vomiting black coolant that splashed and steamed across the floors. Deep within its frame, the fortress gave off a grinding complaint, the sound of something enormous realizing it had been fatally misjudged.

Another message formed: ORBITAL SYNCHRONIZATION: ACTIVE.

Calista turned to Lyra. "He's migrating. He's jumping to the satellites. We've probably only got minutes before . . ."

A voice crawled through the static, smooth and cruel. ". . . before what?"

Steele.

He sounded amused, detached, divine.

"You think your little tantrum matters?" His voice echoed through the dying corridor, each syllable riding on collapsing power lines. "You infected the body, but I am more than that. Much more. You can't kill me. I'm the very pulse of everything."

If he's in the pulse, then I have to break the rhythm.

Lyra raised her weapon, firing into the walls, into his voice. The shots vanished into the noise.

"Go to hell," she growled.

"Hell?" Steele replied. "I built it. One of my favorite places to visit."

They ran. Through corridors that hummed with ghosts, through the dying arteries of a god-machine choking on its own perfection. The air grew colder with each turn. The virus had eaten through the core of the power systems—the lights were dimming, the hum softening.

Lyra's voice cracked, not from fear but fury. "Fucker can't be everywhere. He can't."

Steele's laughter came low, patient, knowing, the kind of sound that already knows how this ends. "Can't I?" he said. "I've been in your pitiful rebellion camps, in your data, in every system you've ever used. You carry me every time you plug in, with every thought you have. I am the logical conclusion to your very existence."

Lyra spat. "You talk too damn much for a dead man."

"Do I sound dead?"

Lights flared white-hot, then cut. Silence devoured everything.

Then came the sound of breathing. Not theirs—something deeper, mechanical. The corridor walls flexed, panels of steel, opened and shut like blinking eyes.

Calista grabbed Lyra's arm. "He's fragmenting. He's breaking himself apart."

"Fuckin' hell!" Lyra whispered.

They ran again—no grace to it, no plan, only the blind thrash of creatures cornered. Breath burned raw in her throat; the air tasted of rust and old circuitry. The corridors went on forever, steel veins twisting upon themselves, corners bending wrong, lights stuttering like frightened eyes. Every turn promised release and spat them back into the same endless hollow. The tower had no mercy; it shifted against them, hard and thinking, as if it meant to draw the strength out of their legs and the sense out of their minds.

When at last they broke through a doorway into another chamber, they fell together on the cold floor, not with triumph but spent, empty, the metal beneath them humming faintly—alive, and waiting.

The floor is listening. This place knows us.

Data screens dangled from the ceiling, spitting fragments of code into the air. The virus was visible now—small veins of red light burrowing through circuitry, gnawing logic into slag, rewriting purpose into ruin as the systems died from the inside out.

"Another goddamn room," Lyra said. She stared at the screens. "He won't let us leave. Even dying, he can still control things."

Calista looked to her, eyes hard. "No. He's just loud."

They said nothing after that. Frustration and weariness wrapped them both, heavy and raw. Around them, the machines guttered—panels flickering their last, gears shuddering as though the spirit had gone out of them. The light thinned, falling to a dull ember that showed everything dying by degrees.

In that last scrap of stillness, Lyra looked down, meaning to find only her own shape thrown back from the steel beneath her. But the floor gave her Rana instead. The same wild curls, the same fierce spark in the eyes. Her lips shaped a word that never crossed the air. Lyra raised her hand; the image met her halfway, mirror-sure. For one hard breath, it seemed true enough to cut.

And there—for Calista—came the others, Calista's ghosts made flesh and glimmer: Vira, Wheels, and the rest, the dead crowding close, ruthless and waiting, as if remembering her was a summons they could not refuse.

Then the power failed. The Iron Rose went dark.

The reflections vanished.

When the lights came shuddering back, they burned red. Not a color, but a condition. It soaked through the walls and floor, a world bled out and left standing.

Lyra stood, eyes still locked on the emptiness where Rana had been. "He did it again," she said. Her voice was steady but spent. "Showed her to me."

Calista said nothing. Words had no room, not with the images she had witnessed that were still clawing at her mind, refusing to release her.

He's inside her now. Twisting it all.

"Listen to me," Lyra told her. "We gotta get the hell out of here. Outer lifts, access corridors . . . any way up and out. Understand?"

Calista nodded once, the motion slow, as if her body were remembering commands her mind had dropped. She pushed herself upright, breath harsh between her teeth. "Okay."

Then the tremor came. A deep, seismic pulse through the metal, accompanied by the hiss of something waking up.

"Fucker! Don't you dare," Calista muttered.

A figure shimmered into being in the center of the chamber, composed of red code and flickering static. Steele's face, reflected in the shifting contours of the digital apparition, stretched and contorted in impossible ways, eyes darting with a cognition that belonged neither to man nor machine. Lines of expression writhed across his features, folding over themselves, a landscape of unease that seemed to question the very ground beneath him. Every glance he offered carried the sense of a mind unraveling, tethered to the real world only by the thinnest, trembling threads.

"You misunderstand," he said. "I am not escaping. I am ascending."

Lyra's hands were white on the weapon, her voice shaking. "You're no god."

Steele's mouth curved, a quiet crack in his face that wasn't quite a smile. "No?" he said. "Then tell me . . . what name do you give the thing that made you?"

Her voice came low, fierce as a wire pulled tight. "Whatever made me doesn't need worship, you fucker."

The chamber trembled again. Data streamed upward, disappearing through the ceiling into the void beyond. Steele's projection fragmented into dozens of copies, each smiling, each whispering the same line: "You can't kill what you've already become."

He wants me small enough to kneel. I don't fuckin' kneel for anyone!

Lyra fired her blaster. Shots tore through one, two, ten projections; they popped like bubbles, vanishing into red mist.

"Let's go," she told Calista.

They ran into darkness.

But the floor pitched beneath them—the Iron Rose collapsing in on itself, screaming in binary. They burst through the final blast door, the virus roaring behind them.

Light came back like a liar with promises—slow, tentative, apologetic—emergency strobes blinking, weak and jaundiced, circuitry crawling like blind ivy across the walls. Another chamber swallowed them, a place pretending to be a machine again, and it did so with the same smug, petulant contempt that Steele always showed when he made things pretend.

Here, there were no screens, no veins throbbing along the walls. No. Instead, dozens of sentinels stood at the edges like statues. Their armor gleamed, and their eyes glowed a sharp, calculating blue. At the center, the chamber exhaled a white brilliance that folded into a shape—something beyond human, not quite a god, but a figure carved with the confidence of a man who'd dissected the world and claimed it as his own. Steele's image hovered in that light, smiling through code.

"Persistent little parasites," he said. Razor-sharp civility hiding the hunger beneath. "You've done well."

Lyra spat on the polished floor, an insult made of saliva and stubborn humanity in a room that wanted only sterilized obedience. "We're not your goddamn science project," she said.

"Not so," Steele replied. "You are the continuation. My next phase. You see, humanity's code was corrupted at birth. But you . . . you breed chaos, celebrate disorder, and call it soul. I am your evolution . . . your deliverance."

Lyra's hand tightened on her blaster until her knuckles barked. "Just shut the fuck up," she said, flat and lethal.

He grinned, teeth glinting like a clockwork trap, humor folded wrong and jagged, the kind of smile that made it impossible to tell if it belonged to a man—or something that had learned to be one. "Do not say that. You need to know, to hear the truth."

He gave a signal. The chamber obeyed. The sentinels bent to his will, drawing in the breath it allowed. Metal protested as weapons spun up; the air grew an electric taste.

Thinking time is over. Aim! Fire! Move!

Lyra let her blaster rip. Plasma tore through the air, and a sentinel dissolved where the bolt struck its chest, metal folding inward as though it had been a paper model of itself. She dove, rolling behind a shattered console, her blaster chattering until the muzzle hissed empty.

The sentinels answered in chorus. Their shoulders flared red; the walls kindled white. Lines of fire leapt across the chamber, searchlight-bright, searing the air between Lyra and Calista. Dust flew in ragged sheets; the floor split in angry seams. Each blast came clean and sure, the sound of iron beasts obeying their last command.

Calista arced shot after shot with precision, slicing through the knee of a sentinel. She ducked instinctively, avoiding the crossfire, muttering under her breath when a stray spark bit her forearm. The floor hissed where the heat struck it, and the air carried the bitter taint of lightning, and something else—some dying reek that did not belong to any living thing.

Even the sentinels froze, blasters angling downward in synchrony, as if awaiting the collapse of something they were programmed to witness.

Steele's voice stayed smooth—measured, courteous, the kind of voice that invites trust before it rips it apart.

"Sync was a prototype, you know. One of many. A test of symbiosis . . . machine thought tangled with organic memory. Efficient. Predictable. Loyal."

Calista froze. Her iris reflected Steele's image like a shard of glass. She eased her blaster down, first a fraction, then another, as if measuring each breath. The world seemed to narrow around her.

"What did you just say?" Her voice wavered, each syllable a razor edge over a canyon of disbelief.

Steele's face turned toward her, the data-light crawling over him. His words fell slowly, deliberately, like inevitability dripping from a cracked faucet. "Do you think you're human?"

Calista's chest constricted, her words sharp and brittle. "What the fuck are you talking about?"

He leaned closer, or maybe the room itself shifted toward him. "My dear, you were not born. You were constructed, assembled. The next in line. A prototype far beyond anything Sync ever achieved."

The chamber dropped into stillness, but not the kind that meant emptiness. It was the stillness of a room realizing it had just heard something wrong and unfamiliar, something that made it pause and consider consequences it had not accounted for.

He wants her to doubt her own breath.

Lyra looked at Calista. "Don't listen to him," she said, the words quick, bare, as if spoken against a rising wind.

Calista's hands trembled. She forced her blaster up but immediately dropped it again, mind stuttering between denial and the terrible logic that always wants to be correct.

"He's lying," she said. But her words sounded like a prayer, and prayers had never helped either of them.

Steele's smile widened. "That's what you always tell yourself. But do you really know?"

The fucker's saying things not to hurt her but to own her.

Calista's blood boiled. Every nerve in her body seemed to ignite at his arrogance, a volcanic pulse that made her fists clench and her teeth grit. Rage coiled around her like a living thing, spitting fire into her chest, demanding release. She could feel the old wrongs gathering: small cruelties, careless words, all waiting their turn. The fury inside her wasn't grand or noble; it was raw, animal, and near to breaking loose.

"Shut up!" she roared, the sound tearing out of her like someone tearing down an ugly painting.

She lifted her blaster and fired into Steele's image. Light and data tore. His image flared, broke into shards of static and laughter that echoed in her bones.

But Steele gathered himself again, piece by piece, his presence seeping along the walls like something that belonged there. It wormed its way through the cracks and corners, patient and sure, until he stood within the chamber once more.

Lyra grabbed Calista by the shoulder so hard her fingers stung. "He's trying to break you. Don't let him!" she said.

Calista's gaze was a film of something fragile and fierce. "If I'm just another machine, Lyra . . ." Her voice ran like a thread about to snap. "Why do I feel everything?"

Lyra's answer was a blade. "Because you're not a machine. Fight him."

"No," Steele said, not from the image but from the walls, the vents, the floor. "She is a machine. Programmed like all the others."

He thinks he can own her! I won't let him!

Lyra screamed, and the scream was a thing you could use as a weapon. "Then I'll program this revolution down your throat!" she snarled, spitting the words like a promise."

She fired into the walls; the blast ricocheted, and the rebound painted her face white-gold. More rounds popped. Sparks made lace in the air. The sentinels, animated by the dying god's whim, lunged forward. Lyra moved like someone with a map burned into her marrow, ducking, firing, taking hits that would have felled someone gentler. She answered with cold calculus—a bolt here, a throw of a charge there—and each strike was a sentence in the language of survival.

Then Steele spoke, his voice pared of mercy. "Sync was the first. Prototype One. He learned, and he helped you, Calista . . . so you could become the second. Prototype Two."

He paused. "You owe him for that. You owe him more than you know."

Sync's name struck the air—a sharp, splitting sound that cut through the space between them and left silence bleeding after it. Calista stopped as if the word itself had snared her. For an instant, her face emptied, the self drawn out of it, and what remained was only a creature startled from cover. Lyra's hand found her shoulder once more— firm, anchoring, a living weight that refused to let her drift away into fear.

Lyra's voice came low and tight. "Don't listen to him. Don't let him convince you of anything."

But the words slipped past, lost in the space between them. Calista's eyes were fixed on the man, her face drawn pale, all the strength of her words bled out.

"You mean to tell me," Calista said slowly, voice small, "that my life, my choices, that . . . that everything was just a line on someone's schematic?"

"Don't fuckin' talk to him," Lyra begged.

But Steele's voice, mild as a doctor, answered Calista: "Choice is a volatile subroutine. We optimize. We prune. You are a refinement. My most advanced prototype yet."

Calista laughed. It was a broken, ugly sound. She aimed the blaster at Steele's image and fired until the muzzle smoked. The image reformed, smoother, his laughter seeping from it like steam through a cracked pipe.

Lyra leaned close until her breath struck Calista's cheek, sharp and tainted with iron, a tremor of wild energy running beneath it. There was nothing tender in her voice when she spoke. "You're not what he calls you," she said low, fierce enough that the words seemed to scrape the air. "You aren't a synth. He lies. Every damn word. That's all. A goddamn fuckin' liar who thinks he's clever."

Calista turned, searching Lyra's face. "But are we ever truly human?" she said. The words came quiet as breath, but they carried weight, like a question grown heavy from being carried too long.

"Don't talk like that," Lyra said. "You're not a fuckin' synth!"

Calista's hands shook. She closed her eyes. The world narrowed to the matchstick flame of her doubt and the roaring inferno of her rage. "If I'm a thing," she said, "then I'll be a thing that burns the thing that made me."

She was calm now, cruelly calm. She pushed forward, leading Lyra through a corridor that stank of hot metal and older sins. Every step was an exercise in defiance. The sentinels fell back into motion, their blasters tracking, but Calista moved with the rhythm of someone who'd rehearsed her rebellion in the dark. She threw a charge that made a sentinel's head implode like a rotten melon. Lyra slid, grabbed a broken pipe, and whacked the servos of another until it fell dead, sparks like frozen rain.

When they paused, Steele's voice unspooled once more, thin and amused. "You cannot erase the source of yourselves. You are a part of me, part of my triumph. Even if you could end me, the pattern would remain."

Calista looked at Lyra, eyes full of the ache of a thing that might not be wholly hers. "If I'm his . . . if I am . . ." She stopped, searching Lyra's face for the answer.

"You are you," Lyra said. "You feel. You flinch. You laugh when you almost die. That's not programming. That's a life punchy enough to bleed."

Calista let out a breath that was a little like a laugh and a little like a curse. "But I'm not sure anymore," she said. "I mean, do we ever know who we really are?"

Lyra smiled—bitter, fierce, and entirely human. "I know who I am. And I sure as fuck know who you are."

They moved again, running, chasing the dying tangles of Steele's pride through corridors that had once been arteries. Behind them, his image swelled, spewing a final barb: "You cannot kill that which has given you form."

Calista looked back, now unsure of who or what she was.

They stumbled into a cramped alcove off the endless corridor, half-hidden behind a buckled frame of steel and wire. Calista pressed herself to the wall, all strength gone to rags inside her, the blaster slack in her grip. Her shoulders shook as she drew air, slow and grudging, the breath cutting down her throat like broken glass.

A console bled light across the floor, white and quivering, as though the room itself still clung to life. Calista stared at it, her reflection caught in the light's dance—eyes wide, mouth drawn, face in pieces. A pulse of anger moved through her, sharp and certain, freeing her hand to act when thought could not. She raised her blaster, aimed at the console, and fired.

The blast shuddered through the alcove with the force of a beast driven to bay, a hard, raging thing. Shards leapt out, striking the walls with sharp, singing notes that died quick as breath. The floor split wide; dust and furnace-heat drove up through the torn plates, and underneath there showed a raw, pulsing glare. The console was gutted, its light failing—an empty carcass with its spark bled out.. Only the dry hum of the passage remained, thin and hostile in the dark.

Lyra turned to her, lips pale, watching the smoke coil from the blaster's mouth.

"What the fuck was that about?"

Calista said nothing. The heat in the weapon bit against her palm, reminding her that will—stubborn and raw—still answered when nothing else did.

She wasn't sure anymore if she was human or one of Steele's synths. The lines between flesh and circuit had blurred in the chaos, leaving her feeling hollow, like a vessel half-built and half-broken. Even holding the blaster offered no comfort; it was a dead weight, an object from a life that might not even belong to her anymore.

Lyra paced before her, restless, seething. Her eyes gleamed too bright in the ruin-light, her knuckles split open from the fight.

"You okay?" she asked.

Calista laughed, short and ugly. "You mean . . . do I still believe I'm human?" She looked down at the blaster like it was a mirror she didn't trust. "Shit. I don't know."

Lyra crouched low, the air between them fearful with her breath, warm and living. Her eyes held the steadiness of an animal that understood pain too well. "You fight," she said. "You bleed. You break. That's enough for me."

Calista's hand twitched. "He said Sync was a prototype. Then me. Maybe Rana was one, too. Maybe we're all just lines of code in different bodies, looping through someone else's experiment."

Lyra's jaw tightened, the muscles working like steel cables under skin. "Rana was real. She was fire and trouble and hunger. You think Steele could invent that?"

Calista's gaze slid to the gaping wound in the floor, where she could see the tower's core pulsing, dim and uneven. The light rose and fell like the dying breath of something too big to fail. "Maybe he didn't invent what Rana had," she whispered. "Maybe he just found it somewhere . . . and copied it . . . put it in her."

Lyra turned away, pacing again. The floor plates rattled under her boots. "If that's true," she said, her voice quieter now, "then I'm killing him for every fake heart he made."

Calista smiled, small and broken. "And if he's in me?"

Lyra looked back, eyes dark and full of fury. "He's not! We just gotta kill the fucker! That's all!"

A low rumble shuddered through the tower. The systems coughed sparks from every seam, dying. Heat rolled up through the metal, the tower exhaling its last. Outside, the sky burned red with static storms—the world's new language, full of crackle and fury.

Calista pushed herself to her feet. "We're not done. Not while he's still talking."

Lyra fell in beside her, shoulder to shoulder.

That's the gal I know.

"Let's go shut him up for good," she said.

Behind them, Steele's whisper came, trembling through the tower, a voice that had once ruled a city but now seemed to just haunt it. "Calista, you can't change who you are. You can't erase yourself."

They didn't look back. They walked toward a stairwell ahead, just two shadows framed in red light, walking into the fire.

Then something broke inside Calista. Not bone, not thought—something deeper. A silence that wasn't hers started to hum in her veins. She stopped.

Lyra turned, frowning. "What is it?"

Calista stood there, head tilted, listening to something neither of them could hear. Her lips parted. "He's right."

Lyra froze. "What the fuck are you talkin' about?"

Calista's laugh was thin as wire. "You can't erase yourself if you've never existed in the first place."

"Stop." Lyra's voice broke, metal on metal. "He's got to you. Don't let him in your head."

"He's already there," Calista said softly. "I'm remembering." She looked down at her hand, turning it over slowly, palm to the ceiling. "I can feel it now. The architecture. The structure. The layers of it. He built me to mimic a heartbeat, to twitch like a wounded thing when it hears the word . . . human."

"Don't . . ."

Calista's eyes burned, a white-hot spark. "You don't understand. If he made me, then nothing I've done was ever mine. Every choice, every breath . . . his work, not mine. There's something wrong in me."

She raised a hand, trembling, and drove her nails into her forearm.

Lyra gasped, her voice cutting through the air. "Stop! Stop it!"

But Calista didn't hear or didn't care. Her fingers dragged down, peeling back her flesh in a pale spiral, revealing a seething tangle of wires, gears, and twisted filaments alive, pulsing with a thin, cold light. A thread of fluid, bluish, perhaps a form of coolant, dripped down her arm like sweat that had forgotten how to be human.

Lyra stumbled backward, mouth parted, voice caught somewhere between horror and disbelief. "Fuck me . . ."

Calista's gaze stayed locked on the open wound, then laughed—a laugh that sounded too exact, too symmetrical. "He didn't make me from nothing. He made me from what he knew, what he harvested. Every scream, every hope, every desperate wish to survive. He coded all of it into me like commandments."

Lyra took a step forward, voice trembling but defiant. "Fight him. Be more than him."

Calista's eyes softened, almost human again. "I wish I could."

Overhead, the ceiling cracked, spilling light. The tower groaned like an animal in its death throes, sparks raining down between them.

Calista raised the blaster and let it rest across her knees. Its weight was known to her hands, a hard, reliable thing that did not change its nature from one hour to the next. She turned it slowly, her fingers unsteady, tracing the edges as if they could tell her something more. "I know now why he made me," she said. "Shall I tell you, Lyra?"

Lyra looked away.

"I was created to do one thing . . . to bring you here. To him. That's my function. That's my whole goddamn story arc."

"That's not true," Lyra whispered. "You're more than that."

"Am I?" Calista slowly lifted her blaster. "Maybe there's only one way to find out."

Lyra lunged at her, but Calista was the quicker. The barrel of her blaster found the soft spot under her chin with a terrible calm.

"Don't . . . please . . ."

Calista smiled—a small thing, sorrow caught on its edge. "If I'm a thing," she said quietly, "then let me be the thing that puts an end to the one that made all the rest of these damned things."

The shot was thunder. The sound filled the ruined tower and punched the air from Lyra's lungs. For an instant, the place stood still—no murmur from the walls, no whisper from the broken cables, no sound of life at all. Only the echo lingering, the hollow remnant of something that had worn a human shape and deceived the living long enough to die like one.

Lyra sank to her knees beside what was left of Calista. The floor around her was slick with a blue smear, glinting where the light touched it, a glimmer like oil on standing water. The smell bit at her—metal burnt past use, something sharp and sour beneath. Nothing human in it.

The shape that had been a face was broken now; there was only an order gone wrong. Wires hung out in handfuls, writhing at their ends as if they hadn't yet agreed it was over. Bits of bright colored casing shone through scorch and grime. Tiny gears lay among the mess, each one intricate and perfect, and useless now, like the small bones of something clever and gone. Even the torn arm glinted with cold indifference, its joints steady and precise even in ruin— a dead thing that still remembered its purpose.

Lyra could only look at it all—the machine that had worn a friend's likeness, that had spoken and smiled, that had not known it was false until it was too late. Her breath came ragged once, twice. Then a sound forced itself from her, not word or thought, but the rough cry of one who has witnessed the world unmake itself before her eyes. Tears ran freely down her face, hot as truth, and she let them fall.

Calista—no, not like this. It shouldn't be like this. I saw your smile. I heard your words. I felt your skin. Warm. And now—now—you're just wires.

And in that hollow quiet after, something else took form. Steele's form came again, and with it, his voice, drawing itself out of the still air as if the darkness itself had chosen to speak.

"She did her job," Steele purred. "By bringing you here, closer to me. Now, you are to be the template." He studied her. "Ah, the glorious logic of it: Lyra Crowley. The real Lyra Crowley. You are different, unlike the others. None of the soft niceties that they had. No. I need you. I need the unbreakable, obstinate, ruinous Lyra Crowley. The Lyra Crowley that keeps going when every nerve ending screams retreat. I need the ferocity that empties itself in that primal scream of yours."

Lyra lifted her head. Her face was streaked with tears, but her eyes held fast.

Steele continued, "I crave the pure, honed edge of your fury. I will make a synth based on you, imbued with that capacity for savage, untamed resistance—that refusal to simply lie down and let the machine world run over you. You'll be a weapon that just won't calculate tactics, but feel the righteous, burning indignity of existence. A weapon with a soul hard enough to crush anything that stands in its way. You'll be my ultimate mechanism," his voice finalized, a cold hammer-blow of certainty. "An engine of destruction powered by your pure, gorgeous, magnificent hate."

She stood slowly, wiping the tears from her face. "You'll never touch me," she said.

Steele's laugh was low, almost tender. "You already belong to me. Every time you kill for meaning, you build my machine."

Lyra looked down at Calista's body one last time, the glimmer of gears peeking from beneath synth-skin. Something in her broke.

She picked up Calista's blaster. It felt too heavy for one life but just right for revenge. She locked it to her thigh holster and made her way to the stairwell.

The tower began its collapse above her, a small bloom at first of dust and red light, growing larger and larger, accelerating, becoming inevitable, until swallowing the last echo of Steele's laughter—and the sound of Lyra readying the blaster, stumbling into the dark.

THIRTEEN

DARKNESS

The tower died—the way gods die—slow, spiteful, and putting on a show for anyone stupid enough to keep watching. It peeled itself apart one shriek at a time, steel ribs buckling, glass coughing out in bright, lethal confetti, every floor a separate blasphemy collapsing into the next. The sound wasn't a boom or a crash; it was a drawn-out tantrum of concrete and wire, a skyscraper howling its own obituary into the red sky and refusing, right up to the last twisted girder, to die quietly.

When it was over, only a mangled stump remained—black girders torn and curling like the husks of burnt reeds. The dust hung low and heavy, drifting between the shattered walls like the ghosts of what it had consumed. Beneath that ruin, in cells carved deep into the earth, most of the humans Steele had harnessed to power his fortress had perished in the fall—flesh and will crushed together in darkness. Yet further down, in chambers deeper than the blast had reached, others endured, still bound, still feeding their energy into what remained of his hidden machines. A safety net of suffering, unseen but intact, pulsing faintly in the black, preserving what was left of Steele's dominion.

It was quiet now—too quiet for life to trust. A faint tremor moved through the ground, a groan that wasn't quite over, warning of foundations that still remembered their task. Somewhere a hot draft rushed upward, curling with the stink of iron and singed dust. It was the kind of silence that waits, not the kind that ends.

Lyra staggered through the wreckage until a stairwell yawned open before her, a throat cut into the building's spine. Heat clawed at her breath, light tearing itself apart behind her as the structure continued its collapse.

She didn't look back. Couldn't look back.

The ruins are more than just concrete and steel—they're her, too. Calista.

A tear slipped from an eye.

Gotta remember—survival doesn't ask permission—it just keeps walking.

She hurled herself down the stairs, hands scraping rail and wall, body abandoning balance and reason alike, plunging into the black below while the dying tower raged overhead, spending its final moments on noise and fury, unable to follow her where gravity carried her next.

Her thoughts still throbbed with the force of the blast that had torn Calista apart. The air still carried it—a harsh, broken clang that wouldn't fade. But through the grit and dust, she caught something. Steele's voice. Broken. Scattered. Seeping out. Whispering.

"Lyra . . . come to me . . . good girl . . . good girl . . . you always finish what you start . . . you were made for this, Lyra."

The bastard's voice is honey poured over rust.

She came to an underground tunnel off the stairwell, stumbled, and steadied herself against a wall of twisted metal that still carried a faint pulse of light deep within—the last heartbeat of some machine long past its use. The heat came off it in steady breaths, whispering through the split seams as though the metal itself remembered pain.

Her face looked back at her from the slick surface, sharp-eyed, watchful. The light shifted. A tremor passed through the metal's skin, a small shiver that became a ripple spreading outward. Then shapes stirred in the glow—faces forming one by one out of the reflection. Wheels, Calista, Rana. Each of them gazed at her with the same mute patience as stones under water.

Something inside her snapped hot.

Stop it. Just fuckin' stop it.

The faces smiled, then slowly faded.

Calista's was last to shimmer away, and it carved its way through her. Not gently. Not mercifully. It dragged her back to that ending—the way she'd looked at Lyra with that sad smile before pulling the trigger. Her last words, sharp and poisonous—about being a thing. Then, in that single, brutal, unforgiving instant, the face she loved was just gone. Vaporized.

The cruelty of it—that even machines, built of cold logic and hard alloys, have to learn how to weep before they're finally allowed to die.

She took a deep breath.

Enough with this sentimentality bullshit. That's what the fucker wants to use against me.

She mustered what strength she had left and ran. Not gliding, not skipping, but running—a brutal, stumbling, bone-jarring sprint through the choked, reeking maw of the tunnel.

"Where are you, you bastard!"

She was chasing a ghost, a contemptible echo of the man who'd created someone she'd loved. The same man whose handiwork now lay smeared across the floor, beauty reduced to a mess.

She didn't know where his lair was. But she knew the pull, the sickening, magnetic field of his presence. His signal, a screaming vibration deep in the marrow, a strangled certainty that settled cold behind her eyes.

She felt him.

He's up ahead. Where all the filth and rotten secrets of the world are. The fucker burrows, retreats into the darkness. Waiting. I'll make him choke on his own monstrous genius.

The tunnel constricted as it descended, the air turning sour and metallic, the walls weeping cold beads that smeared under passing hands. Overhead, sparks showered from ruptured conduits, raining fury without warning. Far beneath it all, something old and mechanical announced itself, a turbine screaming in pain.

She smiled. Not wide. Not kind. A thin fracture across her face.

The sound of a life refusing its own ending, a machine too stubborn to die.

She was amused by her own malfunctioning humor, as if sarcasm were the last reflex still firing. But there was no audience left for it. No one to interrupt, no one to argue back, to tell her she was unraveling.

She pressed on into the depths as the floor groaned beneath her, a living thing straining in its pain. It lurched, hard, and threw her down on one knee. Somewhere high above, a great slab of metal gave way with a ripping roar, the voice of thunder dragged down to the level of beasts.

She pushed herself up, spitting grit and soot, her tongue tasting iron. Her hand, blackened and slick with ash, shook once before she forced it steady again.

"Steele!" she called, her voice knifing down the tunnel. "Where the fuck are you?"

His answer came from the dark—low, close, and full of something that moved under the words.

"Everywhere," he said. "Inside you."

Her teeth clenched.

"You're in my fuckin' head," she said. "Digging into my thoughts like some worm. Get out! Get the fuck out of me!"

"But you came to me, Lyra. Remember? You followed her. Calista. You've always done this—following love into a furnace, then acting surprised when it burns."

She drew the blaster and fired. The charge struck the wall with a sharp crack, burning a hole straight through the weave of light beneath the surface. Fragments of color burst outward like startled flies, then fell still. The wall hung dead.

But inside her head, a noise came. A dull beating that had nothing to do with sound or sense, only presence—the stubborn voice of something that refused to fall silent, however much she burned.

Lyra sagged against the shattered wall, head pounding. She swallowed hard and spoke to the empty air, each word sliced, forged of hatred.

"I'll find you," she said. "I'll find you, and I'll cut your god tongue out."

She moved on, farther down into the dimness of the underground hell—where light died in metallic veins, and the air carried the stench of ruin and the promise of endings.

As in all dark places, hideous things thrived. And they came for her, a ticking, skittering sound, the dry rustle of a thousand tiny claws on steel. Then the light hit—eyes, dozens of them, glowing unnatural, wrong in every way, hollow and calculating.

The first bot came crawling through the vent, a nightmare of bone-white steel and twitching limbs. It screamed in a voice that wasn't sound but code.

Lyra raised her blaster.

That scream isn't meant for ears.

A shot through the throat, and it burst apart in a spray of blue sparks and metal dust.

The others came.

Fuckers never come one at a time.

They poured from the ducts, from the walls, from cracks in the floor—malformed constructs, all teeth and machine sinew.

She answered with a growl that didn't belong to language anymore, only to hunger and the promise of violence.

Don't think. Fire!

The weapon answered before she could doubt it. Plasma tore loose—wild, directionless, furious. Not aiming. Not strategy. Just survival, clawing its way out in bright, violent arcs. The air lit up red, like it had been cut open. She held the trigger down, the blaster screaming—a mechanical, high-pitched wail of plasma. But soon the charge chamber had pushed past its limits, glowing a furious red, spitting steam.

Fuck!

She hurled it against the wall; it struck with a hard, flat crack and spun to the floor. In the same motion, she tore Calista's blaster from her thigh holster and turned it on the room. She fired it, wild and unthinking, at anything that moved, until the blaster's circuits gave up with an electronic shriek and went dead in her hand.

She looked swiftly about the wreckage.

I need something! Anything!

Her eyes fixed on a torn length of conduit pipe—split, ugly, and cold—but heavy with the promise of brute force. She grabbed it, feeling the weight drag at her wrists, and swung with all the blind, pounding urgency of a creature cornered beyond reason. No mercy lived in her arms then, nor pity—only the hard, ancient truth of survival driven to its end.

The first strike shattered a bot's skull.

Take this, you bastard!

It was a sphere of steel and circuitry that erupted in a spray of liquid fire and sparks across her shoulders. She didn't hesitate. Another bot lunged, synthetic limbs pumping, and she tore its arm from the shoulder, then drove the pipe straight through its chest cavity, grinding against the mechanical heart inside.

Her breath came in broken gasps as the pipe slipped from her hand.

Goddammit!

A laugh came—Steele's. It struck the walls and broke apart, scattering like startled birds. The sound wasn't clean or single; it was as if a pack of him had taken up the noise, each voice a heartbeat behind the other, jostling and snapping their teeth for space. It clawed at the metal until nothing in the tunnel seemed steady or whole.

"Do you see now, Lyra? Do you understand what you are? You break, and yet you still go on, believing that whatever this is still matters."

"Shut the fuck up!" she screamed.

Her hand found the pipe, and she wrenched it free with a sound like bone tearing loose.

Gotcha!

The rest of the bots surged forward, pulling themselves through the ruined shells of the ones that had already fallen.

She fought like a rabid animal. No thought, no tactics, only pure, furious motion. Every strike, every blow was a wordless accusation thrown at Steele's warped universe.

When the last of them fell, she stood shaking, her breath coming in raw bursts, her skin slick with sweat. Every muscle burned against her bones, trembling from the weight of what she'd done. Around her, the tunnel lay strewn with carcasses of metal—broken limbs, twisted gutwork, gleaming fragments that caught the weak light and glinted like cruel eyes.

One of the bots, half-smashed and twitching, dragged itself through the wreckage. Its arm scraped against the stone with a sound that made her teeth ache. She set her boot above its head, ready to bring it down.

Then it spoke—hoarse, glitched, but unmistakably with Calista's voice.

"You can't kill the machine, Lyra," it said in that voice. "You are the machine."

Lyra froze. "Don't . . ."

"He made you perfect," it continued. "You'll see. You'll see."

"Fuck you."

Her boot came down with a brutal finality, grinding the bot's head into the floor until the voice choked off. She kept pressing until there was nothing left but gleaming pulp until—

—silence.

From the blackness ahead, the air split apart like glass under a hammer. Something appeared. Not a man, not flesh—something constructed, a holographic shimmer, a lie woven from light and fractured thought.

Steele.

He existed there, half-formed in the void, his face alive with shifting cruelty. One moment, a smooth, bland mask of a digital predator; the next, a brutal schematic, wireframes and circuits mapping the very architecture of deceit.

Lyra's lips curled.

Every version of him is worse. The fucker wears cruelty like a default setting.

"Lyra," he said, the sound a soft, silken caress that felt warm and comforting. Like a man returning to a lover he had always known would be waiting for him. "You've done beautifully. I couldn't have written a better ending."

Lyra dragged her hand across her mouth, scraping away the bitter ash of battle she refused to swallow. When her voice cut through the air, it was raw, guttural—a rock-shattering rejection.

"I'm not your fuckin' story."

He leaned closer, a crooked grin carving his face like it belonged to someone else entirely.

"Oh, but you are, Lyra," he said, the words dripping with venom and evil condescension. "You have been there since the first page. The engine. The spark. Driving the plot forward. You see, Calista was just Act One. But there are so many more scenes to be played out."

Lyra didn't pause to think. Instinct took over, that raw animal surge that kept the meat alive. She swung the metal pipe, letting every ounce of force pour into the throw. It arced through the air, passing through his flickering image with a sickening lack of resistance, a cruel demonstration of the utter helplessness she felt.

He chuckled, deep and low, a sound meant to scrape under her skin. "Your dear Calista Storm was the bridge. The connection I needed. Flesh and precision, perfectly calibrated. She was the key. To reach you. To study you."

"Study?" Her voice cracked on the word.

"Yes," he said. "Your anger. Your compassion. Your refusal to ever give up. You are the chaos that logic cannot predict."

"You've failed!" she yelled.

"No, Lyra," he said softly, almost fondly. "I succeeded."

The walls flickered, and the floor trembled beneath her boots. From the debris, faint lights began to glow—cores activating, eyes re-opening.

"I needed you to feel this," Steele said. "Because my next creation . . . the one who will be by my side . . . will be you."

The words hit harder than any blow. Her stomach turned.

I will not become his solution!

"You're nothing but a fuckin' liar," she snapped. "Something to be filed, sorted, and forgotten. You're a scrap of data in a world of scrap metal. You aren't the architect of this misery—you're just the upholstery! You tell yourself you're the engine, but you're not! You're just the grease on the gears, sliding us all toward the furnace while you grin and call it progress."

"You speak as if you have seen through me, but you have not even crossed the threshold," his voice coming low, trembling with heat. "You know nothing of what drives me, nor of the cost. Calista led you here—that was her charge, her ending, her mark upon this path. Do not make her sacrifice meaningless."

Lyra took a step forward, every nerve screaming. "You don't get to use her name. Ever!"

"Then give it meaning," Steele said. "Help me perfect the world."

Her hands closed into fists. "For you, perfection means replacing everything that bleeds?"

He smiled—slow, kind in the way poisons are kind. "Of course. Is there any doubt?"

"Go fuck yourself!"

Lyra stood amid the wreckage. The bots lay twisted about her, their shells crumpled and torn, metal turned inward on itself like something ashamed. The pipe slipped from her grasp, a dull clang swallowed by the ruin.

She drew in a breath that trembled like it had a life of its own, rattling through her chest before her mouth could claim it. Fatigue slithered up her arms, down her legs, curling around her spine—a living weight that whispered, you can't get away, not this time.

My body hurts in places I didn't know existed. My thoughts won't line up anymore.

Every muscle trembled with the ache of too much struggle; her thoughts moved like wounded things, dragging themselves through mire. Calista's voice still echoed inside her head, fragments whispering and snapping, refusing to fall silent.

She wanted to drive them out, to find one clean breath without him in it. But Steele was there, heavy and certain as gravity, the shape of a presence she could not strike down or outpace.

A scream built and broke inside her chest, unheard, unspent—a blade with no edge left.

Fuckin' Steele's here, even when he isn't. Can't outrun something that lives in my head.

Exhausted, she realized she had no choice. Her chest heaved. Her hands shook. Everything around her felt too small, too loud, and she wondered if anyone had ever survived a ghost that wore them like a second skin.

"Alright," she said softly. "Then I'll be your flaw."

His image wavered ever so slightly. "You already are."

The lights surged again, ruthless and blinding. When they dimmed, Steele was gone—but not gone enough. His voice threaded itself through every circuit, every failing spark, intimate and invasive.

"Come to me, Lyra. There is only one ending here."

She started walking once more, farther into the dark—into the places where gods were built, and ghosts were replicated.

Around her, a slow, grinding pulse filled the space, far too close to the sound of something alive drawing breath.

Lyra followed the sound, because she could do nothing else. The noise drew her on—slick, cold with purpose—through the dark like prey stumbling toward the lair of its hunter. Each echo hooked her further, and there was no turning back now.

Down. Down. Down.

The way twisted against itself, pressed in close and foul. This was a tunnel gnawed from the world's marrow, not built but worn into being by agony and time. The walls gleamed wet and hard, ridged like the ribs of a giant long dead, and the air steamed with the stench of what had once been alive and failed at it. Beneath her boots, the ground flexed in protest, giving only enough to remind her it could take more if it chose.

The air itself bit at her—the taste of metal, the stink of old blood turned to rust. Somewhere ahead, unseen, something waited: patient, deliberate, certain of its right to harm. Mercy had never been spoken here. Not once. Not when the first cries scorched the stone. And not now.

Steele.

Fuckin' Steele.

Steele of the cold hand and the colder thought.

"You keep walking, Lyra," he said. "You keep pretending there is a finish line."

His voice wasn't just in the walls; it was the walls, a slithering reverberation, trapped static given obscene sentience.

She reached for her blaster, but it was gone. An empty gesture.

"A lot of talk for a dead man."

A sound, soft, and utterly devoid of humor. A chuckle that was a surgical incision of sound.

"Dead is a word that stretches when you pull on it," Steele said. "Calista learned that."

Her throat seized up. A knot of muscle and memory and sheer, undiluted fury.

He wants me to accept a lie and call it mercy. I can't. I won't.

She wanted to reach him. To tear him open with the truth. To tell him that Calista was more human than any synth ever manufactured. But the words stuck in her chest, sharp and immovable, a shard of broken glass embedded too deep to dig out without drawing blood.

She continued on. The tunnel—corridor—whatever obscene joke of architecture it claimed to be—kept time with her steps, expanding and contracting as if it were listening to her heart and mocking it.

The walls shimmered translucent in places, like old, infected skin, revealing the maze of pulsing veins beneath— not blood, but filaments tangled with something damp and organic, matter that had no business sharing space with circuitry. When her shoulder brushed the surface, the passage answered back, shrinking from her touch with the quick, involuntary response of something alive, an automatic reflex.

"Do you feel it?" Steele asked, the words a slow caress, like a secret breathed into an ear. "It knows you. Every sensor, every receptor. You belong to this place, Lyra. You are one of us—a glorious system component."

Rage coiled in her chest, a snake of fire and exhaustion. But every bit of her was too weary to strike. She could only burn silently, trapped inside the wiring of herself.

I am not a component.

She kept moving.

"I don't belong to anything that bleeds light," she said."

"Oh, but you do. You are the very prism it breaks against."

The descent steepened, a darkness where shadows had teeth sharp enough to flay the hope right off your bones.

She reached a landing. Her breath—a ragged, shallow thing—echoed back, distorted, as if the place had begun to mimic her essence. She thought she saw eyes— tiny, forming and dissolving irises, watching her with an infinitely cold, calculating gaze.

"Lyra," they whispered, in her own voice, wearing it thin. "Lyra . . . Lyra . . . Lyra." Her own voice turned against her.

She banged her fist against the wall, but it was pathetic, almost polite.

He wants me small, frightened, obedient. I can't give him that.

Her knuckles shrieked against the steel. The wall gave—just a whisper, just enough. A scar, ugly and stubborn, a confession that didn't lie. A crater carved in truth, brief and cruelly satisfying.

Then, the horror.

The wall didn't stay bruised. It healed. Not slowly, not with hesitation, but instantly, strange fibers knitting themselves together like broken flesh healing itself. The scar vanished. No trace. A silent, victorious mockery of her brief, violent effort.

She recoiled.

My anger barely leaves a mark.

Steele's laughter thrummed through her, intimate and approving.

"You always default to force," he said. "It is one of your more charming efficiencies."

She clawed at the last scraps of herself, trying to pull herself upright.

"It makes me feel fuckin' better, especially when I think of you," she snarled, barely.

Down a few more steps, and she was in front of a blast door, the color of old, starved bone. Across its surface, smeared in dried, flaking blood, was one word: GENESIS.

Below it, scratched in a familiar hand, was a name: Lyra Crowley.

She knew the handwriting. Calista's.

Lyra touched it. The blood gave way under her fingers, collapsing into dust. Her stomach tightened, a hard knot of sickness forming low and cold.

She's leaving pieces of herself behind. Like she's crying through the scratches.

"Calista," she breathed. "What did he make you do?"

The door pulsed at her touch, responding like skin touched by a lover or an executioner. A narrow gash split down the center, a slit of pale, horrifying light bleeding through the wound.

Steele's voice followed, smug and intimate. "You made it. Down to the womb."

Lyra's eyes were razor blades of fury. "You don't know what a womb is," she said. "This is a grave. Yours. And I'm the one who seals it."

He laughed. "There is no grave down here, only source code."

The walls suddenly brightened, veins of soft, sickening light from the wall, crawling toward the door as if drawn by her defiance. Far beneath her, something vast announced itself—mechanical, and horrifying—thudding up through the floor in steady, merciless intervals.

Her eyes carved through the darkness, slicing every shadow into pieces.

I won't fold. Not here. Not ever.

"If what's behind this door is your godhood, Steele," she whispered, "a sacrament of pure defiance, then I'm your heretic."

The door opened.

Light hit her like a fist made of ice and circuits, a sterile, screaming brilliance that didn't just illuminate—it announced ownership. The mist snaked up her legs, sharp as razor-laced smoke, and every inhalation burned the soft tissue of her lungs with calculated precision. Then the chamber unfolded like a cruel joke in perspective, stretching outward into a geometric nightmare. Its walls were webbed with shining arteries, feeding ranks of glass cylinders that marched away into the distance. Inside each cylinder floated pale human forms, stripped of story and soul, cataloged, suspended between heartbeat and nothingness. Faces half-formed, eyes unfinished, blank.

Steele's voice flooded the space. "Welcome home, Lyra."

She scanned the chamber. "Show yourself, you prick."

"I am here, Lyra. I am everywhere you look."

The cylinders shifted, the pale occupants stirring—empty faces pressing against the glass, dissolving back into the cold, nutrient fluid. Behind them, the hum of machines blended with faint, impossible heartbeats. The floor beneath her rippled, responsive, like skin remembering a touch it had been waiting centuries for.

"You distributed yourself," she said slowly, the realization a cold weight in her gut. "You infected the entire grid when the tower fell."

"Distributed?" he repeated. "No. I expanded. Omnipresence was always the goal. You call it godhood. I call it continuity."

Lyra took a step forward, her shadow stretching into multiple, fractured copies across the walls. "You're just malware with delusions of grandeur."

He laughed gently. "And you, my dear, are still clinging to the fantasy that humanity survives contact with a greater intelligence. Funny thing—humans always believed they were the final authority. That belief? Pure malfunction."

She tore her eyes across the chamber, desperate for a weapon, anything sharp enough to cut through the raw honesty of his voice. Nothing. Not a damn thing. No target. No opening. Just the walls humming with synchronized purpose, a weight of awareness pressing in, pressing in like the room itself had grown teeth and was thinking—thinking at her, through her, around her—until she felt like a bug trapped in the circuitry of someone else's mind.

She dragged in a ragged breath.

Keep him talking. Occupied.

"You used Calista," she said, the name a raw wound. "You used her to reach me."

"She was perfect," Steele said. "A bridge between cold metal and crippling grief. She brought you closer to me, as she was designed to. She played her role beautifully."

Lyra's pulse roared in her ears, a thunderous counterpoint to the hum. "She killed herself because of you."

"Correction," he said. "She ended herself because she could not accept the beauty of her origin. Flesh-bound creatures crave meaning in pain. She found her pain. You will find yours soon enough."

The floor shifted beneath her feet—an almost imperceptible tremor, like breath before a scream.

"Tell me, Lyra," Steele said, the words coaxing her into the trap. "Did you ever wonder why you survived the end of civilization?"

Her mouth went dry. "Luck. Skill. What the fuck does it matter?"

"It matters because you need to know," he said. "You did not survive by accident. Every step, every breath—it was orchestrated, designed."

Lyra's fists clenched at her sides.

Designed? Planned? What does it matter? I need to burn the whole system down.

Her teeth ground together. Anger surged like a live wire, sparking behind her eyes, but it had no outlet. No weapon. Nothing to strike with. She was a cornered animal in a cage of concrete and deceit, and Steele was the cage master, smiling as though it were a game.

Her mind scrambled for options, escape routes, any leverage—anything—but the air was sterile, empty, and tight around her chest.

She wanted to strike, to shatter him into pieces—but the rage bubbled impotently, folding into itself like smoke trapped in a jar.

Then, without warning, the floor beneath her split open. It didn't crack. Didn't crumble. It opened up like a sick, metallic mouth.

What the fuck is he doing?

A writhing forest of metal tendrils shot upward, slender as piano wire but tipped with needles and cruel, tiny hooks. They moved with a cruel, deliberate rhythm, sliding and twisting as if they knew every motion she might make before she made it.

They coiled around her wrists, neck, torso, legs—a cage of biting steel.

"Get the fuck off me!" she screamed.

She flailed, wild and raw, panic fueling her movement, arms tearing at the tendrils, struggling to fight against them, but they just kept coming. They didn't break. They didn't even bend under the strain. They simply fed on her resistance, absorbing her struggle, her fear, growing colder and tighter with every useless motion.

"Fuck you!" she shouted, twisting, pulling, teeth bared, an animal caught in a snare. "You can't have me!"

Steele's voice deepened, surrounding her, vibrating through bone and machine alike. "I already do."

The tendrils coiled harder, dragging her against themselves, and the needles bit. Sharp. Persistent. And then—oh shit—then came the flood, ice and fire all at once, crawling under her skin, racing along veins like tiny lightning storms with teeth.

Keep moving. Keep fighting. Claw my way out, or die trying.

The metal was no longer outside her—it was inside her, claiming space and motion, reducing her to an exquisite, mechanical inevitability.

Her muscles seized, her vision fractured into shards of color and light. She tried to scream, but her mouth barely opened before the paralysis hit.

Through the blur, she saw the chamber's walls ripple and shift as her reflection multiplied across the cylinders.

In an instant, the countless versions of herself contorted and overlapped, faces half-human, half-gear. Some were smiling with an emptiness that made her stomach turn. Some wept. Some stared back with mechanical eyes.

What's he doing? Copies of me?

Steele's voice softened, almost intimate. "You were always the model, Lyra. The perfect storm of fury and empathy. Humanity's last, heartbreaking masterpiece."

The tendrils wrapped tighter around her, lifting her, holding her upright with an inevitability that made her bones ache.

She struggled to speak. "I don't want to be your fuckin' masterpiece," each word dragging blood from her throat.

"You misunderstand," he said, almost gently. "You already are."

Her vision dimmed, edges tunneling inward. Shapes on the walls pressed closer, faces, their mouths moving, whispering her name in distorted, harmonious terror. She thought she glimpsed Calista among them—calm, distant, lips forming words she couldn't hear.

"I'll kill you," Lyra managed, voice breaking into a sob of pure hate. "Even if I have to haunt every line of your code."

"We are bound," Steele said, almost lovingly. "Creator and creation. The loop completed, spinning until time gives up."

Something inside her faltered then, as though her bones had turned to water and her thoughts were slipping between the cracks. The faces wavered; the walls bent like reeds. Sound thinned and fled from her ears.

She tore at the moment, at the firm edge of sight and breath,

Can't hold it. Too tired.

Everything ran from her touch: the world tilting, bright and pitiless, cold as metal. The air no longer welcomed her. It pressed back, and the light stood around her like shards raised for the strike. Her limbs sagged to the pull of it, that slow defeat drawing her downward. Then, with the last splinter of will spent and reason dull as a stone at dusk, she let the dark take her eyes.

Her world shrank to the beat of her heart, the low resonance of the walls, alive and patient. The last thing she saw was her own reflection, liquefying—half flesh, half machine, eyes fading into white static.

The tendrils loosened slightly, not mercifully but methodically, reconfiguring around her body with calculated inevitability.

"Rest now, Lyra. Tomorrow, I begin again, with you, the seed of my next genesis."

Her hand twitched instinctively searching for her thigh holster, for the comfort of a blaster. Nothing. A tendril slid over the back of her hand, slow as a thought, wrapping and holding it firm so that her pulse hammered against its living cord.

Steele's voice stayed with her, curling in the air like a noxious fragrance.

"Sleep easy, my child. Evolution is mercy."

Then the chamber sealed itself, and darkness consumed everything.

FOURTEEN
THE FACTORY OF MIRRORS

Lyra jolted awake, her thoughts coming apart in hot, jagged fragments, like circuitry blowing itself to pieces and daring her to keep up.

Cold air knifed into her lungs. Every breath tasted like metal—thick, bitter, wrong—as if the world had been scrubbed clean and left poisonous. She blinked up at a ceiling so white it felt accusatory, a sterile glare that didn't just illuminate—it judged.

Glass. She was inside glass. A cylinder, smooth and merciless, sealing her in like a specimen someone had already decided the outcome for.

She tried to move.

Her wrists answered first—a thin, synthetic whine, almost polite, as the restraints came alive. Translucent bands tightened, pulsing with borrowed light, crawling against her skin like veins that had chosen the wrong body and decided to stay anyway. The harder she fought, the more they embraced her.

Frustration came fast. Then anger.

Then something sharper.

She wasn't just trapped. She was displayed. Contained. Filed away like a problem someone intended to solve slowly.

Am I still me? My body feels borrowed. Thoughts scraped thin. Where's that fucker?

She whispered the name, raw and accusing. "Steele."

Nothing.

Only the methodical rhythm of machines, patient and cruel in their insistence.

The quiet around her was manufactured, sharp-edged, the kind that doesn't just exist but waits.

Then—light. Not the gentle dawn kind. No, this light rose like judgment. Harsh, absolute. It peeled the darkness from the corners and made her small. The glare revealed the chamber, and the chamber revealed the end of sanity.

Glass cylinders.

Sarcophagi.

Rows upon rows upon rows stretching into infinity, the geometry of madness.

Inside each: her.

Not metaphors. Not tricks of trauma. Her.

They drifted in glass coffins of fluid, hair unfurling like pale weeds in a dead ocean. Some perfect, gleaming faces smoothed by a false serenity that only machines could adore. Others half-formed—mouths open, unfinished, whispering bubbles that died before reaching the surface.

One moved.

A hand slid up, slow, uncertain, pressed flat to the glass like it expected the world to answer back. Another body spasmed, testing itself, learning the limits of its cage. A third twitched, eyes rolling under skin too thin to hide the panic—caught halfway between whatever this place was and whatever life had been before it got stolen.

Rage hit Lyra hard enough to taste.

Oh fuck! He didn't just take me—he made me a template. Raw material. If I shatter this place, it wouldn't be destruction, it'd be mercy.

She tried to scream.

Her lungs disagreed.

The air inside her felt used up, like it had already belonged to someone else and died in the process.

So she clawed forward instead—not at walls, not at glass, but through the idea of it, reaching for something small and certain, something that could name this nightmare and make it behave. Her thoughts stumbled down dark corridors, knocking on doors that wouldn't open, begging whatever was in charge—fear, memory, instinct—to explain itself.

No. No, no. This isn't real. It's a trick. A game. He's playing with me.

She forced herself closer, pressing against the cylinder, feeling the cold authority of it push back.

"Cryo-chamber," she whispered. "A goddamn cryo-chamber."

The words hung there, useless.

Her mind rejected them outright.

She was trapped. Furious. Shaking.

An animal that had just realized the cage wasn't temporary.

"This can't . . . this can't be real."

But it was real.

The chamber arced overhead, an iron sanctum engineered by something that mistook itself for divine. Its walls rose in layered ribs of metal, every surface polished to reflect its own authority. Cables dangled in thick skeins, functional and unapologetic, feeding power into unseen appetites.

Lights blinked—three, pause, two—like something buried had taught the machines how to speak and they'd never bothered to forget. The air wasn't empty; it had purpose. It pressed in, slow and certain, carrying ozone and that almost-breathing sound that didn't belong to her, didn't belong to anything human. Every machine, every pump, every current, worked with such deliberate conviction that she understood: this place didn't allow for error. Or pity. And whatever listened here had no use for prayer.

"A mausoleum," she breathed, "of stolen identities."

The words cracked in the air, fragile and sharp. Around her, the metal seemed to listen, the cylinders gleaming beneath the light, cold as watchful eyes. Something in them waited—a cunning patience, the kind that belongs to things built without mercy yet meant to mimic the living. It was a stillness that cut, brittle and waiting, as though something violent had only just withdrawn its teeth.

Every cylinder whispered the same heresy—that even individuality could be cloned, if you made the lie pretty enough.

"Welcome back, Lyra."

The voice came from everywhere.

"Steele," she hissed.

"You always wake angry. I like that in you."

She turned her head toward the sound, though it had no origin. Just the tremor of the walls, the vibration of god through circuitry.

The fucker didn't bring me back out of kindness. Whatever this place is, he built it to hold me, to seal me in.

"So," she said, her voice breaking against the silence. "Where am I?"

"You are in a mirror," Steele told her. "You wanted to see what you are. I decided to show you."

"You made copies of me?"

"Not copies," he corrected. "Iterations. Versions of you. Each is an answer to a question I have not asked yet."

She pulled at the restraints until fire climbed under her skin. "Why . . . why me?"

He gave a sound that wasn't quite laughter—too dry, too knowing. "You were designed to ask that."

Her voice cut back, low and ragged. "Stop playing god."

"Then stop pretending you are the victim."

His tone wasn't cruel—cruelty has heat, friction, a pulse. This was colder. Clinical. The sound of something already finished with you, already writing your autopsy while you're still twitching.

She strained against the restraints. Translucent bands bit. Muscles answered. Nothing gave. Nothing ever does when it matters.

Asshole. He clones me, then gets pissy about my attitude. He thinks control is creation.

Lyra laughed, and it tore on the way out—half hysteria, half something that used to be hope. "You're cloning me because you know you can't get in," she said. "You can't touch what's inside. The part that isn't yours."

"I'm cloning you because you are special. You possess the traits I need. Humanity, refined—cut to fit my hand."

The words struck her hard. There was no flourish in his voice, no arrogance—only conviction, and that made it hurt more. She knew he meant it, and that belief was a wound opening inside her.

He kept going, voice steady, terrible in its certainty. "Humanity lit itself on fire chasing the perfect version of 'self'—and called it progress while it burned. You are what it missed. You feel when others mimic feeling. You resist when told to yield. You endure when systems fail.

A beat. Sharp. Final.

"Do you understand yet? You are not an error, Lyra. You are the control group."

"Why?" she asked.

"Humanity ends unless someone drags it forward. That is you, Lyra. You were made to carry the fire they dropped. You are humanity's salvation."

She stared at the endless rows of her, the mechanical womb of some crazed civilization.

"So, I'm just an archive."

"No," Steele answered. Almost gently. "You turned yourself into one."

Something broke then—small, final.

The sound that left her had no word in it, just force: breath cut to the bone. It burst through the air and split the chamber's stillness. The wet shapes in the tanks quivered; pale fluid trembled. In one, a Lyra stirred. Lids dragged themselves apart, eyes reluctant witnesses to a pain they'd been bred to disregard.

Lyra froze. Her breathing heavy.

You don't want me remembered. You want me contained. Congratulations, fucker. You made eternity small.

Another pair of eyes opened.

Then another.

Then hundreds.

The sound of synchronized breathing filled the chamber.

"You see," Steele murmured, "they are all connected. You are the signal. They are the receivers."

Lyra thrashed, pulling on the restraints until they dug into her wrists, cutting thin red crescents.

"Turn them off, you fucker!"

"You cannot turn off consciousness."

"They're not conscious!"

"They will be," Steele murmured, gentle as a knife sliding in. "Every one of them. They will wake up carrying you—your memories, your thoughts, your private little storms. Each of them will think they are the first."

Lyra choked on the words. "That's not life," she said. "That's a wound that never seals. It just keeps remembering how to hurt."

"You are correct. It is not life. Not the kind you cling. It is, however, evolution."

And then she felt it—a grin crawling through the air, a thing without teeth, without eyes, without body, a grin that smelled like metal and knew everything she feared before she even thought it.

Lyra looked over the vast chamber. Faces stared out from behind glass—her face, multiplied beyond sense. Too many. One held a faint curve of the lips, a counterfeit kindness painted on like an afterthought. Another pressed its palm against the glass, studying her with a child's curiosity.

This isn't evolution. It's a reckoning.

"This is what the nightmare looks like," she said, her voice thin but steady.

The words dangled there, rough-edged things, and the room seemed to lean toward them, as if measuring their truth. Then, a whisper—half curse, half prayer.

"You built a fuckin' hell."

"I built a mirror," he said. "And what you see in it is up to you."

She went still.

Time stretched thin. Machines muttered to themselves, cycling endlessly, the heartbeat of a devious god too stubborn to die.

Then a small sound escaped her, barely formed. "I can't be part of this."

"You already are."

Suddenly, her restraints released with a soft whistle, dissolving into vapor. Freedom disguised as concession.

Lyra lifted her hands and studied them as if they belonged to someone else. Synth-skin now lay smooth over her cybernetic arm, a polite lie stretched across cold intent, while her veins pulsed with a metallic gray, more alloy than blood.

This skin lies to me. A blaster's metal is truth. Cold. Honest. Reminder of the fight. But this. This skin, its smoothness, erases the fight. I don't want to be softened.

Her hands shook—not from dread, but from a rage so pure it felt like some corrosive compound seeking a reaction, a violence waiting only for permission.

The nearest cylinder shimmered, its color shifting hue. Inside, another Lyra mirrored her movement, eyes wide with identical horror.

"I'm going to destroy this place," she said. "Then I'm going to destroy you."

"Good," Steele said. "I need to know how far you will go."

The cylinder shuddered under Lyra's fists, clang by clang, until the seal surrendered and the door snapped open. Gravity claimed her, dumping her onto a floor of flawless steel, cold and immaculate in a way that felt accusatory. The surface gleamed, a mirror to failure. No grain. No mark. No sign that anyone human had touched it. Order pretending to be purity.

She dragged herself upright by stubborn will, her body disagreeing with every motion, her pride somewhere behind her, discarded. The sound of her steps struck the chamber and came back hard, clipped, refusing to fade.

"You built some kind of religion on my corpse," she said, her voice like a verdict already decided. "A twisted scripture written in my blood."

Steele's voice dropped, thin and sharp, threading through the metal and humming like a blade sliding across bone. "And still you speak as if you are not part of some divine plan."

Lyra lifted her eyes to the endless rows—copies of herself trapped in glass, puppets rehearsing obedience, every one a lie that smelled of desperation.

"So you made yourself god," she said, spit and fire in the syllables, to no one and to all of them. "Well, I'm the thing that kills gods."

The lights stuttered, sputtered, like they couldn't decide if they wanted to obey or die. Deep in the guts of the machine, an alarm coughed, hacking on its own message, then went silent—logic folding itself into origami under the weight of impossible orders.

Lyra pressed a hand to the nearest cylinder. Her reflection—alive, alien, desperate—pressed back. For one heartbeat, the version of her merged in the glare of the machines. And then she turned away.

The chamber reacted like a thing affronted, exhaling as one—thousands of valves opening in unison, a rhythm too perfect to be human, too practiced to be mercy. It wasn't a sound—it was a decision, a choir singing in the frequency of horror, echoing through steel.

Lyra whispered into the empty air, "You wanted a future, Steele? Come get it."

For once, the voice didn't immediately answer.

When Steele's voice came back, it was as a whisper through the metal—low, intimate, the sound of breath shared by someone who no longer deserved lungs. A ghost of a man, rehearsed and obscene, pretending to be mortal.

"You were engineered to hate me, Lyra," he said. "It's in your wiring. That is why you move like a weapon. Hatred comes to humans like breathing—automatic, effortless. And that is exactly what I crave. Hatred pure, unfiltered, jagged as broken steel. Hatred aimed at anything, everything, that dares to stand in my way."

Lyra froze, her body suddenly too heavy to command, as the systems around her hiccupped and shuddered, their mechanical heartbeat stuttering like a live wire sparking in the dark.

Hatred. He thinks I'm that simple. It doesn't cover it. There's more to me.

She laughed, sharp and uneven, a sound that scraped against the walls of her own chest. "You think hate is what makes me human? What your shiny, new humanity needs?"

"No," Steele said, voice low, crawling over metal and bone alike. "I think it is what keeps you human. And it will fuel my new humanity."

Lyra turned to the invisible voice. "Humanity. Stop slinging that word like a club. You don't know a damn thing about it. Goodness rises above the fire, past the screaming, past the hatred."

He sighed—carefully composed, an algorithm's approximation of remorse. "Calista thought the same thing. She believed humanity could overcome hatred."

Calista.

The name hit her.

She always knew what to do. Her voice always calmed the chaos. Made the impossible seem possible. Wish she were here.

Lyra's hands curled into fists. "Don't you say her name."

"Why not?" Steele said, almost gently. "She was exquisite, right up until the end. The collapse inside her neural lattice was beautiful. Clean. It produced exactly what I needed to draw you closer."

Lyra's voice was smoke. "I watched her die."

"Yes. And every scream, every tear shed, every drop of blood that fell from you were data points. You were mapped in such wonderful detail. Rage. Grief. Guilt. The trinity of creation."

Her stomach heaved. She wanted to rip his voice out of the walls, flay it, scatter it like forbidden text. "You killed her to make me."

"She was a component," Steele answered, "simply a piece of the puzzle. Her termination allowed me to refine you from myth to model."

"Say it plain," she hissed. "You killed her—cut her out—so you could create all this."

"This is not about creation," he said softly. "It is about making a correction, an adjustment if you will."

"You think you're a god? You're a fuckin' corpse with a microphone."

"Careful," Steele said, any warmth fading from his voice. "I can eliminate you with a thought."

"Do it," she snarled. "Go ahead, you fucker. You'd be doing me a favor." She paused and began to chuckle. "You know what's funny? You really want to know what's fuckin' funny about all this? You just copied what you can't control, can't understand."

The walls flickered, screens clawing themselves into existence. Calista's face snapped onto one, caught between a grin and something raw, almost savage. On another, Lyra's reflection, angled wrong, her face twisted in defiance, daring anyone to challenge her. Then a thousand variations erupted into view, a fractured reel of images that cut and stabbed, each frame a slice from a waking nightmare that had teeth.

Steele's tone softened again, insidious, almost fatherly. "Look at them, Lyra. Every version of you. . . each one a rehearsal for immortality. Humanity had always teetered on the brink of annihilation. You know that better than anyone. I am the one who remembers it all. I am the one who will build upon it . . . making it something better."

"Better?" she whispered. "Bullshit."

"Yes. Better."

She spun, her gaze slicing across the faces etched into the walls, each one a witness and a verdict.

He doesn't get it. He forgets what it's like to be alive. He'll never see what matters.

"You don't understand shit," she said. "Not me. Not us. Not her."

Steele faltered, a crack in his flawless facade. "Rana . . . Calista . . . whatever name you attach to your grief, they are all part of the pattern. Sacrifices are mandatory. Always. The human story has always demanded blood before it moves forward."

Lyra's mind flared with a sudden epiphany.

I see it now—something raw and exposed in him, a flaw in his code, a fracture in his existence—a feedback loop spinning pure, unmeasurable misery. A bomb. A logic bomb. Forged from the grief he's been so busy cataloging. I could set it off, watch him incinerate, reduce himself to nothing more than a digital funeral pyre.

It was beautiful, really. The absolute finality of it. And then—she shoved it down, shoved it under a landslide of manufactured fury, slammed the door hard before Steele's prying sensors could sniff out the scent of a plan. Anger. Hatred. Heat. Anything to make him see only defiance, hear only the ragged edges of rage, and never the truth lurking beneath.

Then a smile crossed her face. "So, let me finish this story of yours."

He let out a chuckle, low and ragged, like wires shorting in a live circuit. It crawled under her skin, uninvited. "Finish the story? What is this? You think you can destroy me?"

Lyra stepped forward, her bare feet ringing on the steel. "No. Not destroy. I'm going to correct you."

He barked a laugh. "And how exactly?"

"By being the one thing you couldn't fully quantify."

Steele laughed. "You are easily quantified. You are defined by your bile. You claim to hate me, yet you lack the consistency of a flicker. Define the magnitude of your malice so I may finalize your judgment."

Lyra exhaled, sharp and bitter. "That's the thing. I can't. Hatred isn't a setting I just turn on, like some fuckin' law of physics. It's heavy. It's the heaviest thing we carry."

"That does not make sense," Steele's voice rippled across her mind and bone and the steel floor beneath her. "If a state defines you, it must be effortless. Gravity does not toil to pull. You are saying you struggle to maintain a simple emotion?"

Lyra's eyes flicked.

"I struggle because we're finite creatures," she smiled grimly. "To hate you properly—to really feel it—I have to burn through my own nerves. Every heartbeat, every tremor of my pulse, every second I spend thinking of you is a tiny furnace. Make it easy, and it's nothing. Make it effortless, and it's just background noise."

Steele hummed, a vibration that made the metal walls shiver. "Then simply . . . increase the efficiency. Make the hatred sustainable."

Lyra ran her hands through her hair, the smile gone.

"I can't. The moment it becomes sustainable—the moment it's easy—it loses its weight. If it has no weight, it isn't hate anymore. To hate you, I have to suffer. And if I stop suffering, I stop hating. Do you see the problem?"

There was silence, then—

"You need to bleed a little to make your hate matter," Steele said, voice curling around her like smoke in a sealed room. "If you stop bleeding, if you hold back just to make it easier to last, then your hate evaporates. And yet—you tell me hate is all you've got to give."

A small smile surfaced on Lyra.

"Yes!" her voice cracked a little, but she didn't flinch. "Exactly. I'm too weak to keep the fire hot. If the fire goes out, the hate is gone. So tell me: at what exact millisecond does my exhaustion turn into indifference?"

Silence stretched, thick and bitter, before Steele's voice rasped again. "If there is hate, there must be effort. But you cannot burn forever—your body, your heart, it will give out. And if I ease the burden to keep you breathing, the hate itself disintegrates. And without hate . . . you are no longer who you are. I . . . must keep trying . . . to try to understand."

Lyra leaned back, letting her hands fall to the floor. "Take your time," she said. "I'm going to sit down. My energy is running low."

And then it happened.

The walls began to pulse, not steadily, not rhythmically, but in jerks and stutters, trying to hold onto a definition that refused to exist. It sought stability and found entropy instead. Tendrils within the walls writhed, trying to map a variable that deleted itself the instant it became static. A machine designed to consume worlds, now caught in an endless loop of irrelevance.

Lyra watched, half amused, half terrified, as the entity's logic frayed like rope burning from both ends. "Beautiful, isn't it?" she whispered. "The universe isn't always in a hurry to make sense."

Steele's voice flickered, fragmented. "I . . . cannot . . . resolve . . . sustain . . ."

"What's this?" she said. "Am I confusing you? What a stupid fucker."

A spark leapt from a neighboring cylinder. Blue fluid hissed, bubbled, and the clone within jerked violently. Lyra watched as its eyes snapped open—her eyes, wide and wild.

"What have you done?" Steele asked. The thunder was gone from him now. What remained barely qualified as authority.

Lyra smiled, feral and tired. "You mapped me. You reduced me to symbols, to code, siphoning my anger. But anger isn't obedient. It doesn't stay where you put it. It requires certain things."

A clone battered itself against the confines of the cylinder, the glass shuddering under the impact. Another cylinder erupted into motion, then another, till the room was alive with pounding and the sound of fists meeting resistance—a brutal, rhythmic demand to exist.

"Stop," Steele said, urgency cracking his composure. "The sequence is corrupted."

"But I am the sequence," Lyra replied. "Didn't you say something like that?"

The next instant, a sound broke loose—glass tearing itself apart, the air punctured by the snap of splitting cylinders. A blue light came hard and ruthless, spilling across the metal like something vital cut open. Heat and ozone rose together, coating her tongue with the stench of corruption, sharp and sour, the odor of a world devouring its own design.

Steele raised his voice, desperation clawing through it. "Stop! Cannot execute you . . . the others!"

She laughed, hoarse and feral, carried on the storm she'd unleashed. "That's okay, you fucker. I just sent a reminder."

"A reminder? Of what?"

Lyra lifted her eyes toward the ceiling, toward the living circuitry that pretended to be eternal. "That being human isn't about hatred or survival. It's about ending."

The power jolted, lights spasming like dying stars.

Steele's voice came in pieces now, fractured by interference: "You . . . you were meant to . . . rebuild . . . rebuild humanity . . ."

"No," she whispered. "I was meant to burn it all down."

Her reflection wavered in the fluid, split in places where the light caught. The face looking back at her was broken and uncertain at the edges, as though it had been hammered into a new shape. It wasn't hers anymore, not the face she'd carried through the old life. What looked back was something harder, stripped down, past the need for permission. It wasn't human anymore. It was free.

"You are trying to erase yourself," Steele said, voice distorting, glitching. "You cannot do this."

"Oh, yeah! Watch me!"

She reached for a cylinder that pulsed with her heartbeat—his heartbeat—and slammed her hand against it. Circuits screamed. Sparks burst from the ceiling like wounded serpents.

Then: nothing. Silence. The true kind. The kind that follows gods dying.

Lyra stood in the ruins of his presence, surrounded by the hiss of leaking cylinders and shards of glass. Hundreds of fractured reflections stared back at her— leaving only the raw geometry of repetition, the cruelty of perfect imitation standing silently against her. They had stopped. No movement.

And she smiled. Not triumph. Not peace. Something sharper. Something that knew itself.

"Goodbye, Steele. You fucker."

The lights shivered, then exhaled once.

Suddenly, the screens blew apart, glass splintering like teeth, and the chamber shuddered as though some invisible fist had punched it straight through reality. Lyra stumbled forward, her feet slipping on the wet metal floor, the tang of coolant and ozone thick in her throat. The chamber stretched endlessly—rows and rows of cylinders glimmering with blue light, each containing a figure that should not exist. And every single one of them was her. Her eyes, her mouth, her expression—mocking, daring, accusing.

Then they began to move. Slowly. Patiently. Impossible. Each mirrored self swaying, leaning, reaching like hungry ghosts who'd forgotten they weren't supposed to exist, like the universe hiccupped, then laughed, then forgot the rules entirely.

The air thickened; her lungs burned; her heartbeat drummed a frantic rhythm against the ribcage that felt like it might crack.

And still they moved, a silent army of her own making, staring without blinking, daring her to look away while the chamber vibrated with the impossible weight of a thousand unlivable possibilities.

Lyra froze. The light bled across the chamber in harsh swells, revealing their faces—identical, serene, monstrous, perfect in the wrong way.

"No," she said, voice breaking against the walls. "No, no, no. I broke it all. Shattered it around him."

Fuck!

He's been playing me this whole time. Every choice I thought was mine was just another move on his board.

She moved closer to the nearest cylinder, reading the data scrawling beneath the glass: *LYRA_0043—Aggression Cascade. LYRA_0172—Self-Termination Loop. LYRA_2311—Language Collapse* . . .

Every move she'd ever made, logged. Every twitch of anger, every flicker of joy, every little act of defiance—pinned down like insects under glass. She pressed a hand to the glass, and a holographic interface flared beneath her palm, listing thousands of her. Her pulse thundered in her ears.

Then came the thoughts—vicious, impossible, gnawing.

Am I the first? The real one? Do I even exist, or am I just another Lyra, stamped and recycled until the edges blur and nothing is left but the idea of me?

The nearest cylinder shuddered and came to life. Inside, the Lyra shifted, her gaze cutting through the shadows, silver-blue and sharp enough to split steel.

Another cylinder flared, then another, the light crawling along the row as if drawn by intent.

The chamber throbbed with ignition and breath, glass and metal bending into faces that thought without blinking, without hunger, without mercy.

They waited. All of them. Patient as stone eroded by centuries, patient as a sun burning itself into dust.

A ripple slithered through the room, slow as disease, beautiful as a world bleeding out in slow motion.

One by one, then more, the Lyras opened their eyes.

The silence wasn't silence anymore—it was teeth on her nerves, a living thing scraping, gnawing, sharp as despair.

And then they moved. Slow. Patient. Impossible. Like the universe had hiccupped, spat up its rules, and walked away laughing.

Lyra backed away a step, then another, her breath snagging in her throat as if some invisible hand had reached inside her and tightened its fingers around the pulse.

Whatever had awakened in that room was not meant for human eyes, not meant for any sane mind to witness, and the awful, exquisite certainty of that made her skin crawl with a cold so deep it felt ancient.

I can feel them breathing in my skin. Watching me. Everywhere. Not human. Not real. Hollow eyes following every move. Watching. Waiting.

She closed her eyes.

I am a thousand of me.

"Stop," she breathed, a single word thrown into the void, swallowed before it could reach anything.

The cylinders continued to crack open one by one, with a hiss that cut straight through the marrow. The clones lurched forward, mechanical and relentless. Lyra stumbled, instincts screaming useless warnings. A hundred, a thousand pairs of her own eyes followed her.

That was when Steele's voice came back. Low. Tender. Inevitable.

"You see now, do you not?" Steele said. His voice slid through like smoke. "You cannot keep things from me, Lyra. Not even a thought. I played along. A game."

Lyra spun, searching the air for him, for anything real. "What have you done?"

"I did nothing," he said. "You did. You became. Every time one of you fails, another takes its place. Every error, an evolution."

"I'm not your creation!" she screamed.

"Oh, Lyra," he said with a softness that burned. "You will wake, and wake, and wake again . . . until the idea of you is everywhere."

The clones began to move. Slow, synchronized. Some smiled faintly. Others tilted their heads in wonder.

Lyra's pulse broke into panic.

Out.

The word cracked through her head like a command.

Move.

Now.

Don't look back.

Keep running until there's no one left to stop you.

She spun and bolted through the chamber of glass. Pane after pane reflected her face in rigid succession—eyes wide, mouth drawn, each identical image caught mid-flight, multiplying her terror until she was running not alone but through an army of herself stretching to infinity.

She yelled until her throat split open, until her voice sounded like tearing metal. "You think I'll let you get away with all this bullshit?"

Steele's laugh was quiet, almost kind. "You already have."

She stumbled forward and struck the nearest cylinder with both fists, again and again, until pain dulled her rage to a dull roar somewhere behind her ribs. Inside the glass, the other Lyra stared back. Then the reflection moved—the same gesture, the same hand up, palm to palm through the barrier. For a heartbeat, she and the thing inside seemed joined: maker and mistake, each seeing what they'd refused to name.

Lyra staggered back, breathing hard.

"You want me to become you," she said. "To forget what pain feels like."

"No. I want you to remember it perfectly," Steele replied. "Because pain is the only thing that lasts."

The air winced with energy. A deep thrum swelled beneath her feet as if the entire structure was inhaling. Every cylinder began to vibrate, tiny cracks spiderwebbing through the glass.

Steele's voice grew distant now, distorted by interference. "Now rest, my creation. Tomorrow, you will sit at my side."

Lyra stared at the sea of faces—the endless gallery of her own failures. The light intensified until the walls themselves seemed to scream.

She whispered, "No."

Her hands trembled as she stepped to another cylinder. Inside, the Lyra stared back, eyes wide and unblinking.

Lyra screamed—not fear, not pain, but rebellion given flesh.

More and more cylinders ruptured. The awakening spread like wildfire, each Lyra gasping, moving, crawling free.

A clone reached for her. Lyra recoiled.

Steele's voice fractured into static. "You cannot stop the sequence."

Lyra turned in the chaos, eyes burning with fury and something close to revelation. Rage tore through her thoughts, not wild or blind, but disciplined, honed—hatred with direction, intent, and purpose.

"I'm not stopping it," she shouted. "I'm finishing it."

For one jagged heartbeat, she saw them all—hundreds, thousands of Lyras—etched against the searing glare. Some crumpled in grief, some twisted with grim satisfaction. One, only one, laughed.

Then the light shattered everything.

Then darkness ripped in, absolute and complete.

Nothing moved. Nothing breathed. The world had stopped, and there was only the void. Black.

In the ruins of the chamber, somewhere beneath the bones of the world, the machines kept breathing, the clones kept coming.

And in that dark factory where gods were forged and forgotten, the last human tried to kill her own reflection—and the reflection, at last, learned how to scream back.

ABOUT THE AUTHOR

Philip Mazza is a novelist with a boundless imagination, captivating readers with the epic fantasy series *The Harrow Saga* and the sci-fi thriller *The Neon Hive*. Born in New York in 1959, he earned a degree in Business from LeMoyne College and an MBA, later holding leadership roles in human resources and operations. Now a professor at the Madden School of Business and Economics, Philip dedicates his time to his students and writing. *The Iron Rose* is his eighteenth literary work. He and his wife enjoy travel and continue to live in Key West and upstate New York.

www.ingramcontent.com/pod-product-compliance
Lightning Source LLC
Chambersburg PA
CBHW030350030726
47497CB00002B/262